TANGLEWOOD

Dermot Bolger

NEW ISLAND

TANGLEWOOD

First published in 2015
by New Island Books,
16 Priory Hall Office Park,
Stillorgan,
County Dublin,
Republic of Ireland.

www.newisland.ie

PRINT ISBN: 978-1-84840-430-4
EPUB ISBN: 978-1-84840-444-1
MOBI ISBN: 978-1-84840-445-8

The author wishes to express his sincere appreciation to Mr Thomas Kinsella and to Carcanet Press for permission to quote lines from his poem 'Wormwood', which first appeared in the collection of that title in 1966. The full text is available in the volume *Selected Poems* by Thomas Kinsella, published by Carcanet Press. The author would also like to acknowledge the editors of the *Princeton University Library Chronicle*, where the opening chapter of this novel first appeared, and *The Irish Times*, where an extract appeared.

British Library Cataloguing Data.
A CIP catalogue record for this book is available from the British Library.

Typeset by JVR Creative India
Cover design by Mariel Deegan
Printed by ScandBook AB, Sweden

New Island received financial assistance from The Arts Council (*An Chomhairle Ealaíon*), 70 Merrion Square, Dublin 2, Ireland.

10 9 8 7 6 5 4 3 2 1

Praise for Dermot Bolger

The Journey Home

'Joyce, O'Flaherty, Brian Moore, John McGahern, a fistful of O'Brien's. This is a succulent Who's Who of Irish Writing, and Dermot Bolger is of the same ilk … an exceptional literary gift.' – *Independent (London)*

The Family on Paradise Pier

'Possibly his finest achievement … whether he's capturing the slums of Dublin or the pain of a missed opportunity in love, Bolger's writing simply sings.' – *Sunday Business Post*

Father's Music

'Dermot Bolger creates a Dublin, a particular world, like no one else writing can … the urban landscape of the thriller that Bolger has made exclusively his own.' – *Sunday Independent*

The Woman's Daughter

'A wild, frothing poetic odyssey … a brilliant and ambitious piece of writing.' – *Sunday Telegraph*

A Second Life

'Audacious and moving … Bolger's brilliant conflation of detective story, ghost hunt and history lesson is compulsive' – *Times (London)*

Emily's Shoes

'The writing is so strong, so exact … triumphantly successful – bare, passionate, almost understating the almost unstatable.' – *Financial Times*

Temptation

'It is rare that a man should be so adept and insightful at identifying the preoccupations of a mature woman and mother-of-three, but Bolger does just that in this tender, thoughtful novel.' – *Harpers & Queen*

About the Author

Born in Dublin in 1959, Dermot Bolger is one of Ireland's best known writers. His eleven previous novels include *The Journey Home, Father's Music, The Valparaiso Voyage, The Family on Paradise Pier, A Second Life: A Renewed Novel, New Town Soul* and *The Fall of Ireland.*

His first play, *The Lament for Arthur Cleary*, received the Samuel Beckett Award and an Edinburgh Fringe First Award. His numerous other plays include *The Ballymun Trilogy*, which charts forty years of life in a Dublin working class suburb, *Walking the Road, The Parting Glass* and a stage adaptation of Joyce's *Ulysses.*

Also a poet, his ninth collection of poems, *The Venice Suite: A Voyage Through Loss*, was published in 2012, and latest collection, *That Which is Suddenly Precious*, is forthcoming from New Island.

He devised the best-selling collaborative novels, *Finbar's Hotel* and *Ladies Night at Finbar's Hotel*, and has edited numerous anthologies, including *The Picador Book of Contemporary Irish Fiction*. A former Writer Fellow at Trinity College, Dublin and Playwright in Association with the Abbey Theatre, Bolger writes for most of Ireland's leading newspapers and in 2012 was named Commentator of the Year at the Irish Newspaper awards.

www.dermotbolger.com

PART ONE

March 2007

Chapter One

Tuesday 13th, 1 a.m.

The echo that reverberated from the high-vaulted ceiling, after he used a crowbar to force open the door of this derelict building near the seafront, reminded him of somewhere closer to home, a place he was careful never to return to, even in dreams. The stale air brought him back in time; the uncomfortable silence, the mildewed walls layered in cobwebs patrolled by bloated spiders, the judgemental sense of ghosts observing him amid the dissipated grandeur. Outside, on the deserted road, the night air smelt of salt. His nostrils could always detect this coastal infusion that locals rarely noticed. He had been twenty-five before he saw an ocean. He disliked this tang: it brought back a sea voyage he was determined to put behind him. But when he entered these deserted premises and discreetly closed the door, the mouldy air conjured up memories from which there was no escape.

This Victorian building was the sort of structure into which people could be herded. Old men in long coats made to kneel in one corner, a handful of terrified mothers clutching children tight, toothless grandmothers mutely staring into space as if nothing that might occur here could match previous misfortunes endured decades ago. Cowed villagers who only dared to raise their heads when the bullying voices and taunts stopped, when footsteps retreated, when the click of a steel padlock that sealed an old cinema door from outside gave way to merciful silence. A respite from the men who had hurt them with boots or rifle butts, from threats of mutilation or rape. A silence broken only by a child's muffled whimper, by the departing sounds of the trucks

3

that had ferried the militia to this village, by a crackling hiss, a spurt so soft it was barely audible at first. Then it grew unmistakably into the whisper of fire taking hold. The sound became interlaced with screams from within the cinema as the people locked inside it realised that it was being torched.

He knew that this building in Dublin had not witnessed such screams. Similar horrors never occurred in Ireland. Irish people did not possess the guarded look that hinted at secrets too raw to be spoken of. They smiled too easily, although their smiles were a tactic to keep strangers at bay. Irish history consisted of sporadic historical squabbles which bearded men in pubs droned on about, describing skirmishes in post offices and cowardly shots fired into the skulls of unsuspecting policemen as if such petty assassinations were battles that should fascinate him. Irish drinkers revelled in revealing these nuggets from their national narrative, like infants displaying turds in a chamber pot, anticipating exaggerated praise for the feat.

But the businessman who owned this building did not concern himself with history. Paul Hughes had no interest in his real name, or where he came from. Such a man was invisible to Hughes, and the other men Hughes whored him out to, except as a trusted pair of hands willing to undertake discreet tasks at a cut-price rate. They liked the fact that he rarely spoke, and he appreciated their failure of curiosity, the way they only engaged with the present. In the present tense they had a role for him: to dig foundations and plaster walls so that new apartment blocks could arise. Occasionally, like now, they also needed him to make the past disappear.

In recent months Hughes had dragged old mattresses into this building as an invitation to squatters, but he doubted if anyone had ever slept here. He would, however, check each room: he wanted no murder of a tramp or junkie on his conscience. His conscience had no room left to be lumbered with additional burdens, and besides, he was his own commander here; no longer young, no longer scared and no longer acting under manipulative instructions. The mattresses were also dumped here because mattresses burn easily. Boxes of documents were similarly now strewn about, company ledgers, invoice books, receipts – papers that were not only highly flammable, but possibly inflammatory. Such papers were not his concern. There would be no work for foreigners like him if Irishmen did not possess secrets. And he had no shortage of work, because the Irish were too posh to even burn their own past. Every night for the past week Hughes would have sat at a penthouse window anticipating the sight of flames, but he had explained that the wind must be exactly right to make a conflagration unstoppable. It was important to sound authoritative and prolong the waiting so that clients considered him worth the money.

Now that he had started he wanted the job swiftly done. Kicking open the doors, he shouted before entering each room. If any down-and-out was asleep, the noise would wake them. The living held no fear for him: he had the crowbar up one sleeve and a knife in his jacket. He sprinkled petrol as he walked. The motion brought back a memory of how his mother had longed for him to be ordained as a child. It reminded him of a time when his family needed to share a toilet with six other families, when he used to pretend that the tap water he sprinkled against the walls of the foul-smelling privy was holy water. A time when religion was dangerous. A time he now felt annoyed with himself for remembering as he kicked open the final door on the landing.

Tomorrow this gutted building would be condemned as unsafe, despite the protests of locals, who had campaigned to have it preserved. He could not understand the objections of such people in smug homes: people who paid peanuts to cleaners and nannies. The demolition of this building would provide months of work for men like him, with more work arising from the construction of apartment blocks here. Since acquiring this building, Hughes had rendered it uninhabitable by degrees. But for over a century it had been home to hosts of different people. He could sense their eyes as he soaked the final mattress with petrol. The curtains in this last room once possessed a distinguishable colour, but as he drew them shut he watched his white gloves turn black with dust. For the first time he hesitated, reluctant to turn and confront the watching eyes. He was unsure if they were Irish ghosts from this dwelling or the ghosts who had travelled here inside his head, phantoms who gathered every time he held a lit match aloft.

With his back turned, he struck the match and raised it up. The ghosts just needed to brush against him and this flame would fall from his grasp. There could be no escape: the whole building would ignite. His flesh would catch fire like those herded souls trapped in a place to which he could never return. The flame, however, remained steady, no unliving breath diverting it. When the match almost burnt down to his fingers he extinguished it and turned to walk slowly back out onto the landing. The watchers had not taken up his challenge, but he was not alone: more ghosts than ever thronged each doorway. He felt strangely pure, the way he used to feel as a boy when a priest secretly heard his confession. Halfway down the main staircase he stopped to light a cigarette. Taking a pull, he breathed in the smell of nicotine, richer than incense. Then he tossed the cigarette behind his shoulder, hearing the soft whoosh of petrol igniting on the landing. There was no time to look back: he needed to reach the door quickly and slip out onto the pavement. He had a sense of being watched, but this sense had been imbued into him for two decades, and it would look suspicious to check behind him. So he calmly walked the short distance to the main street of Blackrock, where late-night drinkers would not notice the features of an outsider like him, with his cropped hair and unsmiling face. Behind him on the landing the ghosts were burning, with distorted faces and hideous screams so high pitched that not even the local dogs could hear them. He refused to quicken his step, but also refused to look back in case their souls had been illuminated into shimmering flesh, in case he discovered whether they were Irish ghosts or the ghosts who had tormented him on his journey inside the sealed container that was finally opened in Rosslare port, where customs officials, whose beams of torchlight blinded him, had let him shield his eyes and step down. They had fed him while politely declining to believe the lies he fed them. But they had allowed him enough space to disappear and to invent this new identity for himself in Ireland.

Chapter Two

Ronan

Sunday 11th, 11 p.m.

'Watch the sky next week,' Paul Hughes murmured to Ronan when they found themselves standing together on the smoking terrace of the Playwright Inn on Newtownpark Avenue. 'Red sky at night will definitely not mean *An Taisce*'s delight.' Hughes winked. 'My mum's old friends keep themselves young by lodging planning objections to everything. Maybe, just once, they need to glimpse the majesty of the Northern Lights.'

It was typical of Hughes's sly bravado to drop this oblique hint – sober behind the camouflage of several double vodkas with Slimline tonic – as the two middle-aged former Blackrock College classmates stood far from prying ears. All men were only equal when pissing into urinals or stretched on mortuary slabs. Ireland's smoking ban had initiated a third sphere of equality: pub smokers thrown together under awnings like ostracised sinners, momentarily separated from their drinking cliques. A smoking terrace was a non-aligned zone where a humble chartered surveyor like Ronan could inhale the same secondary smoke as a multi-millionaire property developer like Hughes.

Hughes's wry tone as he absent-mindedly inhaled on a small cigar left Ronan unable to decipher why he was being forewarned. The heritage trust, *An Taisce*, was leading local objections to Hughes's plans to demolish a Victorian building near the seafront. But local objections would cease if an accidental blaze rendered the site derelict. Travellers

7

might move in, or junkies could start using it as a heroin shooting alley. Hughes must be letting Ronan know his plan for a reason. There had to be something in it for Ronan, maybe assisting with an insurance assessment or helping to draft a resubmitted planning application. Tycoons like Hughes had a motive behind everything they did or said.

'You're a lucky man,' Hughes added casually. 'Your new wife is one of the most beautiful creatures I've ever seen.'

'Kim has a lovely personality.' Ronan's tone was wary, though he would have appreciated the compliment from another man.

'Indeed.' Hughes stared serenely ahead. 'Her personalities were the first two things I noticed about her.'

Ronan wanted to punch him. But then again, he had been longing to punch Hughes for twenty years, ever since discovering that Hughes had once dated Ronan's first wife, Miriam, at sixteen. Miriam always laughed and claimed that nothing happened because the teenage Hughes was so nervous that he would have enjoyed more success defusing car bombs than undoing bra straps. Why was Hughes dropping hints now about a forthcoming fire? Was it to give Ronan the chance to inform the police as a staunch citizen, or to remind him that he occupied such a peripheral role on the outer fringe of the interconnected circles of money which dominated Dublin that whatever he knew was inconsequential?

Hughes seemed to be waiting for Ronan to speak. So, to change the subject, Ronan asked about his mother. It was years since Ronan had seen Mrs Hughes, but he retained boyhood memories of once being invited to play tennis on the grass court beside the orchard that occupied half an acre of the vast garden surrounding her Edwardian house off Newtownpark Avenue. The developer turned to gaze at him, and Ronan realised that Hughes had deliberately followed him out onto the smoking terrace.

'Mum is lonely,' Hughes said. 'Shaky on her feet, but too proud to use a stairlift, even though I've offered to install one. Her circulatory problems are bad enough, but she gets depressed rattling around that old house with rotting windows and a vast jungle for a garden. I pay a Polish care worker to come in, but Mum is convinced the girl is stealing from her, though nothing goes missing. She just keeps losing everything: her car keys, her purse, her tablets.... She spends half the night roaming around those cold rooms on her walking stick, refusing to wear the alarm pendant I got her. If she falls, I've no way of knowing. It would kill me to find her some morning at the foot of the stairs. It's a pity she can't find a single-storey town house within walking distance of Blackrock village, close to the church and the coffee shops, where she could meet old friends.'

'There are lots of nice apartments,' Ronan suggested.

Hughes shook his head. 'Apartments are for Poles and proles. Most are bought by investors, which means that I'd never know what skangers might wind up blaring rap music beside her. We need to find her a discreet bungalow tucked away at the end of someone's garden.'

Hughes stared at Ronan, as if waiting for the penny to drop.

'I like my back garden,' Ronan said. 'Besides, I've extended my house so much I've barely room for a pergola.'

'But have you looked on Google Earth? Your neighbour … what's his name … the civil servant who was in school with us … he's got plenty of room.'

'You may be able to buy his house,' Ronan said. 'Chris is bidding at an auction next Wednesday.'

'So the auctioneer tells me.' Hughes laughed. 'It wouldn't feel like a Blackrock auction without your neighbour sweating in the front row. His nickname among the estate agents is Mr Underbidder. On Wednesday he'll live up to his name again.'

'Are you saying he has no chance of getting that house?'

'He can get the house, but not on Wednesday. If Chris is clever and accepts your help, then maybe in a few months' time it can be his, but only after it has briefly had another owner. I can arrange that if you can persuade him to do me a favour. You would be helping him and helping me, and naturally also yourself.' Hughes stubbed out his cigar. 'Nobody should ever leave the table unfed.'

So it was that Ronan didn't smash in Paul Hughes's face, despite his sly remark about Kim's breasts. They were mature adults. In Ireland only small fry acquired business by advertising in the *Golden Pages*. Serious business sought you out on the smoking terrace of upmarket pubs, or when businessmen chanced to stand together, publicly displaying stoic patience as their wives tried on clothes in BT2 in the Dundrum

Shopping Centre, or availed themselves of the complimentary services of an in-store style advisor when shopping at Coast by appointment.

Ronan listened to Hughes's plan and explained the logistical difficulties. Hughes expressed confidence that Ronan would find ways to sidestep any such problems, reminding him how everyone respected him as a man who made difficulties disappear. Ronan would be helping two old school friends, one desperate to buy a house, and the other unable to persuade his stubbornly independent mother to use a stairlift and avoid risking a crippling fall. They didn't shake hands: such gestures belonged to cattle dealers at marts. Instead they put their heads together to share a match as they lit another smoke. Then each stared companionably ahead, contemplating the steps required for them to fulfil their side of the bargain.

Chapter Three

Chris

Tuesday 13th, 1.30 a.m.

Chris noticed the flames shortly after arriving home, when he had undressed for bed but instead crept up the dark stairs to feel close to Alice, though he knew that no welcome awaited him in the bedroom they once shared. At such moments he realised how desperately he still needed her, despite the flinty words they sparked off each other and their terse, simmering silences. Twenty years had not taught him how to avoid the creaking floorboard on the bend of the stairs. The noise sounded loud, but every sensation felt magnified at this hour, including his desire to be held. Maybe he only craved such intimacy now because he no longer felt needed. By being too focused on trying to mind Alice when she was invalided after a car accident, he had missed out on Ireland's bonanza years, with neighbours exploiting tax incentives to acquire buy-to-let apartments in Leitrim or becoming absentee landlords in countries that hadn't existed when he and Alice purchased this small terraced house, just before the Berlin Wall came down.

Chris reached the landing, shaded in sepia moonlight through the open bathroom door. This muffled silvery light made the landing appear frozen in time. It was how Chris felt. Downstairs a fold-out sofa awaited him, a ticking clock and a half-finished bottle of wine. He didn't want to drink any more. But sleep refused to come when he yearned for a fleeting embrace so that the silky after-feel of Alice's skin would linger on his own when he returned to the temporary bed that had become a permanent fixture in their lives over the past six months.

At that moment the bathroom window started to resemble a stained-glass artwork lit by a flickering glow. Red threads of glow-worms flitted across the bathroom tiles. A building must be on fire, somewhere near the seafront, not far from where Chris had spent the previous hour standing outside the Victorian house with the long back garden up for auction tomorrow. One part of him hoped that the fire was coming from that house, so that this decision might be taken from him, with only a smouldering ruin left. He would be the chief suspect, however. This was the eighth consecutive night that Chris had stood, staring in through the windows, torturously pondering his decision.

The vendor always left the blinds raised in the two enormous front sash windows to display the high, imposing ceilings, a sidelamp casting a soft glow over the antique black-marble fireplace. From outside, the house oozed peace and stability, inviting Chris finally to commence a new life there with Alice, but even now he was uncertain if this house suited them. The narrow cul-de-sac was never designed for cars. A preservation order meant that garden walls could not be knocked down to create driveways. It would be a nightmare to parallel park in this constricted space, or have anything delivered. Their surveyor had found a snag list of internal problems, but the biggest problem was that Chris was no longer sure if Alice could be happy with him in any house. Tomorrow, though, after three years of being outbid in auctions across Blackrock, their luck might change. They had always recovered from such disappointments because they still possessed each other, but tomorrow felt different. Alice's belief in him was evaporating; he could not fail her again.

In the light caused by that flickering glow, Chris stared at Alice's closed bedroom door. This door had witnessed Sophie's conception. It overheard whispers of endearment when it shut out the world to let them inhabit a private republic of love, with him the axis of Alice's universe. He could recall the evening last September when this door was first used to exclude him. No angry words were spoken, but he had returned home to find it locked from the inside and felt suddenly like a trespasser. Alice's gradual estrangement stemmed from more than their inability to purchase a house. Worries gnawed at her that she was unable to speak about. Her hormones were in chaos, the menopause causing mood swings. She seemed perturbed that Sophie planned to leave home for the first time to study abroad for a year. But none of these factors changed the reality that Chris grew diminished in her eyes each time he was outbid at auction.

The fire was gaining strength. Tiny tongues were more prevalent against the bathroom window, red blotches like evaporating kisses. Without making a sound that might wake her, Chris pressed his naked body against the closed door. He didn't know what he wanted at this moment; he just could not bear to feel so alone inside his marriage, like a ghost left over from a truncated life. Alice's sleep was precious. If disturbed, she could never go back to sleep. Her need for silence at night had made him feel like a guard constantly on duty, until one day he found that she no longer needed minding. She had emerged from her malaise, transformed into a different woman.

Chris longed for sleep, but he could not bear to go downstairs to endure another sleepless night of totting up figures, interest repayments, mortgage relief, worrying about what would happen if he fell ill and could not provide for Alice and Sophie. He longed to open the bedroom door and lie beside her, touching her breasts, like in the old days, when he could feel her love like a force field enveloping them. He wanted to ask if she was certain that tomorrow's house was the home they had been waiting for. He wanted not to feel so scared, so convinced that whatever decision he made would be the wrong one.

He remained motionless while red flames flitted against the bathroom window and fire brigade sirens broke the silence. His body grew cold, his palms numb. He felt isolated and sexually frustrated. He felt resentful that Alice didn't seem to love him in the same way any more. He wanted to leave her, yet knew that he would never survive on his own. Most of all he wanted to prove himself to her at last by winning tomorrow's auction. Then, once again, he could be the man who climbed these stairs in the dark to open a door into an unlit bedroom, the man who would be made to feel welcome, the hunter after an epic trek who had finally fought his way back.

Chapter Four

Alice

Tuesday 13th, 1 a.m.

Alice woke. She did not know what had disturbed her or whether she would be able to get back asleep. The luminous clock face was turned to the wall. In the past it would stress her to know the time if she woke and discovered that she had only slept for a few hours. Back then, her fear of being forced to endure another sleepless night invariably turned into a self-fulfilling prophecy. Now she was teaching herself not to panic when she woke, never to look at the clock, or, above all, get agitated. The secret was to live in the present, not be perpetually mulling over the past or worrying about tomorrow.

If she started thinking about the house for auction, she was doomed to lie awake. It would almost be as bad as if Chris were in the bedroom, tormenting her with figures, a man torn in two by his desire to please her and an inability to make decisions. When he bid tomorrow, she didn't want him to do so for her sake but for his own, to prove to himself that he was capable of closing a deal. Their relationship was being damaged by his inability to move house or abandon his dream of doing so. After the heartbreak of being outbid at each auction, Alice would resolve never to look at another house, but Chris always managed to sweep her up in his initial enthusiasm for a new property, effusing about it before invariably finding numerous problems to worry about.

Alice yearned to escape from this cramped house and make a fresh start in rooms free from the memories of illness, but most of all she longed to fall back asleep. During the years when Chris shared this bed, she often endured long nights of lying awake, growing so envious of the ease with which he slept that sometimes she succumbed to an unwise impulse to bombard him with pent-up, irrational questions about how he always managed to fall asleep, as if this were a secret he was keeping from her. Waking Chris had never achieved any purpose beyond giving her desperation an outlet. By that stage, Alice was beyond consoling. But Chris hadn't understood that sleep was not a problem she expected him to solve. While they sounded like pleas for help, she had merely repeated her litany of questions out of a need to break the incessant silence on nights when she had feared going insane if forced to lie silently for any longer in the dark.

Waking Chris had always led to a row, her husband anxiously trying to calm her at first, before eventually losing his temper, confronted by an unsolvable dilemma, where whatever he said only made things worse. Chris had always looked trapped on such nights, with Alice begging him to hold her and then resentfully claiming that Chris didn't understand her anguish. Nobody had understood her exhaustion in the three years after the car crash; how sick her body felt after working herself up into a state of panic, afraid of being unable to face another day without sleep. Her very closeness to Chris had caused those intense late-night rows, her dependency on him to solve every problem – a dependency which one counsellor she attended had described as unhealthy.

In those bad years, Chris seemed like a white knight trying to surmount all obstacles, caring for Sophie and driving Alice to the alternative medicine practitioners, in whose hands she had placed all hopes for a cure from that trough of despair, in which she would have welcomed death. Her dependency on him had been a symptom of an illness that robbed her of several years of her life. Now at last she was recovering her strength, and her counsellor kept suggesting that she should step back from the intensity of her marriage to appraise Chris in a fresh light, which might allow Alice to grow in self-confidence. The counsellor had implied that she needed to diminish Chris. But the longer that the saga of trying to buy a house in this frenzied market went on, the more she found that Chris seemed to diminish himself.

Alice was glad that Chris was not lying beside her. It removed any possibility of argument. She recalled the resentful silence in which they used to lie awake after she woke him with her questions. Their simmering hurt had generally festered throughout the following day, until finally they glanced at each other and laughed at their own silliness. Back then, they often made up their quarrel with sex, back when she felt incomplete if any estrangement existed with this man whom she loved. They no longer quarrelled at night because Chris didn't sleep in this room. Alice sometimes wondered if Chris slept at all. She was shocked that a new part of her simply wanted Chris to leave her alone.

For twenty years she had needed his constant reassurance, but recently the pendulum had swung. Now, the less that Alice needed Chris, the more he seemed to need her. Alice felt trapped by his increased need, especially since the shock of discovering that perhaps she could no longer trust him. She doubted if she would ever recover from her devastating sense of betrayal last September when she stumbled upon evidence that Chris may have secretly been seeing someone else. She was so innocent back then that she would have suspected nothing if she had not been perturbed by a sudden furtiveness in Chris's behaviour. She was still chiding herself for being paranoid when some instinct made her examine the pockets of Chris's black suit in the wardrobe, where she unearthed an opened packet of Viagra. Even then she might have not put two and two together if Ronan next door hadn't tipped her off, whether accidently or on purpose. Ronan rarely did anything with only one motive.

During two decades together she had never seen Chris lift a hand to anyone. Indeed, it was impossible to imagine this man, incapable of killing a spider, committing any act of violence. But that September evening – when she came downstairs after making her discovery, trying to keep her voice casual as she asked him where he was going – the way in which Chris so awkwardly lied to her had hurt more than any sickening punch to her stomach. Alice remembered needing to hold on to the kitchen counter for support, her eyes gazing out the window so that Chris would not notice her grief-stricken face while he casually checked for his car keys and disappeared off to meet whoever he was not telling her about. Only once before had she experienced such a stab of hurt, after her first boyfriend casually discarded her within days of Alice surrendering her virginity. Chris's arrival into her life had healed the damage from that rejection which had once shattered her self-esteem. But Chris's lies last September had brought back the pain of that first betrayal, a hurt she was surprised to find still buried deep within her after a quarter of a century. It also brought a realisation that, throughout her life, she was always too innocent, guileless and trusting.

The disappointments endured in auction rooms, and even her years of loneliness when bedbound in this room after a car accident seemed insignificant compared to the hurt she felt last September, listening to his car drive away. The fact that Chris had blatantly lied could only mean that he was seeing another woman. Or did it? With Miriam gone from next door, there was nobody that Alice could confide in, nobody to calm her down over a coffee, nobody to put her fears into perspective when she became overwrought by anxiety. Alice dated her ambiguous feelings towards Chris from that night, not just because he was doing something clandestine behind her back, obviously gripped by some stupid midlife crisis, but because the fact that he was venturing out into an unknown world reinforced her sense of isolation. That was the night when she realised that she would suffocate in this tiny house, perpetually waiting to move unless she also carved out some hidden life for herself too, with new friends, or at least with strangers who didn't instinctively recall old newspaper reports about a car crash whenever they saw her.

Every failed bid at auctions reinforced the sensation of being trapped here, not in control of her life. But Chris's infidelity, or his attempt at infidelity, or at the very least his wilful decision to parcel off some new aspect of his life and keep it secret, had made her realise how she needed to take command of those parts of her destiny that she could control. She needed to overcome her loneliness and restore some of the self-worth that had been decimated by that car crash. Chris's actions in September had planted the seed that if he felt entitled to a secret life then maybe she had the right to have secrets too, provided that they hurt no one. She had become too dependent on a man who seemed overwhelmed by this spiralling new Ireland evolving around them. Before it became too late to experience something of life, maybe she needed to create a private space where, for some brief interludes, she could escape this limbo and become someone unencumbered by the past, even if this someone was a stranger to her true self.

Last September she was too hurt and shocked to articulate her confused emotions. Sophie had been out with friends, but Alice still locked the bathroom door before hunching down onto the floor to silently cry. When she eventually finished crying she left sheets and a spare quilt on the fold-out bed downstairs. Then she had lain awake in the darkness, waiting for Chris to return home and ascend the stairs to find the bedroom door locked. Next morning, when Chris asked what was going on, Alice blamed hot flushes and night sweats and migraines so blinding that she could no longer share a bed with him. She had irritably invented a dozen excuses, praying that Chris would have the intuition to grasp what was really wrong, to understand how deeply his lies had wounded her and to realise that, despite all her naïvety, she was refusing to be played for a fool.

Six months passed, and the evidence suggested that Chris's liaison, if that was what it was, had ceased. When trust breaks down in a marriage, however, you never get it back. Looking back, Alice knew that she should have challenged him at once about his lies instead of inventing excuses for locking the bedroom door. But Alice was raised in a family where no trauma was ever confronted by anything except evasive silence. Despite spending half a lifetime trying to liberate herself from her repressed childhood, she hadn't known how to confront Chris beyond sniping at him in the hope that he would decipher the real intent behind her words. If Miriam had still been next door, she was such a woman of the world that Alice might have been able to confide in her, but she had lost contact with the circle of mothers who were once her close friends when Sophie was in primary school. Even if she had stayed in touch with them, she just didn't know how to talk to another living soul about the anxieties that plagued her.

She was an open person in every other way, too open and too gullible, but Alice could never begin to speak to anyone about her feelings without imagining her dead parents staring at her in exasperated disapproval, perplexed that their daughter might risk making a public fool of herself by deviating from the carefully constructed illusion that everything in her life was perfect. Her occasional outbursts of temper were directed as much at herself for being caged in by this emotional reticence as they were directed at Chris. Her self-esteem was crushed by the realisation that, even at forty-eight years of age, she remained her parents' creation, unable to break free from their frigid restraint and their overarching concern about what other people might say. They had groomed her too well in childhood, stifling her capacity for spontaneous joy, as if unchecked happiness were a disease that she needed to be inoculated against.

These days Chris rarely went out, except to view houses and be racked by indecision about bidding on them. His mysterious paramour must have dumped him on that night in November when he returned home, far earlier than usual, his face white, as if in shock. But perhaps it had never been a proper affair. What if he had been secretly visiting a prostitute, desperate for an outlet for the stress he undoubtedly felt? Maybe in November he had been threatened by a pimp in that seedy underworld. All Alice knew for certain was that, when an almost maternal protective instinct woke her at 3 a.m. last November, she had ventured downstairs to find Chris sitting up, shaking, with a brandy in his hands, refusing to speak about whatever had traumatised him. That night she yeaned to take him in her arms and for everything to return to how it once was between them. But she couldn't do so because Chris had been so tensed up that his body resembled a clenched fist. Something in his expression had made her think that if he were visiting a prostitute, perhaps he had just discovered that he was infected with a venereal disease. She had no proof of this shocking thought beyond his wretched silence, yet it had made her too afraid, or repelled, to reach out to him. Angered by his silence, and by her inability to confront the gulf between them, she had returned upstairs to the room that she no longer needed to lock to exclude him, leaving him to stew with his brandy and his guilt.

Maybe she had been completely wrong about him having contracted a venereal disease, but when a husband refuses to confide in his wife, how is she ever to know? If he had been visiting a prostitute last autumn, did this make his betrayal any better or worse? Was she meant to feel some consolation that he had not unwittingly fallen in love with some younger work colleague in the Department of Jobs, Enterprise and Innovation, that his betrayal had merely involved a financial transaction to allow him a few moments of unalloyed, escapist pleasure? Six months ago Alice would never have known how to answer such a question: back then she knew nothing about clandestine worlds. Now she knew too much, not through personal experience, but by peering over a precipice into online worlds whose existence she was previously unaware of. They had made her realise that perhaps Chris's infidelity had involved neither a romantic infatuation with a work colleague nor a furtive financial transaction. Maybe he had simply ventured into an internet world that she was only learning about, where grown-up people resolved their desires in grown-up ways. They matter-of-factly sought out friends with benefits and other odd terms that Alice would still know nothing about if her sense of panic and betrayal had not caused her to try and see if Chris was leaving any online footprint behind him. This was the strangest irony. She would never have unearthed this hidden world if she had not gone searching in vain to try to find her husband and understand what was happening to him.

What she needed to find tonight was a way to fall back asleep. For two decades her love for Chris was so overwhelming that she could never have envisaged this hollow feeling. But her desire to keep him at bay was only one of numerous new and strange sensations. Her pillow was now soaked in sweat, and her limbs felt flushed. Every day she could feel her body change in ways that perturbed her. These changes insinuated that she was growing old, and yet the more the menopause colonised her body, the more she felt herself regress to being a young girl at heart.

Alice didn't wish to dwell on this contradiction. She needed to fall back asleep. What noise had woken her? It wasn't anyone in the terraced house next door – the latest tenants from Poland or Latvia were mercifully quiet, though you could never be certain how long they would stay, or if some chaotic crew might replace them. She dismissed the crazy notion that Chris could be standing outside her bedroom door, that the noise she had heard might be his fingernails making a barely audible impact on the wood. But twice in recent months she had woken to find him in her room. On the first occasion he lay beside her in bed, his naked body hovering inches away, like she was a magnetic force field he was unable to resist. On the second occasion she found him on the varnished floorboards, wrapped up in a blanket beside her bed.

Turning over, Alice noticed a will-o'-the-wisp light flickering along the edge of the curtains. Curiosity made her peer out the window. In the distance, eerily bright and silent, flames rose from a burning building. The sight seemed coldly beautiful. Maybe this was what her life needed, one huge conflagration to make her feel truly alive. The flames had woken Ronan next door. Alice could glimpse his bald patch through a Velux roof window in his extension. His baldness gave him a monk-like appearance as he appeared to study files on an unseen computer intensely. Alice was amused. Ronan was no monk, and would hate to know that she could blatantly observe his hair thinning on top.

His sprawling extension was new. Three years ago Ronan had demolished a previous extension to build this latest monstrosity, which had initially included a conservatory vast enough to resemble a botanic garden glasshouse. Last year he declared the conservatory to be too cold in winter for his new hothouse-flower child bride and subdivided it, with a partition wall and a solar-panelled roof. This was Ronan all over, perpetually restless, unable to stop tinkering with his property. He was always trying out new ideas – a vast island marooned in the middle of his kitchen, or a walk-in fridge, which had contained 'his' and 'hers' racks for champagne. His innovations were often discarded as quickly as they had been incorporated, but invariably they made Alice and Chris's house seem shabby in comparison.

Ronan's inability to stop redecorating was one of numerous traits that had infuriated his first wife, Miriam. For years Miriam put up with the constant disruption, flattered by the notion that Ronan was trying to build her a dream house. Eventually Miriam realised, or so she told Alice before leaving him, that these perpetual renovations were Ronan's way of corralling her inside a luxurious prison. Ronan's alterations could never be completed. They had been his excuse to remain outside, like a child with an oversized toy drill, waving in at Miriam through triple-glazed windows while he tinkered with whatever adjustments would allow him to avoid having to sit down in one of his refurbished rooms to discuss his collapsing marriage.

Alice had never possessed much in common with Miriam, but it had lifted her heart when that woman used to pop in to laugh about Ronan's latest manic enterprise. Alice had longstanding reasons to distrust Ronan, but at least Ronan did things. Chris was his polar opposite, prevaricating and worrying every decision to death. Chris's innate caution had caused them to miss out on the prosperity being enjoyed by neighbours, who had purchased second and third houses, using those tax incentive schemes that people now always discussed at parties. Everyone in Blackrock appeared to own at least three houses or apartments, while Alice and Chris remained stuck in this terrace they had outgrown.

Had they also outgrown each other? Alice didn't want to think about this. She needed to drift back to sleep, her fist tucked between her legs for comfort. There was a growing dryness down there, a discomfort if she wore jeans. These outbreaks of thrush were making her dress differently – something else for Chris to comment on. '*Whoever you're buying this new underwear for, it isn't me.*' Chris was right: the lingerie that she felt a new compulsion to accumulate was not for his eyes, but this did not mean that she was buying it for other men to see. These skimpy purchases were about seeing herself in a fresh light in the privacy of her own bedroom and learning finally to feel good about her body. For now at least she wanted no man to see her naked, except in occasional fantasies, but she liked the idea that, even with the dreaded landmark of fifty looming, other men might still wish to see her clad in such underwear, that they would stare at her body for once and not at the scar on her right cheek – a legacy of that crash four years ago.

Chris carried too many reminders of the bad years after the accident, when her self-worth had dissipated. Not that she ever possessed much self-confidence: her parents had ensured this with their constant criticism of her personality. She had known moments of undiluted joy as a girl when out with her friends, but all girlish devilment disappeared when she returned home, to where any innocent expression of joy made her appear odd. The hardest thing in her childhood was the knowledge that she could do nothing right in her father's eyes.

Alice knew that his detachment stemmed from the emotional impoverishment of his own upbringing. Based on the few references he'd ever made to his childhood, Alice sensed that her father had rarely heard an expression of affection or encouragement while growing up in Booterstown, in a house 200 yards from where Ireland's first Minister for Justice, Kevin O'Higgins, was shot dead en route to Mass in 1927. Rather than ever recounting any nostalgic boyhood memories, Alice's father had preferred to boast about this O'Higgins connection, as if proud that Booterstown had historically witnessed a much better class of assassination than other suburbs. Her grandparents' house on Booterstown Avenue sounded like a mausoleum, where every unchecked emotion was subsumed into religious fervour, and the sole warmth came from a red bulb aglow on a Scared Heart shrine on the wall.

The only time that Alice ever heard of her grandfather becoming energised by life was during the 1930s, when circumstances briefly allowed him to parade around the suburb in a quasi-fascist Blueshirt uniform, denouncing *The Irish Press* newspaper as a communist organ more red than Stalin himself. The sole glimpse that Alice had of her grandmother's outlook stemmed from the single sentence with which this woman had greeted the return of her daughter, Alice's aunt, Patricia, after that young woman absconded from a convent, two years into a novitiate, realising that she lacked the vocation to be a nun. Alice's father used to enjoy retelling this story, not in any cruel way but unthinkingly, oblivious to the hurt that his younger sister had surely felt when greeted by their mother with the curt remark: 'It would be better for you to come back into this house in a wooden coffin than to bring shame on us like this.'

Alice knew little about her only aunt, not even if the woman were alive or dead. She just knew that the young woman had only remained living at home in Booterstown for a few weeks, pitied and ostracised as a spoiled nun, until she found a position as a clerk-typist in a government department. On the evening she received her first wage packet, Aunt Patricia had left Booterstown without a word to her parents or her older brother, and had truthfully never darkened their door again. Because

Alice's father made no effort to maintain a relationship with his sister, Alice always essentially regarded him as an only child. She had dutifully tried to care for him right up until his death. But now, in this curious reappraisal of her life brought about by the menopause, Alice no longer felt able to forgive him for his inability, even just once, to have praised her when she was an insecure child, desperate for anyone's approval.

When Alice was in fifth year in Mount Anville, the career guidance nun asked each girl in the class what she wished to be. Discreet entreaties were made for pupils to consider whether, like her unfortunate Aunt Patricia years before, they might suspect they had a latent vocation. Information packs were prepared for the standard jobs to which girls aspired: nurse, teacher, air stewardess. Alice's emphatic reply had perplexed the nun: she didn't wish to join the Civil Service or utilise the top marks she always received in foreign languages to train as an interpreter. Nor did she wish to study at UCD, where she might meet a nice husband from Mount Merrion. Alice had admitted to possessing only one ambition: she wished to become a Canadian. She could trace her dream of emigrating to Canada to the intense loneliness she had felt as a girl, lying in bed at night, listening over and over to her scratched copy of Joni Mitchell's album, *Blue* – one of the few albums she could afford. Alice could still recall her surge of emotion every time the needle reached the song 'A Case of You', in which Mitchell's confiding voice described the experience of sitting on a bar stool, drawing a map of Canada on a beer coaster and superimposing the face of her lover over it. The mysterious allure of that dimly lit bar had seemed as far and as magically removed as she could ever get from her childhood prison on Avoca Road. Alice hadn't cared about what career she pursued in Canada; she had just longed to escape from being pawed at tennis club hops and forced to kneel for family rosaries beneath a painting of Jesus proudly displaying his wounds, like a cocky Blackrock College rugby player trying to impress girls at a dance.

Her brief but unbearably exciting first romance, amid the frenzy of the Leaving Cert, almost derailed her plans. But its abrupt truncation, once her first boyfriend extracted every sexual favour he wanted, redoubled her determination to flee. Alice had felt estranged from her parents, exhausted by rows any time she tried to prise some tiny concession of adulthood. So, three weeks after her Leaving Cert results, she boarded a flight to Toronto with money saved up from her part-time job. It was her first time flying alone, her first attempt to evolve into her unimpeded self. She flew with a mixture of terror and anticipation, experiencing every new incident with a dreamlike vividness, the uniformed officials quizzing her at passport control, the taxi ride into the city that cost a fortune because she stupidly missed the sign for the rail link. She was overawed by the size of everything, except the cramped one-room apartment she managed to rent on the eighth floor of a building, overlooking a busy intersection, where traffic passed by as loudly at midnight as at midday.

For one bitterly freezing winter, Alice had hovered on the verge of becoming someone new. Sometimes in dreams she still picked her way through compacted snow to cross the chasm of Yonge Street and stand lost amid the bustle of Union Station, recapturing her sense of wonder at seeing the Royal Bank of Canada skyscraper glint in sunlight, with every window coated in twenty-four-carat gold. She had never experienced such coldness, but also such liberation, in a city where nobody knew the slightest fact about her. Canada was the place where she had hoped to shed the self-image forged by her parents' criticism. During that winter Alice often thought she would never feel warm again, returning late at night from her waitressing job to hear a hubbub of strange accents through the apartment's thin walls, going to bed wearing all her clothes because she could not afford to turn on the heat. Yet despite the wind chill she had always needed to be out walking and absorbing new sights, observing how Canadians seemed to be open but often camouflaged their inner feelings behind wide smiles.

Everything was bigger there, even the male dishwashers arriving for work in lumberjack shirts and brown Kodiak boots. Her fellow waitresses, in their Day-Glo shades of polyester, always described their weekends as 'awesome'. They found everything 'awesome', even the fact that Alice couldn't find the margarine in the fridge on her first day, unaware that Canadian margarine was bright orange. The tea tasted as dreadful as sawdust, the chocolate weak and sugary. She was unable to join in conversations in work about characters in a soap opera called *The Young and the Restless* because she couldn't afford a television. Whenever she passed electronics stores with displays of televisions in the window, however, Alice had always paused to gaze at the screens until she could at least put faces to the characters that her fellow waitresses gossiped about.

One evening, she was the only soul braving the cold when she spied a basement hardware store down an alley off Yonge Street, with a display of wooden handmade house-name signs in the window. Loneliness made her descend the snow-covered steps and enter the shop, the shrill bell above the door causing the elderly proprietor to look up. She knew that he recognised her loneliness and didn't mind the fact of her having no real business there.

'I just wanted to look at your signs,' she said shyly. 'They're beautiful.'

'My dad taught me to carve. There was nothing he couldn't do with wood.'

'I'm charmed by the name of this place.' She pointed to an oak sign for a place named Tanglewood. 'Does it exist?'

He laughed. 'I hope so, or I won't get paid. Tanglewood is out by the lake. A bunch of swells lived there in mansions when I was a boy. Then Polish migrants started building smaller wooden homes out there. The Poles were honest, hard-working folk, but I'm not sure the swanks welcomed them as neighbours. The place is filled with old trees and plenty of space to breathe. Go along the harbour till you reach Lake Shore Boulevard, and then past Sunnyside until you're almost at the Palace Pier Park. It's not worth the trip in this weather though, when everything is covered in snow. Wait till spring. Where do you hail from?'

'Ireland.'

'Do you think you'll stay here?'

Alice had blushed, afraid that her next sentence would sound idiotic. 'Did you ever feel something in your bones and just know it's going to be true?'

The man nodded. 'I felt that way the first time I met my late wife. We were only seventeen, but I could see our whole future in that moment.'

'The only thing I know about my future,' Alice confessed shyly, 'is that one day I'll walk down these steps again and order a sign like this for a home in Tanglewood.'

The man unexpectedly took her hand in his, her first true human contact since arriving in Toronto. Alice loved how he hadn't laughed but replied solemnly, as if making a vow. 'I'll esteem the job of making it a privilege, Miss. I won't have forgotten your face, and we'll laugh, remembering this freezing day that would make anyone feel lonesome in their bones.'

The sincerity in his voice kept her warm for days afterwards. Toronto possessed nightclubs and discos, but Alice knew she would not meet her soulmate there. She was not prepared to let herself be used by a boy again.

On icy weekends she was often the only passenger on the ferry that chugged out to the small islands hugging the city shoreline. There were hints of spring on the Sunday when she walked from Hanlan's Point to the edge of Ward's Island, past closed amusement parks and shuttered restaurants, until she was unable to bear the cold any longer. She could envisage these islands filled with bathers when the warm weather came. Everywhere would reopen then, and there would be more possibility of meeting strangers who might become friends. Being abroad was harder than she had expected, but when spring came to these islands she would lose her shyness and emerge from her chrysalis.

When the ferry back to the city docked at Queen's Quay that afternoon, her fingers were so stiff with cold that she could barely hold the telephone when an ingrained sense of familial duty made her halt at the telephone booth by the ferry terminal to make her token weekly call home. She longed for whatever semblance of warmth could be conjured from the two-bar heater in her flat. Cradling the phone and observing the handful of passengers boarding the next ferry, at first she had only half-listened to her father, who always made any incident sound impossibly grave. Then his words sank in, and Alice watched the ferry sail back out towards those islands and leave her ensnared in the childhood world she had fled from. In numb panic she quit her job, lost the deposit on her flat and spent any remaining savings on an overpriced flight home. She hadn't wanted to waste a single day, even though the doctors who discovered the cancer had given her mother three months to live.

After four months away, the house on Avoca Road felt like a drab museum of the childhood from which she was desperate to escape. She had formulated questions she was determined to ask her mother. This woman had never let Alice see into many corners of her life – corners Alice hadn't concerned herself with when fleeing the unspoken suffocation of home. She had imagined returning one day as a fully fledged adult, when she and her mother might commence a relationship as equals, but once she stepped across the threshold, Alice was reduced to being a child. She never asked her mother any personal questions. She lacked the words to frame them, and knew that her mother would regard such intimacy as impertinence. Instead, they had said nothing of significance, sitting in an unnatural silence, conscious of time ticking past. What Alice recalled about her mother's death wasn't the terrible pain the woman endured as bones protruded through her skin, it was the shocking banality of the conversation, the labyrinths of avoidance in which callers got lost. Yet she became aware of how much her parents could convey to each other without seeming to say anything. They possessed an intricate code of restraint by which they registered inexpressible emotions. Her abiding image was of her parents stoically holding hands – one lying in bed, the other seated on a chair – awaiting death as quietly as if waiting for a 46A bus to go and see Maureen Potter in the Gaiety.

After the funeral, neighbours spoke about the tragedy of her mother's death and the depth of her father's grief, which led him into a succession of mental hospitals, where doctors experimented with cocktails of drugs to patch up a man who had lost his reason to live. Nobody noticed Alice's tragedy at having been forced to return home to a country towards which she possessed no feelings. Her dreams of a new life in Canada had to be put in abeyance. How could any daughter abandon a father who was reduced to being a helpless figure, wandering hospital corridors in a dressing gown? Only once had Alice allowed herself to dream of escaping. It was on the evening she made her one, and only, visit to her Aunt Patricia, whom she had met for the first time when that woman made a cameo appearance at Alice's mother's funeral, and told Alice that she lived in a rented one-bedroom apartment in the Mespil flats near Dublin's Grand Canal.

Looking back, Alice realised that she handled this visit badly, not thinking through the implications of what she was asking her aunt to do. In her desperation to escape back to Canada, she had convinced herself in advance that Patricia would welcome her suggestion. Although surprised by Alice's unexpected visit, Patricia was initially friendly. During the first fifteen minutes of their conversation her combative, self-reliant aunt had asked Alice more probing questions about her ambitions in life than her parents had asked throughout her childhood. Alice had found the conversation liberating and disconcerting. Patricia didn't treat her like a niece but as another single woman, albeit one thirty years younger. It was the sort of conversation between equals that Alice had dreamed about returning to one day to have with her mother. Alice had been unable to stop gazing around her aunt's small flat, wishing that she could be magicked back to her own far smaller flat in Toronto. But the atmosphere soured when Alice blurted out her grand notion that Patricia should give up her cramped flat and keep her brother company by moving, rent free for life, into that Avoca Road house so recently visited by death.

'Are you crazy?' her aunt asked. 'Or maybe you think I'm crazy, that I'd give up my independence to skivvy for a stranger?'

'He's no stranger,' Alice had protested, 'he's your brother.'

Patricia shrugged dismissively. 'I think of William as my ex-brother. That's a lie in fact: I never think about William or our dead parents at all. I just spotted your mother's death notice in the paper, and curiosity made me attend her funeral. I wanted to see if they had managed to turn you into one of them.'

'Into what?'

'A true Prendeville, constipated by respectability.'

'That's my father's family you're criticising,' Alice had said defensively, knowing in her heart that she was using indignation to cloak her embarrassment at having allowed herself to concoct this fairy-tale solution, where an estranged brother and sister would live happily ever after.

Her aunt's sigh had displayed a sad exasperation. 'Family guilt is an emotional ball and chain. If you don't flee now, you'll drag this guilt around with you all your life; its shackles will cut into your skin. If you want to describe your father and his posse of maiden aunts as your family then that's fine, just don't presume to call them mine. My mother told me that I was as good as dead to them on the day I fled that God-awful convent, full of squabbling nuns addicted to novenas and to looking down their noses at each other. You'd swear that Jesus was a strong farmer's son who would only choose them as brides according to the number of acres their fathers owned. I should have had the guts to leave that convent sooner. I knew within a day that I was no nun. I also knew within an hour of returning home that I was no Prendeville. When my parents cut me dead, with your dad too much a eunuch to say a word in my defence, they set me free. At the funeral you told me you're longing to get back to Canada. Why aren't you on the next plane out of here?'

'How can I leave?' Alice had asked, distressed. 'My father is a broken man. Somebody has to mind him.'

'Because neighbours will think badly of you if you don't?'

'Because he's helpless. It would be unnatural not to worry about what will happen to him.'

Aunt Patricia lit a cigarette. Alice had sensed that her flinty gaze was forged by deep hurt. 'You come here pretending to be Florence Nightingale, but you're really trying to play pass the parcel. William is fifty-seven years old, in a comfortable job where he's never had to make one hard decision. If he had found the courage to stand up for me when our parents savaged me for leaving that convent, then he might have actually grown up. It's a miracle he conceived you at all because the man's balls have never dropped.'

'I don't want to hear such talk.'

'You need to hear it. If you want to help him, force him to take responsibility for his life. Your mother never stood a chance. She was a naïve young typist from Ringsend, startled by his proposal, propelled up the social ladder into the respectability of Blackrock, where her new neighbours called her Mrs Prendeville to her face and The Ringsend Slapper behind her back. She gave my parents a new purpose in their old age, to reshape her with sighs of disapproval until they sucked any spontaneity from her and cloned the type of daughter they never had. I'm sorry that she's dead and William feels depressed. He has every right to be. But he's hardly unique. We all get depressed at times. I know I do.'

'How do you cure it?'

'Everyone's different.' Aunt Patricia had taken a drag from her cigarette. 'But personally I've never known a dose of the blues that can't be cured by a weekend bender of irresponsible sex and drink, three or four times a year. Maybe it cures nothing, you can't cure life, but it sure as hell always makes me feel alive for a long time after.' The woman seemed amused by Alice's shocked expression. 'What's wrong, child? Do you think I've no sexual needs? Women my age are only reaching our peak. Men are pitiful creatures; they go sexually downhill in their twenties. I don't deny that sometimes I get lonely here, not so much for physical contact as for simple things like having someone to share a bowl of soup with in companionable silence after a long day. But God forbid that I ever lived the sort of life that your poor mother lived and only ever knew sex with one man. You need to be able to compare the experience to know you haven't been short-changed.'

'My mother was happy with my father,' Alice had replied, out of her depth, and aggrieved that this woman would discuss her mother like this.

'How do you know? Did you discuss sex with her?'

'No, but at least a man asked her to marry him.'

This unfair, cutting retort had been meant to conceal Alice's acute embarrassment, but Aunt Patricia didn't seem offended. Instead she laughed, enjoying Alice's pluck in standing up to her. 'What makes you think men didn't ask me? They never formed a queue, but three different men proposed. Two of them I loved, though one was a rogue. The third was a thoroughly decent man, but dull.'

'And each time you said no?'

'I wasn't so much saying no to them as to giving up my independence. Back then a woman needed to leave her Civil Service job the day she got married. A married woman couldn't apply for a passport or open a bank account without her husband's written consent. I'm not saying your mother wasn't happy or that William wasn't a kind husband, but being happy or not doesn't change the fact that once she put on a wedding ring she become utterly dependent on him. Love doesn't always last. I took a decision that I'd rather be lonely at times then dependent on any one man, especially if his attitude might change when I was no longer lying between his sheets but down in his kitchen, washing skid marks from his underpants.'

'That's disgusting.'

'It's reality. At my age I've no illusions left. Men aren't queuing up to marry me now, but if I feel like it I can still spot men who possess a bit of jizz and are happy to spend a lost weekend in my bed. I'm what people call a homewrecker, though I don't see any of the men rushing to leave their wives. The odd man crawls back here occasionally like a wounded dog, but they do their howling on the front step, because the advantage of living on the second floor is being able to tell them to bugger off home through the intercom. I leave them severely disconcerted, because I perform acts that wives rarely bother still doing, after a year or two of washing skid marks from their underpants.'

'I should never have come here.' Alice had risen, mortified and desperate to escape. 'I had no idea what you're like.'

Aunt Patricia had stretched out a hand to linger on Alice's fingers. 'And you think you know me now? How can you know anyone after ten minutes? You're too young to even know yourself yet, child. You think me harsh, but I'm only as hard as my parents made me. They only took me in after I left the convent because, while I had lowered their social standing by not taking my final vows, they were worried that neighbours might think even less of them if they turned me away. But they never welcomed me back as a daughter. Even if I had gone off and married a stockbroker from Vico Road, I'd have remained a failed nun in their eyes. Poor Patricia. I bet that's what your father calls me, a verbal tic picked up from them.'

'I've never known much about you,' Alice had confessed.

'Now you do. What you see is what you get. I'm not a helpless spinster, desperate to find a niche to crawl into. I love my little flat and my job. I carved out for myself the right to be happy years ago. I'm no longer part of your family, and you don't have to be either. Forget about what other people think of you, or if you're not careful you'll get trapped into nursing your father's grief for the next thirty years. You will get no thanks for it. William won't even see the sacrifices you're making; he'll merely think you're doing your duty as a daughter.' The woman leaned forward. Alice had felt deeply uncomfortable, as if asked to take sides in a quarrel that dated back to before she was born. 'You came on a wild goose chase if you think I can be coerced by guilt into looking after a man who has never needed to learn how to boil an egg. Listen to me, woman to woman. Your only duty is to yourself. I harboured a secret hope that one day you and I might somehow become friends, but unless you return to Canada I'm going to be disappointed. I'm not saying let him rot in John of God's; I'm saying you should help him to finally take responsibility for his own life. That's the greatest gift you can give him. Now, how are you fixed for cash?'

Alice had sat back down, shocked by the frankness of the question. 'I didn't come here looking for money.'

'I know. You and I both have our pride. Even if you were starving, you'd never come looking for cash. You're my closest living relative, my next of kin, I suppose … but I promise never to be a burden. You'll get no calls from the police thirty years from now to say that I've gone demented and am living here with seventeen feral cats. But I want to help you. I have post office savings. These days my blowouts are few and far between; I'm mainly content watching *Coronation Street* on telly. I bet you spent every penny you have flying home at short notice. Did William offer to refund the price of your flight?'

'He has too much on his mind,' Alice had replied, her hurt rekindled at how her father never thought to offer.

Aunt Patricia raised her eyes dismissively and reached for her handbag. 'I'll get my coat, and we'll have coffee in the Royal Hibernian Hotel in O'Connell Street. I love the foyer there. Afterwards I'll buy you a ticket to Canada at the Aer Lingus booking office, a twelve-month open return. It means that you can leave in a few weeks' time when you have things sorted out here, and if Toronto doesn't work you can fly home for free any time in the next year. I've not been much of an aunt so far, so consider this as my first, very belated gift to you.'

Alice had barely possessed the bus fare back to Blackrock. Her father was so mired in grief that it was impossible even to ask him for money for household bills. Most evenings she needed to walk to John of God's because she couldn't afford the bus fare. Aunt Patricia's unexpected offer was so overwhelming that Alice hadn't known how to respond, being as unaccustomed to generosity as to praise. Her aunt was offering a solution to her financial problems, but not to the problem that burdened her: what to do about a drugged father rendered as helpless as a child by grief.

Could Alice really have left him in that state, like her aunt had suggested? More than two decades had passed since the evening Alice sat in that flat on Mespil Road, and her future suddenly hinged on one decision. But in recent months this was the question she kept returning to whenever she woke like this at night. Had she taken the conscientious decision by staying, or had she merely been too cowardly to return to Toronto and search for a new job, when Aunt Patricia's offer meant that her aspiration could suddenly be transformed into reality. Alice couldn't remember how long she had sat in that flat, so overwhelmed by the weight of this decision that it seemed like no words would ever come.

Finally, Aunt Patricia grew inpatient. 'What have you to lose?' she urged.

Alice had just lost her mother. She suddenly felt that if she got back on a plane to Canada she would lose a sense of her identity. Confronted by Aunt Patricia's ultimatum, the vast anonymity of Canada scared her. A few months previously she had loved the fact that nobody knew her as she walked through Toronto, but that night in Mespil Road she had felt that, if she emigrated again, she would become truly homeless. Although Alice had constantly quarrelled with her late mother, they had retained a shred of closeness. If she were to emigrate again, though, she would never feel comfortable about returning to a house where only her father lived if she found Canada to be too lonely. Not that her father would turn her away, but how could you pick up the pieces in a relationship that barely existed? Alice had also begun to wonder if Aunt Patricia's apparent concern for her was actually a way of using her as a pawn, achieving victory over her estranged brother by luring his daughter onto a plane. Alice knew that she didn't love her father, but how could she abandon him in that state? Therefore, she had brusquely left her aunt's flat, never to return or to contact the woman again.

She had been determined to escape back to Canada one day, but only on her own terms and with her own money, after helping her father to regain the strength to live an independent life. Instead, during the following months, when her heart was truly in her boots, she met Chris, and miraculously, Chris's love saved her from descending into a trough of despondency. She had danced at school discos with Chris, liking him and sensing that he liked her, but while still at school she had needed a more extrovert boy to draw her out from her shyness. In the malaise after her mother's death, however, with her father's depression threatening to swamp her, Chris became her sanity and rock. From the start, Alice knew that there was nothing that Chris would not do for her. After six months her father was released from St John of God's Hospital. He spent his first few weeks at home sitting in an armchair, staring at the living-room window as if the glass contained an apparition of the Blessed Virgin. He was sufficiently embedded in the higher echelons of the Civil Service to have no need to keep regular working hours beyond making brief cameos to register his continued existence. Her father had ignored the vast collection of big-band records he once loved to listen to and the golf clubs he used to clean before every round. He thanked Alice for each meal she prepared, while stating that all food now tasted like cardboard. Then, beyond commenting on how pale she looked, he essentially ignored her existence.

By then Alice had found agency work as a temporary typist, shunted around a succession of solicitors' offices. Chris's flat in Belgrave Square in Monkstown became her sanctuary and refuge, the foreign land to which she migrated to escape from her father's unbearable sadness. She brought a hot apple tart wrapped in a tea towel in the basket of her bicycle on the night when she told Chris that she was ready to lose her virginity. She needed it to feel like a loss of virginity to block out that previous occasion when she had let herself be used. Chris had made love carefully and slowly, asking no questions about the absence of blood afterwards. Chris would not have cared if Alice had a dozen previous lovers; his only anxiety was not to hurt her. But Alice had cared. She wanted that night to be a fresh start. A tiny nagging voice – it sounded suspiciously like Aunt Patricia's – warned her that this habit was inherited from her parents – the idea that if you avoided mentioning something unpleasant, it would eventually feel like it never happened.

She had felt truly loved when Chris first entered her body, and truly pleased to give him such obvious pleasure. But she was also surprised and underwhelmed not to feel more pleasure herself, despite all the mystique surrounding sex. Chris did not swamp her with the same almost frightening ecstasy she recalled from her previous encounter, although, because her first boyfriend had got her gratuitously drunk, perhaps Alice only had imagined this rapture. What Chris gave her was an enormous feeling of well-being. His arms enveloped her protectively. He seemed wise and could make her laugh. For the first time in her life, Alice had felt special and truly loved.

Over the following months, Chris had regularly called to Avoca Road, often insisting on cooking for the three of them. It was a clever ploy. Chris knew that her father would feel an obligation as a host to rise reluctantly from his chair and keep their guest company in the kitchen, marvelling at the ease with which Chris cooked. Praising the flavour of each dish, her father would then, almost without noticing, become drawn into their preparation. Soon her father began to boast, with a childish sense of wonderment, about the simple meals he could cook. After they ate together, Chris often spent hours sitting with her father, drawing the man out of his silence by patiently discussing the most inane subjects, until one day her father had announced that he felt well enough to return to work full time.

This was the moment that might have allowed Alice to escape from Ireland, but during her months of walking with Chris in Dalkey, or allowing themselves to be cut off by the tide on the hidden White Rock beach so they could daringly make love outdoors, all she could recall about Toronto was the coldness of her flat. Chris had morphed into her new Promised Land. In recent years Alice had discovered that mentally she had she never left behind the vast spaces of Canada. Her time in Toronto had been tough, with barely enough money for food despite the long hours worked. She had felt desperately lonely there, but would have overcome her loneliness if her mother had not become ill. This riddle had begun to perplex her more and more, the mystery about what type of person she might have become if she had been given the chance to forge a new identity in Canada.

Alice knew that she desperately needed to fall back asleep. Often, when half-awake like this, she allowed her mind to fantasise about her unlived Canadian life. Rocking herself gently, she closed her eyes to watch the small ferry sail from Queen's Quay back out to the islands on that pivotal Sunday when she had phoned home. She could see the receiver dangling in the vacant phone booth as her father's puzzled voice asked if she was still there. In her fantasy world, she was not listening to his news about her mother's illness; she had not even had time to hang up the receiver in her haste to race back through the turnstile before the gangplank was raised and the ferry sailed again. Closing her eyes now, she could feel the boat sway beneath her and the wind bite her cheek. She knew that this same memory was being recalled by another Alice, who was drifting asleep in a wooden-built house in Tanglewood, Ontario. The other Alice, whom she wished to be. The braver Alice, who had reboarded the island ferry that Sunday before it voyaged back out into the churning waves. That illusionary ferry was charting its course. She could feel the swaying guard rail press comfortingly against her as it brought her out towards those pleasure islands with closed down arcades due to reopen in spring. She fell asleep at last, her eyes fixed on the intriguing promise of the distant horizon.

Chapter Five

Sophie

Tuesday 13th, 1.30 a.m.

I often consider that March night, when Dad was about to bid on yet another house, as marking the end of my childhood. Not that I was a child any more. I was a woman of nineteen when I woke, conscious of a red glow brightening my bedroom window. A building was on fire. I opened the curtains. The flames seemed distant. Everything felt distant that night. Before previous auctions my stomach had always been a knot of anxiety and guilt. I didn't want us to move from my childhood home, and yet I desperately wanted my parents to be happy. For weeks I was keeping my head down, trying to occupy an emotional no man's land amid the force field of tension about the auction.

Standing at that window, I felt disconnected from all that stress, realising that I was essentially grown up. Tomorrow's auction wouldn't affect my future. After years of dreading my parents moving, my life was moving on without them. Not that I didn't love Mum and Dad profoundly, but I was exhausted by the need to be their buffer, feeling I had to try and steer them back towards the intimacy which flowed naturally between them when I was younger.

That night I knew I could no longer carry the burden of being their bulwark. I was preparing to leave home to find a summer job in Italy before commencing an Erasmus year at the Università degli Studi di Urbino. I was leaving the safety of my childhood bedroom for a walled medieval city, famed for its Gothic and Romanesque churches. You never truly grow up until you leave behind the people and rooms you love most. As a child, what I loved most about my bedroom was the view from the window. During a seminar in my first year in UCD, a lecturer mentioned how a certain Greek poet always stood at a peculiar angle to the universe. The phrase stayed with me. I realised it was how I had always lived – at a peculiar angle to everything in Blackrock.

I recognised this divergence at fourteen when I first kissed a boy at the Wes disco and felt a peculiar sensation of emptiness. His hands didn't feel like sandpaper. Sandpaper would suggest roughness. But when he tentatively caressed my lower back, my skin felt like being massaged by a deli worker still wearing plastic gloves after filling a wrap. The boy stirred no emotion in me until I felt a stab of envy towards him after I later saw him kiss another girl in a skimpy skirt. I realised that it was her lips I longed to kiss, her fingers I wanted to caress my naked back. I wasn't scared at having outed myself to myself at that disco, just mildly self-critical that it took me so long to recognise the sexual angle at which I stood to the universe. In that moment I grasped why I used to love being babysat by Emer and Lauryn, Ronan's two daughters, who had always spent their evenings padding around half-naked, experimenting with their mother's Pout lip gloss until Miriam pouted off, escaping from Ronan's oversized mansion.

I was even born at a peculiar angle to the subtle crease-marks that map, in visible and invisible ink, the intricate layers of class distinction in Blackrock. My bedroom window surveyed two worlds. We lived in the last house in a 1920s' council-built terrace, with back gardens long enough to be allotments, built when Blackrock still retained its stubborn status as a one-carthorse independent township. Back then my window had overlooked the crumbling boundary wall of an eighteenth-century villa, whose elderly owner, as a young bride, saw her gardens dissected by the Dublin–Kingstown Railway. Forty years later her heart was dissected by the death of her three grandsons in the Great War.

Mr Jennings – our original next-door neighbour on the terrace itself, an elderly bachelor who cycled everywhere on an ancient bicycle, still tending to people's gardens in his eighties – once told Mum that sixty years ago you would barely have known if anyone still lived in that villa. The only signs of life were a weekly delivery of groceries from the Protestant firm of Findlater's and the emergence of the old lady's Austin Box Saloon through the gates every Sunday, when she nosed her way at a snail's pace to attend the Church of Ireland service in Booterstown. But once a year, on Remembrance Sunday, a Union Flag flew from her wall in an act of silent defiance against a changed world.

When she was found dead in the 1970s, developers broke through the gates during a bank holiday weekend to illegally demolish the historic villa, which had a preservation order on it. In its place they erected five-bedroom detached houses, built in an architectural style that might be described as mock-Tudor, semi-Georgian, Irish-Twentieth-Century-Grotesque. Scandinavian-style internal open planning added to the architectural confusion. The houses were not cosy to live in, but would have been great locations in which to shoot an ABBA video. Ronan, who had been in school with Dad, purchased the detached house that bordered our property – at a peculiar forty-five-degree angle. This allowed me to grow up watching the quarrelling quartet of Ronan, Miriam, Emer and Lauryn snipe at one another in their pyramid-shaped garden, the end of which opened onto a laneway, to which our garden had no access.

This meant that we weren't posh, but we now bordered on being posh, on one side at least. Not that I envied our posh neighbours to our left for having gleaming kitchens the size of Ukrainian grain silos. I preferred our homely, cluttered kitchen, with Mum and Dad bumping into each other when trying to cook. When I was young they found this an excuse to laugh and hug. This is how I remember my childhood, Mum complaining good-humouredly about our house's smallness, yet declaring that it would take a lot to shift her from her cosy love nest, where Mr Jennings, to our left, used to present us with fresh vegetables from his garden, passed over the wall, until the evening when Dad glanced over the same wall to find the old man peacefully slumped, propped up by the fork that he had been using when silently overcome by a heart attack. The terrace lost its sense of history after Mr Jennings died, and his son in America allowed a letting agency to move in a succession of often noisy tenants. But we were still near everything

– the library, the Dart station and Blackrock's two shopping centres, where I covertly observed leggy teenage girls purring with pleasure at being covertly observed by teenage boys.

It was five minutes by car from Gran's house – Dad's mum – who let me twirl around her bedroom in silk scarves so old they resembled trinkets captured by the crusaders. It was ten minutes from Granddad's house – Mum's dad – and fifteen from John of God's Psychiatric Hospital, into which Granddad booked himself twice a year. Or perhaps Mum booked him in. As a child I never understood what the building was or why Granddad sat there for weeks in an armchair, suffused with an inexhaustible, tangible sorrow. At six years old I thought St John of God's must be a castle. At eight I imagined it was a luxury hotel. At nine I boasted in class about my granddad staying in a palace, and ran out the school gates in tears when older girls made jokes that Granddad was 'a Lula in the loony bin'. I couldn't tell if Mum was angry with me or with them as she drove home, veering distractedly between lanes of traffic, her knuckles a white shade of fury, as if the steering wheel were someone's neck she wished to strangle.

It would be impossible to want to strangle Granddad, who did an irrevocable amount of damage without possessing a scintilla of malice. He seemed like a black hole in space that gradually sucks all energy into its infinite depths, from which nothing re-emerges. He possessed no living relatives except us. Or at least I forgot that he ever had any relations until years later, when, amid all the good wishes flooding into my Facebook page on my nineteenth birthday, I received a friend request from a Patricia Prendeville. I eventually figured out that this had to be Granddad's ancient sister, who resembled a small ball of indigent fury on the sole occasion I had ever encountered her. When I showed it to Dad he told me to delete it and say nothing to Mum, assuring me that he would ensure the old lady never bothered me again.

When I was small, Granddad accepted widowhood as a fossilised state, a terminus where he sat in a suit and tie, patiently waiting for God to remember to collect him. I saw him as such a solitary figure that it was hard to imagine he had ever been anything other than an only child. He rarely had much to say, but this never hindered him from repeatedly saying it. I could see how he drove Mum demented, while she constantly drove him to medical appointments.

To be fitted for the hearing aid that was so expensive he refused to wear it in case it got lost.

To collect him for memory tests he forgot to be ready for.

To correct him patiently when he started forgetting my name, or sometimes called me Alice and called Mum by his late wife's name.

Mum was deeply tolerant and caring with him, but very occasionally frustration overcame her. She would lose patience with him, then get angry with herself for being angry. But one afternoon I saw Mum not get angry, but get lost. We were late as always for a medical appointment, and halted at traffic lights on the Stillorgan dual carriageway. When the lights changed, Mum didn't move. She stared through the windscreen, in the same way as Granddad beside her was staring into space. Watching them gaze distractedly ahead, I noticed a facial resemblance, though I knew Mum would be annoyed if I mentioned this similarity. I was used to Mum's temper, which rarely lasted long, and was made up for with kisses afterwards. What scared me at that moment was that she was oblivious to motorists beeping behind us. The lights went red, and Mum continued to stare ahead. Only when they turned green again and the agitation of car horns reached fever pitch did I find the courage to lean forward and shake her shoulder. She looked at me distractedly, then changed gear and drove on.

'Where were you, Mum?' I asked, scared. 'You were miles away.'

Mum smiled, though I couldn't fathom her answer. 'I was in Canada.'

Mum never mentioned Canada again, but that Christmas she purchased a kitchen calendar with pictures of Canadian cities: Saskatoon, Vancouver, St John's in Newfoundland. She never let me turn over the colour photograph until the first of the month, rationing each vista so their novelty could sustain her imagination. I was then at an age to begin to wonder what Mum did. Some classmates had mums in full-time jobs, while others parroted the mantra that 'Mummy works in the home'. No girl called their mum a housewife. You only heard such a stone-age term, like 'coloured folk' or 'shoulder pads', on old television repeats. One night I asked Mum what she had wanted to do as a girl. The vehemence in her one-word reply upset me.

'Emigrate.'

'But you have me and Dad here. You don't still want to emigrate, do you?'

Mum had laughed, tucking me into bed after reading aloud from my library book.

'Don't be silly,' she had said. 'You're my life now; you mean everything to me.'

A Polish girl, Monika, joined my class during my last year in primary school. Our mothers ensured that we made her welcome, and they welcomed her mother into the public fringes of their world. Every day that autumn my classmates raced around the playground in Blackrock Park while a hard core of mothers congregated on two adjoining benches, volunteering in turn to fetch takeaway consignments of tall skinny lattés. I'm unsure who enjoyed this stolen hour more – us girls, or our mothers, who seemed to be permanently convulsed with laughter. Mum so adored being part of these long, gossipy chats, finding herself at last among a circle of friends, that we were invariably the last to leave.

One afternoon, as I balanced on top of the wooden maze, I glanced back at Monika's mother on the bench. She seemed to be at the epicentre of the gathering, laughing whenever the other mums laughed. Yet, from the angle at which I was observing her, I could discern how, despite trying to hide it, she remained an outsider, an immigrant pretending to be attuned to the unselfconscious camaraderie of the other women. Some mothers were best friends, others disliked each other, but all were bound by class, age and background. That same afternoon I glanced towards Mum, and it was like seeing her for the first time. Although she also sat at the core of that huddle, her face betrayed the same anxiety as Monika's mother, a sense of trying to keep up with the flow of jokes, but being always a second behind. It made no sense; Mum was born in Blackrock; but at that moment it was like she was playing a part, and this was not her true life. She looked like an immigrant who belonged elsewhere, though not even she seemed aware of it.

Mum didn't work outside the home when I was small. She found this isolating, but would never let anyone see her when she had the blues or felt the walls were closing in. She lived for Dad to come home, or for Miriam to call in and bitch about Ronan. Mum had brains to burn, she just lacked confidence. She claimed never to have paid attention in school, but remained fluent in French and Italian. Ronan possessed no actual friends, which was why he adopted Dad as a press-ganged sidekick, but he had numerous business acquaintances who occasionally called in to ask Mum to translate legal documents. Ronan offered to help Mum set up a small translation bureau, yet even as a child I sensed that Mum never trusted Ronan.

It was through Ronan that she met Vicky, the latest French wife of a diminutive Glenageary barrister, who, by virtue of an inability to decline any photo opportunity, no matter how inane, was called a 'celebrity barrister' in the newspapers. I preferred Mum's assessment of him as the sort of middle-aged man with expensively reattached hair who regularly trades in his wife for a younger model. The funny thing was that Vicky was far older than him. He had the awestruck look of a goatherd after waking to find a sophisticated Marianne Faithful type blowing Gauloise smoke rings at him in a wryly resigned but possessive tone. On his sole visit to our house he boasted about her three previous failed marriages, as if he were the possessor of a vintage Rolls–Royce with illustrious past owners. Vicky never mentioned him at all, beyond confiding to Mum that, on her first morning in Glenageary, she went through his house to quarantine every pair of his underpants. She burnt them in the back garden, telling neighbours who complained about the smoke that it was not a bonfire but an exorcism.

Vicky understood clothes. As a former Parisian fashion photographer, she retained contacts with continental rag-trade wholesalers willing to supply stock to a small boutique in Blackrock, aimed at the high-end market. This was soon after Gran died, and Dad and his sisters sold her red-brick house on Temple Road, just before the property boom took off. Dad inherited enough to buy the forty per cent stake Mum was offered in Vicky's new boutique on Main Street. Dad never saw it as an investment: he recognised it as a lifeline for Mum, a way to make new friends and feel fulfilled by becoming a partner in a business.

For Vicky, the boutique was an excuse to fly to fashion shows in Europe and meet old friends and lovers while sourcing stock at high discounts. Vicky transpired to be a tough businesswoman down to the tips of her fingers, which were as long as a concert pianist's. But for Mum, the position of becoming a co-owner and the manageress of a boutique offered her a new role beyond that of being a mother to me and a daughter to an elderly father who was slipping into dementia.

No teenager set off to do their Leaving Cert oral Irish exam with as much trepidation as Mum had set out with on her first day to open that shop. Dad and I needed to reassure her, soothe her nerves and give her confidence. I was then in second year in secondary school. After school I sometimes slipped into the queue of elderly pensioners, who companionably compared ailments while waiting to collect their pensions in the post office opposite the boutique. I would stare across at Mum living out her new life, on public display through the boutique's window with its immaculately dressed mannequins. I could even glimpse the discreet inner sanctum, where well-heeled customers sat on elegant chaises longues, sipping complimentary coffee.

I loved watching Mum take centre stage in this new version of her life. I didn't feel neglected when going home to an empty house, I felt relieved, realising that I'd always sensed a void in Mum's life, which I tried to compensate for with manifestations of love. Therefore, when surreptitiously passing the boutique, I felt a parental pride. Even at that age, I often felt like the real adult in the house, trying to sustain some equilibrium in my parents' volatile relationship. Dad could never do enough for Mum, and Mum was intensely grateful for every tiny thing. But each tiny thing invariably seemed slightly wrong in her eyes. It was nearly perfect, and she knew that Dad really tried to get it perfect, but despite her expressions of gratitude he would sense her disappointment and take it personally. He never grasped that her disappointment wasn't intrinsically with him or his gift, it was with her life. How could he buy the perfect gift for someone who was ever present and yet simultaneously absent from our lives? Even while doing something with us, Mum was generally somewhere else in her mind, worrying about irrational fears, which magnified due to her inability to confide in anyone.

But during the year when she managed that boutique, Mum was utterly present in her everyday life. Vicky infuriated her with constant demands, yet gave her huge confidence by insisting that Mum could easily handle the various crises with creditors and suppliers from which Vicky generally absented herself. Left with no choice, Mum discovered that she could. The mums from my old primary school paid initial visits to the boutique to finger the expensive garments. One joked that, if she had an affair with the Aga Khan, this was definitely where she would shop for silk knickers. As Mum mixed in new circles, she gradually lost contract with those sociable mothers with whom she had been friends.

Mum's customers lived in detached houses, with no street numbers but ornate nameplates on pillars beside electronic gates, women lured into the boutique by curiosity, hoping to glimpse Vicky, whose name regularly appeared alongside her husband's in the gossip columns. Good things happened to Mum in that year, but bad things too. Mum was naïvely innocent and easily swayed. She encountered women with a different version of what constituted 'normal' life. They impressed or overwhelmed her, they infuriated or amused her, they flattered and sometimes patronised her, they gave her a fragile new confidence, but also a new shame. On the first morning she set out for work she still viewed our small house as a love nest, but increasingly she began to see it through her customers' eyes as a quaint terrace in which no normal person could live, especially when raucous tenants frequently occupied the rooms on the other side of the wall, or at least no normal person in the context of what passed for normality amid her well-heeled clientele.

Vicky encouraged her to accept invitations to evening soirées in customers' homes. A soirée is essentially a party without cocktail sausages. Mum was scared to go alone, so I became her chaperone. But we got our roles reversed one evening in Leopardstown, soon after that boy kissed me with his cold fish tongue at the Wes disco. My gaze must have lingered too openly on the bare legs of a teenage girl lazing on an ornate bench in the crowded back garden. When I went inside, the two downstairs loos were occupied. I slipped upstairs to use a bathroom there, and was cornered on the stairs by a sixteen-year-old girl in a short skirt. She dissected me with an amused languid stare.

'She's too young for you,' she said, 'so stop making eyes at my kid sister.'

'I wasn't.'

She kissed me suddenly, her lips tasting of champagne.

'Liar, liar, your pants are on fire. Or they will be shortly. I'm not too young for you, and you're exactly the right age for me.'

She held my hand tight when I tried to pull away.

'I know what you are. You know it too, even if you pretend you don't.' Her voice was vaguely patronising. 'You should see the view from my bedroom. It's even better when the curtains are drawn.'

She never drew the curtains. Perhaps she liked the risk, or maybe she knew that nobody in the garden could see so far back into her enormous room. If I had not already known that I was a lesbian, then I certainly knew it after the twenty minutes we spent there, while below in the garden Mum awkwardly tried to mingle with other guests around the marquee. The girl came three times under my inexperienced fingers, silent, nonchalant climaxes. As I came for the first time under a girl's touch, I panicked when she pressed a pillow over my face, then realised that she was trying to prevent my loud cries reaching the guests below.

'Try not to frighten the horses next time you come.' She caressed me and then skipped off the bed. 'Get your mother to splash some cash on your boobs, they could use sculpting. But don't let a surgeon touch the hood on your clitoris: you have a clit to die for.'

I got dressed and ventured towards the window. I could still feel the taste of her tongue inside me. My left nipple was bruised. I had not expected sex with another girl to be rough, but I was so young, indeed too young, that I didn't know what to expect. I felt grown up and strangely lonely. I also felt guilty, not about the sexual acts I had committed, but because I could spy Mum alone in the garden, lost among those rich women. She was clearing messages from her phone to give the impression that she was busy doing something. She looked in need of rescue. My phone would have several frantic messages. I looked back at the older girl, who had got back into bed.

'You may have a big house,' I said, 'but I am a better person than you.'

She laughed, kicking off the sheet to flaunt her naked body. 'Feast your eyes. Which part of you is better?'

'I'm just better. And my Mum has more class than the whole lot of you.'

I raced downstairs and out into the garden, but Mum was too busy to ask where I had been. Granddad was on the phone yet again to complain that nobody had called to see him in days.

Granddad, with whom Mum and I had spent an hour before going to this soirée.

Granddad, whose care attendant was due to call at half eight to help him to bed.

Granddad, who had become hopelessly marooned in recent weeks after a tiny fuse blew in his brain so that he could no longer keep track of time.

The responsibility of minding him drew Mum and Dad closer together, yet his death would be the first step in the process that seemed to draw them apart. What happened on the night of his death was like a tiny crack in an ice floe which gradually widened until, on the March night of that fire, a faint noise on the landing made me open my door an inch. It was the first time I saw Dad naked. No man could ever have appeared more naked than he did, his eyes closed and his forehead helplessly pressed against the closed door of the bedroom they once shared.

Chapter Six

Ronan

Tuesday 13th, 1.15 a.m.

It was late. Ronan needed to go to bed. So why was he frozen at his extension window, staring out at the ghost of himself looking back in? Even with every lamp extinguished, his reflection still blocked off the outside world, forcing him to scrutinise his features in the triple-glazed glass.

He was watching the sky like Paul Hughes had suggested, but Hughes's arsonist could burn down half of Blackrock for all Ronan cared. The fire would never reach here. This detached house had been smaller when Miriam and he started their life together. It was built with a tapering garden in the 1970s, when architects took drugs on field trips to Scandinavia. Initially it was a house they could not afford, but sometimes you can't afford to miss out on what you can't afford, a fact that Chris next door seemed unable to grasp. Ronan had spent decades correcting the design flaws, remaking each room to reflect his self-image. He had doubled the square footage, with Jesuitical use of retrospective planning applications to retain additional features. No expense was spared, and the only external presence allowed in was light. It gave Ronan particular pleasure that his late father would not only hate this house, but be unable to decode its extravagant minimalism.

Ronan needed to sleep, but he couldn't, not yet. He was pondering ways to activate Hughes's plan if Chris failed at auction tomorrow. But thinking about Hughes was merely another way of remembering Miriam at sixteen, even if it meant imagining her with another boy. Miriam was gone, after years of incessant recriminations, leaving Ronan free to start afresh in middle age. He had done so judiciously, rebuilding his life with the same attention to detail with which he remodelled this house. He was envied by contemporaries still mired in acrimonious relationships. He had made his problems disappear. So why could he not focus on the benediction of what he possessed, on the miracle of sharing his home with the most beautiful woman he had ever slept with?

Kim had long gone upstairs. She always went to bed before him. He had never known anyone to undress with the tranquillity of his second wife, who could wash her face, comb out her long hair and don a silk nightdress while barely making a sound, immersed in her thoughts. Ronan wasn't certain what his Filipina wife thought about, nor was he certain what she thought about him. He knew what other couples thought about them from the sly glances that men his age gave Kim, followed by the acrimonious glances of their wives. He knew that entering a room with his young bride changed how he appeared in people's eyes; he just could not fathom how he appeared in Kim's eyes. After eighteen months of marriage he knew less about Kim now than on their wedding day.

Early in their relationship he was overwhelmed by an influx of sensations; the absolute pertness of her nipples, the sweetness of her small breasts, her sexual generosity, her compliance. This seemed an odd word, but it fitted. Not that Kim was compliant in any sense of being coerced; it was more that she seemed infinitely malleable, anticipating his desires without him even daring to ask. She was innocently naked in enjoying her own pleasure. She loved what his tongue's perseverance could achieve. Ronan would happily lie between her legs for eternity, teasing her clitoris with his tongue until she came. His tongue possessed infinite patience, because this put less pressure on other parts of his anatomy to perform like the stud he had once been. When Kim finally came, she always did so in a way that truly excited him. She came with all her body, her legs shaking involuntarily, her arms thrown back across her tightly closed eyes, her hips buckling so much that he needed to grip them with both hands to allow his tongue to keep orbiting her pertly inflamed clitoris.

Kim's pleasure was absolutely complete, and it absolutely and completely excluded him. It took Ronan a while to realise this. At first there was just the wonderment of possessing a second wife. He had survived the bitter break with Miriam by reinventing himself. He was in love with a younger woman, who seemed in love with him; somebody who gave him the deepest pleasure, for longer and more often than he had imagined possible in recent years. Yet during her crises of pleasure he had started to see how she withdrew from him. Not only did her eyes remain closed, but her essence became sealed. Her body might be nakedly exposed, but she withdrew into a private sphere during those seconds as she came in a soundlessly self-contained orgasm. Locked outside, Ronan could never be certain about what she felt, or whom she thought about, during such moments.

It was ten nights since they last made love. Not that Kim betrayed any unwillingness. The uncertainties existed in Ronan's mind. As he moved away from the window to enter his office and sit at his computer, he heard a creak of bedsprings overhead. He could envisage Kim drowsily turning over. All he needed to do was walk upstairs, strip naked and curl in against her. When his hand slipped beneath her nightdress she would turn automatically towards him. That word was the problem: *automatically*. Not obediently. Obedience implied a different type of relationship, it implied power or domination. Not passionately, because he recalled how Miriam had been passionate, littering his neck in love bites in the abandon of lovemaking, bodies glued together in the universe of their old double bed. *Automatically* implied a more muted response; it implied acceptance. It implied that they would make love if Ronan ventured upstairs, and they would not if he stayed down here. It implied that neither outcome would leave Kim better or worse off. It left Ronan feeling obscurely cheated.

He had taken a gamble in middle age and won, so why did he increasingly feel that he had lost on some unfathomable level? After Miriam fell out of love with him, their situation became impossible. But he had tackled the loneliness of separation like he tackled every problem life threw at him. He had refused to settle for the bitter silence that permeated his childhood home, where his parents spent their last decades communicating through unspoken codes of disapproval, his father only referring to his mother as 'that woman'. His parents' sour compromise of a marriage was no different from hundreds of unions endured in an era when respectability ranked above happiness, where all emphasis and effort went into maintaining an appearance of harmony. Ronan could no more imagine his mother ever leaving his father than he could imagine her having an orgasm. The Blackrock his mother had been forced uncomfortably to try to blend into was a fossilised statelet, dowdily respectable and possessing an acute self-awareness of its niche within the social stratosphere, neither a Dublin suburb nor an independent township. It had existed like an annexed Czechoslovakia, a buffer zone controlled by the Dun Laoghaire ratepayers to keep themselves apart from the sprawling populace of Dublin, who possessed postal codes, poor dental hygiene, and never washed behind their foreskins.

His parents would not recognise today's Blackrock, its young people jamming The Wicked Wolf pub at weekends to blow more cash in a night than it would have taken their grandparents a year to save. Main Street throbbed with the perfumed aphrodisiac of prosperity, rooted and rootless, seductive and insatiable, unchaste and oddly adolescent. Lines of S-Class Mercedes–Benzes and lines of cocaine. Long-legged trophy girlfriends drinking exotic beers from long-necked bottles, their dress sense as uninhibited as if they and their boyfriends owned the world. They had such self-confidence that, if magically transported to any bar on earth, they could hold their own for the few moments it would take to discover an old school friend there who knew a girl who once slept with a boy who once attended the same Montessori as them.

Ronan had possessed the balls not to be left behind by this juggernaut of contemporary Ireland. He had refused to let his life be soured by the fact that marriage can be a feast where the dessert is served first. He had held on to this house by remortgaging it massively to be able to buy Miriam the small Edwardian house she craved in the part of Sandymount uncontaminated by Ringsend. He had acquiesced in letting her solicitor fleece him, then succumbed to the indulgence of drinking himself stupid for a month before he started his life again, like his father did after his business in Dublin went bust when Ronan was a boy.

His father had restarted from scratch by going to England in the 1960s, digging ditches and unashamedly slaving for subcontractors while calculating how to undercut them. Ronan's way of restarting had been to go on the internet, posting his profile on dating sites. Like his father, he learnt the rules quickly. Loneliness was a commodity controlled by supply and demand, like any other. He learnt not to be over-nice to the women he met for awkward coffees, as this came across as pushy; not always to pay for every meal; and not to compliment a good-looking woman on her appearance, as she would have heard this too often as a try-on. He learnt to be wary of Russian girls whose profile photographs were too perfect, and avoid Irish women his own age, because they carried excess emotional baggage and reminded him of his ex-wife.

The route to success was to make women laugh, but with Kim he had sensed an immediate difference. He did not need to make her laugh or employ charm to impress her. After an initial awkwardness during their first meal, any discomfiture between them ceased. In her reserved quietude he could sense Kim's willingness to accept him for what he was; part sophisticate and part buffoon, imperfect and impulsive, affectionate and exasperating. Here seemed to be the miracle of a younger woman who understood that it was Ronan's myriad contradictions which made him tick. Kim possessed such understated beauty that, midway through their first meal, he had abandoned any hopes of them ever becoming sexual partners. Instead, he had felt genuine concern for her, angry when she revealed how her landlord was illegally rigging the electricity meter in her bedsit, anxious about the dangerous route she had to walk home from the hospital, where she worked as a nursing attendant. His feelings contained the same protectiveness he used to feel towards his daughters, until Emer and Lauryn moved out, unable to cope with their parents' rows. He was so fatherly after the meal, escorting her to her bus stop and waiting until the bus came because he didn't trust the youths loitering nearby, that it never occurred to him to attempt to kiss her. Kim needed to turn back, after ascending the step up onto the bus, to kiss him and whisper that she hoped he might like to phone her again.

Kim had accepted him for what he was. Within six months they were married. She was not actually as young as she looked, or as she had first told him, but she was still young enough to make him sometimes feel he was committing a semi-incestuous sin, like sleeping with one of his daughters' friends. Her beauty stranded him in a position that most men his age only fantasised about. Maybe this was the problem: the tangible acquisition of your dreams robbed you of the right to fantasise. Some nights while Kim slept Ronan lowered the duvet to kneel and gaze at her, utterly beautiful and utterly foreign, her body impossibly perfect, as if porcelain had softened into flesh. Curiously, he would feel no sexual desire when gazing at her on such nights. How could you covet what you already possessed? Instead, he felt a curious ache. It was as if Kim had materialised from inside his imagination – an artist's impression of sensuality inadvisably conjured into actual flesh and blood. What if the acquisition of paradise robbed you of the urge to strive towards the next unreachable horizon? Gazing at her sleeping body he felt obscurely swindled by reality, robbed of any craving to touch her breasts because they were so readily available.

Did tycoons like Paul Hughes possess this same sense of feeling somehow cheated by the actuality of seeing all their dreams come true? Behind the high-octane talk about property in the Playwright Inn, Ronan sometimes noticed a perplexed look cross a speaker's face, perturbed by a malaise they could not articulate. As boys playing rugby they had been indoctrinated to be unafraid of getting hurt as they rucked and mauled to find the space to surge into the open, fighting off every tackle because the momentum that drove them forward was like the surge towards a sexual climax. Nobody could stop them reaching that try line, even if they died in their efforts to ground the ball triumphantly. But what happens if you have already won everything and there is no longer a sense of achievement in facilely raising yet another silver trophy in the air?

The real world wasn't like rugby anyway. It had no fair-minded touch judges or bonds of comradeship with teammates whom you imagined would be your friends forever. You were alone. Customers set you crippling targets. You helped colleagues if you could, but screwed them if it was necessary to get ahead. There was no applause or good losers as you learnt to do whatever was needed to build a nest for those you loved. This was the brutal reality of being an adult with loved ones and dependants. Once it had been Miriam and the girls; now it was Kim. But if you sometimes needed to get your hands dirty, you owed it to your loved ones never to let ugly truths intrude into the sanctuary you created for them, never to let them see any blood or shit or muck carefully cleansed from your fingernails after you did whatever was needed to protect and provide for them, and then stepped back into their lives, never permitting yourself any wince or grimace that might betray the pain you had been through.

Ronan was brooding when he should be in bed. He just needed to walk upstairs and Kim would make him feel young by turning her body towards his. But this was a lie. The truth was that Kim made him feel old. His former rugby teammates were growing old, his generation successful beyond their wildest dreams. Naturally, not everyone was rich. There were those once-cool dudes in leather jackets who for years had kept reappearing in Blackrock bars like Halley's Comet, trailing stories about their apparent success in Australia or New York; arty types who had claimed there was nothing here for them in what Bob Geldof called 'a 'banana republic'. Ronan remembered Geldof getting expelled from college, a few years ahead of him, for being an opinionated prick. But Geldof had balls, and Flemish entrepreneurial blood, which was just as well, because he couldn't sing for fuck.

The guys of Ronan's generation who stayed through the grim 1980s and 1990s had taken risks, purchasing decrepit Victorian houses off Stradbrook Road for a hundred thousand punts, and watching them soar in value to three and four million euro, guys saddled with mortgages and smelling of baby vomit, forced to endure the taunts of wannabe Geldofs home from New York during the 1990s, with sharp suits and attitudes, droning on about film deals that never actually happened. The guys who remained in Ireland had reshaped Geldof's banana republic, lobbying for European grants and American jobs, rewriting corporation tax laws to please major US firms and annoy US administrations, allowing multinationals discreetly to Bed and Breakfast their profits in a fashionable European capital. His generation had refused to kowtow to Boston or Berlin, but by playing the US off against Europe were now rich beyond the dreams of their parents. It was his emigrant classmates who looked like the fools now, coming home not to parade their wealth but to marvel at what they had missed. They rarely mentioned their unmade films any more, but moaned that every barman in Blackrock came from Poland.

Ronan was a bit-player in Ireland's jackpot extravaganza, his separation agreement having almost bankrupted him. But he had re-mortgaged and retained his house, and after Chris fucked up at auction tomorrow he would be poised to persuade Christ to get involved in the plan that Paul Hughes had suggested in the Playwrights. He would help his neighbours, and help Hughes, who had hinted that some investment opportunities might miraculously open for Ronan if one favour begat another. He would invest his share of the profits in a unit-linked fund in Kim's name alone, creating a considerable nest egg, which would allow Kim the freedom to walk away if she found it impossible to live with a man whom Miriam always claimed it was impossible for any woman to live with.

Ronan left his office and walked back to the extension window. There it was at last, a distant glow of flames. Hughes's site was on fire – a dirty business, but how the real world operated. Staring out at the fire scared him, however, because, regardless of the angle at which he stood, he could still see his own reflection in the glass, and now the red glow made it appear that his heart was burning, like in those childhood pictures of the Sacred Heart. The sensation was eerie and indescribably lonely. He wanted Miriam to call him away from the window, telling him to come to his senses and go to bed.

He stepped back, knowing he was drunk. Miriam was gone. He longed to creep upstairs and lower the duvet to gaze wondrously at Kim's body. He wanted to kiss her exposed nipple so softly that his gesture of love would not wake her. Then he longed to cover up her nakedness and slowly lower the duvet again so that, by magic, he might for a few seconds glimpse Miriam asleep in the shapeless, sexless, baggy pyjamas she always wore. Now that Miriam was irrevocably beyond his reach, what he wanted most of all was to curl in beside her for just one moment, knowing that if she woke she would not bother to turn, barely registering the comfortable familiarity of his presence.

Ronan re-entered the inner sanctum of the walled-off section of the extension that he had converted into his office, or, as he preferred to call it, his study. Sitting at his computer he clicked the mouse to close the spreadsheet – his calculations of the costs involved in Hughes's scheme, and what profits to accrue to everyone. He listened, but there was no sound of Kim leaving the bed like Miriam used to do, coming down to ensure he wasn't working too late or drinking too much. He clicked the Google search engine, its history ready to be wiped as clean as a soul after confession. Ronan had no interest in porn models or domination, and an abhorrence of anything involving children, but the danger in this infinitely expanding cyber universe was that you never knew what would appear. You clicked on one image and your computer was redirected onto a random thumbnail gallery of unsought pictures, images so numerous you could never take in everything that appeared. A click on another tiny thumbnail sent you hurtling through more vast galaxies of random faces and snippets of home videos captured on camera phones, an expanding limbo where you never knew what was real or staged.

As a young man Ronan had enjoyed smuggled copies of *Playboy* when such magazines were banned in Ireland. He had felt an intellectually superior sense of arousal when perusing the experimental Parisian eroticism of Henry Miller or Anaïs Nin. But Nin's novels contained narratives; they were escapism from which one could escape. The internet was a kaleidoscope without beginnings or ends, an interconnecting web primed to draw you in with erotic triggers. In this sphere where outside problems were suspended, a moment's curiosity could turn into four hours when all sense of reality was abdicated, when you become so enraptured in arousal and self-disgust that everyday cares couldn't reach you. It was a world where Ronan felt like a fly trapped on flypaper, eternally breaking his promise to download only one more glimpse into the lives of strangers.

Ronan had possessed no interest in internet pornography until the final year of his marriage to Miriam, when they rowed so constantly that their daughters screamed at them to make up or break up. Back then there seemed some emotional justification for turning on his computer to allow himself a respite from reality, a method of release that demanded nothing back. But what possible excuse had he now, when Kim awaited upstairs? What could he search for that could match

Kim's tactile actuality? Ronan was not trying to find something, but momentarily to lose something: himself. With the excuse of a collapsing marriage stripped away, he was forced to recognise these computer sessions for what they were. These sites let him cruise in a comfort zone, an addict whose conscience and bothersome moral compass was switched off. These images were heart-numbingly intimate, yet utterly impersonal. Amateur, home-shot galleries provided glimpses into mundanely bizarre lives, a network of loneliness, with everything revealed and nothing felt, with judgement suspended and emotion numbed by the public manifestations of intimacy that these couples needed to display.

Their demonstrative passion reminded him, in a warped way, of his parents' outward respectability. These worlds were utterly different, and yet, at some level, there was the same sense that everything was being done for show, presenting a façade that betrayed no cloud of unhappiness. In the anonymity of cyberspace the whole world became transformed into your prying neighbour. Instead of framed pictures of diocesan pilgrimages to Lourdes, couples on the net tried to convince outsiders that everything was harmonious in their lives through exaggerated orgasms and slow-motion money shots sprayed across women's angelic faces. The potential illegality of these sites, plus the hurt they would cause Kim if she knew, allowed him to experience danger at a surrogate distance. Marriage to her had not cured his jaundiced obsession. He had proved to the world that he was a success, so why was he overwhelmed by the sense of being a fraud at heart on nights like this, when he sat mired here until dawn?

Maybe he was two different people. When among other men, his competitive impulses kicked in. He was the competitor with a side bet on every hole in golf, the golfer who would sell his soul to win a 'closest to the pin' contest. People thought they knew him, even if they didn't always like him. In the public world, winning and losing was clear-cut, but alone at this computer he was robbed of every persona he adopted with outsiders. There was no logic to hide behind when bombarded by this maelstrom of images, just curiosity and a lack of responsibility. Here, he no longer needed to think. He could sink deep into himself until he reached the bedrock, with everything simplified down to his most basic and base desires. No responsibilities or pretence of goodness could touch him. Everything was on display, yet could be made to vanish with one click. In this zone, all recriminations ceased. There was no sense of time in the barren loop of home movies filmed in Alaska or in Spanish hotels or Asian shanty towns. With one click he could stare at blowjobs filmed for fun by teenagers on their mobile phones and then see loving recordings made decades ago by honeymooners who were possibly now dead. Every private image had slipped free of its natural orbit and was destined to circulate randomly forever, like particles of intergalactic junk.

Ronan hated himself for being trapped in this zone. He hated this need for oblivion, from which only Miriam could ever save him. He wanted God to strike him dead. But there was no God, merely heart attacks. No matter how exhausted his body grew, the fatal chest pains never came. Ronan had no idea how long he would remain imprisoned here until reluctantly he cleared his search history. He would have rendered himself impotent. Consumed by self-disgust, he would vow to be strong enough to kick this habit tomorrow night. It might be dawn before he finally curled up beside his young bride, reunited with her, and yet knowing he was utterly apart. Even then, he would be unable to sleep, trapped between two worlds.

Chapter Seven

Chris

Tuesday 13th, 2 p.m.

This was the moment. Chris could put it off no longer. He had paid for a private survey, had his solicitor scrutinise the deeds and discussed funding with their bank manager. These were stratagems to postpone his decision, but here he was again, sitting beside Alice at another auction. Chris couldn't tell if anyone seated nearby was there to bid against him. He was uncertain if he wanted to bid himself. This was his tragedy, to have become a punch-drunk boxer. The stress of trying to buy a house in this frenzied market had mentally exhausted him. Seven times in three years they had been beaten at public auctions. On five occasions they lost out when forced into Dutch auctions, coerced into delivering final bids in sealed envelopes.

He had lost track of how often they were outbid in private treaty sales. These were the most torturous. Some estate agents took days to respond, while others rang back within moments of Chris's latest bid to claim that other viewers had bid more. It was impossible to know if these counter-bidders existed or if he was being bled into bidding higher. Alice and Chris were convulsed with trepidation each time the phone rang, unsure whether the call would cause elation or despair, if the agent might congratulate them on having their bid accepted or announce how they needed to find another two thousand euros to remain in the bidding war.

The property market was a world of smoke and mirrors where nobody told the full truth. Even in the seeming transparency of this auction room, the vendors' friends could be primed to kick-start the bidding. He had seen it before, competing hands eagerly nudging the price towards an undisclosed reserve, after which they withdrew, having panicked any real bidders into a feeding frenzy.

Sophie had remained at home, studying in her bedroom. She rarely gave any house her parents looked at more than a fleeting glance. She was the only one who still loved their small home. Sophie went quiet whenever they bid on a house, retreating to her books and music in her room because she could not bear to watch her parents bicker in the terse wait for Chris's capitulation when the price disappeared into the stratosphere. Once, when it seemed they had finally secured a house, until their surveyor discovered a snag-list of structural faults, Chris found Sophie silently crying in her room. She was sixteen back then. He stroked her hair, reassured her that she would quickly grow to love her new home, and she looked up and whispered, 'You don't really want to move either. Be honest, you just want to please Mum.' What he wanted was to win back Alice's respect.

Chris looked around the room, feeling torn in two. Whatever he did today would leave either his daughter or his wife intensely unhappy. Three houses were scheduled for auction. Often voyeuristic neighbours attended, curious about what price their own homes would fetch. Occasionally the vendors sat in, but more often they waited in an adjoining room. Chris counted thirteen individuals or couples who might be potential bidders. He was surprised to recognise Paul Hughes in the back row beside a bored-looking businessman who seemed preoccupied with completing the sudoku in *The Irish Times*. Hughes caught Chris's eye and nodded, one old Blackrock College boy to another, then resumed answering messages on his leather-cased iPhone. Chris was sure that Hughes was not bidding on the house. Hughes had started off by acquiring a portfolio of rental properties, before specialising in landmark developments that combined residential and retail units. The labyrinth of companies through which he concealed his assets meant that nobody knew what he owned, but if newspaper reports were correct about him owning the seafront property which burnt down last night, he was displaying a Zen-like serenity at his loss.

Two couples in the front row clutched brochures for a property in Rathmines, so acutely conscious of each other that Chris suspected they had locked horns in previous bidding wars. The younger couple behind them were probably after the artisan cottage in Harold's Cross, along with the guy in his twenties, wearing jeans and a scruffy T-shirt. But Chris had been wrong about such fellows before. His mud-stained boots suggested he had just walked off a building site. He looked like he lived in a bedsit, but could already own a portfolio of properties like the rented house next door to them, Romanian tenants; paying his multiple mortgages. Irish people were buying property so young and so fearlessly that the young man might already be a millionaire several times over.

Alice, seated beside Chris, said nothing, but he could sense her tension. Chris would do the bidding because, as Alice said, he knew about the different types of mortgages and what they could afford. He was still agonising over every problem. The road was so narrow that you needed to reverse into the tightest parking space. But if parking were easy, such a Victorian property would be beyond his price range. Alice claimed that he obsessed about problems. She was right, but she could not reverse park into any tight space. The house was a mile from all the shops that were currently a five-minute walk from their present home. In future, even buying a litre of milk would involve a car journey, with no guarantee of regaining your parking space unless you placed unneighbourly cones outside your house.

The auctioneer started to read out legal documents relating to the sale. Chris felt consumed by terror. With nine per cent stamp duty to be paid, they might never be able to resell it unless prices continued upwards. Prices were rising by twenty per cent a year, but at some stage this madness had to stop. His irrational fear of negative equity had held him back in the past, watching houses change hands for what seemed like fortunes. In hindsight he would have made a financial killing on any of those houses if he had displayed enough testosterone at the time. Was this the house to risk everything on? If he got ill, could he service such an enormous mortgage?

Chris needed to focus on the positives: the old leaded church window in the bathroom; the extended kitchen with recessed spotlights and a double oven built into shaker-style wooden units; the way in which, when standing outside that house at night to gaze in through the enormous sash windows at the soft lamp light, he could envisage a different life, with him and Alice at ease with each other again.

The auctioneer's attempts to open the bidding were met by silence. He dropped the price, extolling the house's virtues, trying to cajole an opening bid. Chris wasn't going to be first. In the past he had shown his hand too early. Let the auctioneer sweat for a change. If nobody else was interested he might get it for a knockdown price. His throat was dry, his body tense. Alice gripped his hand so tightly he knew she was scared. Their shared fear made them feel close. The auctioneer beseeched the crowd until finally a woman in her early thirties who sat alone raised her hand. Her bid was ninety grand below the published guide price, which was probably fifty grand below the hidden reserve. Only after they reached this mysterious figure, known just to the auctioneer and vender, would bids on the house be formally binding.

If it came to a bidding war with this woman, Chris felt he could win. She shook with nerves already. He waited a while before raising the price by five thousand. She looked disappointed, but increased her bid by another five. Chris did likewise. As he suspected, just the pair of them were involved, slowly nudging the price to thirty thousand above the published guide. Chris felt a cocktail of adrenaline and dread each time he bid, and a mixture of disappointment and secret relief when she counterbid. He couldn't cope with this pressure, yet he didn't ever want to put Alice through this agony again. He thought about the snags his surveyor had found. What if there were other structural problems he had missed?

When the woman bid again, the auctioneer announced that the house was officially on the market. From now on, the vendors had to accept the highest bid. Once Chris or the woman lost their nerve, the gavel would descend three times, with the house sold. Alice never spoke, but her fingers gripped his hand fiercely. The woman started to increase her bids by only a thousand euro, running out of steam and money. The house was his, but would cost sixty thousand euro more than the published guide price. They had already surpassed the figure that Alice and he had agreed on as their absolute maximum. Maybe he could get it by increasing the woman's bid by just one thousand, but, like a matador sticking in the knife, he loudly increased his bid by five thousand, to dishearten the woman and prove to Alice that he was willing to go all the way.

He could sense the tension throughout the room. Everyone present was transfixed by this escalating battle of wits. Every eye focused on him, except for the woman, who stared ahead, white-faced. Chris knew she was defeated. He felt a sudden panic, a desire for her to make one final bid and take this chalice of debt from him, but the woman merely lowered her head. Alice's fingers cut deeper into his palm, but he didn't care if she drew blood. He had been tested and not failed her. Here was their fresh start.

There was a surge of elation as the auctioneer banged the gavel once and twice. Then the businessman in the back row beside Paul Hughes lowered his *Irish Times* and spoke for the first time, calmly increasing the bid by ten thousand euro. Chris looked back. The man seemed relaxed, as if Chris's joust with the woman was only an entertaining prelude to the real auction. Chris needed to think, but was emotionally too exhausted. If they cancelled holidays for several years and if he ignored his surveyor's advice about urgently addressing the structural crack, he could mount a final bid just above the businessman's offer, but Chris felt too drained. He had bid well beyond his maximum. The whole room awaited his decision, apart from the woman, who silently cried. They had been locked in bitter rivalry, now they were both jilted. He looked at Alice and muttered, 'I'm sorry.'

The auctioneer brought down the hammer, and everyone erupted into applause. The vendors appeared in the doorway, giddy with pleasure. Paul Hughes caught his eye. As he passed he patted Chris's shoulder. 'Don't lose heart,' he murmured sympathetically, 'there could be a twist in the tale yet.' The businessman never glanced at Chris as an estate agent led him into a side room. There was a giddy buzz of conversation. Chris wanted to sympathise with the woman bidder, but she had already left. Strangers consoled him as if at a funeral. Beside him, Alice remained silent.

Then the auctioneer banged his gavel to attract attention. He read out the particulars of the next dwelling for auction, and Chris and Alice were forgotten about. They left the building in silence and emerged amid afternoon shoppers on St Stephen's Green, Alice one pace ahead of him. He caught up and took her arm.

'I'm heartbroken,' she said quietly, 'but I bet part of you is secretly relieved.'

'I bid every cent we could afford and more.'

'I can't do this any more.'

Chris wanted to reply, but there was nothing to say. Alice knew him too well, and she had already walked on.

Chapter Eight

Sophie

I had a dream about Mum once, set in the Northwest Territories in Canada, formerly called the Yukon. The landscape was an expanse of ice and teeming snow. I was waiting for Mum to collect me, while Inuit families slid past on sleds of wood and animal bone, drawn by huskies whose tongues hung out to catch the snowflakes. When Mum finally materialised, she possessed no dog-drawn sled; she was barefoot and shivering in a nightdress. But it was not her goosepimpled flesh that chilled me, it was her fierce determination as she inched forward, shoulders cut open by rawhide straps harnessed to the massive block of ice she was dragging behind her. After I woke I sensed that Dad and I were part of this ice block, and so were her unspoken anxieties. But the overwhelming burden of it was the weight of responsibility at being the only child to a father too emotionally retarded ever to make her feel good about herself.

The golden year in Mum's life, when she attained a new identity in her mind as a hesitant but welcoming boutique manageress, was also the year when the weight of being a daughter truly dragged upon her. Phone calls from Vicky in Vienna about stock and cash flow, calls from Granddad at 3 a.m. to complain that he had been sitting up in the cold for hours waiting for the care worker to make his breakfast, consignments of cocktail dresses from Rome, urine-stained sheets to be washed daily in our Bosch spin-dryer, overdue invoices with French and Italian postmarks, rotas for care workers tasked with dispensing Granddad's medication. Mum's hurt at discovering that Vicky was privately selling their best stock to friends for cash, which made the books impossible to balance. Battles with Granddad over every tiny cheque that needed to be written as he incessantly claimed that his care workers were robbing him. Mum's inability to get Granddad to sign over power of attorney. Mum's inability to extract straight answers from Vicky.

Mum was trying to give Granddad assisted independence in his home for as long as possible, but he was no longer safe alone. She had his name down with numerous nursing homes, but only once did a bed become available. Modern nursing homes were being built as tax-break investments, bright as opulent hotels, but this was a gloomy Edwardian house in Dun Laoghaire, with an obstructed view of the harbour. They phoned to say that a room had just become available, and we had first refusal until five o'clock. Mum closed the boutique and took me for support. It was pointless to bring Granddad, who had no intention of moving anywhere. We were directed towards a second-floor room, and told that the manager would join us shortly. We were so busy examining the faded curtains pulled shut and the spartan furnishings that only when Mum stopped beside the bed did we look down and see the corpse of the former occupant, eyes closed, hands folded around rosary beads as she awaited collection by an undertaker. We fled without speaking to the manager.

Something had to give. I was the cause of it, without wishing to be. Another reason why Mum grew to hate our small house arose from the fortnight she spent trying to mind Granddad there after the situation in his own house became untenable. Waking him at 8 a.m. (though he claimed it was midnight) to get him up, changed and fed; to put on another wash of wet bedclothes and leave him in a comfortable chair before racing to open the boutique. Closing early for lunch so she could run home, unsure if he would still be there or if he had wandered back to the steps of his own home; he often found his way back there to sit in the rain. Dad begging Mum to lie down as she grew increasingly stressed. Dad trying to settle Granddad into bed while the old man loudly praised him as a wonderful son-in-law, unlike 'poor old Alice', who could never do anything right.

That fortnight possessed the qualities of a nightmare. One afternoon after school I passed the boutique and glimpsed Mum in her public window world. The boutique had three customers, none interested in buying anything. Friends of Vicky, they chatted animatedly on the chaises longues, sipping the rich coffee Mum provided, but otherwise ignoring her as if she were a waitress. Every few seconds Mum washed her hands distractedly at the scented soap dispenser. I was studying *Macbeth*, but Mum was not trying to wash away invisible bloodstains. Amid the soft lights and flickering candles she was desperately trying to rid her hands of the stink of urine and the specks of porridge she needed to wipe from Granddad's chin after feeding him breakfast.

On another afternoon I arrived home to find Mum in our hallway, furiously arguing with a stern-faced elderly woman who smelt of cloying talc and cigarette smoke. Granddad had again slipped away from the comfortable armchair where Mum left him, and this woman had been passing Granddad's house by chance when she spied him sitting on the cold steps there, bewildered as to why his dead wife was not at home to answer the door. The stranger was stridently hectoring Mum about how it amounted to cruelty that Granddad was not being properly cared for in a nursing home. Mum was shaking, engulfed by an almost primeval fury as she screamed that she would accept no lectures on how to mind her own father: she had been minding him for twenty years without help from anyone. Both women were so overwrought and intent on shouting each other down that it took them several moments to register my presence. They went silent. The stranger studied me with a forensic gaze that I found disconcerting.

'So this is Sophie,' she said.

'Stay out of my life,' Mum snapped. 'And stay out of hers. It's a bit too late to turn up now, crying crocodile tears when all you really want is to stir up trouble. Why don't you offer to pay for us all to get on a plane this time and leave your brother alone, sitting in the cold in wet trousers on his doorstep on Avoca Road!'

Granddad was sitting peacefully back in his armchair, oblivious to the loud voices. The stranger left and Mum hunched down against the wall, so convulsed with tears that it was several minutes before she answered my question about who the intruder was. Finally, she looked up.

'That was my Aunt Patricia. Trust her to pass her brother's house at the worst possible moment. It's the first time she's taken an interest in him in decades.'

'I'd forgotten you have an aunt,' I replied. 'You never mention her.'

'I don't have an aunt,' she said bitterly. 'That woman is dead to me. After my mother died, when I was barely older than you, I asked for her help once, and she wasn't there for me. But she can go to hell now if she thinks she has the right to parachute in and play any part in our family. I want nothing to do with her, and you and your dad are to have no truck with her either.'

I didn't ask any more because Granddad was soaked to the skin, having wandered off without even a hat. The priority was to get him dry and keep him safe. No night was undisturbed during Mum's desperate attempts to keep him living with us. The smoke alarm went off at dawn when he decided to boil potatoes for dinner with no water in the pot. He grew increasingly angry with Mum, although unsure of her identity. Whoever she was – wife, daughter or mother – he was convinced she kept playing tricks, changing the hands on every clock. This deeply placid man became possessed of a furious rage, an instinctive terror at sensing reality slip beyond him. Mum and Dad tried to shield me, but I would wake at odd hours, finding the silence as scary as any blaring television. I never knew what to expect when opening my bedroom door. One night I crept downstairs, drawn by a sound so faint I knew I was not meant to hear it. Outside the downstairs toilet, I recognised Mum's weeping. I tapped on the wood. Her whisper told me to go away. I pushed the door open. Mum knelt, crying. Granddad was half-seated on the toilet, his fists tightly clasping the handrail Dad installed for him, but he could neither haul himself to his feet nor let go of the rail without falling back. His lower body was naked.

'He's had another accident.' Mum could barely raise her voice above an exhausted sigh. 'He can't help himself. I can't help him either. I've no energy left. He needs professional care, but he just sits in complete denial.' She looked up. 'Go to bed, Sophie. You're too young to see this.'

'I want to help,' I said.

'Then make me a promise. If I ever get like this, find a way to put me out of my misery and make it look like suicide. I mightn't be able to say it to you by then, but it's what I'd want. I'm losing my sanity watching him lose his. It would kill me to think of you having to go through this torture with me.'

'Let's get him to bed, Mum,' I said quietly, wetting a towel that I knew would go straight into the bin. 'Then you get to bed; you need to sleep.'

By badgering the hospital, Mum got Granddad's next appointment at the geriatric unit in St Vincent's pushed forward. She dressed him that morning as if for an ordinary check-up, but we knew – even Granddad, amid his confusion – that it was not. Dad took the day off work to go there with Mum. At school, I could focus on nothing. Afterwards, Dad called it the hardest thing he ever did, necessary and urgent, but it felt like the ultimate betrayal. Mum refused to talk about it. When they saw the doctor, Granddad accused Mum of playing tricks. He pulled himself together as always when confronted by a figure of authority, but Mum insisted on the doctor repeating his questions until it became clear that, behind this last, desperate bluff, Granddad barely knew his own name any more.

The doctor's secretary asked Admissions to search for a bed. Granddad was now formally in the system, or would be when the golden ticket of a bed was found. He was en route to becoming a bed-blocker that the hospital could only get rid of by finding a nursing - home bed. One nightmare was over, but Mum knew that another was only beginning. There would be months of daily visits and arguments with hospital social workers, who were being constantly pressurised by their line managers into trying to persuade Mum to take him home. Yet, no matter how unhappy Granddad would be at finding himself in a ward, or how angrily he would peer out from his bed, awaiting his first glimpse of Mum so as to demand that she bring him home to where his wife was waiting, Granddad would be looked after in hospital. Or he would be whenever Admissions freed up that magical bed so that he could formally become a patient.

No bed became available that day. At 6 p.m., only Mum and Granddad and Dad remained in the previously packed geriatric clinic. Contract cleaners washed the floor around them. Granddad continually asked why he was still there, complaining of being fed up and hungry. Vicky kept constantly phoning Mum, angrily asking about a consignment of new dresses Mum had hidden away, knowing that, once Vicky found them, they would disappear, privately sold for cash, which Vicky would pocket, despite their landlord growing increasingly hostile about overdue rent.

The doctor's secretary switched off the lights. My parents' last remaining option was to bring Granddad down to sit among the junkies and drunks queuing in the reception area of the Emergency Department. They wheeled the bewildered man, now in a hospital wheelchair, down long corridors into the maelstrom of Accident and Emergency. The triage nurse explained that he was in a queue for admission, but if he left the hospital he would lose his place. No doctor in A&E would attend to him. No nurse could help, unless to assist with bringing him to the toilet. They would do their best to get him onto a stretcher before the night was out, but it would be tomorrow at the earliest, when the Admissions office reopened, before there was any chance of a bed.

Dad persuaded Mum, who was reluctant, to go home to rest and leave him with Granddad. When Mum rose, Granddad shouted that surely to God she didn't plan to abandon him. I had food waiting for her, but she barely ate and barely spoke. I bullied her up to bed, though I could not persuade her to get under the sheets. Dad kept texting to ask how she was. After an hour, I checked upstairs. Her light was out, but she still lay fully clothed on the bed. Her eyes were open. I took her hand.

'What sort of daughter have I been?' she whispered.

'A great daughter,' I said, 'and a great mum.'

'I've never been able to do anything right.'

'That's ridiculous. Who told you that?'

'My parents. Every day of my childhood.'

'What was your mum like?'

'She stored up complaints like cardigans to keep her warm. I wasn't an easy child, my head in the clouds. I loved her, she loved me, and we fought like cats and dogs.'

'You've always been good to Granddad.'

'No matter what I do, I feel guilty because I don't love him. I feel nothing for him except responsibility.'

'You're exhausted, Mum. You need to sleep.'

'I can't sleep for long, otherwise your dad will need to sit there till dawn. Putting Granddad into hospital feels like the cruellest thing I've ever done.'

'It's what's best for him. You know it's the only option.'

Mum squeezed my hand tightly.

'Granddad doesn't know it. Isn't life crazy, Sophie? Look at the age I'm at, yet I'm still desperate for his approval, hoping that just once, before his mind shuts down, he'll say something nice.'

'I think you're wonderful. I love you, and so does Dad.'

She held my hand tighter. 'I resent your dad at times.'

'Why?'

'The whole world thinks he's Mr Perfect. He's so busy being Mr Perfect for everyone that often he has nothing left to give me when he gets home. Just once I'd love him to do something stupid, to come down to my level, because I can't compete with a good man perpetually making halves of himself to please everyone. He'd sit in that hospital all night and feel happy to think of me asleep in bed. But how can I sleep, thinking of him setting standards I can't match? I'm not perfect.'

'We love you as you are.'

'I hate who I am. You get to bed. I'll go back in at midnight and send your father home. He has work tomorrow.'

'What about the boutique?'

'Vicky can go to hell, or she can actually go in herself and do a day's work. I imagined I was going to be her partner, but she's simply using me as her skivvy.'

I kissed Mum's forehead. I closed the door of her darkened room and stood for a long time on the landing. I knew something special had occurred. Amid her anguish, Mum had just for once let me glimpse her inner world. I went to bed but could not sleep. At midnight Mum left. An hour later I heard Dad come in. He would have tried to send Mum back home, but she had worn him down. He sat downstairs, and I knew he was drinking brandy. Finally, he came up. I opened my bedroom door. I had never seen Dad so tired; he had spent hours listening to

Granddad's terrified complaints. He looked at me and tried to say the words: 'Go back asleep,' but he was too exhausted for any sound to emerge.

He closed their bedroom door. He would fall asleep within seconds and not hear his fifteen-year-old daughter slip out into our back garden. Next door, a light still shone in Ronan's office. I wheeled my bicycle through the side passageway, then started to cycle. The Rock Road was quiet, Booterstown Marsh to my right. At the light at the Merrion level crossing, motorists glanced out at me cycling alone. Mum would be furious, but I wanted to be there for her and for Granddad in his agonised bewilderment.

I found the entrance to the Emergency Department by the sound of raised voices. A young mother cradled a six-year-old girl in her arms. The child's skin looked mottled under the harsh lights, her demeanour listless. The mother had recently scrubbed vomit stains off her coat. The security guard was trying to explain how St Vincent's Hospital could not treat minors and she needed to drive to Our Lady's Hospital for Sick Children in Crumlin, but the mother had minimal English, and in her distressed state was incapable of comprehending his words. Perhaps she was unable to piece together the complicated night-time journey across a foreign city when her child needed urgent attention. Her accent sounded like Monika's mother from primary school. I risked using the Polish greeting I had learnt from Monika.

'Cześć.'

She glanced around and addressed me in a distraught onslaught of Polish. I shook my head, conscious of being the centre of attention. Unable to reply, I addressed the security guard.

'The child should at least see a nurse.'

'Obviously, as a precaution.' He seemed perturbed by my appearance. 'Then we'll print a Google map. But you couldn't bring a child into this bedlam. There are more drug users inside than in the Tour de France.'

He was reluctant to admit me into the inner zone that served as a holding pen for less critical cases, but something about my bearing made him relent. I spied Granddad in a wheelchair. Mum sat beside him. Granddad wasn't asking her to bring him home any more. He seemed asleep with his eyes open. Maybe this wait had pushed his mind over the edge. He looked unhinged; Mum simply looked demented. Granddad seemed to have disappeared into a sphere beyond feeling, leaving Mum to feel the horror intensely for them both.

A girl in an impossibly short skirt stood directly in front of Granddad, shrieking into a mobile phone. Her boyfriend had gashed his skull during a fight outside the Tribe nightclub in Stillorgan. He needed an X-ray, but due to his low priority this might take hours. The girl kept beseeching the person on the phone to collect her, otherwise she would not get back into Tribe for last drinks. Granddad stared at her naked legs and the skirt, which revealed the curves of her buttocks whenever she swayed in agitation. But I don't think he understood that anyone around him was real. Mum was staring at another young girl collapsed on the floor, people stepping over her unconscious body. I sat on the plastic chair beside Mum and took her hand. She glanced at me, too tired to be cross.

'You shouldn't be here,' she said.

'None of us should be.'

The young Polish mother had negotiated her way into this zone. A triage nurse tried to find space to do an examination, asking the child – who seemed more awake, but still dazed – to bend her neck and look up at the bright lights. As the nurse questioned the mother, the child stared fearfully around and saw me. I waved. After a moment's hesitation, she waved back with a tentative smile.

'She's too young to be here,' Mum said, noticing the child.

'And Granddad is too old.'

The child waved again. This time Mum waved back, holding her gaze until rewarded with a glorious smile. It looked like they were engrossed in a childish game, temporarily forgetting the horror of their surroundings. Then a young doctor passed by. Mum touched his coat, and he stopped. Exhaustion returned to Mum's face. She pointed to the unconscious young woman.

'That girl shouldn't be lying there,' Mum said.

'It's where her friends always dump her. She's safer on the floor: she can't fall off anything.'

'It's chaos in here.'

He shook his head. 'Trust me, it only becomes chaos when she wakes up.'

'They promised my father a stretcher.'

'The situation keeps changing. We don't know who will arrive in the door. Unfortunately, your father isn't a priority.'

'But every drunk is?'

'We patch up people and ship them out. Hopefully by dawn a trolley will be freed up.'

'He desperately needs rest. It could be 10 a.m. before he gets a proper bed.'

'You're being hopeful.' The doctor checked his bleeper.

'They promised me that once the Admissions office reopens he'll be prioritised.'

'He will be.' The doctor looked exhausted. 'We just don't know what other priorities will arise. I'd be lying if I made any false promises. I can't even promise that he won't still be sitting in this chair when I come back on duty tomorrow evening.'

'He's soaking; he's in his second pair of wet trousers. If he's going to receive no attention, let me take him home for a few hours' rest and a change of clothes. I'll have him back in this chair before the Admissions office reopens.'

The doctor shook his head. 'If you take him away he loses his place in the queue. I didn't invent the system, and I'd gladly shoot whoever did, but I'm forced to work it.' His bleeper went off. 'I'll come back out when it's quieter. We'll find him somewhere to lie down if at all possible.'

The doctor walked away. The girl in the short skirt had moved on. I took Mum's hand. 'Go home for a few hours,' I said. 'I don't mind sitting with Granddad.'

Granddad stirred from his stupor and looked blankly after the doctor. 'What did the conductor say?' he asked. 'Will this bus ever reach Blackrock?' He peered at Mum, his voice expressing genuine concern. 'You look too tired for a girl your age. Your mother will be cross with me for having you out this late.' He screwed up his eyes in the fluorescent glare to stare at me. 'Is your friend stranded in the snow? We'll phone her parents when we get home. They'll be worried.'

I patted his knee. 'You know me, Granddad, it's Sophie.'

'Have they taken you hostage too, Sophie?'

'You're not a hostage, Granddad.'

'Am I dead, Sophie? I'm dead tired and soaked. Who'd have thought you could wet your trousers in purgatory?'

I looked away: I didn't want Mum to see my tears. I needed to be strong for her in this hellish place with harassed staff and people having shouting matches or moaning in pain. The Polish woman seemed reassured by the nurse. Her daughter waved to Mum as the mother carried her towards the exit while trying to study a map showing the route to the children's hospital. Mum watched them leave and stood up.

'Follow them out, Sophie,' she said. 'Walk quietly through the exit.'

'I'm not leaving you here with him.'

'We're bringing him with us.'

I looked at her. 'He'll lose his place in the queue.'

'He won't.' Mum gripped his wheelchair. 'It's such a shithole of a country that nobody will notice he's gone. We take him home for a hot meal and some sleep, then we wheel him in like we're only bringing him back from the bathroom. Nobody will notice.'

'It's against the rules.'

'They can stick the rules up their fucking arse.'

I'd never heard Mum curse before. The F-word sounded terrible from her lips. She weaved a path through the packed benches, and I followed, scared by her agitated matter. I knew not to argue; her face possessed a look of rigid determination. The security guard let her out the doorway, thinking she was bringing him to a toilet. Suddenly we were outside in the moonlight, wheeling him towards the multi-storey car park. Mum had parked on the second tier, but now the concrete edifice was empty. I tried to help Mum push the wheelchair up the slope, but she wouldn't let me. She radiated a manic energy, as if pushed beyond her limit.

We reached the car. She beckoned me to help get Granddad into the passenger seat. He had not spoken since we left the hospital, but now he became agitated as we lifted him out of the wheelchair.

'Who's kidnapping me now?' he demanded.

'We're bringing you home,' Mum snapped. 'Let me get your seat belt on.'

'Go to hell, whoever you are. You won't tie me down.'

Twice Mum snapped his belt shut, and twice he forced it back open. Finally she had to abandon trying to strap him in. She motioned me into the back seat and started the engine. Mum moved off, rooting in her purse for the car park ticket as she approached the incline down to the lower level. There was no danger in the deserted car park until Granddad glanced across at her in amazement.

'What are you doing, Alice?!' he cried out. 'You're too young to drive. Let me show you how.'

His hands grasped the steering wheel as we emerged onto the lower tier. Startled, Mum screamed at him. The concourse looked deserted until I noticed the Polish mother standing beside a Fiat Punto, still trying to puzzle out the Google street map. The back door was open, and she was about to strap the child into the booster seat, but the girl stood beside her. Mum and Granddad shouted at each other. Amid this distraction, Mum's foot slipped. The accelerator roared as the car shot forward, careering wildly as two sets of hands struggled to possess the steering wheel.

I saw the Polish mother look up, terrified by the noise. The child should have been equally scared. Perhaps she was panicked into running in the wrong direction, or perhaps everything seemed so strange that she could not comprehend the danger and, in a dreamlike state, ran towards us. I cannot say what happened: the car's jerking motion threw me backwards. This saved me from serious injury. I was sprawled across the back seat, and therefore was merely thrown against the front seats when the car rammed into a concrete wall.

Dad tried to protect me when the inquest occurred: he turned off the radio and ensured that none of the newspapers carrying Mum's photo entered the house, therefore I don't know how far the child's body was carried by the car before it hit the wall. I know that the main collision occurred on the passenger side, so even if Granddad had been wearing a seatbelt he might not have survived, or he might have endured a living death, with ruptured organs. I got tossed forward with such force that all strength was expelled from my body as I lay, winded, on the back seat. But when I finally managed to scramble up, I immediately knew that Granddad's neck was broken. His face stared back at me from an angle that was utterly wrong.

The safety airbag in Mum's steering wheel probably saved her life, but it didn't save her from injury. She was unconscious but alive, a streak of blood on her cheek. I wanted to ask how she was. I wanted to tell her I loved her, but even if awake she would not have heard me over the blaring car horn, which summoned security men, who came running, speaking into walkie-talkies. For a moment – how long does a moment last in altered time? – I was not conscious of the child crushed by the tangled bonnet. There seemed to be two separate worlds: my world inside that crashed car, and the world outside, where the Polish mother cradled her dead child, comforting her in words I could not comprehend. Only a few feet divided us, but we were not aware of each other. Our worlds collided when a paramedic forced open the car door. The car horn sounded even louder, yet the woman's cries were audible. I tried to put my arms around Mum's neck, but other arms reached in to lift me away from the carnage inside the car and bring me into contact with the horror outside it. The paramedic gently placed me down. I didn't feel like an adult any more. I was a crying child, encircled by awkward men, all desperate to comfort me and yet conscious that my body possessed too many curves for them to rock me in their arms.

That was four years ago. Mum gradually recovered from her physical injuries, but sank so deep into herself from the trauma that Dad and I didn't know if she would ever smile or get out of bed unaided again. Initially, I was terrified that she was paralysed. She suffered multiple fractures and blood complications. These were factors in her inexplicable exhaustion. But her malaise was more than physical. She was burnt out, not only from that crash, but from the strain of minding her father. Only now, when he was dead, had she enough time to suffer the repercussions of those years of constant anxiety. She had too much time. Her confidence was shattered by the looming court case and its publicity. Doctors assured us that she would fully recover her strength and be left with just a minor scar on her face; they just weren't certain of when. I sat on her bed most evenings, trying to help select a memorial card for Granddad or reply to letters from his neighbours and work colleagues. She wouldn't let me help with the drafts of the letter she wanted to send to the Polish mother, drafts I found crumpled in the bin, crying after I secretly read them. I don't know if she ever managed to send that letter; the crash became something we could never discuss.

Mum was convinced that everyone blamed her. Her injuries meant she had to stop managing the boutique, though unpaid suppliers continued to chase her after Vicky traded in the celebrity lawyer husband for a richer suitor. Most of Granddad's inheritance from the sale of the Avoca Road house went to the Mill Hill Missionary Fathers. Dad used the small sum left to Mum to pay the back-rent on the boutique and other debts Vicky had run up in the company's name. It was a pipe dream to imagine that Mum would ever be able to reopen that boutique on her own, but Dad felt she needed something tangible to look forward to as she strove to get well. I'd come home from school to find Mum staring out her bedroom window, pop music blaring through the wall next door when a new set of tenants had moved in – four college students who never seemed to sleep. Mum needed to lie still, ignore the music that always continued until Dad called in to complain at 1 or 2 a.m., and stop fretting about the inquest. When it occurred, Brygida's mother – we discovered that this was the dead child's name – stared at Mum, but never addressed her. In the following months I lay in bed beside Mum, devouring library books about Italian architecture and dreaming about Italian girls. Miriam would call in with coffee and delicacies. Then one day she called in to announce that she had found the perfect divorce lawyer, recommended by Vicky, in the same tone as if declaring that she had found the perfect dress.

Mum was lonely after Miriam left. But she could ache with loneliness even when we were holding her hand and saying we loved her. I dreamt about seeing the Sistine Chapel. Mum dreamt about being able to walk as far as her closed-down boutique. Her enforced rest made her grow to hate her bedroom, a prison where a succession of loud strangers laughed or quarrelled or made love on the far side of the wall. Dad promised we would move to escape these memories when Mum improved, but during the years of Mum's slow recovery, Ireland became Europe's economic miracle. Everything the Irish touched sparkled like gold, and property was the most mesmerising gold dust of all. This was why Dad failed at that auction in March, when I lay on my bed, waiting anxiously for them to come home. My thoughts that day were primarily about how I was finally about to view Florence and the other cities I used to read about when lying beside Mum. I didn't know that Mum was also about to acquire a new view. I looked out my window that afternoon and wondered why Ronan was standing in his garden, gazing intently at ours. Our neighbour had run out of schemes to maximise every gold-dust inch of his property. He was staring into our garden, having devised a scheme to devour every inch of it as well.

Chapter Nine

Chris

Tuesday 13th, 2.45 p.m.

Neither of them knew it, but their future was decided that afternoon when they lost again at auction. Alice was too distraught to speak for most of the journey home, beyond saying 'That's the last auction I'm ever going to sit through. I can't bear having my hopes crushed again. If that house went for that price, then prices are just beyond us. Maybe we had a chance two years ago when you were finding fault with house after house, but we lost our chance and are becoming a laughing stock. Auctioneers barely hide their smirks when they see us turn up at viewings. Can't you see? It's finished.'

Chris was too scared to ask what was finished, even though he found it hard to conceal a guilty sense of relief at not having been launched into an inconceivable stratosphere of debt. Alice's drained voice sounded nothing like the demonstratively affectionate and warm woman she always had been until recently. She stared through the windscreen, and Chris was glad he could not see the abject despair in her eyes. He would have preferred her to be angry. Alice's anger was always temporary. She was highly strung, and he was accustomed to occasional rages or glacial silences. In the past these were quick to melt away because Alice used to hate allowing any quarrel to come between them. What scared him now about her silence was how it seemed to convey a resolute indifference. He longed to take her hand, but an impenetrable force field separated them. As he turned the corner onto their street, Chris made one final effort at conversation.

'I did my best. I nearly had a heart attack bidding so high.' His hands were shaking. Only after auctions ended did he realise how traumatic and physically draining they were.

'I'm not saying you don't try, Chris, but you don't really have it in you.'

'Please don't say that.'

'It's not a criticism; it's simply your nature.' Alice stared ahead. 'But you're a good provider, and a good father to Sophie.'

'Am I not a good husband?' he asked tentatively.

Alice took so long to reply that he thought she was ignoring his question. 'I never said you weren't,' she eventually responded in a neutral voice.

'It's a long time since you said I was.'

'You're a good man, Chris, but you lack courage.'

'I lack money. House prices like today make no sense to me.'

'How come they make sense to all the other men who outbid one another, men willing to accept that this madness is the price of things in Ireland? Nobody needs money to buy houses nowadays; banks write cheques to cover any mortgage, no matter how massive. Maybe today's price was beyond us, but it's all the other houses that went for far less that I can't get out of my head. How many times have you been mad keen on houses, only then to find enough flaws to worry about so that you worked yourself up into a state of paralysis before we even bid? These last couple of years you've been like a bird stuck on a ledge, too scared to fly ... or too preoccupied.'

'Preoccupied by what?'

'How can I tell what goes on in your life?' She looked at him. 'There was a time when we never had secrets.'

'What secrets do you think I'm keeping from you?' he asked, puzzled, but also wary.

Alice retreated into tense silence. He knew how hard she found it to talk about what was really going on in her mind. At such moments he always felt occluded, frantically trying to second-guess what was troubling her. Chris pulled in to their driveway and left the engine running. Soon he would need to tell Sophie the news. Alice would go straight upstairs to bed, the curtains pulled and her light out.

'You used to call me your saviour when you were ill. Now I can't even tell how you feel about me.'

Alice looked at him. 'After that car crash I desperately needed a saviour to give me hope. But my growing so dependent on you wasn't good for either of us. I lost years of my life to that accident.'

'And what sort of life do you think I had,' Chris asked, 'bringing you from doctor to doctor, struggling to raise Sophie?'

'We raised Sophie together.'

'And we can make up for those lost years together.'

'Maybe you've started making up for them already.'

Alice looked away, and Chris felt a stab of anxiety. 'What do you mean?'

'Can you imagine how helpless it felt to lie in bed? A woman left alone all day can have the queerest thoughts.'

'What sort of thoughts?'

Alice gripped the door handle, anxious to end this conversation. 'Thoughts I dismissed until six months ago.'

'What happened six months ago?'

'Maybe you were trying to break out of a rut. I don't know. There are days when I feel that I barely know who you are any more because at times I barely know who I am myself now.'

Her voice betrayed such a wounded vulnerability that Chris risked taking her hand.

'Another house will come along,' he promised. 'We'll solve this problem.'

She held his fingers tightly. 'Not all problems are solvable, Chris. That's why I can't talk to you about these changes I feel inside my body. They have me so confused that I'm scared. At times I feel like I'm not thinking rationally any more, then at other times I say to hell with being rational. I was responsible and dutiful all my life, thinking that after my father died my life would finally take off. But at the end of it all, where did rationality get me except stuck in this endless loop of crushed hopes at failed auctions?'

'The next time we enter an auction room we'll walk out having made the winning bid,' Chris said. 'I promise you.'

She looked at him and shook her head. 'I'm not asking you for promises. With prices like today we just have to live with the fact that we've missed the boat. What I can't live with is how you can't let go of that dream. From now on, if you want to look at more houses then you do so on your own. I just haven't the strength to face having my hopes raised again and then dashed.'

'I promised you a house,' he said doggedly, 'and I'm going to keep that promise.'

'How? By scrunching yourself up into a ball of tension, frowning over rows of figures that will never add up and snapping at us if we refuse to believe in you? I'm thrilled that Sophie is about to go off for a year and live out her dreams by seeing Italy, but one part of me is jealous. I wanted so much to see the world at her age. I'm getting old, and it feels like I'm still waiting for my life to begin. I'm frightened to find myself one day like my mother, lying in a bed waiting to die, realising that I've experienced so little of life that I won't know if I've been short-changed by it.'

'You're not old.'

'Then why is my body betraying me by changing? It's the one thing I can't forgive: betrayal.' Alice disentangled her fingers from his.

'Who has betrayed you?'

'Vicky for one, visiting me in hospital to promise she'd run the boutique until I recovered. The only thing she ran up was more unpaid utility bills, transferred into my name.'

'I looked after those bills.'

'You handled everything. But you did enough talking about it afterwards, calling me stupid for signing the forms Vicky brought into the hospital without reading them first.'

'I never called you stupid.'

'You did so under your breath when you got frustrated. Maybe you never said it aloud, but I know you so inside-out that I could hear you think it.'

'Vicky fleeced her ex-husband too, despite his rumoured brilliance as a legal eagle. Maybe you and I are just too trusting.'

'Maybe you still are, but my eyes have been opened.'

'What do you mean?' he asked anxiously.

Alice drummed her fingers agitatedly on the dashboard. He wanted to take her hand again, but knew that she would snatch it away in frustration at the inability to express whatever was truly bothering her.

'I'm going inside,' she said. 'We're on public display here.'

'Today was just a setback,' Chris said softly. 'Other couples got ahead of us on the property ladder when you were ill. We have to play catch-up.'

'I don't want to play anything except tennis,' she replied. 'I'm joining a tennis club, somewhere away from here where I can make new friends.'

'Tell me which club you want us to join and I'll put our names down.'

Alice gazed at him. 'Do you think me too helpless to even join a tennis club on my own? Why can't you just leave me alone?'

'Is that what you want, Alice?' he tried to keep his voice even and not betray his desolation. 'I barely know what you want any more. Do you want me to leave? Is that it?'

'I want space to breathe. I want to be myself, and I can't seem to be myself any more when you're around.' Alice took a deep breath and lowered her voice. The detached gratitude in it stung him. 'I appreciate everything you've done for me, Chris, but maybe I need to learn to do things on my own two feet.'

There was so much that Chris wanted to say in reply, so much love he wished to express, and so much hurt. He wanted to describe how the loneliness of sleeping in a spare bed cut into his soul. He wanted to talk about his sexual frustration, and how, when he sometimes snapped, it was because this seemed the only way to reach out when he longed to be held by her. But he said none of this because Alice was gazing at Ronan, who had emerged from his front door.

'What is he doing here?' she whispered.

'He has a right to stand in his own driveway, Alice.'

'He has come out to gloat. You deal with him. I can't talk to anyone.'

Chris moved the car forward to park so close to the front door that Alice could walk inside without appearing overtly rude. He had no such option. He wanted to talk to Sophie – often they felt like conspirators – but instead needed to walk over to the wall where Ronan waited.

'I have champagne in the fridge,' Ronan said, 'but Alice's body language suggests I might be unwise to produce it just now.'

Chris tried to summon a smile. 'You're not rid of us as neighbours yet.'

Ronan nodded sympathetically. 'I could have told you the outcome before you left for the auction.'

'Don't you start on me, Ronan. Alice is heartbroken.'

'The bush telegraph tells me you tried your best. Give her time and she'll see that.'

'I keep telling Alice these house prices make no sense.'

'What does she say?'

'With each failed bid I've become the opposite of an oracle. I genuinely believed I had that house today.'

'What did you feel?'

'Terror at shouldering such monumental debt, but at least I'd have proved to myself that I was no coward and I could compete with other men.'

Ronan climbed companionably across the low dividing wall. 'You need to prove yourself to nobody, least of all yourself. You stood no earthly chance of winning that auction.'

'What do you mean?'

Ronan glanced towards his front door. 'Second wives can be as tricky as first ones. We're like guilty schoolboys out here. I'm dying for a cigarette, and Kim hates me smoking. I promised to give them up. Can I sneak a smoke in your shed?'

Chris thought of Alice lying in her darkened bedroom now, enveloped by despair. Even if he went indoors, there was nothing he could say to her. With Ronan, one clandestine cigarette could turn into an hour-long conversation, but he nodded for Ronan to follow him through the side gate and down the long back garden to the shed at the end, which had needed refurbishing for decades. It was crammed with leftovers; things too valuable to throw out, but which would never be used again. Unlocking the door, Chris surveyed the debris of his life. Ronan followed him in. Sitting on an old milk-bottle crate, he offered Chris a cigarette. Shaking his head, Chris walked back to the doorway and spied Sophie at her bedroom window. She raised one hand in a covert greeting, and Chris discreetly nodded. Sophie moved away as if not wanting to spy on them. He wondered if she would risk going in to console her mother.

Staring up at his house brought back a memory from when Sophie was small and he and Alice always got a babysitter on a Saturday night. Arriving home early once, Chris had parked their car up the street, and – play-acting at being teenage lovers in search of privacy – led Alice down to this shed. He could remember that the curtains were open in the dining-room window, the babysitter framed by the television's rays as she sat on the sofa. If this girl had approached the window she could probably have made out their shapes kissing in the shed doorway; Alice's blouse unbuttoned so he could touch her breasts as, half-laughing and deadly serious, Alice made him come with her hand. It was an adolescent parody, yet also a stolen moment of true love. Chris recalled them trying not to laugh as they crept out the side gate to enter the house by the front door, unsure if ivy leaves still stuck to their clothes. This was how close they had been fifteen years ago, or even fifteen months ago. Could they ever get that closeness back?

Ronan joined him in the doorway, staring at the ornate pond surrounded by jagged rocks at the V-shaped end of his own garden.

'That house went for a crazy price today, but the guy who outbid you could have paid twice that and still make a fortune. He's been waiting two years to pounce on that house. He's a developer who owns the adjoining house, and two other houses on the next street, whose long gardens back onto that garden.'

'Who told you this?' Chris asked.

'Paul Hughes tipped me the wink. You remember Paul sitting behind us in school in his owl-shaped glasses?'

'I remember he was a little wanker.' Chris was unable to conceal a touch of envy at contemplating how much Hughes was rumoured to be worth. Hughes had been sitting beside the winning bidder today. He must have texted Ronan afterwards to inform him how high Chris had bid.

'A little wanker who could never get a dance at the Wes disco back then.' Ronan luxuriated in the inhaled smoke before exhaling. 'Now wannabe models anxious to get their names into the gossip columns can't get a dance off him when he starts splashing out on Krug Grand Cuvée in the VIP area of Krystle Nightclub. It's amazing how your sex appeal can be increased by simple things like laser eye surgery, an expensive hair transplant, an estranged wife who has invented a career as an agony aunt purely on the basis of being dumped by you, and the fact that you own a dozen major sites currently in development.'

'One of Hughes's sites burnt down last night. I saw the flames.'

Ronan winked. 'I suspect Paul saw them too.'

'What are you saying?'

'Paul knows everything that happens in this town, even before it happens. He knows that the house you lost at auction today will come back on the market in six months' time – minus half its long back-garden. The adjoining houses will also be for sale, with their gardens all similarly cut in two. Plans are being lodged to build a dozen town houses in a newly created square in the space the developer is going to free up.'

'Local residents will object.'

'No doubt a few old dears will enjoy blue-rinsed orgasms of indignation in their china teacups, but the government is desperate for the stamp duty on each house sold. The developers are keeping Ireland solvent, generating the income to pay teachers and nurses. Residents always object, and local councillors huff and puff on their behalf, but those same councillors genuflect in front of developers in their rush to snatch their share of the tax spoils. The County Council keeps raking in a fortune in building levies.'

Ronan inhaled the smoke again, savouring this tiny illicit pleasure like he relished every pleasure. Tipping the ash against the door frame, he turned to Chris. 'That's what you were up against today; whizz-kids thinking outside the box, realising the potential of every remaining sliver of land. If you want to buy Alice a house, you need to do likewise.'

Chris longed to go indoors and tell Alice that they had been outbid by a developer. Such news might bring some sort of solace. 'What are you saying, Ronan?'

'Whizz-kids don't just see the existing streetscapes, they see possibilities. Take your garden, for instance.'

'What about it?' Chris peered out at his lawn, which needed cutting.

'The Town Commissioners who built your terrace designed these gardens as allotments. But no one needs a garden this long these days. It's why every homeowner with a corner site has built a town house in their side garden.'

'My garden is landlocked, Ronan. Are you suggesting I build apartments and ask buyers to tiptoe through my side gate to reach their beds?'

Ronan placed a hand on Chris's shoulder. 'I'm suggesting you knock down this shed and build a well-designed, single-storey town house in its place. I'll donate a spear of land from the end of my garden, from, say, two yards below my rock pond to my back wall, which we can knock down. This will give you just enough space to build a cobble-lock driveway on it, with access out onto the lane. The town house can be screened behind a nice-looking limestone wall that will divide your garden in half. That way neither Alice nor Kim will have to see the town house, or the old lady pottering in and out of the back lane.'

'What old lady?' Chris asked.

'Next time you enter an auction room you'll have an extra quarter of a million Euro in your back pocket, enough to frighten away the big swinging dicks. You and Alice will be the couple the estate agents open the champagne for, begging you to pen your signatures on the contracts.'

'I asked what old lady?'

'Paul Hughes's mother,' Ronan replied, as if delivering the *coup de grâce*. 'It's too dangerous for her to continue living alone in her crumbling Victorian house off Newtownpark Avenue, but she's too proud to even let Paul install a stairlift. She's on the lookout for a tasteful single-storey town house, a stone's throw from Blackrock village. Paul and I worked it all out on Friday night. He even got his top architect to email me some provisional plans.'

Chris turned, angrily. 'You drew up plans for my garden?'

'Only a rough outline. And remember, it involves both our gardens. Still, it's your decision; I'm merely the matchmaker. Mrs Hughes loves this part of Blackrock, and Paul will pay twice the going rate to keep her happy. He can afford to. He has outline permission to convert her old house into six apartments and then erect a three-storey apartment block on her old orchard and tennis court. For this to happen, she needs to be rehoused somewhere where she'll be happy. You have him over a barrel, Chris! You're sitting on the last few square inches of downtown Blackrock that somebody hasn't already developed. This is how deals happen; I'm trying to help you and Alice.'

'By buying half my garden from me?'

Ronan shook his head. 'If we put this town house in my name, then Miriam's lawyers can come back in and fleece me again for my share of the profits. I want to earn a discreet nest egg that Kim can squirrel away in the bank in her own name only; something she can fall back on if I die and legal hissy fits arise over my will. I'm not as young as I was, and to be honest, though never say this to Alice, Kim has sexual appetites that I'd have been hard pressed to satisfy at twenty-one. Some nights I think I'm going to die in bed of a heart attack and die happy, but I'd die happier if Kim had money that Miriam knew nothing about.'

Ronan looked away, and a realisation came to Chris. *Ronan can't get it up any more.* He was convinced of this because he could remember Ronan as a young man, playing his way through a succession of conquests without bragging or making one indiscreet comment about any girl he slept with. Ronan's discretion back then was in such contrast to his libido that Chris suspected that he'd had a dozen other girlfriends in addition to the ones that Chris knew about. For Ronan to make such an unprompted boast about his sex life now was the closest Chris had ever come to hearing his neighbour inadvertently confess to experiencing pain. Even Ronan's messy divorce had been passed off with bravado as heralding a new adventure. It felt blackly funny that here they were, two friends whose fortunes had gone in opposite directions, and yet, as they might have crudely put it during their school days, neither was getting a sniff of sex. What other aspects of Ronan's life were grand illusions, propped up only by empty boasts?

'You want me to build the town house?' Chris was incredulous. 'I know nothing about building, and I'm not into that kind of risk.'

'There is no risk.' Ronan scrutinised him. Was this admission about his sex life untrue? Had it been dropped into the conversation to make Chris feel they were equally in the same boat? Ronan was always three steps ahead, incapable of letting his right hand know what his left hand was doing. 'We have a guaranteed buyer lined up, willing to pay over the odds. All you and Alice need to do is sign this planning application form.'

Ronan produced an envelope from his pocket. 'I had it drawn up, just in case, along with a deed transferring the end of my garden to you for a peppercorn sum.'

'You said you only had rough drawings.'

Ronan shrugged apologetically. 'Time weighs on my hands. We can knock down this shed and dig out and lay the foundations while we're waiting for planning permission. I'll become your silent partner and site foreman. I pay for all materials – I can source things at the right price – and I pay the workers with my cash. We'll use a guy called Jiri, a Romanian workman that Hughes recommended. Jiri is only two years in Ireland, but he already has a network of tradesmen moonlighting for him. They can finish their shifts on official sites at half four and start here at half five. In the summer evenings they'd throw up a town house in a flash. There's no risk for you: I'm paying for everything.'

'And getting what in return?'

Ronan tapped the envelope gently, teasing Chris's curiosity.

'Do I look like Mother Teresa? After Hughes buys the town house for his mother, I get refunded all my expenses. After that we split all the remaining profit fifty-fifty. It's a fair deal.'

'You get fifty per cent for building a town house in my garden?'

'In your landlocked garden, which is worthless until I give you access onto the lane. My share of the profits is for the land at the end of my garden, plus the use of my contacts, my cash, my expertise and my balls of steel in putting this deal together.'

'Alice will want nothing to do with any illegal tax dodge.' Chris felt scared by this turn of events. He needed time to lick his wounds after the public humiliation of today's auction. Alice was right that he was useless at decisions, and he had no desire to have a new one thrust upon him now.

'Everything on your end is strictly above board. But after you pay capital gains tax on the profits, if you decide to give me, in cash, half the remaining proceeds as a finder's fee, then whether I declare this on my income tax return is not your responsibility. You and I will only have a gentleman's agreement. Everything on paper will be in your name, so I'm the person placing my complete trust in you.'

'Neighbours along the terrace will lodge objections.' Chris was desperate for any excuse.

Ronan gave him that same boyish devil-may-care grin he could recall from when they had been schoolmates up to mischief.

'Fuck them. You don't even know the names of the current tenants living next door to you. And the rest of the terrace won't be your neighbours for much longer after you make a small fortune on this deal. There's a precedent established three streets away, where two neighbours built a house that straddled both their gardens. For the Planning Department, setting a precedent is like losing their virginity: they're not always happy about it, but they can't get it back. It's your decision, but do you want to keep dragging Alice to auction after auction and see her hopes crushed? You're sitting on a gold mine you never knew about. For Alice's sake, it's time to cash in.'

In the male world of this shed, Ronan's proposition made sense, but up in Alice's bedroom every flaw would be exposed, and most especially the fact of Chris being daft enough to trust Ronan.

'I'm no good at this sort of thing,' Chris pleaded. 'Besides, Alice will never go for it.'

Leaning against the door frame, Ronan gave a conspiratorial shrug. 'That says it all, doesn't it?' His dismissive tone made Chris angry.

'For once say what you mean.'

Ronan shrugged again. 'I don't need to, do I?'

'I've had a tough day, Ronan. I don't need you being snide.'

Ronan lit another cigarette and slowly exhaled the smoke. 'I'm scared of my wife too. I illegally park on the hard shoulders of motorways to step out from my car and sneak a smoke in case I leave any smell of tobacco inside. I'll finish this fag and chew a packet of mints before I go inside.' He gestured apologetically. 'I wasn't being snide; I'm trying to help you make a decision. It's not me you need to have this argument with.'

'Stay out of my life, Ronan.'

'We're old friends: an old friend can say things you mightn't want to hear. Alice might respect you more if you actually did something.'

Something had been troubling Chris since his conversation with Alice in the car. He was reluctant to mention it here, but needed to know.

'Last autumn there was a woman I met a couple of times, remember?'

Ronan turned and nodded, cagily. 'What about it?'

'Did you ever say anything about it to Alice?'

'I backed up your story that you and I had gone to the driving range, just like you asked me to.'

'And you said nothing else?'

Ronan shrugged. 'I don't get involved in in other people's business. Would Alice really kill you if she knew?'

'I was going to tell her. It just got too complicated. It didn't end the way I expected.'

'It ended very beneficially for Sophie.'

'Sophie knows nothing about that business, not for now at least, and neither does Alice.'

'Do you think she suspects?'

'She suspects something, but I don't know what.'

'Alice can't suspect there was anything sexual going on. She knows you're too sensible for anything like that. Besides, I only needed to cover for you three times, and your third visitation ended rather abruptly as I recall.'

'I should have been straight with Alice from the start. I got greedy … not for me, but for Sophie. It was easy money … there's no such thing as easy money, is there?'

'You could tell Alice now. Surely to God she'd be pleased for Sophie.'

'She'd be furious with me for having gone behind her back. Things aren't great between us just now. I was going to tell her today if we won that house at auction. She'd have been so euphoric she'd have forgiven me anything.'

'Do you want my advice?'

'No.' Chris shook his head. 'I just want to know that you didn't say anything else to Alice that might have roused her suspicions.'

'What do you take me for? I was your friend years before I ever become your neighbour.' Ronan stubbed out his cigarette and glanced back into the shed. 'If you won't build a town house, then at the very least hire a skip. You can park it in the lane and drag your junk through my garden. There are paint cans here going back to the last cholera epidemic in Blackrock.'

Ronan stepped into the sunshine and went to scale the wall.

'Listen, I'm rattled,' Chris said apologetically. 'Don't take offence.'

Ronan turned and looked at him. 'You needn't have any fears about me saying anything to Alice. She has barely exchanged a dozen words with me since Miriam left. Alice never took to Kim. Marriage break-ups are messy. I know the signs, and the lonesomeness after.' He held out the envelope containing the planning application. 'I'm not telling you to sign this application; I'm just suggesting you read through it. You'll be doing Hughes a favour. In today's Dublin, favours beget favours. The developer who won the auction today owes Paul a favour. Once he gets permission to annex the gardens for his new development, he plans to resell the house he bought today. Hughes can ensure that it's sold to you on the quiet. It might be missing half its original back garden, but it will going for a price you can easily afford. Think of how stunned Alice would be if you could hand her the keys to it without her even having known that it was back on the market. You could tell her pretty much anything then, and she'd forgive you. This could be a clean start you've both been looking for.'

Reluctantly, almost against his will, Chris took possession of the envelope Ronan was holding out. His neighbour nodded.

'I'm not just offering to help build a town house, Chris: I'm offering to help save your marriage.'

Ronan gripped the wall with surprising agility, scrambled up to balance on the top and then disappeared, leaving Chris alone with his decision.

Chapter Ten

Sophie

Tuesday 13th, 3.30 p.m.

Mum didn't say much when I went in to her, but I was used to her silences and we didn't really need words. I knew they had lost at the auction and she was lost in a trough that was not as deep as in the bad years, but which at that moment surely felt as deep, because Mum experienced every emotion intensely. When she was happy she could not conceive of unhappiness; when she was sad it felt like the whole world had been transformed into a landscape of despair.

I slipped off my shoes and wordlessly got in beside her. Her shoulders hunched up, resentful of my intrusion. Then her hand reached back to grasp mine and I spooned into her like when I was a child. Lately we were constantly squabbling, but we both knew that, when we weren't mad at each other, we were mad about each other. I'm not sure how long I lay there, holding her hand, not saying a word. Time never had any meaning in Mum's room. I didn't know how much they had lost the auction by, but if I possessed any money I'd have given every cent for Dad to feel able to join us in that darkened room, all three of us snuggled up one more time, like when I was young and this bed was the safest sanctuary on earth.

Eventually, Mum turned over and kissed my forehead. It was her way to intimate that she loved me and wanted me to leave her alone now. I closed her door softly and returned to my own bedroom. The door was ajar. Dad sat on my bed. He didn't hear me approach and was so absorbed that he didn't see me. He looked like the loneliest of men as he stared down at an unopened brown envelope, turning it over in his hand like a lost soul.

PART TWO

August 2007

Chapter Eleven

Chris

Sunday 5th, 2 p.m.

The workmen were shouting and hammering in the garden. As he listened, Chris realised that this was how Alice and he had communicated for weeks – above incessant banging and the piercing screech of electric saws. At least the cement mixer was idle – one token concession to what should be the quietness of a Sunday afternoon in an August bank holiday weekend. The hammering ceased suddenly. This was good. It meant that he would hear if Alice came upstairs and caught him opening the wardrobe to remove the envelope from the pocket of his sombre black suit.

Alice loved his tweed suit and would never touch this black one that he wore only to funerals and interdepartmental meetings. Over the years this had made it his repository for possessions that embarrassed him. Its pocket contained the remnants of a packet of Viagra purchased last August. To work properly, these tablets had to be swallowed an hour before sexual activity commenced, but intimacy with Alice – when it used to occur – had always needed to happen spontaneously, a casual touch sparking a passionate embrace, often with Sophie the width of a bedroom wall away. The increasing infrequency of their lovemaking had left his body in a quandary, never knowing when it might be pressurised to perform during hurried intercourse that could end as abruptly as it began. Last year he had noticed how anxiety was progressively causing him stage fright during these trysts that came out of nowhere. Three times in the weeks after purchasing those expensive blue tablets that he had felt embarrassed about asking his doctor to prescribe, Chris had tried to anticipate Alice's mood by slipping upstairs to swallow one. On each occasion the atmosphere of the evening had changed, leaving him feeling frustrated and foolish, unable to confess his folly to Alice when the last thing he wanted was for her to feel that he was no longer naturally attracted to her.

He discreetly checked that the packet with its single remaining tablet was still there, and then opened the envelope to count out the thirty thousand euro in cash that he had withdrawn from their building society on Friday. He hated keeping secrets from Alice, but an unmerciful row would erupt if she knew that he was lending Ronan their savings. This was not even the first tranche: three weeks ago Chris had reluctantly handed over a similar sum to his neighbour. But there could be no third tranche. Their savings were decimated. All that remained were some savings for Sophie, which were so secret that not even Sophie knew about them yet. The hammering resumed. Chris concealed the bulky envelope in the leather jacket he wore and went downstairs.

Before he even opened the kitchen door he sensed that the presence of the workmen today would put Alice in bad form. This anxiety about her mood, which he constantly felt since the building started, had become a self-fulfilling prophecy: even if Alice were happily singing at the sink, Chris's look of apprehension invariably soured her humour. She didn't turn from the window now when he entered. The innocuous comment he had formulated to break the ice died as he stared past her shoulders at the chaotic scene in their garden. It was a jumble of rusted building equipment, heaped bags of cement and mounds of sand covered in plastic sheeting. Cavity blocks and oddments of planks were being sorted by Jiri's ever-changing army of workmen, all stripped to the waist and shouting in foreign tongues.

'The whole crew is out there,' Alice murmured with resigned exasperation.

'I'm as desperate as you to see the back of Jiri,' Chris replied.

'I can cope every weekday evening when they clamber over Ronan's wall at six o'clock like marauding pirates, is it too much to want to have some privacy on a Sunday?' She turned to face Chris, an onion half-sliced on the chopping board. 'Other couples are off at the beach enjoying the bank holiday weekend.'

'I'll happily bring you to the beach after lunch,' Chris replied.

'You hate the beach.'

'I'll bring you anyway.'

She resumed chopping the onion. 'I don't need bringing. If I decide to go out later, I'll just go.'

Chris noted this first hint of her intention to go out tonight. It had become a regular pattern on recent Sunday evenings, with Alice growing defensive if asked where she was going.

'Jiri's men will be gone soon,' he said. 'They're tidying up before a plasterer skims the final section of wall this evening. Ronan wants the scaffolding off the site by tomorrow.'

'It's not a *site*, it's our back garden.'

Through the window Chris saw Jiri emerge from under the scaffolding. His sidekick, Ezal, walked behind him, like a faithful younger brother, although Ronan claimed they were from different countries.

'Look how much work they've done in just six weeks,' Chris said. 'Are they really interfering with your Sunday so much?'

'They will be,' Alice replied, 'when Ezal knocks at the back door, badgering you for the loan of something. Jiri's men barely own a set of tools between them.'

'Real builders cost a fortune and charge VAT. There's a three-year waiting list for them and a six-month gap when they disappear off to another job. Paul Hughes was spot on when he promised Ronan that these lads would show up every evening.'

'And every evening I go out to the garden to try and befriend them,' Alice said. 'I offer them food, but they refuse to even accept a cup of tea.'

'Maybe they think it's charity,' Chris said.

'I don't mean it as charity, it's courtesy and simple hospitality because they are guests in my garden. They're surely hungry and exhausted after doing a full day's work elsewhere, and I hate to think that the most I can get them to accept from me is a glass of water. It's like I don't really exist in their eyes, it's like our garden is Ronan's property because he's the one paying their wages.'

'They're good workmen,' Chris said.

'I'm not denying it. I've never known any men to work so hard, tipping away by torchlight till midnight, with you pleading with them to keep the noise down as if it makes any difference to how the neighbours hate us. They seem like nice men, and I wouldn't have a word said against them, but just for once I'd like to cook a meal without being on public display with men stripped to the waist staring in at me.'

Chris risked laying a hand lightly on her shoulder. 'Another woman might enjoy the view,' he teased, 'her private Chippendale show.'

Alice ignored his hand. 'I'm in no mood for jokes.'

'These days I rarely know what mood you're in.'

'What does that mean?'

He removed his hand and stood beside her. Chris hoped she would look up, but her eyes remained focused on the chopping board.

'There was a time when you shared every thought in your head, Alice.'

Something plaintive about his voice made her turn.

'People change.' Her voice was soft, as if comforting a child. For a moment she looked like the Alice he had married. Then she looked down at the vegetables again and said, 'I need to finish this before they barge in.'

'Alice, stop cutting me out of your life.' She didn't reply, even when he repeated her name softly. He stepped away in exasperation. 'Enjoy your Chippendale show: you've certainly no interest in seeing me strip off any more.'

'Whoever those workmen are, they're not sly,' Alice said quietly as he reached the back door.

He quelled an angry retort, guiltily cognisant of the envelope in his pocket. Two months had passed since Sophie had left for Urbino to get a summer job and immerse herself in Italian before her autumn classes started. In her absence the house was quiet, and Chris knew that they both missed her. He walked back to put his arms around Alice.

'We're on display,' she said quietly.

'Can I not even give you a hug any more?'

He sensed a frustration so deep within her that she seemed near tears.

'Not with half of Eastern Europe watching. And I'll remain on show after they're gone, with a Noddyland bungalow in my garden.'

'It's a town house,' he said. 'After we erect the wall we won't be able to see Mrs Hughes, and she can't see us.'

'I remember Mrs Hughes in her beautiful old house. She'd let us in to pick apples in her orchard when I was small. A proper lady, my mother always called her. How can someone like that adjust to living in a cubbyhole?'

'People grow old.' Chris felt uncomfortable at defending something he was equally uneasy about. 'Her house isn't safe any more. Paul Hughes kept her living there independently for as long as he could.'

'Just long enough to secure planning permission to build on her home.'

'I'm not defending him. I don't know what he's like.'

'I danced with him at rugby hops,' Alice said. 'Other fellows at least waited for the music to start before trying to paw you, but Hughes was always in a hurry and only out for himself.'

'You can't judge everyone by their hormones at seventeen.'

'People say he's in massive debt, struggling to stay afloat until he makes a fortune from developing her home. I don't like us playing any part in parking a confused old lady at the end of our garden. It doesn't make me feel good about myself.'

'It won't be our garden much longer,' Chris said. 'With our share of the profit we'll be gone, I promise you that.'

Alice looked out the window as Ronan emerged from next door to converse animatedly with Jiri. 'I'd respect you more if you stopped promising things you never deliver.'

Chris removed his arms and stepped back, hurt. The sight of Ronan made him uneasy. His neighbour was waiting for the cash that would draw Chris deeper into what had been meant to be a simple transaction.

'You could show some belief in me.'

Alice's tone softened. 'I desperately want to believe in you. I was so lonely as a girl that I never thought I'd find anyone to love as much as you.'

'What's changed?'

Alice was silent for a moment. 'I don't know.' She turned to face him, looking as vulnerable as the day they first met. 'It's a matter of trust. Why can't I get the thought out of my head that there are times when you lie to me?'

The weight of the envelope felt immense now, the bulge in his jacket pocket huge. How had he ever let himself get manoeuvred into this situation? He noticed Ronan impatiently glance in the window and panicked, wondering if Ronan had spoken to Alice. No, that would make no sense, even if Alice liked to paint their neighbour as Machiavellian. This cash was a matter between Ronan and him.

'What makes you think I have?'

'Then answer me with a simple yes or no,' she said quietly. 'Have you ever lied to me?'

His reply was Jesuitical – another word for cowardly. He was not lying to her about this money in his jacket, because she had not asked him about it. If she asked him, here and now, he would tell the truth and face the consequences. But Ronan had sucked him so deeply into this deal, which was so near its endgame, that he had no choice but to keep funding it with their savings or risk losing everything. When the town house was sold and he could show Alice the profit, then he would confess every single detail to her. After the auction in March she had said that he lacked the courage of other men who could make deals. Even if it required a temporary deception to do so, this time he was going to prove himself.

'I've never lied to you,' he replied softly.

She looked at him in silence, and then turned away to stare out the window towards Ronan and the workmen.

'What's wrong?' he asked after a moment.

Alice shook her head. 'I don't know,' she replied, a quiet hurt in her voice. 'These past months I feel there's something broken inside me. I used to love the end of our garden, how it gets the sun in the evening.'

'You used to love lots of things. You used to love me.'

Alice's voice was barely a whisper. 'I still love you; maybe I'm just not *in love* with you.'

'What does that mean?'

She turned, so upset that she was close to tears. 'It means there are times I feel I just can't breathe with you around me. I feel suffocated by our closeness. Maybe we've been too close for too long, and that hasn't been good for us. I hate seeing the pressure you keep putting yourself under. At times it's like I'm watching you go to pieces in front of my eyes.'

'Well maybe that pressure isn't just coming from me. You're the one desperate to move.'

'But I was also willing to accept that we never will. You can't let the dream go. It's ceased to be just about a house for you, it's like a test in your mind. But I'm not asking you for some grand gesture … what I need from you is more than just bricks and mortar. I still care for you. Maybe I'm not always good at showing it any more, but I worry about you setting yourself goals that you can't achieve.'

'Look out that window and tell me I can't achieve anything,' Chris replied, hurt.

Alice turned to gaze at the frenetic scenes in the garden. 'I was so excited when you came into my bedroom that day about the idea of building a town house. I wasn't excited for myself or about what profit we might make, I was excited for you, that you going to take on something that it would be good for your self-confidence and give you a sense of achievement. I was a hundred per cent behind you, remember?'

'Then why did you so quickly turn against it?'

'Because I realised that none of it was your idea the moment you told me who your silent partner was going to be. I knew in my heart then that you weren't really building this town house for you and me, but because you've never been able to stand up to Ronan. No matter what half-baked scheme Ronan concocted he'd find a way to play on your weaknesses until he'd twisted your arm.'

'If it's such a bad idea, why did you co-sign the planning application?'

She shook her head. 'I just hadn't the heart for another argument … that's all we seem to do these days. Maybe I'd figured that whatever we end up with can't be worse than what we have now. If this was your idea alone, Chris, I'd be out there mixing cement myself. But I don't trust Ronan. From the start I said that I'd sooner go into partnership with a snake.'

Chris glanced out at the daily interlopers into their lives. If the workmen could overhear, they showed no interest in the domestic drama being played out at this kitchen window. Alice turned away.

'From the way he's looking in this window, Ronan is getting impatient to talk to you. The sooner you go out to him, the sooner that man will be out of my garden. His wife should have left him years ago.'

'Ronan has a new wife.'

'A Filipina child bride is not the same thing as a real woman who could stand up to him.'

'Kim looks pretty real to me.'

'When Miriam was next door I had one friend on this street. I'm lonely here now. I didn't think I'd miss Sophie so much.'

'You've loads of friends on this street.'

'Not since we started building that house. It's why I needed to go as far as Cabinteely to join a tennis club where none of the members had lodged an objection to our planning permission.'

'Is that where you're going tonight?' Chris tried to keep his voice casual.

Alice grew guarded. 'I haven't even decided if I will go out. I decided nothing, but I might meet some friends for a drink.'

'What friends?'

Alice resumed dicing the onions, indicating that the conversation was over. 'I've the right to know people you don't know, strangers who don't automatically think of me as the woman involved in that crash. Now go out and get rid of Ronan. It's hard enough cooking in front of hungry men without having him smirking in at me as well.'

Chapter Twelve

Ronan

Sunday 5th, 2.30 p.m.

Small African nations have negotiated independence treaties with less debate than Chris and Alice were having in their kitchen window, leaving Ronan stranded in the garden trying to stall Jiri and his apparatchik, Ezal, whose version of small talk meant no talk.

Jiri he could deal with. Jiri reminded Ronan of his own father: a man who didn't waste words, but who had possessed the ability to walk across an empty stretch of land and intuitively price any job without recourse to quantity surveyors or anything other than a pencil and an envelope. His father took it as a personal insult when Ronan qualified as a quantity surveyor. But there again, his father had taken everything in life as an insult after unwisely being persuaded, aged sixty-six, to accept a generous buyout offer for his construction company from a rival firm, with a clause prohibiting him from starting up any competing business for a decade.

Ronan's father had been banished to God's waiting room – the fairways of Killiney Golf Club – where he endured his purgatory of enforced retirement by scowling at lady members or any venial sinner guilty of slow play. He fought bowel cancer for three years, not so much from a discernible love of life as a determination to outlive the clause in his contract. If he couldn't cheat death, he longed to cheat his rivals by establishing a new business, because what was a man's purpose in life if it did not involve building something up or tearing something down?

Ronan had been gutted when his father abruptly sold his business shortly after Ronan qualified. It was the *generalísimo's* public declaration that his son was not made of the right stuff and the firm would never become J. J. Cox & Son Construction Ltd. The fee-paying education which Ronan's mother had wanted for him – partly from a desire to see him succeed, and partly so that she could hold up her head on equal terms with the other mothers in Frascati Park – had softened Ronan up in his father's eyes. Perhaps they had been too alike, equally stubborn and unable to communicate with each other. All fathers want to see something of themselves in their sons, but Ronan had never wanted his peers to see anything of his father in him, especially when growing up as a teenage rebel in an ostentatious fish tank like Blackrock. They had rowed incessantly after his father returned from London to focus on building projects in Dublin. If they had worked together, maybe they would have been at each other's throats. But the tragedy was that they never had a chance to merge their contradictions and perhaps achieve something exceptional, which might have earned Ronan the parental respect he had craved.

Ronan had inherited a third of his father's estate, with his sister receiving the same and Opus Dei being the final bed partner in an unholy threesome. Since then he had dabbled in small deals, some going pear-shaped and others making him spectacular profits. But if his father had shown confidence in him, or stuck a shovel in his hand rather than an expensively earned BA, Ronan might not now be only a bit-player. He could be up there with Paul Hughes and Sean Dunne and Johnny Ronan. He could match any of them in terms of balls and brains, but they had been lucky: they merely needed to grapple with banks and rival consortiums. He would have needed to compete with his father's shadow from beyond the grave, but had refused to give that disgruntled ghost the satisfaction.

The older he got, the more Ronan realised that the qualities he most hated in his father were qualities he needed to fight within himself. His father's meanness with the money he hoarded made Ronan determined to enjoy spending cash on his loved ones. Miriam might have often wished to strangle him, but she never needed to run from room to room, like his mother in Frascati Park, turning off radiators before his father returned home. Ronan was a more balanced and fulfilled person than his father, so why was the old miser's judgement still important to him?

Ronan's father was not a man whom people had liked, but he was an employer all workmen instinctively trusted. Ronan trusted Jiri implicitly, so it felt like another slap from beyond the grave that Jiri obviously didn't trust him. One reason for Ronan being late with their agreed payments was that Jiri was completing the town house ahead of schedule. Ronan had not expected to need to find so much money so quickly, or that another investment opportunity would severely erode his cash flow. However, this was not the day to fall out with Jiri: Ronan needed the scaffolding gone by Tuesday morning. He would find a way to keep his side of their financial bargain. The important thing was not to let Jiri, or his sniffer dog, Ezal, know that he had problems in raising cash.

Ronan glanced around at Jiri's workmen cutting lengths of guttering, fixing in place the windowsills and digging foundations for the dividing wall midway down the garden. Chris's voice rose from the kitchen, not loud enough to distinguish the words, but enough for Ronan to register his neighbour's agitation. Neither Jiri nor Ezal looked up, but it was obvious that they had heard.

'Your neighbour seems a nice man,' Jiri said. 'What does he do?'

'He does nothing, but files it away in triplicate,' Ronan joked. 'He's a civil servant in the Department of Jobs, Enterprise and Innovation.'

Jiri and Ezal pondered this remark, scrutinising Ronan with such inquisitorial seriousness that he felt he had lost face. Flippancy was not among the national characteristics of whatever nation Ezal hailed from, though Ronan had ceased trying to prise any personal information from him. Nobody on this site worked harder than Ezal. He was perpetually alert and cognisant of everyone who came and went, yet Ronan couldn't shake off the sense that one part of Ezal's mind was permanently elsewhere, as if the activity occurring around him were a mere sideshow to whatever thoughts truly preoccupied him. In contrast, Jiri seemed immersed in the practical steps of whatever job next needed to be done, so focused on the here and now that it felt as if his own past were of no more interest for him than the buildings in Ireland that he had helped to build, and then forgot about as soon as he had been fully paid. Jiri and Ezal seemed an unlikely duo, yet Ronan had never known two men to work so well together. Their continued gaze unnerved him as he tried to lighten the mood.

'To get ahead you must work for yourself,' he said. 'Like you, Jiri. Just how many men work for you now?'

'None,' Jiri replied quietly. 'I am a bricklayer. I just happen to have friends who help me with odd jobs.'

'You sound like my Dad.' Ronan wished to hell that Chris would hurry up. 'He always played his cards close to his chest. You'll end up owning half of Ireland in a few years.'

'I'll be gone.'

'Gone?' Ronan laughed. 'Dublin is a boom town for a man like you.'

'There'll be no more apartments to build.'

'Why? We'll hardly run out of space.'

Jiri went silent as the back door opened and Chris emerged. Ezal spoke for the first time: 'You'll run out of people able to afford them.'

Ronan steered Chris away from the workmen. Walking past Alice's destroyed flower beds, he lowered his voice. 'How's Alice?'

'Sick of men gazing in through her window.'

'Tell her it's great that men still lust after her.'

'You tell her.'

Ronan laughed. 'I suffered enough matrimonial war wounds. I should be entitled to an active service pension.' He halted, out of Jiri's hearing and out of Alice's eyeline. 'Have you got what we discussed?'

Chris anxiously glanced towards the kitchen window. 'I've had it in my suit pocket all weekend. I hated hiding it from Alice.'

'Did you tell her?' Ronan couldn't prevent anxiety entering his voice.

Chris stared at him. 'Do you think Alice would trust you with our savings?'

Ronan shrugged. 'Nobody leaves money on deposit any more. Money needs to be out in the world earning its keep.'

'I've never taken risks with our deposit for a house, or at least not until you badgered me into emptying our savings account. Our deal was that you would fund this town house.'

Noting the anger in Chris's tone, Ronan needed to tread carefully. 'That's still the deal,' he assured him. 'I'm paying these workmen in cash.'

'But you never said it would be my cash.'

'I'm not paying them with your cash.' This was what Catholic theologians called a statement made with strict mental reservations. 'Your cash is being used to buy cut-price materials. We're ahead of schedule and under budget.'

Chris didn't look convinced, but Ronan knew that Chris needed to let himself be convinced. None of this would be necessary if Paul Hughes had delivered on his promised schedule of advance deposits on the town house. But it was as much in Hughes's nature to play hardball as it was in Chris's nature to be compliant. So far Hughes had not only stalled on the date of each proposed payment, but had subtly turned the tables by opening up new investment avenues, allowing Ronan access into high-octane circles he could normally only fantasise about. On the three occasions when Ronan entered the Playwright Inn, expecting to extract a cheque from Hughes, he had ended up writing Hughes a cheque instead. This entrée into the consortium developing Hughes's childhood home would pay huge dividends in the medium term, but it meant that cash flow was becoming increasing messy. Hughes was famous for stretching out payment with everyone, but later today he would definitely need to pay Ronan the next stage of the agreed deposit because Mrs Hughes had already approved the town house plans. Mrs Hughes had even helped – albeit reluctantly – to select the furnishing and tiny hi-tech kitchen. The company fitting kitchens in Hughes's latest apartment development was supplying it at cost price. This afternoon Ronan planned to cut through Hughes's prevarications and emerge with a cheque. But project management involved taking one step at a time. The first step was to prise cash from Chris.

'You promised that Alice and I wouldn't have to pay for anything,' Chris said. 'If we're under budget, why are you broke?'

'I'm not broke.' Ronan laughed at the notion. 'I'm encountering unanticipated but beneficial cash flow problems. Things are progressing so quickly that I need to pay Jiri faster than expected. His men may be workaholics, but they're also a mistrustful shower of bastards who like cash up front. I was planning to buy materials on credit at a builders' providers I know, but Jiri has the inside track on a site going bust. He can source us roof tiles, oak floorboards, quality windows and ornamental brick for the dividing garden wall that Alice will love. Some developer is desperate for cash. With your extra cash we can buy materials for a fraction of their value before a receiver impounds everything on his site. I'll be able to pay you back every cent you've loaned me, at a thirty per cent interest rate, and still make far more than originally planned.'

'Where's Jiri sourcing the stuff?'

Ronan shook his head. This time there was no mental reservation: Jiri was refusing to say.

'It's untraceable,' Ronan assured him. 'Not even the fraud squad can fingerprint a cement block.' He put a hand on Chris's shoulder and looked him in the eye. 'This isn't the Civil Service now. You're out in the real world where people cut corners to get jobs done. The sooner we finish, the quicker Hughes signs the contract.'

Chris stared back as if still seeking some excuse to vacillate, and then furtively reached into his pocket to hand over the envelope. Ronan glanced back to check if Jiri was watching. Jiri was supervising a job inside the town house, but Ezal stood outside, rolling a handmade cigarette. The Serb or Croat or whatever he was gave no indication of having seen anything, but Ronan knew that he had observed this handover.

'If Alice finds out, I'm finished,' Chris said quietly.

'Alice will think you're a hero after we pull off this sale. Why don't you both call over tonight for a drink?'

'Alice is going out.'

'That's nice. Who with?'

Ronan kept his tone casual, but knew how loaded the question was. Chris betrayed an anguished look of bewilderment. It was a glimpse into a loneliness that Ronan recognised. In between Miriam leaving and meeting Kim, Ronan had nearly drunk himself to death, privately at night with only a computer and self-loathing for company. Miriam was a flinty and robust survivor. Indeed, it hurt Ronan that Miriam was surviving so well. Alice and Chris were more vulnerable. They belonged together and would never survive apart.

'Some friends from her new tennis club.' Chris tried to sound convincing.

'Then call in yourself,' Ronan said kindly, 'I have a bottle of Hennessy XO. It would be a mortal sin to open it alone.'

Chris laughed to break the tension. 'We'll see.'

Ronan watched Chris walk back into his house. His genuine guilt at having to cajole cash from his neighbour was replaced by a familiar adrenaline rush at having resolved yet another stumbling block. He ran through a mental list of tasks. The next step was to ensure that a plasterer came today. Jiri emerged from the town house, as if Ezal had summoned him by telepathy.

'Are you certain you can source everything on the list?' Ronan asked Jiri, mentally dividing Chris's cash into what he could get away with paying Jiri now and what he needed to retain to dole out during the week.

'I keep my promises,' the Romanian said, 'unlike certain people.'

'I hope you don't mean me.'

'You are a straight man.'

Ronan began to count out the banknotes. 'Do I know this developer who's in trouble?

Jiri shook his head. 'I doubt if you know him at all.'

'What time will Andrzej come at to plaster the wall?'

'Andrzej is sick today.'

Jiri pocketed the cash as he spoke. To Ronan this felt like another slap from beyond the grave. His father would never have handed over the money until certain that the plasterer would arrive as promised. Ronan glanced sharply at Jiri and Ezal to show that he would not be taken for a fool.

'Andrzej is your best plasterer. If Andrzej was dying, he'd rig up a bed on that scaffolding rather than miss out a half-day's pay. You have him working on another site, don't you?'

Jiri refused to be drawn. 'Another plasterer will come.'

'I need this scaffolding taken down tomorrow.'

'It will be. This new plasterer is good.'

'Phone him to make sure he's coming.'

'I have no number. Ezal told a bricklayer on his site to tell him he is needed here today. He was here once before, helping to knock down the old shed. Ezal vouches for him. If Ezal says he's reliable, he's reliable.'

Ezal nodded.

'Has he a name?'

Ezal shrugged his shoulders, and it was Jiri who replied. 'Someone told me his real name is Pavle, but these days he calls himself Joe.'

'Do you even know where he is from?' Ronan asked.

Jiri glanced at Ezal, who shrugged again, uninterested. 'Serbia perhaps, or Kosovo. If a man doesn't say, I don't ask. Some men you don't question about their past.'

'He keeps to himself,' Jiri added. 'Men in his hotel say that he never sends home money or phones anyone. He moves between sites, disappearing whenever he's earned enough money, and turns up somewhere else using a different name when he's broke. All I care about is that he's a good plasterer.'

'All I care about is that he turns up. It's urgent.'

'Have I let you down yet?'

'No.'

It was Ezal who spoke, almost out of turn. 'Then you know that Jiri doesn't work with men who let him down.'

Jiri turned away, removing the wad of banknotes from his pocket. The other workmen lifted their heads from their tasks, brushed their hands on their trousers and gathered around him.

Chapter Thirteen

Ronan

Sunday 5th, 3 p.m.

Kim was downstairs. Or at least Ronan thought she was. Her movements possessed an unobtrusiveness that he found oddly disconcerting. Miriam had always occupied a room in a way that allowed no doubt as to her presence. Even if her radio was not blasting out her favourite easy-listening stations, partly to drown out pop videos blaring from televisions in the girls' rooms, Miriam's presence in the house had been absolute. Even her silences had simmered loudly. Or maybe back then, with three bickering females corralled under one roof, everything was loud: loud hysterical laughter, loud rows, or loud reaffirmations of affection. Even sudden outbreaks of silence from the girls' rooms had been loudly suspicious.

When outside this house, Kim could also be loud. Ronan had witnessed this transformation early in their courtship, when he accompanied her to a karaoke Asian restaurant in Capel Street and saw her personality change as she joyously greeted old Filipino friends. She could appear so girlish in those unguarded moments, her face radiating such unstrained delight that Ronan had felt an ache at being reminded of how his daughters used to greet school friends excitedly during nights out.

Maybe it was this reminder of his estranged daughters that had made him so uncomfortable during those impossibly loud gatherings. He had tried to blend in for Kim's sake, pleased to see her happy, and pleased that she seemed proud to introduce him to equally animated foreigners, with names too complex to remember or too simplified to be true. But he could never relax in that alien world, listening to strangers uninhibitedly parrot the cloying lyrics of mid-Atlantic mush in poor English overlaid with attempted American accents. It was a world where he never understood what to say or wear, and always wound up feeling defensive for not being in command of the situation. He was unsure if his discomfort had sprung from an intrinsic sophistication or a sense of inhibition, an inability to let go in case anyone, even in a restaurant packed with foreigners, sneered at him for making a fool of himself. After a time, Kim stopped suggesting that he accompany her, tacitly acknowledging that she could not be truly herself when burdened by his unease. Ronan never prevented Kim from going, but after their marriage she went less frequently, and finally not at all, despite his encouragement, as if she no longer fully belonged to that world, or any world.

Taking off his jacket now, Ronan counted out the remaining cash in Chris's envelope. He felt uneasy in case Kim came in. Not that Kim would confide in Alice. Indeed, one reason for him masterminding this town house project was the hope that, after Alice moved away, Kim might feel less lonely if she managed to befriend a new next-door neighbour with no legacy of loyalty to Miriam. Opening the custom-fitted mirrored Sliderobe wardrobe that ran the length of their bedroom, Ronan examined his array of suits and jackets. He felt unsure about how to dress for this drink with Paul Hughes. Business meetings were easy: he possessed an armoury of half a dozen suits to be utilised to impress, blend in with or intimidate people. He instinctively knew what to wear when attending a client consultation, or taking his wife to dine at Restaurant Forty One on Stephen's Green, but he was unsure of what to wear today, not knowing if his latest lunchtime drink with Hughes represented a casual encounter or a business summit. Would it be a quick progress report, or descend into a confrontation? Bobby Fischer would have gone insane more quickly if forced to play chess against Paul Hughes: Boris Spassky had at least conceded that he and Fischer were playing chess. With Hughes, Ronan found it impossible to know if he was confronting a master tactician cultivating the persona of a spiv, or a spiv attempting a poor impersonation of a master strategist.

Ronan's uncles had also been sly men who shied away from straight sentences and wallowed in ambiguity. As a youth he had hated their expeditions to Dublin to visit their self-made brother, cadged whiskey fumes on their breath as they winked as if taking it for granted that Ronan understood that the true intent of any sentence they uttered bore no relationship to the words actually spoken. In contrast, Ronan's father was straightforward in his dealings. Ronan had expected Hughes to be equally straight, beyond the invariable token bluster. Maybe Hughes was straight, and the three missed deadlines to pay a deposit on the town house were tests, initiation rituals into the big boys' world. This made Ronan feel that he was being toyed with. Hughes had no legal duty to invest money towards the town house until it was time to sign final contracts, but when Hughes initially pitched this plan there was an implicit understanding that he would bankroll the project in a series of cash advances once planning permission was granted.

On the first occasion when Hughes initiated him into his drinking circle of business associates in the Playwright Inn, however, Hughes had kept loudly repeating that this backup funding was available if Ronan found the financing of such a small project to be beyond his own means. It was a cleverly worded ploy, publicly hinting to every drinker at the table that Ronan had limited resources. It had left Ronan with no option but to assure Hughes that he could easily fund the town house. The only card he was able to bring into play in that unacknowledged poker game was to insinuate to the company that Chris's wife was proving awkward, and therefore the sight of a signed cheque from Hughes might settle her nerves. Ronan had felt guilty at making a mocking joke at his friend's expense by pointing out that Chris no longer possessed a shed to sleep in if Alice kicked her henpecked husband out of bed.

When the obligatory laughter had subsided, Hughes recalled with a conspiratorial wink how Alice had never changed: it had been awkward merely to get a dance off her at rugby hops years ago. To general hilarity he wondered if the Sacred Heart Nuns at Mount Anville had trained Alice to protect her breasts like they were the relics of Saint Thérèse. Shrewdly hijacked in this way, the conversation had quickly descended into tales of boyhood conquests of Mount Anville and Alexandra College girls. One drinker present claimed to have cadged a dance from the inspiration for Bob Geldof's song 'Mary of the Fourth Form' – a legendary object of lust for Blackrock boys of their generation, who had later gone on to become the Taoiseach's personal assistant. Ronan hated such old-school nostalgia shit. He never understood why balding men with hip flasks turned up like lost sheep at Leinster Senior Cup Rugby Finals to support schools they had left thirty years ago. His father's money had purchased him a foothold in this world, but his social background ensured that Ronan was always made to feel like an outsider at school. Ronan's reference to Alice's objections in the Playwright Inn had seemed to turn the funding of the town house into a public test, with Hughes determined not to be dictated to by some Mount Anville girl he had been unable to shift at a dance.

On the three prearranged payment dates since then, Hughes had never offered cash, as if amused to see how Ronan would outfox Alice. In lieu of payments up front, Hughes had instead offered to roll these payments up into a small stake in the consortium he was putting together to develop the site of his mother's house, on condition that Ronan match each agreed advance payment with a similar cash sum. Instead of receiving the hundred thousand euro of working capital from Hughes for which he had budgeted, Ronan had gradually handed over to Hughes another hundred thousand euro, freed up from his own savings, from cashing minor pension investments, and more recently by using money borrowed from Chris. This meant that Ronan had built up an equity stake of two hundred thousand euro in Hughes's consortium. This was registered solely in Kim's name, although as yet his wife had no knowledge of this nest egg, which would triple in value from the moment the first sod was turned on Mrs Hughes's old tennis court, with an eager queue forming to buy the apartments off the plans.

The unexpected chance to invest in this development had initially felt like a reward, one old school friend initiating another into the outer orbit of the crème de la crème business circles that were reshaping Ireland, with bogtrotter government ministers content just to hold on to the tails of their coats and bask in the reflected glory. But recently Ronan was starting to wonder if it could possibly be a sort of cock-tease. The town house was progressing faster than Ronan could have envisaged, so why did he have a foreboding that the project was somehow falling apart? Ronan always prided himself on being able to read the signs, but in this case the portents made no sense. All Ronan knew for certain was that, if he could not extract a cheque from Hughes today, the only cash he had left to work with was whatever remained in that envelope prised from Chris.

It was a month since he posted contracts for the sale of the town house to Hughes. Twice they had talked by phone, with Hughes airily blaming inefficient PAs and mounds of documentation clogging his desk. But a signed contract was different from a gentlemen's agreement: the ten per cent non-refundable advance due on signature would repay every cent Ronan had borrowed from Chris. In previous meetings Ronan had been reluctant to lose face by demanding money from Hughes. He had written cheques that he knew would struggle to clear, merely to prove that he was a player too. But maybe he misread the rules of the game at this level, and had lost face by lacking the balls to insist on Hughes producing his chequebook on day one. The initial capital that Hughes had promised to finance the town house was now inextricably ring-fenced into Kim's stake in his consortium, but there was still a considerable sum due on signature of the contract. Today, this shadow-boxing, from a multi-millionaire so cocksure of his own wealth that so far he had never even offered to buy a round of drinks, needed to stop.

Ronan stared into the mirror at the tie he had carefully selected. He took it off and undid the top button of his shirt. He wasn't walking into the Playwright overdressed, and nor was he going in with a begging bowl. He had kept his side of the bargain. It was time for Hughes to deliver. He would get straight to the point, producing the spare copy of the contract which his solicitor had given him, and would only leave that pub with a signed contract and a cheque. Happy with how he looked, Ronan walked downstairs. Kim was in the kitchen. She had taken a lamb joint from the American style De Dietrich fridge freezer, and was starting to prepare it at the island unit with its polished granite worktop. The natural-stone-tiled floor glistened with light from the semicircular side window, with the long seat built in beneath it. The sound was muted on the plasma TV high on the wall. He could never tell if these silent glimpses into other lives were meant to keep Kim company. She looked up and smiled.

'You look well. What time will you be back?'

'It's just a quick meeting.' Seeing Kim made him want to bring her with him. It was too nice a Sunday for anyone to cook, and especially for someone he loved to have to cook for him. Kim's presence would make talking to Hughes difficult, but he would find a way to get a few moments with him alone. 'Come with me. We'll go somewhere nice to eat after; it will save you having to cook.'

'I like cooking for you.'

'I like treating you.'

'I don't need treating,' she said, though he saw that she was touched. 'Besides, eating out is expensive.'

Ronan lightly kissed her forehead. 'As long as I'm here you need never worry about money,' he promised softly.

Kim reached up on her tiptoes to kiss him on the lips. She held his face between her hands and looked seriously into his eyes. 'I want a husband not always killing himself working. Must you meet this man on a Sunday? Just for once, stay home and relax.'

'You told me you never saw your father relax in Manila.'

'My father could never afford to. It made him old before his time.'

Ronan stepped back to allow her to see him more clearly. His tone was teasing, yet deadly serious. 'You don't find me old, Kim, do you?'

'Would it matter? I married you because I love you as you are.'

'It matters to me. I don't want to think of you stranded with an old crock.'

She teased him, letting him off the hook. 'You are no old crock. You sometimes prove it three times a night. I think they named that pub, the Wicked Wolf, after you.'

He smiled. 'Who are you, Little Red Riding Hood?'

'I am one exhausted woman afterwards: satisfied, content.'

Ronan held her tightly. Marriage was a series of descending steps: you found a woman willing to lie beside you, and then, in time, willing to tell white lies to you. Early in their marriage there had been nights when he so truly satisfied her that Ronan had felt in danger of suffering a heart attack. Kim's presence had initially removed a dark cloud. It was not age or self-doubt or addiction that had robbed him of his manhood in recent months, it was the stress of this town house, the lies he needed to spin, and the pressure always to show the world a confident face. His libido would change when he got Hughes's signature on the contract. When he regained control of this project he could go to bed with a clear conscience, knowing that he had created financial security for Kim. Whenever he held her in his arms and felt the urgency of her heartbeat, the pain of his divorce and his daughters' estrangement ceased to exist. At such moments it felt as if his past were a sequence of events that occurred to someone else: a car careering down a pier, hitting the water with such force that he considered himself doomed, but he had freed himself from the wreckage, forcing his way up with bursting lungs to crest the waves and gasp for air amid the salty spray. She might not know it, but Kim had been his rescuer, the stranger who plunged in to hold him aloft as he recovered his breath in the miracle of survival. He looked down. Kim was observing him wryly.

'I wonder where you go in your mind,' she said.

'Acapulco.'

Kim laughed and stroked his hand. 'This is what you are truly the master of.'

'What?'

'Evading the subject.'

'Put that lamb joint away. I want to bring you out to a nice restaurant.'

'To show me off.'

'That's not fair,' he protested. 'I enjoy having you with me.'

'You enjoy how men look at me. I don't enjoy their wives looking through me.'

Ronan stroked her hair. 'Ignore those sour, wrinkled old bags.'

'Is that what you used to call Miriam?'

Ronan discreetly withdrew his hand to indicate that she had crossed a line. 'Miriam was different: I loved her.'

The pause before she replied seemed like a glimpse into an inner world from which he felt excluded. 'Sometimes I wonder if you still do.'

'You're the only person I can be truly myself with. I cannot afford to let anyone else see what I'm thinking. Now I need to go; I have a beautiful young wife to provide for.'

'Money is not why I married you.'

Ronan stroked her hair one last time, enjoying its silkiness. He felt an overwhelming desire to leave Paul Hughes waiting and take her to bed instead, to spend the afternoon doing what he wasn't sure that his body would allow him to do.

'I can't afford not to care about money,' he said. 'I'm fifty-one; you're thirty-two. If I die, then my insurance policy will provide for you. But I'm self-employed, and if I get sick you need investments to fall back on.'

'I can go back to work.'

'As a nursing attendant? I won't see you exploited again. Our profit from this town house goes into an account on your solo name.'

'I'm not asking you for anything.'

'You never do. That's why I'm doing it for you.'

'Then let me do something for you.' She took his hand. 'Don't sit up drinking tonight. Come to bed and just lie still. You always try to give me pleasure, but you don't know the pleasure I get from pleasuring you.'

Ronan stroked her hand. 'You always please me. You'd please me more if you'd come out for lunch.'

She shook her head. 'Go to your meeting.'

He produced his car keys. 'Do me one favour: keep an eye out that Jiri's plasterer turns up. That scaffolding must come down tomorrow.'

'Why?'

'Just trust me, it must.'

Kim looked hurt. 'That's no answer to give a wife.'

'I didn't mean it like that,' Ronan said apologetically. 'I just mean it's nothing to be concerned about. You're sure you won't come out?'

'I'll have dinner waiting.'

'I won't be long. I hate to think of you having to wait for me.'

'I don't mind waiting for my husband. If you knew me, you'd know that.'

'I know every inch of you.'

'I wish I knew you properly.'

She looked so serious that he laughed. 'You know me inside out, Kim.'

'I don't know what would make you happy.'

Ronan jingled his car keys. 'That's easy. I'll be happy if Jiri's plasterer shows up.'

Chapter Fourteen

Alice

Sunday 5th, 7 p.m.

Chris didn't even need to speak for Alice to feel the burden of his presence in the doorway. She sensed his intrusion and felt rattled. She didn't need him watching her with his hangdog expression, when she was only half-dressed and still only half-decided about whether to go out. She didn't turn, but by shifting her weight in the chair she surveyed his reflection in the dressing-table mirror.

'I'm late already,' she said. 'What do you want?'

'Just to say good night. You never like if I disturb you when you come in after midnight.'

'You do it anyway, like you're lying awake, checking what time I arrive home at.'

She sensed how Chris longed to cross the varnished floorboards and place his fingers on her bare shoulders, to kiss her neck like in the old days, gently cupping her breasts, which had never looked as full as in this new bra. Her gaze warned him to stay back. But he didn't need to approach to make Alice feel violated. She longed to cover her bare shoulders. She wanted him gone from her room, and – the reckless thought came – maybe from her life. She didn't know what she wanted. Nothing felt clear any more. This afternoon she had given him one final chance to tell the truth about whatever he was up to last September, but as usual he denied having ever lied to her. It hurt to be taken for a fool, but she knew in her heart that this didn't give her the excuse to do something stupid or reckless. It wasn't revenge on Chris that she was seeking. Going out like this was not about him; it involved finding out things about herself.

For two decades she had possessed a fixed sense of her identity as an inoffensive wife and mother, friendly to everyone, anxious to please and do the right thing. But the crash had pulverised Alice in ways she had barely been aware of during the years when the after-effects of trauma left her so poleaxed that she could barely rise from her bed. Only now was she starting to understand how Brygida's death had affected her in ways that she lacked the vocabulary to confront; how – simply to survive – she had created a mental block around those events in which a part of her soul had died, alongside Brygida and the bewildered father she was trying to mind.

Lately it was not her father who plagued Alice's thoughts, but his bitter harridan of a sister. Alice found herself constantly recalling the single occasion when, at eighteen, she approached Aunt Patricia, naïvely hoping the woman might move in with her brother. Instead, Aunt Patricia had mocked Alice for being crippled by conformity.

The older woman had boasted about her active sex life and disparaged Alice's mother for dying without knowing if she was cheated by life for having only ever slept with one man. Back then Alice had dismissed her aunt's disrespectful remarks as stemming from bitterness at being rejected by her family. Maybe Patricia had been right and Alice was a true Prendeville. But maybe her aunt's remarks had been designed as a time bomb, intended to tick away inside Alice's mind, corroding any future marriage with a loaded and unanswerable question. Alice wished now that she had possessed the courage at least to try to talk openly to her mother before she had died. Maybe then she would know if her mother had felt cheated at the end for having experienced so little of life.

How much more did Alice know about life than her mother? Her mother had seemed so old when she died, prematurely aged by her conservative clothes and by having married a staid man, fifteen years her senior. But it shocked Alice now to realise just how young her mother had been – now that she had reached the same age her mother was when she died. What did a woman need to know to be able to say that she had truly lived? Alice wasn't sure. All she knew for certain was that if she didn't get up from the mirror and leave the house soon, then, for tonight at least, she would lose her courage or foolhardiness. Life should not be so complex. Her evening had not felt this complicated until Chris barged in to stand there, eyeing her naked shoulders like a voyeur.

'I don't deliberately lie awake when you go out,' he said. 'I'm just not used to you staying out so late. I find it hard to fall asleep until I know you're safely home. I'm the same when Sophie goes out at night.'

'Sophie is a child.' Alice couldn't prevent herself turning to face him, though this made her feel more exposed. 'What do you think will happen to me?'

'Nothing. But as I don't know the names of the people you're with, I wouldn't know who to phone if you didn't return, if you were in a crash, say.'

'I only crashed one car in my life,' Alice said.

'You know I wasn't talking about that.'

'Then how come you still think I can't drive?'

His eyes couldn't help staring at her new bra. She would have felt flattered once, but now his gaze made her feel like a hooker on display. Why could he not have looked at her with such longing during her years of illness? Not that she would have been able for his physical advances back then, but why could he not have coveted her when she was at her lowest ebb, with no sense that anyone would ever find her attractive again?

'You're a safe driver,' he agreed. 'It's drunks breaking red lights that I worry about. I try to fall asleep, but be honest – wouldn't it be worse if there were nobody here to worry about you?'

Chris was right. Alice hated coming home to spy his light still on, but what she hated most was when Chris forgot to leave on the small lamp with its welcoming glow in the porch. On such nights she would sit in her car and feel excluded, shivering at the sight of the house in darkness. In her heart Alice knew that she could never live alone. She would never bother to cook a proper meal or go to bed without someone badgering her eventually to do so. This was what had disturbed her most during that visit to her aunt years ago, how she had dreaded the thought of ending up alone in a small flat like the Mespil Road one. Even if she couldn't decide how much she still loved Chris, she knew that she still needed him, if only to rebel against, like she never rebelled against her father.

'I mean no harm,' Chris added in a conciliatory tone.

'I know.' Her voice was equally soft. The thought of being without him scared her sufficiently to dissipate any resentment at his appearance here, when she was trapped by indecision in front of this mirror. Now it was Alice who wanted to embrace him, but she couldn't do so in case one embrace led to another. It would be cruel to lead Chris on after resolving to end the physical side of their marriage last September. She could still recall her panic after checking the purchase date on the chemist's sticker on the hidden Viagra packet, and realising that, whoever he had used the three missing blue tablets with during the weeks since the packet was purchased, it had not been with her. No opportunity for lovemaking had arisen during that period. But not even her fears about this betrayal could halt a sudden rush of memories from the years when she unquestioningly trusted him. It made her feel even more trapped, half-naked and with her face half made-up. His next sentence cast him back into the role of jealous jailor.

'I just find your new friends strange. You always talked non-stop about every person you met, chatting away about what everyone said on a night out. Now you snap if I even ask who you're going to meet.'

'I've told you, it's just some girls I play tennis with in Cabinteely. What's the point in telling you about people you don't know? They're a bit dull. We talk girly talk, so there's not much to say about them.'

'If they're so dull, why have you met them every Sunday night for the last six weeks?'

The clock was ticking. Alice's sense of self-confidence, engendered by these new clothes, was evaporating.

'I want some sort of life, Chris. Isn't it about time you got one?'

'I had a life with you. We did everything together. When you were sick I'd lie beside you in bed watching films. When you felt able to go out, we'd go walking together. When did we last take a walk, Alice?'

'I can't walk anywhere in Blackrock without passing a house I set my heart on, only for us to lose it at auction. I appreciate all you did in those tough years, Chris, but our roles have changed. I'm no longer an invalid who needs looking after.'

'What do you need?'

'My own space to breathe in.'

'It feels like you're pushing me out of your life.'

'You make me feel like a prisoner. It's like you're always spying.'

'I'm not spying. Promise you'll come for a walk some night.'

'I've told you, every street contains a signpost to our failure.'

'And every house went for mad money we didn't have.'

'And you think the people who bought them were millionaires?' she asked. 'Explain to me how folk no richer than us can own three and four properties. I'm not looking for a posh house, I just want a normal house away from Ronan's prying eyes and away from the constant fear that new tenants will move in next door and hold raves every second night, like that time two years ago where the letting agent needed a court order to get the tenants out. I want to be able to go to sleep not having to worry about who might start partying on the other side of my bedroom wall.'

Alice turned to face the mirror. She took a deep breath, trying to recall where she was in her preparations before Chris ruptured her mood. How had their marriage come to this? By lying to her again this afternoon he was pushing her out into this world. She could barely recognise the man in this mirror, any more than she recognised the half-dressed woman staring back at her.

'It's not really about moving house,' she said, trying to find some way to make him understand.

'Then what is it about?'

'If you can't guess, then I can't tell you.' She wasn't being cruel, but she was inhibited and tongue-tied, scared of being hurt again if he fed her more lies. What she was contemplating doing with a stranger felt easier than trying to confront her husband openly. Alice shifted position until his reflection was no longer in her eyeline. She covered her shoulders so his eyes were not drawn to the bra she had spent an hour agonising over in the Honey Trap Lingerie Boutique in Dun Laoghaire. If Chris had been sexually satisfied with her alone, he would never have gone wandering last September. These Sunday night excursions had initially stemmed from a childish sense of retribution, a temptation to peer at danger without becoming implicated in it. She had never expected her curiosity to spill over into anything more tangible. But Chris's betrayal had exposed deep scars of inadequacy, a need to discover if some other man might find her sufficiently attractive to take such a risk for her. Alice needed to stop dwelling on why, after agonising for hours, she had persuaded herself to go out tonight. She needed to recapture that confident glow of pretending to be somebody different, which she had felt before Chris invaded her bedroom.

'Tell your friends what it's all about.' Chris backed out of the doorway. 'They obviously mean more to you than me.'

'I don't even know if I like them.' Alice didn't know if she was addressing Chris or her own reflection. 'These days I barely know if I like myself.'

'Talk to me, Alice.' Chris re-entered the room, his tentative voice barely above a whisper.

'You're destroying everything. I was looking forward to going out.'

'I'm not stopping you.'

'I don't feel like going out now.'

'I want you to go out. I want you to be happy.'

'Then stop plaguing me with questions. If I'm late they'll think I'm not coming and won't wait.'

'What do you mean?' He sounded like a barrister unearthing a clink in her evidence. 'These girls will still be in the pub whether you're early or late.'

Why had she relaxed her guard, yielding to this instinct to confide in Chris?

'They sometimes change pubs during the evening,' she said.

'Why can't you just text to see where they are?'

'Why can't you stay out of it? And stop staring like my body is a piece of meat.'

'For God's sake, Alice, you're my wife.'

'That doesn't give you the right to ogle me.'

'I was just thinking that it's great you're looking so well.' He paused angrily, and then added, 'I'll leave any ogling to whoever you bought that bra for.'

'I brought this bra for myself.'

'And the suspenders and garter belts tucked into your drawer?'

She couldn't stop herself rising from her chair in annoyance. 'Have I no privacy?'

'The woman I married was never interested in dressing like that.'

'Maybe you know nothing about my needs. I buy lingerie for *myself*, to feel good about *myself*. Sometimes I think I married a man who's paranoid.'

'Lately I think I married a stranger.'

Alice wearily sat down again at the dressing table. 'I'm late. I have to go.'

'Because some man is waiting?' She could see that Chris was hurting. 'I have a right to know.'

'I've told you. My friends from the tennis club are waiting. Do you want to see letters of permission from their husbands allowing them to go out?'

She turned to the mirror to resume applying her make-up. She heard nothing for so long that she hoped Chris had retreated downstairs, but then his voice came again, sounding lost.

'Is our marriage over?'

'No,' she replied quietly.

'What state is it in then?'

'I don't know. I'm simply trying to live in the present. You're trying to make me have a conversation I'm not able for.'

'We need to talk.'

'Why? You always say the same things. Even at the inquest you took the coroner's side.'

'Coroners don't take sides,' Chris said. 'They make findings of fact. It wasn't your fault you lost control of the car: your father grabbed the steering wheel. The coroner just said you were unwise to remove him from hospital at that late hour. He was losing his mind.'

'I was losing my mind sitting with him.'

'I know. I sat with him too.'

'You'd still be sitting there, afraid to say boo, politely hoping to attract a nurse's attention. At least I took a decision.'

'Your father's seat belt wasn't fastened.'

'There you go again, taking the coroner's side. In your eyes whatever I do is wrong.'

'That's not true. I'm going downstairs.'

Alice felt another hot sweat coming on. She wanted to end this conversation but her mood swings were so extreme that they frightened her.

'I lost years feeling guilty for something that wasn't my fault. Now my reflection tells me that I'm getting older and running out of time.'

'For what?'

Her inability to reply provoked his next words. 'At least you are getting older.'

'Say what you mean,' she replied, equally quietly.

His voice became egg-shell hesitant. 'Just that there are worse fates than sitting in front of a mirror searching for wrinkles.'

Alice walked to the window. She detested this half-built townhouse. But it was preferable to the sight she had occasionally seen during the years when illness left her quarantined in this room – a sight never mentioned in case Chris suspected she was going crazy. She stared out for so long that Chris thought she was ignoring him.

'What makes you think that Brygida doesn't grow older?' she asked finally. 'I see her less often, but she has grown into a truly beautiful girl.'

Chris approached but seemed scared to touch her. He followed her gaze.

'There's no one out there,' he said.

'I don't see her in our garden any more. That was only at the start, when she needed to come looking for me.'

'I attended her funeral,' Chris said softly. 'You know she's dead.'

'I only know that for years I kept seeing her.'

'You've never mentioned this.'

'Would you have believed me?'

'I would have got you help.'

'Twice my father stood at the end of our garden, holding her hand. A kindly man bestowing on a dead child the affection he always withheld from his own daughter. It wasn't fair.'

'It wasn't real. We had one doctor treating your physical injuries with a cocktail of drugs while a second doctor was prescribing a different cocktail to treat the mental effects of the trauma.'

'There was nothing wrong with my mind.'

'I never said there was.'

'You implied it so often that I used to think I was going mad.'

'Alice, the list of medications they had you on would make anyone hallucinate.'

Alice turned from the window. It was a warm August evening, but she shivered, exposed like this. She wanted Chris to go away. Yet she also wished they were spooned into each other, like when they used to confess their fears in the dark. That child's ghost was the first secret to come between them. Alice had been ashamed to confess to seeing her, with Chris already so burdened by her physical and psychological collapse. Maybe this was where the cancer of secrecy started: inexpressible anxieties festering into petty rows, fissures widened by the icy silences that followed.

'I thought she was angry with me for ending her life,' Alice said. 'Now I think she was just shy and lonely in the after-life and recognised that I was equally shy. At first the apparition scared me: then it became oddly comforting to see her from this window. I'd be alone, waiting for you to come home or Mariam to come bounding in with all the local, bitchy gossip.'

'Did you tell Miriam about these visions?'

'Don't be daft. Miriam is as shallow as her airhead daughters.' Alice absent-mindedly traced a heart on the window pane. 'I think the child loved her mother too much to ever haunt that poor woman. But she and I are like twins. Twins never care how much we hurt one another because we're really only hurting ourselves.'

'Tell me you don't see her any more.'

'Last year I saw her go up an escalator in the Dundrum Town Centre, surrounded by chattering schoolgirls. I had no idea if they saw her too. She never looked back at me but, if she had, I'd have smiled: I think that's all she ever wanted. She'd smile from the end of our garden, a smile to break your heart. I only started to recover when I found the courage to smile back, so we felt like co-conspirators.'

Alice sensed Chris's caution as he framed his words: 'Did you ever think that maybe it was a manifestation of guilt?'

Alice walked back to sit at the dressing table. She slowly did up the buttons on the blouse she had agonised over choosing.

'I felt so guilty for years that part of the reason why I was too exhausted to leave our house was because I just couldn't bear having to run the gauntlet of seeing neighbours pass judgement on me with their eyes when I walked along the street. The therapists were reassuring during their expensive consultations, but every night when I lay here I felt truly alone, reliving that crash. The day my recovery started was when I realised that the child didn't blame me. It was she who ran straight into the path of the car, not understanding the consequences.'

'The apparition wasn't real,' Chris said, 'it was caused by whatever cocktail of drugs doctors had you on.'

'Her ghost was real to me. I saw what I saw. But I no longer see her: I'm seeing someone else.'

'What do you mean?'

Alice glanced up and felt a surge of panic.

'One day when I saw her from the window, I put both my palms on the glass and said aloud: "Let's forgive each other, let's both move on." Brygida held her palm aloft too and smiled and then her ghost simply disappeared, or at least stopped haunting my imagination. I swore on that day to stop beating myself up over every single thing. I've been through hell and back. That's why I need to go out and do things. Can't you see? I'm too scared to stand still in case I end up going backwards.'

'Those years were hell for Sophie, and me too,' Chris said. 'I'd have walked across broken glass to help you get better.'

'And yet some days you looked like a jailor entering my cell with trays of food. It killed me to hear you slave away in my kitchen, burning one dish after another, when I longed to be down there cooking for you and Sophie. You brought up my meals, but at times I'd feel you withholding your forgiveness over that child's death. That's why you're up here now, trying to ruin my night.'

Alice knew that she was being deliberately unfair, but she needed Chris to get annoyed. If he became angry it would shatter her feelings of closeness to him and give her the strength to go out. Instead, he looked like a lost soul.

'I only came up here to say goodnight,' he said.

'I hadn't even finally decided if I were going out yet.'

'Well, you've spent long enough getting dressed.'

'More fool me for thinking you'd let me escape carefree for one evening,' she said, more bitter with herself than with him.

'All I want is for you to be happy.' Chris knelt beside her. 'It kills me that you'd ever see me as a jailor. Please go out and see whatever friends you want.'

'It's too late,' she said, tearfully now. 'I can't go now.'

'Why not?'

'You've killed the joy of it.'

'I'm not leaving this room till you promise to go out.'

She looked away, upset that he looked upset. How had she allowed her life to get so convoluted that Chris would feel hurt if she stayed in and she would hurt them both by going out?

'All that matters is that you feel well again,' he insisted.

Alice reached out to grip his hand tightly, determined to stay in now and bridge this chasm by talking openly to him. But then he stroked her fingers and realised that something was missing.

'Your engagement ring is gone,' he said with sharp suspicion. 'Your wedding ring too.'

'I can't wear jewellery these days,' she said defensively. 'It brings out my skin in a rash. I've tried hydrocortisone cream, but it doesn't work. Dermatitis ... another symptom of the menopause.' She looked at him tenderly, trying to find a way out of the mess she had ensnared herself within.

'Maybe I won't go tonight, Chris,' she said. 'These people I was going to see ... they're not really our sort of people.'

'You have to go,' he insisted. 'If you don't, I'll blame myself. I'm delighted you've made new friends.' He hesitated as he rose, scared of her reaction if he tried to kiss her, then pressed his lips softly to her forehead. 'I'll try to be asleep when you come back, but if I'm awake I won't come up and disturb you. I'm calling over to Ronan now to get out of your way. Just tell me you don't see that child's ghost in dreams any more.'

'That's in the past.'

'Anyone would have queer dreams, isolated in a bedroom. You go out and have a wonderful evening.'

Alice watched in the mirror as he walked away. She saw him descend the stairs and leave her utterly alone, staring at herself. She didn't move for several minutes, but sat in judgement. She didn't want to approve or condemn. She just wanted to do what she had promised herself: to live in the moment. This is who she was: an ageing woman needing to discover certain things about herself. She was late, and yet she could not hurry. Whenever she hurried she got flustered and everything took more time. Staring at her face in the mirror, Alice slowly applied a final layer of make-up so that the scar on her right cheek was almost invisible to anyone who didn't know that it was there.

Chapter Fifteen

Ronan

Sunday 5th, 7.30 p.m.

Ronan allowed Kim to answer the doorbell. It bought him time to eavesdrop from behind his study door and prepare an appropriate persona for whomever the caller was. He was still so shaken from his conversation with Paul Hughes in the afternoon that he was relieved to hear Chris's voice. Chris he would handle. Kim was offering to prepare a fresh carafe of coffee and bring it down to the study. She declined Chris's entreaty to join them.

'I've promised to Skype my sister,' she said, and smiled with sudden embarrassment. 'We're grown women, continents apart, yet we sit staring at each other on the screen, laughing about silly things like two children again sitting on a wall.'

Ronan opened the study door, having willed himself into jocular mode.

'Are you finished chatting up my wife?' he joked.

'Kim is promising me the best coffee in Blackrock.'

'I'm promising the best cognac,' Ronan replied. 'It's imperative we polish off that bottle of Hennessy.'

'Why?'

'So I can smash it over Jiri's head. Jiri is becoming more Irish than the Irish. He's making Irish promises … his plasterer never arrived. Though it wasn't even Jiri's plasterer but some geezer Ezal recommended, maybe because he was getting a cut on the side. You never know, you can never trust anyone.'

Kim and Chris exchanged the barest glance, but it was sufficient for Ronan to know he was slipping. At one time he could easily consume four brandies without anyone noticing.

'I'll have one brandy with my coffee,' Chris said, 'then you're on your own.'

'Some partner you are, leaving the heavy lifting to me.' Ronan laughed and retreated into his study, lingering inside the doorway to catch Kim's anxious whisper.

'I think his meeting went bad. Try not to let him drink too much.'

Ronan pretended he had not overheard. He wanted to give Chris no opening to ask about Hughes. Ronan felt less panicked now than four hours ago. Four hours was as long as it should take a man to pick himself up from a disappointment. His father had claimed that the man who could not see new opportunities after four hours was a weakling succumbing to self-pity. He turned to Chris. 'Sit down. The night is young, and Kim makes exceptionally good coffee.'

'You're a lucky man.'

Ronan poured them each a brandy. 'We make our own luck.'

He saw Chris eye the measures. 'Go easy.'

'You'd never survive doing business in Russia: every deal is sealed with a glass of vodka.'

'Thank God we're merely Blackrock oligarchs. How did the meeting go?'

Ronan shrugged dismissively. 'Even in school Hughes was a little wanker.'

'What does that mean?'

'It's time you and I started to think like auctioneers. Auctioneers always want more than one fish to bite. The real sport only starts when several fish get tangled up in an auctioneer's net.'

'We're not using any auctioneer. We already have a buyer.' Chris sounded alarmed.

Ronan knew this situation needed to be handled with tact and alcohol. 'I'm just saying that if Hughes decides to play hardball, we're building a house a lot of buyers would kill for.'

'We've agreed a clean sale with Hughes. There's talk that the market could fall.'

'From columnists trying to flog newspapers and RTÉ reporters whose hairline receded at the same time as their Workers' Party membership lapsed. There'll be a soft landing eventually, but even that won't come for another decade.'

He paused as Kim entered and set down a tray containing coffee and home-made shortbread biscuits. Ronan enjoyed Chris's inability to hide his pleasure in gazing at her. Kim smiled at Ronan.

'Don't be too late coming up.'

'I won't keep him long,' Chris promised. 'Good night, Kim.'

'Say hello to Alice for me.'

The men were silent as she left. Miriam would have chatted for ten minutes, but not caused Chris to lose his train of thought. Ronan knew that Chris had momentarily forgotten the town house, unable to conceal a look of loneliness occasioned by Kim mentioning Alice.

'It's funny,' Chris observed. 'I live next door, yet I feel I don't really know Kim. I thought she was shy at first, but it's more than that. What is it about her?'

'You're asking me?' Ronan lowered the plunger in the carafe. The coffee smelt exquisite, conjuring up an unbidden memory of the first time he could afford to stay in a good hotel with Miriam, their wide-eyed enjoyment at the newness of it all.

'You married her,' Chris said. 'If anyone knows her, you do.'

'I thought I knew Miriam.'

'Kim generates serenity. No disrespect, but serenity wasn't a word I associated with Miriam. Living next door was like being forced to overhear a blow-by-blow commentary on your marriage. Now it's like living beside a Trappist monastery.'

'Did Miriam and I sound that bad?'

'Like a heavyweight world title decider. Even Don King would have hidden among the towels in the hot press.'

Ronan handed him one of the John Rocha Black Pico cups that had been Miriam's favourites.

'It was hard for Emer and Lauryn to grow up listening to us. I don't know why we bothered shouting; we already knew what the other was going to say. Half the time it wasn't fighting, it was foreplay.'

'You must have had one great love life then, that's all I can say.'

Ronan laughed. 'We had our moments. Air traffic controllers needed to divert low-flying planes whenever Miriam would finally decide to reach orgasm.'

'What about Kim?'

Ronan appraised him with a hawk-like stare. 'That's a very personal question.'

'And thoughtless too. I'm sorry.'

Chris's embarrassment allowed Ronan to top up his neighbour's brandy snifter without Chris protesting. It caused Chris to forget about Hughes, even if Ronan could not afford to. Tonight he needed to juggle a dozen problems, and was wary of hasty solutions. It would take the patience of a master strategist to allow the right scenarios to evolve.

'People think Kim is shy,' Ronan said, 'but she's self-contained, she wants nothing. That's the hardest part of our marriage. I haven't a clue what to give her. I only say this to you because we go back a long way.'

Chris laughed. 'I remember you selling rolled-up herbal tobacco to first years who were convinced it was dope.'

'The school should have asked me to teach entrepreneurship rather than suspend me. That's what my dad told the headmaster when he summoned us to his office. It was the only time Da took my side in anything. He snarled like a lion protecting its cub. Father Flaherty was used to parents threatening court injunctions, but he'd never encountered a father who seemed ready to fuck him through the window.'

'I hope Flaherty refrained from his habit of summing up the situation in Latin.'

'He tried it, and Da snorted and gave him the hard-boiled eyes look. I was up to my neck in trouble, yet it was the first time I felt Da was proud of me. To be honest I'd been a bit ashamed of him until then, or anxious not to be seen with him in school, where everyone else's dad was on the verge of taking silk or tipped to be a government minister. That day we didn't walk out of Flaherty's office together, we swaggered. Flaherty had fey blue-blooded features that made Louis le Brocquy look like a Bulgarian weightlifter on steroids. He didn't believe his students needed to be entrepreneurs: their daddies possessed sufficient influence to effortlessly sew up their futures.'

'Paul Hughes obviously learnt some entrepreneurship there,' Chris remarked. 'He owns half of Dublin.'

Ronan couldn't stop his bitterness from spilling out. 'All Hughes has ever built are consortiums of investors, old school chums trusting him with borrowed lucre. Everything he owns is mortgaged twice over, except his stupid pigtail.'

'Is he still buying our town house?'

'Do we really want to sell it to him?'

'That's the only reason we built it.'

'We built it to get you and Alice out of here so that Alice need never look down her nose at Kim again.'

'Alice never looks down her nose at anyone.'

'Really?' Ronan eyed him caustically, employing an unflinching stare he had seen his father use to disconcert men.

'Alice misses Miriam,' Chris said warily. 'That's all.'

Ronan nodded, switching his gaze to empathy. 'I miss her too,' he said gently. 'Not that I'd let Kim know that. But when you lose something, you don't get it back. Remember that.'

'I can't get a straight answer out of you tonight,' Chris said, draining his snifter. 'But before I hit the road, just tell me one thing. Do I need to worry about Hughes?'

'I'll answer all your questions, but what's your hurry? Alice has gone out. Where did you say she's going?'

'She's meeting people from that new tennis club in Cabinteely.'

'Mixed doubles in the dark, is it?'

'That's not funny.' Chris betrayed a frayed defensiveness. 'Alice has the right to a life of her own.'

'So do you. I'm only teasing. You need have no fears there. Alice is a good woman.'

'I know she is.'

'Then let's have a toast to Alice and Kim. Hold out your glass.'

Chris shook his head. 'Honestly, I'm grand.'

'You needn't be scared. I won't tell Alice on you.'

'I'm not scared.'

Ronan approached with the bottle. 'Hold out your glass and prove it.'

Chapter Sixteen

Chris

Sunday 5th, 11 p.m.

It was eleven o'clock. Chris couldn't remember when he stopped protesting that the measures were too large and he wanted to go home. This was Ronan's house, where Ronan set the pace. Just this once, Chris was determined to keep up. Only loneliness awaited next door, where he would sit fretting about where Alice was. Tomorrow was a bank holiday: he could lie in and nurse his head.

He had stopped trying to talk business: he would get no answers tonight. He enjoyed Ronan's blustering company in small doses, but was secretly always relieved to escape. Being with Ronan involved unspoken tests of masculinity, which Chris seemed predestined to fail. When Ronan set his eye on anything he went for it, maintaining that the only two qualities needed in life were a brass neck and steel balls. Ronan always got what he wanted because he never bothered to question the why or wherefore. He set himself goals. When he fell, he got up and started again. At school, the word 'no' never existed in his vocabulary. Chris could recall him at discos, hitting on girl after girl and being rejected. But by night's end Ronan would invariably slip away with a willing girl to a garden shed or front room. There was no boastful exaggeration about it next day. Once Ronan got what he wanted, it was already forgotten in his desire to extract the maximum from life.

In the decades since leaving school, it seemed to Chris that Ronan had never failed at anything because he didn't recognise the concept of failure.

Some business ventures had collapsed, but Ronan seemed to regard these as mere stepping stones and invaluable learning opportunities. Even his failed marriage had been turned into a fresh beginning. Miriam used to give Ronan stability; now Kim gave him a renewed aura of youthful recklessness. Kim smiled a lot, but didn't say much when Chris was present. It was as if she saw life as a sequence of negotiated compromises, down payments on happiness. Chris wondered at how it must feel to be viewed as a mail-order bride, with other wives in Blackrock claiming that Ronan wasn't mature enough to cope with a real woman. Kim looked real to Chris, though he would never confess to Alice that he found her attractive.

Did Kim love Ronan? This was a mystery Chris could not decipher. Did Alice still love him? It was a question he felt too scared to answer. Recently, whenever Alice withdrew into moods of anxious retrospection, she often said that he should get himself a life. This was what he was doing, drinking with Ronan because he had nowhere else to be. It was easier for women to develop friendships in middle age. Women went everywhere in packs, to the theatre or book clubs. You couldn't ask another man out for a meal. You played golf with them or drank in pubs and invariably ended up listening to strangers talking shite.

They had finished the Hennessy. Now Ronan produced a more expensive brandy from his oak-panelled drinks cabinet. Chris covered his snifter, but Ronan simply poured a triple measure through his fingers. Accepting defeat, Chris laughed. Ronan's latest project seemed to be to get them as drunk as possible. Alice would hate to see Chris like this, knowing he'd feel thoroughly sick tomorrow. But maybe it was time to start doing things that Alice would disapprove of.

Where was she tonight? It was madness to imagine her seeing another man, yet Chris had never heard of these new friends before. *I wouldn't want to live without you in this world*, Alice used to say during the bad years after the car crash. *You're my sanity.* Her need had been so intense back then that often Chris felt suffocated, hiding his exhaustion as he rushed home to try and lift her spirits. He was delighted that she had recovered, but only now did he understand the depth of her previous love. He understood it by becoming acutely aware of its absence.

He thought that Kim was asleep, but she re-entered the study to tell Ronan she was going to watch television in bed. With the satellite dish on the back wall, she could choose from hundreds of channels. Chris wondered if the programmes sometimes reminded her of the Philippines: episodes of *Friends* bringing back memories of sitting in a crowded Manila kitchen, laughing with sisters in a world far removed from the queen-sized bed and wall-mounted giant plasma screen where she now watched reruns of those same episodes. Kim was nineteen years younger than Ronan, and looked ten years younger than her age, but she was no meek child bride. Ronan sometimes hinted that she was capable of flying into tantrums which made Miriam's outbursts seem mild in comparison. Chris found it hard to imagine Kim being angry. In his drunkenness he also found it hard to stop imagining what her body must look like now as she undressed above them. He didn't want to dwell on what it must feel to know that a willing partner awaited you in bed, with recriminations banished by eager kisses.

Chris had often heard Miriam and Alice discuss Ronan's various escapades: the weekend he disappeared, the used condom Miriam found in his golf bag, and the final straw: when Miriam came home to discover her toothbrush still wet, having recently been inside another woman's mouth. Miriam would joke that Alice was lucky to have married a saint. Maybe this was the problem – women didn't want saints. They might not want total bastards, but they wanted men of action. Chris sipped his neat brandy, allowing it to transport him into a mellow state. Ronan was talking bullshit, but Chris was only half-listening as he examined the architect's drawings for the town house on Ronan's desk. He loved their sense of order, neatly executed lines of elevation, locations of vents and drains, internal widths of rooms.

'Houses look so uncomplicated on plans,' he said. 'Clockwork worlds with no people arguing inside them.'

'Ours doesn't just exist on paper,' Ronan replied. 'It's almost finished. We've even beaten the jumped-up official who appeared on Friday.'

'What official?'

'A safety inspector who was visiting apartments being built in Monkstown. Inspectors rarely notice a job this small, but the Gauleiter spotted our scaffolding by fluke. He declared it was in violation of safety standards and closed us down.'

'You never told me this.'

'If builders followed official standards, half the sites in Ireland would be shut. The roof was finished, and we were a few hours away from having the external walls plastered. Civil servants never work bank holiday weekends. That's why I've been pressurising Jiri to finish the plastering. I'll make him get Andrzej back here tomorrow. What's the point in dismantling scaffolding to erect it again for three hours' work? We'll have the job finished and the scaffolding gone by tomorrow afternoon. When the inspector returns, he'll have nothing left to close down.'

'What if Andrzej doesn't come tomorrow?'

'I'll plaster it myself now if you're worried. You can sit beside me on the scaffolding, a flashlight in one hand and the bottle of cognac in the other.'

'I've no head for heights, especially on unsafe scaffolding.'

'It's perfectly safe. The safety inspector was merely justifying his overpaid existence.' Ronan rose. 'Come on.'

'Hang on,' Chris protested, 'we're not plastering anything at this hour.'

Ronan laughed, selecting two cigars from an antique wooden box. 'The only two things getting plastered tonight are you and me.' He opened the door into the conservatory and strode towards the French doors that led to the garden. 'I'm sneaking out for a secret smoke. Follow me, and bring the cognac.'

'I've drunk enough.'

'*Au contraire*, you've drunk too much, and that means a last dram and a Cuban wouldn't kill you.' Ronan lit his cigar on the patio and released the smoke into the air. He placed the second cigar and a box of matches on the step. 'Light this outdoors; let's keep the lady of the house happy.'

'I need to use your bathroom first.'

'Join me in christening the town house wall. Or piss in the bushes. Why did God invent bushes if it wasn't for tall men who get caught short? But no peeping at my bedroom window. I've warned Kim about walking around in her underwear, but do wives ever listen?'

'I wouldn't spy,' Chris said hotly. 'What do you take me for?

Ronan took another puff and glanced back in through the conservatory doors with the teasing laugh Chris remembered from school.

'Someone crucifying himself for feeling the same desires as any ordinary man.'

Ronan disappeared into the moonlight. If Chris lit that second cigar, his throat would be as sore as his head tomorrow. Still and all, he picked up the brandy bottle, took the proffered cigar left in the doorway and pocketed the matches as he followed Ronan outside. He was surprised at how unsteady he felt. Any light was gone from the summer sky. Chris's bladder was full, but he felt too lethargic to join Ronan at the town house wall. Placing down the brandy, he unzipped his fly in the shelter of a cherry blossom tree. As he unleashed a stream of urine he noticed that the blind was indeed not fully down in Ronan's bedroom. Kim – or at least the lower half of her body – was visible, clad only in white knickers. He suspected she was folding an item of clothing as she bent over the bed. It was impossible to quell a surge of desire. Her light went out suddenly, and Chris felt disappointment, and then the unnerving sensation that Kim had not gone to bed, but was peering out through the blind, making him no longer the voyeur but the spied upon. A shuffling noise, like a dragging sound, came at the end of the garden. Suddenly his unease increased as Ronan let out an agonised cry. Startled, Chris adjusted his fly, frightened that Ronan had caught him inadvertently spying on his wife. The man's voice came again from near the town house, this time barely above a whisper.

'Sweet Jesus. Chris, come here quick.'

Finding the gap created in the wall, Chris entering the mayhem of his own garden. He could locate Ronan only by the glowing tip of a discarded cigar. His neighbour was hunched beneath scaffolding in the passageway beside the town house. Chris had never seen Ronan so distressed, rocking back and forth.

'What's wrong, Ronan? Say you're not having a heart attack.'

'I'm scared shitless. What are we going to do?'

'About what?'

Ronan peered up. 'Use the light on your phone.'

Ronan pressed his body against the town house wall. In the weak light emanating from his phone, Chris could discern rubble and empty cement bags littering the narrow passageway. A discarded workman's boot lay amid the debris, still laced up and coated in cement dust. The light went out on his phone. Only when he re-hit the button and knelt beside Ronan did Chris realise that this boot contained a human foot. He could see the shape of a leg, and then a torso. He pushed past Ronan to shove the bags aside, coughing as a cloud of cement dust stung his eyes. A man lay face up, features unblemished, startled eyes opened wide.

'He doesn't look hurt,' Chris whispered.

'He'd disagree with you if he could,' Ronan replied grimly. 'He must have fallen backwards off the scaffolding. You can see where his skull struck that blood-stained rock. We were planning to clear this rubble once we got the scaffolding down.'

Chris lit one of the matches in his pocket, and saw how the man's skull had collided with a jagged rock that lay nearby. Ronan was trembling.

'When Jiri promises to send a plasterer, one arrives.'

'Is this our plasterer?' Chris asked.

'Who else could it be?'

'You mean he's been lying here all evening?'

'How do I know? I was taking a piss when I glanced down and saw his face. I covered him up as best I could and called you.'

'Why put a bag over his face?'

'I couldn't bear to look at his eyes.'

'And an empty cement bag was the best you could find?'

Ronan looked up, the incredulity of the remark stinging him into recovering some composure. 'This isn't a field hospital, it's an uninsured building site.'

'We need to phone an ambulance.'

'I'm sure you're right.' There was the barest pause, an indecipherable intonation in Ronan's tone. 'That is, if you are sure.'

'What are you saying? The man is dead.'

'Then how will an ambulance bring him back to life?'

'I'm going to be sick. Why did you get us this drunk?'

'Sober up quick and think coldly before you call an ambulance. You'll be living with the consequences for the rest of your life.'

Chris lit another match, and studied the workman's features. He looked in his late thirties, but could be older. His jet-black hair was obviously dyed.

'Are you sure he's dead?'

Ronan motioned Chris forward. 'Check for yourself.'

Chris knelt, initially too scared to touch him. If the workman was in a coma, every minute was vital. But Chris knew that the man was dead. Had he died instantly, or spent hours suffering alone in this cramped space? His icy face was covered by such a film of cement dust that Chris's fingers left a trail across it. As he stepped back, queasy and disorientated, the ground swayed. He leaned against the town house for balance before quietly vomiting, and then looked at Ronan.

'What's his name?'

'I don't know for sure. Half of these fellows don't use their real names. They're illegal immigrants surviving on their wits, cash in hand and no questions asked. Jiri says he's a loner who drifts between sites. Ezal sent him a message through that grapevine they use, asking someone to ask him to finish off this wall, but I'm not convinced that Jiri was certain he'd turn up.'

'We need to phone Jiri.'

Ronan watched him carefully. 'I thought you wanted to phone an ambulance first. It's your property, your call.'

'What are you saying?'

'Just be prepared for the consequences.'

'For once, Ronan, say what you mean.'

'If you're hell-bent on phoning an ambulance, call one.'

'Are you saying I shouldn't?'

'It's in your nature to always do the right thing. I'm just asking, what good will come from doing the right thing tonight? The moment you summon an ambulance you're going to bring down every safety inspector on our heads. We're all fucked then, most especially you and Alice.'

'All that counts is that a man is lying dead here.'

'And how will it help him that you and Alice will lose everything you own after being dragged through the courts? I'd give every cent I have to bring this poor devil back to life.'

Chris hunched down, shaking, using the wall for support.

'I doubt it.'

'You'd be right to doubt it. I'd give a great deal, but not everything, and neither would you, if you're honest. Does it count for nothing that Alice's life will be destroyed? There was a closure order on this site, remember? You're in breach of it.'

'You said the scaffolding was safe, so how come he's lying here?'

'He could have tripped or had a heart attack. All we know for certain is that you and Alice will be held responsible.'

'I've had nothing to do with running this site,' Chris protested.

'I know that, but legally the buck stops with you. His death happened on a site on your property, with the planning application in your name. Millionaire developers use teams of lawyers to make sure they're never caught. But the tabloids love scapegoats, and the headlines will scream about your greed killing an innocent man. Alice's health was destroyed after her name was in the headlines because of the crash when she killed that Polish child. How do you think that dragging her name into the tabloids again will bring this man back?'

'You won't get away scot-free either,' Chris said, barely able to think as panic engulfed him.

'I won't deny being a silent partner,' Ronan agreed. 'Morally I'll accept a share of the blame, but no document links me to this site. The end of my garden is even transferred into your name. Nothing changes the fact that he fell from dangerous scaffolding on your land, and your house insurance won't cover the compensation. You'll not be buying Alice a new house; you'll be flogging your old house just to pay the legal bills.'

Chris tried to stand up and free his brain from a cloud of alcohol.

'My head is spinning.'

'Make it stop, Chris. Phone the cops or phone Alice. But just don't expect life to ever be the same after you make that call.'

The mention of Alice chilled him the most. He could deal with the legal consequences, but he couldn't face telling Alice. Whatever Ronan was suggesting was wrong, but he didn't even know what it was.

'Cover his face,' Chris said. He sat still, then slowly lifted his head to stare at Ronan in the half-light. 'What are you suggesting?'

'If this guy had a family, he had cut all contact with them. But that won't stop swarms of relations miraculously materialising for any court case. You wouldn't even know if they're relations or scam merchants. Jiri thinks this guy never showed up. I phoned him earlier to complain that he hadn't.'

'You phoned Jiri without checking out here first?'

'I could see from my window that nobody was working on the scaffolding.'

'When did you really find him?' Chris asked, suddenly suspicious. 'Have you got me drunk deliberately? Alice warned me that something would go wrong if I got involved with you.'

Ronan gripped Chris's shoulders. 'Just once, think for yourself. Nobody can make this decision for you, unless you want to implicate Alice by making her an accessory. I found him dead just now after wandering down here for a piss. But who's to say if he ever turned up? Who would notice if he disappeared, like Jiri says he often does?'

'You're crazy.'

'A man hiking on a bank holiday weekend could fall and bang his skull. I know a spot in the Wicklow Mountains where he mightn't be found for days.'

'Are you saying we dump him somewhere?'

'If grieving relations show up we can make an anonymous donation through a priest. His family will be millionaires back wherever they belong. They can have all the profit from this town house.'

Chris's legs felt too weak to properly stand up. He stared at Ronan.

'I never liked you, you know that? Since we were kids I've let you bully me.'

'I don't like myself either, Chris. But I do whatever is needed to protect my family. I'm not bullying you. I'm trying to protect Alice from losing her home.'

'Alice hates you.'

'At least she doesn't think I'm a wimp.'

'You learn to mind your tongue.'

'And you learn to think like an immigrant and face tough decisions head-on. Have you heard Jiri's men talk among themselves with their pidgin English? It's all about the price of a big skip or small skip or the hire of a dumper truck. In every conversation they're working out the bottom line. That doesn't make them gangsters, it means they live in the real world, where life is a series of problems to be overcome so they can send money home. They'd walk through fire to protect their families. You've always been able to take the safe route, but sometimes we all need to do things we're not proud of. Now, just for once, think like an immigrant.'

Chris knelt beside the corpse. He wanted to close the man's eyes, but was afraid to touch him again.

'I am who I am,' he declared. 'I'm calling an ambulance.'

'Then I respect your integrity. But do one thing first … call Alice and tell her.'

'I will.'

'What's stopping you?'

Chris opened his phone, but his hand shook so badly that it fell onto the rubble. He picked it up and tried to dial Alice's number, but his fingers felt paralysed. Ronan reached across to take the phone.

'I'll do it. Here, I think it's dialling.'

Chris snatched his phone back before the call came up on Alice's phone. He found himself crying, unsure if it was for the dead workman or himself. He covered the man's face with a sack and looked at Ronan.

'Alice must never know. Now what do I do next?'

Chapter Seventeen

Chris

Monday 6th, 1 a.m.

Chris had never driven a car when drunk before. Yet he felt more sober now than when placing the workman's body in his boot twenty minutes ago. The main drug coursing through his veins was a pulsating terror at the enormity of this. His fingers smelt of the rubber kitchen gloves they wore when moving the man. His palms remained so sweaty he needed to wipe them on his shirt to grip the steering wheel. Not that he knew where he was going. Every time he reached a junction he automatically swung left, so the car journeyed in a continuous loop up Carysfort Avenue, onto Annaville Terrace and back onto Newtownpark Avenue and Temple Road. On the third loop the vehicle came to a halt halfway up Carysfort Avenue. Chris was too paralysed by his inability to think to drive any farther. Ronan remained resolutely silent in the passenger seat, refusing to offer leadership.

'Is this where you plan to leave him?' Ronan said finally, gazing out at the deserted street.

'And where do you suggest we dump him?'

'We're not hitmen dumping someone … we're citizens trying to manage an unfortunate situation we didn't create. There are a dozen peaceful places where we can relocate his body.'

Ronan drummed his fingers against the side window. Even after they had disposed of this body and Chris reached home, it would no longer feel like home. Any last remaining intimacy he shared with Alice would be gone. This was too enormous a secret to keep, yet too grave to share.

'I'm going to be sick again,' he announced quietly.

Carysfort Avenue was deserted. He knelt on the grass verge and vomited. The grass had recently been cut by the resident outside whose house they had stopped. It matched the manicured lawn. Chris stared towards the lamplit drawing room window, which illuminated a vacant tableau of domestic bliss. Ronan emerged from the car.

'There's nothing left in my stomach,' Chris said. 'But I still want to keep getting sick.'

'This is classic Fine Gael Neighbourhood Watch territory. Some Blueshirt is probably watching us through binoculars.'

'I can't get back into that car.'

Ronan shrugged. 'Fair enough. Knock on that door and ask can we bury a corpse, name and nationality unknown, in their flowerbed.'

'Don't get fucking smart.'

'Then stop pretending this isn't happening. Drive wherever you want. Alice always says you're too easily bullied. Here's your chance to be the boss. I'll go along with any decision you make.'

They had been parked opposite Blackrock Garda Station for fifteen minutes. Occasionally a squad car arrived or pulled away. A late-night dog walker passed them without a glance. Ronan was smoking, letting the permutations circulate in Chris's head. The death was accidental, but they had been negligent about safety procedures, hiring uninsured workers and contravening a closure order. Property developers got away with erecting estates on floodplains, using shelf companies to control offshore bank accounts. Chris had no legal team or expertise. He would be crucified.

The sensible and moral step was to enter the police station before he sank deeper into trouble. But maybe he was already in too deep. How could he explain being panicked into moving the corpse and driving it around, with ten times the legal alcohol limit pulsing through his bloodstream? Or explain the spade that Ronan had placed in the boot, offering Chris no clue as to its possible use? An interrogating voice in his head demanded to know how he could have done anything so stupid. It was no barrister's voice: it was Alice in one of her furies. With Alice, everything operated in pendulum swings. The process of emerging from her chrysalis had necessitated turning him from an oracle into a fool. In helping Ronan to place the dead body in his boot, he had validated her opinion and would forfeit any last shred of respect she felt. Ronan remained silent, abandoning Chris to his private Gethsemane. Across the road, a police cell awaited, with statements, blood tests for alcohol levels, yellow police tape sealing off the town house to be forensically examined as a potential crime scene. Chris could face those. What he couldn't face was Alice.

'Where in Wicklow?' he asked quietly.

Ronan stubbed out his cigarette. 'There are steep paths down to the waterfall at the Devil's Glen. Anyone could trip and fall there.'

'It's thirty miles away.'

'Exactly. Near enough, yet far enough.'

Chris tried to restart the car, but his hand shook too much. Ronan cupped his hand around Chris's fingers, helping him turn the key.

'You've made up your mind,' Ronan said, 'now it's time to act.'

The road towards Dun Laoghaire was once a route of childhood escapes, cycling trips to the swimming baths with a towel and togs, or bus trips to Bray with teenage girls. Now, it held the quality of a nightmare. The carriageway was quiet as Chris stared ahead. Twice his phone rang. He knew that Alice had returned home and was puzzled by his absence. Maybe it was no harm if she got a taste of what it would be like if he weren't always there. The silence in the car remained unbroken as the N11 entered the steeply forested Glen of the Downs. But the silence had a deepening undertone. Chris kept listening for sounds from the boot. He glanced at Ronan. Even if not caught, they would be linked by this secret forever.

'Why did we take my car?' Chris finally spoke.

'My boot is full of rubbish.'

'I'm low on petrol, but if we stop at a garage we'll be on CCTV.' He paused. 'I never thought I'd ever say such a sentence.'

'You'll have enough petrol. Turn left here.'

It was a slip road that brought them onto a flyover. Ronan indicated a small road at a roundabout, barely wide enough for two cars to pass.

'Where are we going?'

'You need to trust me, Chris. After tonight we'll know enough to incriminate each other.'

'When we sell the town house and I move away, you never contact me again.'

'It's some way to bury any friendship,' Ronan observed.

Chris glanced across. 'We're burying nothing, so why put a spade in the boot?'

Ronan shrugged. 'Just in case.'

'Of what?'

'Slow down. There's a tiny turn to your left.' Ronan waited until Chris manoeuvred down the lane. 'Our workman fell when hillwalking. It's simple, no crime and no punishment.'

'He's hardly the sort to go hillwalking,' Chris said grimly.

'You're being racist. You know nothing about him. The next turn is so small you could miss it.'

Chris halted and peered down a lane so overgrown he was unsure his car would fit down it. It had been tarred once, but the potholes were so huge that little proper surface remained.

'Steer by the ridge of grass growing down the centre,' Ronan advised. 'Go slowly and the branches won't scratch your paintwork.'

'I thought we were going to the Devil's Glen?'

'In the Devil's Glen a hillwalker could easily testify that the body wasn't there at nightfall. I know a spot where he won't be found for days.'

Chris cautiously drove down the unkempt lane. His problem wasn't steering, it was staying awake. The adrenaline of fear had deserted him. All he felt were the after-effects of alcohol coursing in his bloodstream. There was nothing left in his stomach, but he still had to resist an urge to vomit. Nothing seemed real, yet every sensation felt artificially heightened. He yearned for fresh air, but was afraid to lower his window in case a trailing branch caught him in the eye.

'I feel I'm being manipulated,' he said.

'I'm just forcing you to get your hands dirty like the rest of us,' Ronan replied. 'If you weren't such a goody-two-shoes, Alice wouldn't need to go looking for rough trade.'

'Mind your fucking tongue,' Chris snapped.

'I'm saying what you're thinking. Any boy who does classics instead of accountancy at school thinks the world owes him a living.'

Chris was lost. Without Ronan he could never find his way back here. He didn't feel an equal partner, yet Ronan was right: subservience was a role he craved to avoid responsibility. His head throbbed. He longed to sleep. He needed to keep driving and pray that this nightmare would end. But it could never end. The fear of retribution would always remain.

'Switch off your headlights,' Ronan ordered. Chris saw a cottage ahead, light spilling from a window and illuminating a hand-painted sign that read: *Private Road. Turn back.*

'How do you know this place?' he asked.

'I just do.'

The steep lane allowed Chris to cut the engine so that the unlit car glided past the cottage. When it slowed to a halt 200 yards farther on, he started the engine again, aware of how cold the car felt. It didn't seem right to turn on the heat with a corpse in the boot. He shivered. The small house from which Alice was sending him unanswered texts seemed like a world to which he could never return. Doubts tormented him. What if the man had been pushed from the scaffolding? What if some quarrel had been settled that Chris knew nothing about, a drug deal gone wrong? This man might not even be their plasterer. With no police investigation, he would never know if this was some stranger who had been killed elsewhere, his body dumped on Chris's property. The moonlight was barely sufficient to steer without headlights. The road was a mud track. To their right, a windbreak of pines had been felled, leaving a gash in the dark forest. The path petered to a halt at an old drystone wall, with gorse bushes precariously sprouting up through gaps where stone sections had collapsed. Chris cut the engine once more. Ronan produced the brandy, took a slug and thrust it towards him.

'Dutch courage,' he said.

'I've drunk enough.'

'If I need a small drink, you need a large one.'

Chris took a lengthy slug, letting the alcohol burn his throat. He handed back the bottle.

'Are we really going to do this?' he asked.

'What do you think?' Ronan stared through the windscreen. Chris sensed that his neighbour was as scared as him.

'Ronan … when we get back to Dublin ….'

'None of this ever occurred.'

Ronan's voice was loud, but even a bird's wings would sound loud in this darkness. Both men got out of the car.

'This stone wall guards against a sheer drop onto rocks in the river below,' Ronan said. 'Take a look.'

Chris moved forward cautiously. So many segments of dry stones had collapsed during storms that the wall was treacherous. He selected a gap and, gripping a bush for support, peered down at jagged boulders fringing a small river below. The sight was unnerving. He went to step back and felt Ronan's arms pin him and inch him closer to the edge.

'What are you doing?'

Ronan's whisper was inches from his ear. 'Exploring the boundaries of trust. If you fall you break your neck. All it takes is one shove.'

'For fuck sake, Ronan, let me go.'

'If I let you go, you fall. Your future hinges on how much you trust me to ease you back off this ledge. So, do you trust me?'

Ronan's tone sounded playful, like words whispered in some sex power game. Was this the reason why Miriam left? Had there been a hidden edge of their private lives that Chris and Alice never saw?

'I came here, didn't I?'

'But what happens when you sober up and your conscience gnaws at you? Can I trust you? I'm in total control now, but once I relax my grip you can destroy my life any time you decide to open your mouth. So answer me this: were you ever unfaithful to Alice?'

'Mind your own fucking business.'

Ronan's grip tightened. 'Everything about you has just become my business because we're suddenly sharing a secret. So tell me: have you fucked another woman in the past twenty years?'

'No.'

'Surely you've wanted to.'

'Wanting and doing are two different things.'

'That leaves you singularly unpractised in the ordinary black art of everyday lying. How do I trust you not to blab all this to Alice?'

'You've no choice.'

'I have: I can fuck you over this wall.'

Ronan leaned forward so they both almost fell. The mud was slippery. Chris tried to regain his footing, but felt the loose stones give way. He screamed as Ronan's hands let go. Then a second later – or maybe just a terrifying fraction of a second – Ronan's arms clasped him again, binding them so tightly that if Chris fell, they would both fall. Gradually, Ronan found sufficient strength to ease them back. He relaxed his grip only when they collapsed on the grass in front of the parked car.

'You could have killed us both,' Chris gasped. He struggled to his knees and swung his fist to catch Ronan on the face. Ronan winced and then grabbed Chris's fist in a vice-like grip.

'That's more like it,' he said. 'Your balls have finally dropped.'

'Just fucking stay away from me,' Chris hissed. Prising his hand free, he walked over to the car. Opening the boot, he stared in at the body covered with plastic sacks. He needed to think clearly, but Ronan's voice was goading him as his neighbour rose to his feet.

'Alice can keep secrets. She was a sweet kisser; hot to trot the summer we did our leaving certs. The most perfect nipples, shy to come out, but hard as nails when they did. I bet she's never told you we dated. I never understood her becoming pals with Miriam: it was Miriam I ditched her for. Miriam put me through hell before I even got her bra off, but I like a challenge, and Alice was too easy. She only tried to move to Canada because she couldn't bear to watch Miriam kissing a boy she still had ants in her pants for.'

'Shut the fuck up. I've always hated your fucking guts.'

'Then I'll give you your chance for revenge.' Ronan stepped back so that he was now standing on the muddy gap in the wall. 'I'm at your mercy, one push and I'm gone. Alice's real reason for wanting to move is that she can't stand living so close to a man she hates herself for still fancying. A man can always tell with any woman he once fucked.'

'I said shut up.'

'If you intend to destroy my life, then don't do it by blabbing to the cops about a workman who means nothing to either of us. Kill me now, for Alice.'

'Don't call my bluff because I might just push you.'

'Maybe I want a way out. I've fucked up. I'm worth far more to Kim dead than alive.'

'You live in a mansion.'

'A house simultaneously mortgaged to the hilt with three different banks. Managers don't even bother asking for house deeds any more. They're too busy counting their commission.'

Both men were startled by Chris's mobile phone ringing.

'Alice is worried,' Chris said. 'I'm never out this late.'

'She'll be more worried when she discovers that all her savings are gone. Paul Hughes has fucked us both over. After I met him yesterday afternoon I wanted to drive my car straight into the sea at Bullock Harbour. Instead of being the guy who constantly takes care of everyone, I wanted to be selfish and kill myself.'

'Are you saying my savings are gone?'

'You're slow, but you're not deaf.'

'I will fucking kill you.'

'Face it, Chris, you can't tie your own shoelaces.'

Chris reached into the car boot, the spade clanging against the metal door as he removed it. Up on the wall, Ronan twitched with sudden nervousness.

'What do you need the spade for?'

'You say you want to die. Why should the rocks down there get the privilege of cracking open your skull?'

Ronan turned to survey the fall. 'It's tempting, isn't it? If I were found dead up here than at least I won't have to return to Kim empty-handed. But I haven't got the balls to jump, and you haven't got the balls to push me.'

'I never thought I'd have the balls to drive a corpse up here.'

'Then hit me with that shovel.' Ronan's voice sounded devoid of emotion now, dreamlike, drunken. 'Afterwards, toss the poor bastard down on top of me. It will look like we got into a fight and both fell. Kim will hit the jackpot with my life assurance policy, and even you should be able to flog that town house on your own for a huge profit. So, have you the courage, or are you a timid nobody like your dad was?'

'You speak about your father like he was a giant,' Chris said angrily. 'I remember a tight-arsed, miserable fucker spitting up phlegm in the doorway of the Avoca House like he was on a Kilburn street corner.'

'My dad had balls to burn,' Ronan replied quietly. 'Ask Alice about the size of mine. No woman forgets the first cock she was fucked with.'

'Alice was a virgin when we started going out.'

Ronan laughed, staring down again at the drop. 'She was still a virgin in one orifice anyway, despite all my persuasive charms.'

Chris stepped forward. The temptation to raise the spade was overwhelming, a welling up of old resentments now congealing into hatred.

'I'll smash your fucking skull.'

Ronan stumbled drunkenly, needing to spread out both arms to regain his balance. 'You lack the guts. A real man would have split open the skull of the smarmy businessman who keeps boasting to Paul Hughes about Alice chasing after him, so infatuated with him that she's making a public mockery of you every Sunday night.'

Both men screamed as Chris surged forward, slamming the spade down – at the last moment – inches from Ronan. Sparks lit up the darkness as dislodged rocks scattered down the cliff. Ronan would have fallen if Chris had not instinctively grabbed him, unsure if they would both tumble over the edge. He fell backwards onto the wet grass, with Ronan's weight landing on him. Chris expected a tirade or a fist in the face. Instead, Ronan gasped for breath. But Chris sensed that his breathlessness was partly a ruse to allow both men to adjust mentally to a subtle power shift in their relationship.

'I thought you were going to actually kill me,' Ronan said, almost in awe.

'Who is this bastard that Hughes claims is chasing after Alice?'

Chris's mobile phone rang again.

'Forget Hughes's gossip and ask yourself, would a woman who doesn't love you ring this often?' Ronan asked. 'Alice is sick with worry.'

Both men listened to it ring out into voicemail. The night silence returned.

'What did Hughes say?'

Ronan shrugged. 'Do you think that a crook like Paul Hughes knows your wife better than you do? He made some snide comment about Alice. He'd probably seen her drinking with people in a pub. Hughes is a shit-stirrer. Alice loves you, and if you didn't love her you wouldn't be up here trying to sort out this mess.'

'If you were dating Alice, years ago, before I met her, why tell me this now?'

'Maybe I was trying to provoke you into pushing me over that cliff. Even I get moments of weakness … at times I feel buried alive under all the shite of responsibilities and debts. Maybe I needed to play Russian roulette to clear my head. I put the barrel to my skull with your finger on the trigger and I survived, because you're about the only true friend I have. Now I feel ready to start afresh. Suicide is the coward's way out.' Ronan stared into his face. 'Fuck Hughes, fuck everything. No matter how bad things are, you and I are not cowards, are we?'

Chris pushed Ronan's weight off him. Panting, he rose.

'If we're going to empty this boot, let's do it.'

'You have balls to burn.' Ronan gingerly eased himself up. 'Alice got lucky when she met you. Miriam always said so.'

'Shut the fuck up, Ronan.'

Ronan opened the passenger door and took out the brandy.

'Not for me,' Chris said.

'It's for me.' Ronan took a massive slug, gasping when he lifted the bottle from his lips. He was shaking as he produced two pairs of plastic gloves, handing one pair to Chris. 'You take his legs.'

The corpse seemed stiffer and heavier than earlier. Ronan struggled under the weight of the upper torso. They reached a gap in the stone wall. Chris didn't look down at the man's face. There was no counting to three, no prearranged signal. They simply let go and watched the corpse tumble awkwardly down, until eventually it came to rest amid rocks by the river. Chris picked up the spade and returned to the car.

'Get into the car,' he ordered. 'And just for once, don't say a fucking word.'

Chapter Eighteen

Chris

Monday 6th, 2.30 a.m.

They were silent for most of the return journey – fellow conspirators, custodians of each other's fate. Chris would never be free of Ronan while they each shared this secret. A sickening level of alcohol coursed through his bloodstream, but he had never felt more sober. He glanced across at his neighbour. How could he have been crazy enough to hand over their life savings to this man? He felt robbed of far more than that cash saved up for their future. He no longer possessed any sense of being the person he was yesterday, no longer immersed in the petty quarrels of an ordinary life that now belonged to a stranger. He had tried to protect his old life by committing this criminal act, but Chris realised that he could never fit back into it. Ronan stared impassively ahead. He is waiting for me to crack, Chris thought. He knows I'll never be a real man on his terms. How many secrets did you need to possess to be a real man? What other tests of masculinity had you to pass? The ability to twist rules, to cheat tax men and outwit officials, to conduct affairs and – most importantly – achieve a state of amnesia where you absolved yourself of all past sins?

He finally broke the silence as they turned off the N11 onto Clonkeen Road.

'What really happened to my life savings?'

Ronan's voice was wary. 'I won't lie: your first €30,000 went straight into Hughes's pocket a few weeks back.'

'Were you crazy?'

'I was greedy. Some opportunities seem so good you need to gamble everything. Hughes offered to let me buy into the consortium developing his mother's house. The site alone is worth millions. He said he wanted other investors involved in fronting it, so he could stay in the background and not be accused of ripping off his old dear.'

Chris looked at him. 'I gave you our money in good faith.'

'And I invested it in good faith, knowing that even a small stake in his consortium would quadruple in profit. We would finally be playing at the top table. I made you a silent investor because I couldn't raise enough cash elsewhere on my own, but I was convinced that we were guaranteed a massive return.'

'I didn't want a massive return; I wanted to build a small town house with no risk. How about the second €30,000 I handed over yesterday?'

'€10,000 was used to pay Jiri's men back wages, as they were getting a bit mutinous and mightn't have taken away the scaffolding before the safety inspector returned. I gave Jiri the remainder for materials he has been sourcing for us dirt cheap. It was only afterwards that I found out where he was getting the stuff. For weeks Paul Hughes has been ordering his site foremen to flog everything that isn't nailed down. He's been squirrelling away cash before the banks appoint a receiver. Hughes is stony broke. He told me this to my face at our meeting yesterday, joking about the reawakened love he feels for his previously estranged wife, the agony aunt, ever since he transferred all his performing assets into her name. I could have killed the bastard. I've wanted to kill the runt for years.'

'And did you?'

Ronan shrugged his shoulders, looking more deflated than Chris had ever seen him. 'Nobody swings their fists in the Playwright Inn. My father would have though. My dad would have strangled him. But I'm not my father. I just sat there and accepted his news, like a jilted girl who realises she only has herself to blame for believing the blandishments of some conniving smooth-talker. I should have felt angry, but instead I felt cheap and stupid for having allowed myself to be used. When he nodded at his empty glass and said he wouldn't deny me the chance to boast to my grandchildren that I had bought Paul Hughes his last drink in the Playwright Inn, I meekly went up and purchased him a double vodka and Slimline tonic. Then I walked out the door with whatever dignity I could and hunched down beside my car, where no one could see me, and vomited up my guts.' He looked across. 'I screwed up big time, pal. We're in a hole, but I'll get us out of it.'

'What will happen to Hughes?'

'Receivers will seize control of his sites next week. I thought Hughes was too big to fail, but his plans to develop his mother's house were actually his final throw of the dice. He has borrowed money all across town on the strength of that deal, offering small-fry investors like me a share in his consortium because the banks and the big players all deserted him. He has been spending whatever money he can raise to pay Peter to bribe Paul to keep his sites ticking over while waiting for this development to take off. It was high risk, but his gamble might have paid off if his mother hadn't rumbled his real reason for downsizing her into a town house in your back garden. Paul's problem was that he never legally owned his mother's land; he just presumed that the old dear would sign any papers he put in front of her. But even at her age, Mrs Hughes turns out to be one tough broad. Don't forget that she was a Protestant who had to convert to be allowed to marry her husband at a grim ceremony with no witnesses allowed in a sacristy. Slights like that make you flinty. Paul sent her a mother's day card last March. She replied last month with a solicitor's letter. She barely knows what year it is, but brittle old ladies with Protestant blood are different to us. Even when they're half gaga they still know the true value of land.'

'So she's not moving into our town house?' Chris asked, although he already knew the answer.

'She is not. She's after getting herself made a ward of court, and in the process she changed her will to disinherit the little bastard.' Ronan looked across. 'We'll find a buyer; we just need to finish the town house first. How good are you with a shovel?'

'Tell me you're joking.'

'We're not too proud to do a bit of donkey work ourselves. Hughes going bust may help us, because lots of Jiri's men will lose their jobs. I can't pay any more wages up front, but they will keep working for us if we dangle a serious cash bonus for them when they finish. We can still sell the town house for a fortune once we find two fools willing to throw their hats into the ring.'

'And what if we don't?'

'We will. Auctioneers don't want to spook buyers by admitting that the market is slowing, but Blackrock is still Blackrock. You'll get back every cent.'

'I've lost more than money,' Chris said.

Ronan nodded. 'I'm sorry about that, but your innocence is like your virginity: it becomes a burden if you keep it too long. We all lose it as part of discovering how the world works.'

'I always knew how the world worked. I just never knew what I'm capable of.'

'Good men do bad things to protect their families,' Ronan said. 'We need to put this behind us.'

Chris stared at the road ahead. Twenty-four hours ago news of his squandered savings would have devastated him, but now it barely registered. The image that plagued him wasn't even that of a corpse staring up from the bottom of a Wicklow ravine: it was a teenage Ronan kissing Alice, his fingers unbuttoning her blouse, his fingertip teasing her nipple erect. That was thirty years ago. How could he be seized by irrational jealousy at a moment like this? But he gripped the wheel with both hands to resist a temptation to punch his companion. He stayed silent when Ronan told him to turn right onto Kill Lane, although this would take them away from Blackrock. Chris drove through empty streets as instructed until they reached the seafront at Monkstown. Ronan ordered him to park a hundred yards from the Dart station. The man stared out at the shuttered building.

'I monumentally fucked up,' Ronan said, so quietly it felt like he was addressing himself.

'You did. Alice and I scrimped and saved for years to get that money together.'

Ronan looked at him, baffled. 'You'll get your money back. I fucked up when I let Miriam slip away from me.'

'Don't you love Kim?'

'I tell her I do, but it just feels different.'

'Do you think the man we dumped over that cliff ever loved anybody?'

'Nobody starts life expecting to end up as a migrant worker in a foreign hostel.' Ronan paused, embarrassed. 'Chris ... about what I said up in the mountains ....'

'And you afraid I'll go to the police?'

'Forget about the workman.' Ronan looked uneasy. 'Go to the police if you must, but just don't ever tell Alice or Kim that I stood up on a ledge like a coward, spouting nonsense about wanting to die. Sometimes, when the pressure gets too much, I feel that I'm cracking up. I say and do stupid things. But I'm back in control. When Sophie returns home from her Erasmus year it will be like none of this ever happened.'

'That's one huge lie,' Chris said quietly.

'I know, but it's the lie we're going to live by. There's something else you need to know: Paul Hughes never mentioned anything to me about Alice and any smarmy businessman.'

'Then why did you say he did?'

'To provoke you. When I'm stressed I can be an arsehole.'

Ronan looked so earnest, so anxious to convince, that Chris couldn't be convinced. Chris just wanted to be alone. Only then could he begin to make sense of everything.

'Why are we stopped here?' he asked.

'Flick open your boot.' Ronan opened the passenger door. 'We need to get rid of everything linking us to this.'

There was a row of recycling containers near the Dart station. Ronan removed the black plastic sacks from the boot and put them in the litter bins. He then put the plastic gloves in the chute for recycled clothes, and walked back to the car. By the time he opened the passenger door he seemed to have restored his confident persona. He did not get in, but leaned down to address Chris.

'It's important to put your clothes in the washing machine first thing in the morning. Don't do it now or make any noise parking your car that might wake Alice or Kim. I'm going to walk home. I need to clear my head. I'm not saying we did the right thing, but what's done is done. There's some brandy left. Have a slug if you need it. It's better if Alice doesn't see you, but if she does it will help if you're not shaking like a leaf.'

Chris watched him walk away. Now that he was alone, his body shook so violently that it took several minutes to start the engine. Chris drove slowly, focusing only on arriving home. When he parked outside his house he saw a light still on in Alice's bedroom. Was she waiting up for him, anxious or furious? He went upstairs and found Alice asleep, propped up by pillows, her fingers still holding the book she needed to finish for her book club. He knelt by the bed they had shared for years, the bed where he was now no longer welcome. He took the book softly from her fingers and placed it on the dressing table. He kissed her forehead, pulled up her quilt and clicked off the bedside lamp. Then he closed over the door of what was now her room. He stood in the doorway of Sophie's bedroom, missing his daughter, and yet relieved that she wasn't here to judge him. He had let Sophie and Alice down, and, just as importantly, he had betrayed himself. Entering the bathroom, he stared into the moonlit mirror until he averted his eyes, forced to look away. How could a man face his wife when he couldn't bear to face himself? Chris walked downstairs in the dark, and kept walking because he no longer belonged in that house. Closing the front door softly, he got into the car. He restarted the engine and drove towards Wicklow.

Chapter Nineteen

Alice

Monday 6th, 9.30 a.m.

Chris had been here during the night. Alice knew this by how her book was neatly placed on the dressing table. It was where Chris always put her book if he found her asleep and was scared of waking her by making space for it on her bedside locker. Her locker was crammed with vials of homeopathic remedies to help cope with the changes of life, with creams for hot flushes and abdominal cramps and dryness, with snippets of advice from magazines, and ornaments that seemed childish, but cheered her spirits on mornings when she awoke to the effects of Seasonal Affective Disorder – the winter blues, or whatever shades of blue were induced by being interminably hemmed in beneath grey clouds in this godforsaken country.

Days of sunshine did more to lift her spirits than the paraphernalia of remedies she hunted down in health food stores. Ironically, the sun was shining this morning, but Alice felt a sense of foreboding. She knew her husband's every mood, but above all she knew his predictability. No day passed without small acts of kindness. He was still unable to resist gently touching her hair every time he passed, even when unsure if she would be annoyed by this repetitive gesture. She was more shocked than Chris by the harsh words she sometimes uttered, words she didn't mean, but often she felt lost inside such a knot of frustration that she needed an outlet for the uncertainties plaguing her, the mood swings that scared her as much as they startled the husband she cared for with such passionate and contradictory infuriation.

Sophie had always been their shield. Alice worried about the emotional damage inflicted on Sophie by constantly having to mediate in their fractured relationship. She had overheard words no child should hear, though Alice consoled herself that many children heard worse during rows between parents. This was one fact of life that recent months had taught her: it was impossible for an outsider to know what goes on in any marriage.

Some days Chris appeared too scared even to kiss her. It was not her fault. He always seemed to get affectionate or need reassurance at precisely the wrong moment, when she was changing to go out or had steeled her mind to do so. He would invade her space, making her feel guilty when at her most vulnerable and defensive. Until last September Alice could have never imagined withdrawing from Chris's embrace. She hated herself afterwards, but there were moments when she needed to shut him out. She didn't feel like this all the time. Some mornings she longed to feel him beside her in the bed. But she had made her husband too petrified to attempt to kiss her. Something once spontaneous had become a source of tension, with Chris hovering in doorways, trying to summon the courage to approach.

They had always both been far too sensitive, easy to bruise and quick to brood, but at this moment Alice desperately wanted him here. She wanted to shake him and demand to know why he hadn't answered her phone calls. But mainly she wanted to hug him. She had been scared since coming home in the early hours. Last night was different from previous nights, when she would resent his intrusion into her room after she returned. Last night she had wanted to slip into his makeshift bed, not to make love, but just to ask him to hold her silently in his arms.

But his car had been gone on her return. This was so out of character that she had felt scared before even opening the front door. She knew he had called in to Ronan, but it was too late for them to be in some pub. She had stood alone at her bedroom window, staring down at the Velux window of Ronan's study. Ronan's house was in darkness, yet Alice had felt sure that, wherever Chris was, Ronan was manipulating him. When it reached 4 a.m., and her calls remained unanswered, she had been tempted to phone the police or ring around the hospitals. She had planned to do so if he were not here when she woke, but the sight of her book carefully placed on the dressing table and of her bedside lamp switched off changed everything.

Chris must have knelt by her bed while she was asleep. She suspected that he had kissed her during those moments, when she could not object. Then for whatever reason he had got back into his car and departed, leaving no note to explain where he was going. Maybe it was on an errand to a builders' supplier, press-ganged into doing yet more donkey work for Ronan, but Alice didn't think so. Chris had a fetish for leaving notes, even if only driving to the garage for milk. Something was seriously wrong. You could always sense this with someone you loved, and the irrational dread she felt at Chris's absence made her realise just how much she did love him.

Had her attitude towards him last night caused his flight. She refused to beat herself up. She had spent too many years making herself sick with stress over every small thing. But she kept envisaging Chris's empty car parked at the end of a pier. If anyone had tipped her husband over the edge, she felt certain it was Ronan. She searched the house for any clue to Chris's whereabouts, then hurried next door, so agitated with anxiety that she only realised she had kept her finger on the buzzer when she heard Kim's hurried footsteps in the hall. She stepped back, meaning to apologise. But when the door opened, she felt overcome by resentment, not at Kim, but at the fact that Miriam wasn't there, one of the few people able to calm Alice down when she got this scared. The slender Filipina stepped back, distancing herself from Alice's obvious distress.

'Is Chris here?'

Kim looked perturbed. 'Why would he be here?'

'If I knew I wouldn't need to ask.' Alice voice rose. She knew Kim spoke perfect English. But it wasn't her words that she wanted the young woman to understand, it was her palpable terror, the unassailable certainty that something was wrong which you only sensed if you had lived with someone for twenty-five years.

'Why are you angry with me?' Kim's puzzled tone conveyed concern, yet Alice suddenly sensed that Kim's quietness was a weapon to be deployed more skilfully than any of Miriam's tantrums. Under the Filipina's penetrating gaze, Alice felt like an irrational child.

'I'm sorry, Kim, I'm not angry with you, I'm flustered,' she apologised. 'Will you fetch Ronan for me?'

'Housekeepers fetch things. I'm his wife.'

Kim's tone remained impeccably courteous, and as impenetrable as steel. Ronan emerged from the doorway of his study. Alice recognised his quizzical look of wounded innocence. He had always deployed it when covering up something during their brief courtship.

'Where's Chris?' she demanded.

Ronan held out his hands like a magician convincing an audience he had nothing concealed up his sleeve. 'Probably gone for a walk. Have you tried calling him?'

'I kept calling all night until I fell asleep. He never answered.'

'Was he out all night?'

'You tell me.'

'You know Chris. He'll turn up.'

'I know him inside out. You were with him. What were you both doing?'

'Not much at our age.' Ronan chuckled, and then looked more serious. 'We had a few drinks. At midnight Chris decided to take a drive. There was no talking him out of it, so I tagged along to keep an eye. We just chewed the cud, reminiscing about old times. You remember old times, don't you, Alice?'

'Chris would never drive when drunk. I could always tell from your face when you're holding something back.'

'And where were you, Alice?'

'That's none of your business.' Alice couldn't prevent herself from sounding defensive.

'Chris needs alcohol to loosen his tongue. He's worried sick about you for some reason. Even hen-pecked husbands have a right to get drunk occasionally, or do you deny him that too?'

'Stay out of our lives,' Alice warned.

'If I hadn't got into his car with him God knows what he might have done,' Ronan said. 'I persuaded him to stop at Seafort Parade; the pair of us sitting at the Martello tower, staring across the bay like a pair of teenagers. He poured out his heart. I tried to get him to answer your calls, but he didn't know how to phrase the questions he wanted to ask you. At 3 a.m. I tried to take his car keys, but when Chris gets upset he can be stubborn. Last night he was stubborn as hell.'

'I don't believe a word you're saying,' Alice said.

'Why would I lie?'

'You've spent your life lying so instinctively that you barely notice yourself doing it. You won't twist me around your finger like you twist Chris.'

Kim stepped forward, trying to ease the tension.

'Alice,' she said, 'I'll make coffee and we'll sit down calmly.'

'This has nothing to do with you, Kim.'

Alice didn't mean to sound dismissive: she was just trying to wrestle a semblance of truth from Ronan. Kim didn't raise her voice, but there was steeliness in her reply.

'You are in my hallway, calling my husband a liar.'

'I've known Ronan as a liar since before you born.'

'If my husband says he doesn't know where Chris is, then he does not. If you are worried, call the police.'

'Don't do that,' Ronan advised hastily.

Both women gazed at him.

'Why not?' Alice asked.

'He'll lose his licence if you say he was driving around drunk,' Ronan explained. 'We had a row after I tried to take his car keys. You lose your temper and get over it a minute later, Alice. It takes a lot to make Chris lose his temper, but when he does he needs time to recover. He gets embarrassed and annoyed with himself. Most likely he's gone for a walk to work off the drink. I'll take a drive and try to spot him.'

Alice turned to Kim, needing an ally. 'Can't you see, Kim, I'm just scared,' she said quietly.

Ronan stepped between them and reassuringly stroked her shoulder. 'Give Chris time and he'll come home. He loves you; you're all he talks about. That's the full truth.'

Alice looked down at his hand on her shoulder. 'When was the last time you told anyone the truth? You might fool someone innocent like Kim, but you don't fool me.'

It was Kim who spoke next, in a tone that brooked no disobedience. 'I wish you to leave my home now, Alice. You won't find your husband by insulting mine.'

Ronan wanted to escort Alice to her door, but a sharp glance from Kim told him to remain where he was. Kim watched from the doorway until Alice was out of sight, then closed the door and leaned against it. Ronan gave a despairing shrug. 'When Alice gets irrational she flies off the handle. I mean, what could I tell her?'

Kim gazed up at him with the most piercing stare Ronan had ever endured. 'You could have tried to tell the truth.'

Chapter Twenty

Chris

Monday 6th, 11.30 a.m.

Chris woke to an anxious tapping against the driver's window. The stifling heat through the windscreen told him it was midday. He had never known a worse hangover, his head throbbed, his tongue raw, his body so dehydrated that he longed to plunge his face into a mountain stream. He could now barely recall restarting his car in his driveway and heading back towards Wicklow, though he remembered encountering commuters making the long haul from Gorey and Arklow, employees of call centres or shopping centres that opened on bank holidays. This sight should have reminded Chris that he also faced bills and responsibilities, but, although barely able to stay awake, he had been driven forward by an overwhelming, primeval need to redeem himself. Maybe he counted for little in this Ireland where everything was measured by possessions, but in his own mind he had become a true nonentity, a stranger to himself, when he allowed a workman's corpse to tumble down a moonlit slope. Driving back into the mountains at dawn, so jaded he could barely prevent his car from swerving between lanes, he had possessed no clear directions about how to relocate the body. There was just a curious certainty that, somewhere up in these hills, the ghost of his younger self awaited, standing sentinel over that corpse like a guardian angel with a torn wing.

The caustic rapping reoccurred against the window, forcing Chris to open his eyes in the sun's glare. The car was like a glasshouse, the steering wheel too hot to touch. Looking around, Chris realised he had driven into a ditch on a remote mountain road. He could vaguely recall the car leaving the road in slow motion, freewheeling to a halt after he ran out of petrol. He had scarcely registered the fact that his side wheels had subsided into a drain before he blacked out into unconsciousness.

Chris rolled down the window, as much from a fear of suffocating in the sweltering vehicle than from any desire to address the elderly woman in a tweed riding jacket who peered in at him. The stink of brandy on his breath mitigated her initial concern, but he still looked sufficiently well dressed for her to be perturbed.

'Are you all right?' she asked. 'Have you had an accident?'

'I ran out of petrol.' His tongue was so parched that his words were barely comprehensible. 'Have you anything to drink?' She stepped back, and Chris realised she had misconstrued his meaning. 'Water, I mean. I need to take a tablet.'

This was a lie, but the reference to medication might make his demeanour seem more excusable.

'I have a small bottle in the Land Rover,' she replied.

Her vehicle was parked in front of his. Chris wondered how many other cars had passed while he slept. Where was he? He had known, from the moment he knelt by Alice's bed to remove the book from her sleeping hands, that he needed to undertake this journey. The problem was that he had lost all sense of direction. All these small roads looked the same. Chris possessed a vague recollection of the sequence of turns Ronan had instructed him to take after leaving the motorway, but had no idea of how far he had travelled before his car ran out of petrol. Even if he had managed to stay awake, Ronan's route was so deliberately convoluted that there was no guarantee Chris could ever find his way back there. This had been Ronan's intention. They had probably doubled back along a maze of roads to add to Chris's disorientation. Ronan regarded knowledge as power. He needed to be in control. He would only have brought Chris to that cliff when certain that his neighbour could never locate it again.

The woman returned with a small bottle of mineral water. Chris raised a closed fist to his lips as if swallowing a tablet, then he drank with a savage thirst, knowing that a dozen such bottles would have no effect on how dehydrated he felt. The woman watched him closely. She had the accent of people who open their ancestral gardens to the public during National Heritage Week in exchange for tax breaks.

'Do you want me to drive you to a garage?' she asked. 'I keep an empty five-litre fuel can in my car.'

'I'm fine.' Chris attempted to hand her back the half-empty bottle.

She waved it away. 'You've been drinking, but you're no drinker: you haven't a drinker's nose. You look like you're in shock. Are you sure you haven't had an accident? This road goes nowhere, except into the mountains, where it barely becomes a road at all.'

'I'm looking for a lane that ends beside a drystone wall guarding against a steep fall to a river,' Chris said. 'There's a cottage nearby, which has a sign that says *Road Private*.'

The woman shook her head. 'There's nowhere like that around here.'

'Maybe you haven't lived up here long enough.'

'Locals referred to us as blow-ins until comparatively recently … the 1920s, I believe. But I know this mountain, and I know when someone is unwell. Now if you get into the Land Rover I'll drive you to a garage or a doctor.'

Chris looked around, failing to identify any landmarks from last night.

'Thanks for the water,' he said, 'but I prefer to walk.'

The woman sighed in exasperation. 'You're just being stubborn now.'

'It's not stubbornness,' Chris replied quietly. 'It's penance.'

He watched the woman shake her head as she returned to her vehicle. It had tweed blankets in the back seat, probably smelling of dog hairs. He was tempted to let her drive him to where he could get a bus or taxi to Dublin. But back to what? To Alice? To staring out his bedroom window at the spot where the workman died? Chris knew where he wanted to go back to: a place and time that was no longer there. He longed to stand in the shadow of their demolished old shed, feeling ivy against his back on the night when Alice passionately kissed him while their babysitter sat framed by the television's glow. He could recall Alice's blouse undone, her intake of breath as his fingertip encircled her nipple, that same nipple Ronan had colonised long before him. This last thought came unbidden, a flush of jealousy souring his most intimate memory. Had Ronan even robbed him of a true understanding of his past? The only thing Ronan could not steal was the sense of who he had once been. The man Alice fell in love with would never have taken part in last night's events.

Chris opened the car door and stepped out into the mountain air. He had never felt more alone. The woman had driven away. He should have asked her for some aspirin; such women always carried first-aid kits in their glove compartments big enough to stock a small field hospital. This merciless sun would quickly burn his skin. The only thing he took with him was her small plastic bottle, hoping to find a stream where he could refill it. When driving here, his plan had been somehow to haul the corpse back up that cliff and replace it in his car boot, then drive to a hospital and alert the police. With his car broken down this was no longer an option, but if he located the body he could phone an ambulance and give them a rough indication of where he was. As a child he often fantasised about being a heroic figure emerging from the mist cradling a rescued child. Such innocent fantasies were gone. The most he could hope for was to be allowed to atone for his sins by descending that cliff to see if he could press shut the eyelids of the dead workman.

Chapter Twenty-One

Alice

Monday 6th, 1 p.m.

The house had never seemed so empty. Alice was used to being there on her own. During the bad years she spent too many dark mornings there alone. But back then she had known that Sophie would soon be home from school, or Chris would arrive in from work. Today the sun was shining and Alice had the energy to drive anywhere she wished. With no sense of when Chris would return, however, sitting around felt like waiting in limbo.

Where was he? Alice was spoiling for a row, yet longed to put her arms around her husband. Despite her contradictory emotions, and some occasions when she felt that she couldn't be in the same house as him, Chris remained her true husband. The very word *husband* was invested with a sense of permanence. In sickness and health, and they had known both. For all their estrangements, there was nobody on earth who understood her better. This was the most distressing aspect of recent months, the fact that she could not confide in him when she felt at her most vulnerable, adrift inside a false world of artifice where she now realised she could never belong.

Driving home last night, she had been certain that Chris would be lying awake, and had prepared a shield of words to ward off every query. The only thing she had been unprepared for was his absence. How could he not be there when he was the anchor she depended on, able to rail against his cumbersome love because she knew that his love was so strong she would always remain held firm by it? Chris had only been missing for a few hours, so why was she so scared? The way that Ronan fobbed her off had fuelled her suspicions. But whatever row the men had, the town house was not the tipping point that caused his disappearance. Alice felt paralysed by a fear that she had pushed her husband beyond a point of return.

Eleven o'clock became twelve o'clock and then one o'clock, the day becalmed with bank holiday dullness. More workmen arrived, as they invariably did. She heard Ronan's raised voice in the garden complaining about a plasterer, but could not hear Jiri's quiet reply. It seemed unimaginable that Jiri would ever lose his temper. His stoicism made Ronan sound adolescent. From her window she could see Ezal discreetly observing the exchange, maintaining the sardonic silence with which he took in everything. Alice sensed that Ezal was the only man there aware of her presence as she sat alone at the kitchen table. He never looked towards her, but Alice felt he was cognisant of her distress. She could phone neighbours for support, but how could she discuss Chris's absence with anyone when she did not know what was really happening?

A replacement plasterer arrived. After this man finished plastering the wall, he spoke quietly to Jiri and then disappeared, along with Jiri and most of the workmen. Only Ezal remained with one helper, dismantling the scaffolding. She was glad of his presence: it meant that she did not feel utterly alone.

Alice lost track of how often she watched the kettle boil without having the heart to pour water into the teapot at her elbow. She was waiting, paralysed with fear. Finally it came: the ringtone of the house phone. She let it ring for long enough to make any casual caller hang up. The fact that it kept ringing meant that it could only be Chris, or the emergency services to say they had found his body. She lifted the receiver quickly now, afraid that the ringing might stop.

'Hello?' Alice said timidly.

'Are you all right?'

Alice would only have been all right if it was Chris's voice on the line. This young woman sounded concerned, but perhaps emergency personnel were trained to sound concerned without betraying too much in their tone. How did they break bad news? Surely the fact that they were phoning was good: if Chris had been found dead, the police would call in person to her door.

'Is he okay?' Alice asked. 'What's happened to him, just tell me.'

'Mum, are you feeling all right? Is Dad with you?'

'Sophie. Is that you?' Was Alice too stressed to recognise her own daughter's voice? The child sounded scared. Alice took a deep breath, needing to pull herself together for Sophie's sake. 'Don't mind me, I was miles away when the phone rang, finishing my book for the book club.'

'Is Dad with you? Can you put him on?'

Alice took another deep breath. Sophie's voice calmed her, giving her a role to play as a reassuring parent. 'Your dad has popped out,' she lied. 'Ronan has him run ragged, racing around to builders' suppliers. They're like two boys building a toy fort. I'm not sure what time he's home at. But how are you? How are things in Urbino?'

Alice grew worried again. It was unlike Sophie to phone. Twice a week she Skyped them, though Alice hated being on public display on Skype. She preferred the phone, where if you were feeling low no one could see you. But could Chris have texted Sophie in Italy? Maybe their daughter knew more about what was happening than Alice did. There was silence on the line. Then Alice realised it wasn't silence: Sophie was softly conferring with someone.

'I was hoping you and Dad were both in,' Sophie said eventually. 'Urbino is more than good. It's absolutely brilliant, it's … *awesome*.'

Sophie used this word in a jokey manner, though Alice sensed the joke was not intended for her. She was relieved at her daughter's high spirits, and heard another girl's barely suppressed laugh in the background. Sophie's call had nothing to do with Chris's disappearance. The child sounded so enthused that she momentarily forgot about Alice's earlier frantic tone.

'You'd love Urbino, Mum,' Sophie continued. 'It's magical. We moved home yesterday. We found the most dilapidated tiny flat, with wooden shutters and ancient floorboards. It's like something from a 1950s' film. I've posted pictures on my Facebook page, get Dad to show them to you.'

'I thought you were sharing with four girls,' Alice said. 'Did you all move?'

'Think of the maths, Mum. Five girls into one flat just won't go.'

This time the carefree laugh in the background was unmistakable.

'Who is that with you, Sophie?'

'I wanted you and Dad to say hello to someone. There are just two of us in our new flat, me and Jessie. Jessie's my ....' Sophie paused. Alice knew her daughter well enough to sense that this pause was intended to convey something. '... flatmate. We're together ... in this flat. You'd love Jessie, Mum. She's from Canada, a remote part, like Westmeath with snow. She'd like to say hello ... will you say hello to her?'

Alice glanced out the kitchen window. Ezal and his helper were such swift workers that they had moved the dismantled scaffolding into Ronan's garden and were lifting it over the back wall into the laneway. They would be gone soon. Sophie must have sensed Alice's sudden disengagement because she repeated her question in a slightly hurt tone. Alice needed to concentrate. For whatever reason, this was important to their daughter.

'I'd love to say hello to Jessie.' Alice tried to sound chirpy.

There was some whispering, and then a young Canadian voice said, 'Hello, Mrs Macken, it's a pleasure speaking to you.'

'Please, call me Alice.'

'Sophie tells me you lived in Canada once.'

Alice laughed, embarrassed. 'People have spent longer in Toronto on holidays than I lived there. It was mercilessly cold, but I loved it. I never wanted to come home.'

'My aunt lives there, but I'm a small-town girl, not a sophisticated cosmopolitan like our Sophie. Sophie speaks better Italian than I speak English.'

The Canadian laughed as if teasing Sophie. Alice felt slightly uneasy about her possessive way of referring to Sophie, but this could be a generational thing. Alice liked this girl's openness and so she laughed too, feeling an unexpected phantom pain at hearing a Canadian accent. It brought back so much: the accents of strangers on Toronto's streets, and her sense of expectation at Sophie's age. She was glad Sophie had made a new friend.

'Is your flat nice?' Alice asked.

'It's beyond nice, it's awesome. Sophie wants to say something. Goodbye, Mrs Macken.'

'Goodbye, Jessie.'

Sophie was back on the line, her practical side calculating the price of the call, her protective side recalling how scared Alice had initially sounded.

'Is everything okay at home, Mum?'

'Everything is fine, love.'

'And is Dad really at a builders' suppliers?'

'Ronan has him fetching and carrying. Still, the town house is almost finished and looks great.'

'And are you okay, Mum?'

'You know me, Sophie. I just hate bank holidays when nothing's happening. Your friend sounds lovely.'

'She is lovely.' Sophie paused. 'I've got to go. I need a proper chat with you and Dad, but not by phone. Next time I'm home, eh?'

'Of course, pet, we'll always have time to chat.'

'I love you, Mum.'

'I love you too, pet.'

Then the phone went dead, the house so tomb-like that Alice felt acutely conscious of being alone. The second workman had disappeared. Ezal was stripped to the waist as he balanced the final pieces of scaffolding against the wall. He was about to slide the poles over the wall and then climb into the lane to arrange everything for collection. Then he would be gone. With the scaffolding removed, Alice could see the town house properly for the first time. The interior needed to be finished, and her garden was a mess. But Chris had built this for her. Alice had refused to engage with it out of self-protection, having had her hopes dashed too often. After all her disappointments, she had been too scared to believe that anything good could happen. But now she could properly see what her husband had achieved.

She still thought that Paul Hughes's mother would find the town house small. Mrs Hughes possessed a gentleness, which Alice respected. She had borne her husband's early death with dignity. Her gentility was never lessened by seeing her son's antics splashed across the social columns. While Paul Hughes was seducing girls half his age by flying them in private planes for intimate dinners in Tangiers – one hand entwined in theirs and the other texting details of the cost involved to the press – Mrs Hughes had been queuing in the post office like every other pensioner, and then slowly wheeling her trolley around Blackrock shopping centre. Only in recent years, when her arthritis grew so bad that she could barely grasp her antiquated linen shopping bags, had she succumbed to the luxury of taking a taxi home.

Last month Alice had been surprised to receive a phone call from Mrs Hughes, asking Alice to visit her. The woman asked her to say nothing to Chris, and spent the first half of the visit reminiscing about how Alice, as a girl, had sometimes shyly called in to ask if her friends could use the tennis court, and would always come away with the gift of a bag of apples from the orchard. Alice had expected to be quizzed about the town house, but instead Mrs Hughes had asked Alice if she would drive her to Molesworth Street in Dublin. Her son had set up a taxi account for her, but she had private business, and she trusted Alice. Alice drove her to one of Dublin's oldest firms of solicitors, where the receptionist served Alice coffee while she waited on an antique sofa in the hallway. Afterwards, when Mrs Hughes suggested a second coffee, Alice had expected her to visit the Westbury Hotel or the Four Seasons. Instead they went to a tiny cake shop in Donnybrook, where Mrs Hughes knew the waitress by name, and where she again asked Alice to keep their 'little excursion', as she called it, private.

Alice was determined to walk around to the lane every morning to make Mrs Hughes feel welcome during the short period when Chris and she would remain living here. Seeing the town house stripped of its scaffolding, Alice now no longer possessed any doubt that they would move. If Chris had the courage to build this, despite the objections of neighbours, then surely he would be the last man standing at the next auction. Why, then, had Chris disappeared? What if he had done something crazy? Alice needed to think rationally, but it was hard to be rational on her own. An overwhelming fear consumed her. Ezal was heaving the final piece of scaffolding over the wall. She couldn't bear to be left alone. Alice opened the back door. The manic way in which she ran down the garden must have startled Ezal, though he gave no sign of it. Ezal perched on the wall as if trying to ascertain what she wanted.

Then he dropped down into the garden, one hand reaching out to pluck his shirt off the wall.

'You will excuse,' he said. 'I am not dressed for company.'

She tried to look away, but her eyes were fixated by his naked torso. Not by his muscles, dappled with beads of sweat, but by an old wound on his ribcage. She wanted to touch it in childish fascination.

'Is that a bullet wound? I've never seen one before.'

His eyes followed her gaze. 'You still haven't.' He seemed gently amused. 'That is only a stab wound, badly stitched up.'

'How did you get stabbed?'

'I was in the wrong place. Sometimes we don't get the choice to be in the right one.'

'Where is your home?'

'I share an apartment with Jiri in Carrickmines, overlooking the M50.'

'I meant before that.'

Ezal carefully donned his shirt. 'I have no home.'

'Everyone has a home, even if you don't want to return there.'

'How can you return to a place that no longer exists on a map, or at least not under the name you once knew, or as part of the country you were born into? I am sorry to disturb your bank holiday. The men collecting the scaffolding later will only come into the lane.'

'Are you hungry?'

'Thank you, no.'

'Thirsty?'

He paused. 'If a glass of water is no trouble?'

'Would you like tea?'

He glanced around to check they were unobserved. Alice wondered what exactly he thought she was offering. It might be safer to bring the tea outside to him.

'Tea would be good,' he said. 'But not poisoned with milk.'

Alice started speaking before she fully planned what to say. 'Will you do something for me? This is hard ... I never before ... you see, I have no one.'

She stopped. Ezal said nothing. Alice couldn't stop herself suddenly imagining him naked. He would be utterly silent in lovemaking, concentrating on his pleasure, and then on giving her more pleasure than she had ever known. There would be no cajoling lies or male bravado. It would be a serious business. Every aspect of life seemed serious to Ezal. He would come with an economy of breath, but only when certain she had climaxed more than once. If she beckoned him into her empty house it would be a secret he would never mention to a living soul.

'What is it you need?' he asked, with solemn solicitude.

She banished these insane thoughts from her head, not sure where they sprang from amid her frenzied agitation. 'My husband is missing. I don't know where to look. I need your help to search for him.'

Ezal nodded slowly. 'If that is what you need.'

Chapter Twenty-Two

Chris

Monday 6th, 5 p.m.

This had to be the road. How many false leads had he followed before stumbling upon it, after spending all day tramping down potholed lanes where signs read *Road Private*? Half of Wicklow considered their roads to be private, though Chris suspected that this was probably the half of Wicklow where half of Dublin lived. He had felt exhausted when he abandoned his car, but had since passed beyond weariness into a state where his feet moved of their own accord, propelled more by agitation than any remaining energy. He had not encountered a single walker, though occasionally a car passed, children's faces peering back at him through rear windows. His sole companions were clusters of sheep roaming the hillside, coloured blotches of dye identifying their coats. Several times he knelt to immerse his face in brownish streams of water that tasted of peat, hoping the icy shock would soothe his headache. Each time, he shook his hair, like a dog shaking its wet fur, rested for a few moments, and then walked on.

But now he instinctively knew that he was on the correct track. He spied the windbreak in the forest to his right, and then the half-collapsed drystone wall came into view. The grass was curiously undisturbed where he parked last night. There was little trace they had been there. If he kept his mouth shut and turned back, he might still escape the consequences of his acts. Alice had stopped phoning, and even Ronan's number no longer kept coming up on his screen as Chris ignored every call. He had barely found this place in time; his phone was emitting warning bleeps that the battery was low.

He looked around. There were few distinguishing landmarks Chris could use to help an ambulance crew to pinpoint his location, but skilled mountain rescue teams could probably work with the barest information. He could always try knocking at the cottage back down the track to ask where he was, but there was no car outside the cottage, and the curtains were shut. This suited him, as he didn't want onlookers when the police came to arrest him. Chris steadied his nerve before confronting the spectacle of the corpse that had come to rest here last night, face upwards. Memories of that man's accusatorial stare had haunted him all day. Grabbing hold of the sturdiest section of wall, he carefully mounted the muddy bank to look down. The fall was as steep as he remembered, but to his astonishment the body was gone. The shock of this disappearance almost made him lose his footing. He felt a sickening sense of having been duped: this body could not be gone unless someone had moved it, or the corpse had risen from the dead. This last thought was ludicrous. But if hillwalkers had discovered the body, then Chris would now be gazing down at a crime scene sealed off with tape, a white tent covering the dead body while police awaited the state pathologist.

Was it possible that the man was never dead? His body had been cold, and surely nobody could survive this fall anyway? Chris looked behind him, half expecting to spy the workman there, eyes cold with hatred, a rock in his hands. But Chris was alone, and convinced that Ronan had already returned to tamper with the body. Ronan had known not to trust him. Hiding the body put Ronan back in control. How could Chris confess to a crime without a shred of proof? While Chris had been wandering across Wicklow, Ronan could have placed the body back beneath the faulty scaffolding on Chris's property, or abandoned it somewhere. Chris felt robbed of something he could not properly define. Not guilt, because guilt remained, but robbed of the retribution that was his due. In his exhausted state he realised that part of him longed to be found guilty of a definable crime and confronted by the finality of a slammed cell door.

Perhaps he would still be punished. Ronan could be stitching him up. Ronan was the ultimate survivor, impersonally ruthless when protecting his territory. Chris was certain of nothing any more. He peered down, searching for any clue on the rocks below. Could Ronan have filled the man's pockets with stones before dragging his body out to sink it in the deepest part of the river? Chris would never know unless he went down. He started his descent, but found the route too steep and was forced to turn back. As he did so, his footing gave way on loose stones. He had no time to call out. Chris's last memory was of a blue evening sky turning upside down.

Chapter Twenty-Three

Alice

Monday 6th, 5 p.m.

Alice didn't know if the hatchback belonged to Ezal or Jiri. The back seat was crammed with tools and copper piping. Alice was shaking, though not as badly as when she sat downstairs earlier, listening to the power shower in the bathroom, unable to stop imagining Ezal's body beneath the jets of water. She didn't know how she could think such thoughts, but she felt so agitated it was a struggle to think straight. Maybe she had needed to visualise Ezal's nakedness to block out thoughts of Chris's body submerged in a hotel bathtub, the water dyed with blood. Had she pushed him over the edge by subconsciously bestowing on him the role of the person who always had to solve her problems? Had he not understood that on most occasions when she quarrelled with him she was really quarrelling with herself? Her disappointment wasn't with their inability to change house, but with her own inability to change how she saw herself. All the subterfuge of these Sunday night excursions were part of a fantasy where she had imagined that, for some brief spell, she could escape from being the person shaped by her parents' incessant criticisms. Chris was simply too close to her, too entwined in her very being, not to get caught in the crossfire, where any criticism of his weaknesses were really deflected self-criticisms of her own flaws. Why had she punished the one person she loved for not living up to the impossible expectations she heaped on him?

If she spied Chris strolling along at Bullock Harbour she would strangle him for putting her through this search, but Alice felt certain that she would not find him. She glanced across at Ezal, who was concentrating on trying to spot Chris's car among the vehicles parked along the road. Ezal had been driving without complaint for two hours, parking illegally on footpaths when they checked public seafront car parks and hotel forecourts. He never asked why Alice wasn't calling the police, nor did he attempt to solicit any more details than the bare facts she outlined. Any opinions he had he kept to himself. Even amid her anxiety, Alice was annoyed that she looked a mess. She had barely managed to comb her hair. Stress was making her look old.

She could not tell what age Ezal was. The routine of physical work meant that his body lacked one ounce of fat. Nobody had seen them leave together, and Alice realised that she knew nothing about Ezal. He could drive anywhere, do anything to her, and there would be no witnesses, yet she felt safe. At first it was because she sensed an innate decency within him, but then she realised, with growing unease, that it was because, at some level, Ezal simply wasn't there. He patiently answered the anxious questions she seemed unable to stop repeating. He was alert to every passing car and male figure in the distance. But she realised that, fundamentally, his thoughts were elsewhere. Maybe this emotional separation came from whatever trauma had occurred that made him claim to have no true home. If Chris didn't return, Alice would emotionally be homeless too. Her phone rang, Ronan's number coming up. A call from Chris was the only call that she was willing to take. She wanted no more lies or manipulation. Ezal glanced across as she ignored the ringing phone.

'Who is it?'

'Ronan.'

'Ronan is ....' Ezal searched for a phrase. Alice wondered if it would be a term of abuse. Only when the phone stopped ringing did Ezal continue. 'Not a bad man ... but a little man.'

Alice glanced out her window. After searching all the familiar places, she had asked Ezal to drive wherever he thought a man might go. She had expected him to venture farther along the coast towards Bray, but instead he had strayed into parts of Dublin that she barely knew existed, a maze of endless apartment complexes off the M50 where everyone looked foreign. Was this where he lived; sharing a functional apartment with Jiri, buying food in shops with foreign signage, stocking up on beer in a Booze-to-Go outlet? An unscalable cliff of rooftops stretched ahead of her. Was this really still her native city, with place names and accents alien to her? The last time she felt so lost was as a girl in Toronto. She was exhausted. She looked at Ezal. There were no fantasies now of seeing him naked, no guilty thoughts of imaginary passion. Only one pair of arms could make her feel safe. If she could not touch Chris, then she wanted to finger the clothes in the wardrobe that retained his smell. Chris must be home by now. God had punished her enough. This new Dublin that Ezal was driving through looked vast and unknowable. The man sensed her unease and looked across.

'Tell me he's not dead,' Alice said. 'Tell me he hasn't done anything crazy, that you think he'll turn up.'

Ezal placed his fingers on her arm for the barest fraction of a second. 'Trust me,' he said, 'everyone shows up again.'

Alice stared ahead. 'Could you possibly bring me home, please?'

Chapter Twenty-Four

Chris

Monday 6th, 11 p.m.

The sky was ablaze with gargantuan stars when he woke. The base of his skull hurt, his joints were stiff, and his throat felt raw. He did not reach out for Alice. Chris knew that he was not in bed, and if he were, she would not be there for him. He knew precisely where he was. What he didn't know was how long he had lain here unconscious. His watch had stopped, its glass face smashed in the fall. Luckily no bones felt broken, although the only word to describe his condition was flattened; not just physically but mentally, so it felt difficult to summon enough willpower to rise.

His phone battery had died. Chris could only guess at the time. It might be 11 p.m. or 4 a.m. All he knew was that he needed to call Alice to reassure her, but even if his phone still worked, he didn't know what to say. His car had probably been located by now, but nobody seemed to have come looking for him. Not that Ronan would implicate himself by leading anyone here. The cliff that Chris had tumbled down looked impassable: there was no way he could scale it. His only option was to go in the opposite direction and try to cross the river by clambering between the boulders irregularly strewn amid the rapid current.

Tentatively, Chris waded out towards the first outcrop of rock. The water was freezing, yet its coldness restored his senses as he cupped his hands and drank, not caring if it was safe to do so. Perhaps it was crazy to cross this river in the dark, but he welcomed the necessity of focusing his mind on a task that left no room for other thoughts. Initially the distance between boulders made it easy enough scramble onto the next one. But midstream he reached a juncture where there seemed no way forward, and yet he was unsure if he could find a route back. His body ached from his earlier fall, and the additional grazes picked up each time he clambered awkwardly onto a rock. The water gushed so loudly that it seemed not only to hem him in but to pound inside his skull. Spray filled his nostrils and drenched his clothes until even his bones felt chilled. He needed to look away from the hypotonic torrent, within which not even the strongest swimmer could survive.

This felt like his worst nightmare, like God mocking his lifetime of indecision. He seemed to face a choice between death by drowning if he moved, or by hyperthermia if he remained clinging to this rock. He had no idea how long he was crouching there, frozen with terror, but unless he overcame his paralysis, he would lose his foothold and be swept into the swirling torrent. The next boulder seemed impossibly beyond range, but an instinct for survival made him leap towards it in the moonlight. He grazed his palms and ripped his trousers as he somehow reached the boulder, scrambling to get a grip on the soaked, mossy rock. But his exhilaration at having accomplished this suicidal leap was so overwhelming that it was several moments before the physical pain registered, and he became aware of a gash on his thigh. He struggled to catch his breath and fight against a dangerous urge to pound the slippery stone in triumph.

More treacherous leaps lay ahead, but with each jump Chris seemed fuelled by daredevil bravado. The secret was to stop thinking and ride this adrenaline rush. Each time he leapt through the air there were additional grazes when he landed, but finally his feet sank into bulrushes on the far bank. The rushes gave way to swampy bog that sucked at his shoes as he tried to find firmer tufts of coarse grass. He was freezing and his body ached, but he had successfully crossed over.

Ahead lay a dark hillside with tightly planted spruce pine forests. If the workman had somehow been restored to life, this was the only route he could have taken. The notion was ludicrous, but it seemed equally impossible for Ronan to have hauled his body back up that cliff. Chris had never felt so lost, yet oddly exhilarated. Old rules no longer applied.

That dangerous river crossing had freed him from being crippled by caution. Maybe all he needed was to be alone and answerable only to himself, without the additional weight of Alice's fears.

The stars still seemed unnaturally bright, a map of constellations he lacked any ability to read. Even if he could steer by them, he had no idea of what direction to take. He reached the forest and stooped to enter, blindly holding out his hands to prevent low branches from snapping back into his face. The ground was uneven, the undergrowth so dense that sometimes he needed to crawl. Initially he thought he was wandering randomly, but then he became convinced that a pattern existed to this journey, that his life over recent years had been leading to some sort of rendezvous out here in the dark. He no longer felt alone, and had the irrational sensation of summoned ghosts closing in. He was weak from hunger and wondered if it was possible that he could still be concussed. Or perhaps exhaustion was making him hallucinate. Not just the exhaustion of the past twenty-four hours, but a culmination of the stress caused by the inescapable realisation that his marriage had reached a crisis point.

Out here, he now felt certain that he was surrounded by the dead, that his parents and grandparents were with him in this forest, alongside ancestors whose features he had inherited. He was no longer a lost soul, but part of a chain of lives. Everything he was experiencing had already been experienced by them. He might be lost in this wood, but he was not alone. True isolation was sitting in gridlocked traffic on the Rock Road, listening to inane DJs and fighting against a sense of being eternally impeded, of being just another commuter shunted towards a glass office. True isolation was sharing a house with someone while being separated by an invisible wall of ice, a litany of slights making it impossible to traverse the few metres that divided you from the person you loved.

Out here, there was nothing to impede him, so long as he kept brushing aside the low branches. He sensed that the summoned ghosts walking behind him had become visible, yet he knew that he was not meant to turn around in case they scattered like startled deer. He no longer worried about the throbbing pain at the base of his skull: he was too focused on leading this expedition towards a still unidentified rendezvous. He wondered again, though, if he were suffering from concussion, because he became aware that he had emerged from the forest without any recollection of having left it. He was striding through a clearing where the ground rose so steeply that he soon began to seek footholds to ascend a slope so severe that normally he would never dare to attempt it.

Maybe he was experiencing a nervous breakdown. He began to feel the scratches where branches must have snapped against his forearm. Or had his nails caused them? Had he scratched at his wrists while walking, in atonement for having let Ronan manipulate him? Perhaps his rendezvous involved being brought to confront the workman's ghost that was also wandering through this darkness in search of retribution. Chris could not blame Ronan for what had occurred; he needed to take responsibility for his own actions.

A creeping white mist covered the hillside. Chris had never felt so cold. The ground flattened out as he attained a rough plateau. A huge rock stood at the centre. Chris instinctively knew what this was a Mass rock, where the outlawed body of Christ was raised in Penal times, far from prying authorities. Half-starved people had climbed here at dawn, silently taking paths known to mountain sheep, having fasted all night to kneel barefoot before a fugitive priest. Chris had long ago ceased to believe in any religion, but he accepted that this was where his ancestors had led him. Slowly, he walked forward to place his hands on the Mass rock. He took a deep breath, feeling foolish, even though he knew that the only souls watching him were the dead.

Chris closed his eyes and slowly turned. As a tiny child he used to be scared at night that ghosts might appear if he peeked out from beneath his bedclothes. Now he was scared of something worse. Opening his eyes, he saw his fears confirmed. Arrayed in silent ranks around him there was just emptiness. No ancestors or ghosts of kneeling Mass-goers were summoned by his distress. The white mist was receding. Before him a succession of valleys led back to the city, where his wife was surely frantic. Chris was freezing and starved and inescapably alone. Every act he had committed since leaving Blackrock was insane. He had drawn attention to himself by disappearing, while Ronan was probably keeping schtum. All that Chris was doing up in these mountains was running away from real problems. In Dublin there was an unfinished town house and a marriage that he needed to save. It was time to confront that reality instead of conjuring up phantoms in the dark.

He didn't know if he had the strength to descend this rocky incline, his legs so jaded that he could barely contemplate another step. But staying here was not an option. He turned to take a final look at the Mass rock. As he did so, he saw a figure walk towards him through the remnants of mist. Chris recognised him at once. He let him approach, wondering if the figure would even notice him. He knew his identity because of something Alice once said when they used to lie awake, confiding their innermost thoughts. *'You'll think I'm crazy,'* Alice once confessed, *'but I'm convinced that a second version of me exists. It's the girl who wasn't lured home from Canada by guilt. One winter afternoon she took the ferry back to Toronto alongside me, but she walked on past the phone box where I stopped to dutifully call home. It wasn't that she didn't love her parents, but she had her own life to lead … the life I might have led. My soul spilt in two that day: she walked on with my dreams, and I returned here to my responsibilities. I'm convinced she lives in a place named Tanglewood. Some nights if I can't sleep I close my eyes and imagine my other life. I walk around her house and touch her clothes. I put my head on her pillow and finally fall asleep.'*

Chris realised that he was staring at the unencumbered version of him; the Chris who lived in a parallel existence where he had made all the brave choices, the man who risked leaving the Civil Service for a private sector job with huge rewards. Chris recognised him because in his youth he had anticipated becoming this fearless man. This is the person I might have become, Chris thought; a gleaming success with stock options, contemplating early retirement and winters in an investment apartment in Portugal. This figure looked too real for Chris to be hallucinating, but Chris knew that he could not be real. The elegantly groomed daemon came face to face with him. There were questions Chris longed to ask: was Alice happy in this parallel existence? Had they retained their inalterable closeness? But Chris said nothing because this mirage could not see him: this man was too busy staring ahead towards the next challenge, with eyes that reminded Chris of Ronan's eyes.

Chris backed away as the figure passed and found himself staring up at the array of stars. He realised that he fallen over from weakness or hunger. Was he still concussed, or had he suffered brain damage in that fall? Chris scanned the hillside to see if the mirage had disappeared. A trick of the moonlight made it seem as if the figure had splintered apart into a dozen figures, each one dividing in two again at each fork in the track. Perhaps these specks of movement on the hillside were only wisps of mist, and his mind had disintegrated after years of trying to hold everything together. All he knew for certain was that he was going home to force Ronan to reveal the shallow grave where he must have buried the workman's body. No matter what consequences arose from calling the police, Chris would no longer feel split in two. He would accept responsibility and win back possession of his former self.

Chapter Twenty-Five

Ronan

Tuesday 7th, 1.30 a.m.

All day he had felt stressed and exhausted, yet now, when it was long past midnight, Ronan seemed physically unable to go upstairs. For an hour he had stood in this unlit conservatory, staring out at that accursed town house and willing Chris to appear. Lately there were numerous such nights, when he felt afraid to slip into bed beside the warmth emanating from Kim's sleeping body, scared that sleep would stand him up. Only once had he allowed anyone to stand him up. He remembered the torment at sixteen of waiting for two hours outside Dun Laoghaire Town Hall for a Loreto Dalkey girl, trying to look nonchalant while his humiliation grew.

It proved to be an important lesson. He had rarely let himself be humiliated in the decades since – or at least, not until he discovered how Paul Hughes had duped him. He remembered Hughes as an acne-strewn teenager, envious at dances as Ronan smoothly notched up conquests. Not that Ronan was ever callous with girls. With one exception, he remained on good terms with most of those he once slept with. Often he passed them, besieged by teenage offspring in the Dundrum Town Centre, or towing their husbands through January sales. Generally he was rewarded with a secretive half-smile of recognition, acknowledging a more innocent era.

But what Paul Hughes had done to him, and countless other investors, was different. Hughes had courted the gullible, and then truly fucked and forgot them. Ronan had never seen himself as gullible before, but he now felt like a naïve girl, sweet-talked, used and discarded. It was bad enough investing his own money in that worthless syndicate, but he had never done anything as dishonest as gambling away Chris and Alice's savings, even when committing the range of misdeeds that men are sometimes required to do to support their families. He had always slept soundly afterwards – too soundly for Miriam, who, as time corroded their relationship, complained that he snored. If he did, he had earned the right to snore, after providing Miriam with financial security by shovelling whatever unglamorous shite life required him to shovel, cutting those corners that quantity surveyors need to cut to earn repeat business in a booming economy.

Were another man's snores keeping Miriam awake tonight? But of course, toy boys didn't snore or complain or grow tired: their chiselled, manicured nostrils matched their chiselled marble cocks. Ronan knew he was being unfair. Miriam wouldn't consort with toy boys, but was still attractive enough to draw admirers. He wondered if she often slept with men, and if she compared their lovemaking to his. Most of all, he wondered if she missed him, despite her claims that he was impossible to live with. Miriam had been the one impossible to live with during their final years, when she increasingly drove him demented. Yet, at vulnerable moments like this, he desperately missed her. He had started to miss her from the very moment that he was relieved finally to see the back of her. Miriam would laugh at this, recognising the sort of contradiction which drove her daft. Ronan missed that exasperated laugh.

But this was one lesson that divorce had taught him: only physical separation allowed you properly to untangle the complex layers in your relationship with the partner who once shared your life. He did not miss their endless rows in later years, their entrenchment behind absolutist positions, the uncharted minefield that passed for daily life in a house where angry remarks could never be defused. He had been angry with Miriam during these outbursts, but mainly angry with himself, locked in a battle against his own failings. Miriam was such an essential part of his being that she bore the brunt of his anger without grasping that it was not directed at her. She was caught in the crossfire of an intractable civil war simmering in his soul. When this erupted, he couldn't prevent himself spewing insults, because she was his essential conscience, the sole part of him that was good. Miriam's inability to recognise this pain within him felt like an affront at such moments. Some men write poems to their wives to express their indivisible bond. When not bombarding Miriam with tokens of love, Ronan had only been able to express his need for her through screaming rows.

He had never shouted at Kim. They could prolong a silence after some mundane row, but they never fought with a fury so intense it felt like foreplay. His numerous acquaintances – apart from Chris, he possessed no actual friends – said that Kim suited him perfectly because he had never looked happier, but in his soul he knew he did not love Kim with the same intensity. He never possessed an urge to shake her in frustration, praying that she might decipher this fury as his only way of reaching out. He had often longed for Miriam to fuck him senseless during such rows, but the rows were never really about sex: they were about his need for someone to hold him until he felt secure and they could laugh about his intense vulnerability. Miriam had understood this insecurity early in their marriage when they forgave each other's irrational outbursts. This intuitive closeness had only withered when they were cast into the roles of protagonists during separation court proceedings.

Ronan had remarried quickly: without someone to care for he would drink himself to death. A second marriage was an unexplored peak, and, like a poor version of Hillary and Tenzing, he could leave no Everest unclimbed. But only now, released from the pressure cooker of his first marriage, did he feel that once again he was the man with whom Miriam originally fell in love. Miriam was liberated from having to live with his menagerie of competing personalities, but she must surely miss the boy she first encountered: vulnerable behind his cockiness, shyly revealing dreams that felt achievable because she believed in him. By the end, their love had been obscured by resentments. Their silences had congealed into paper, and this paper started to display the discreet watermarks and embossed letterheads of legal firms specialising in divorce. Their past ceased to be a treasure trove of shared memories, but an inventory to be fought over, some solicitor performing an autopsy on each possession, reducing it to a notional monetary value.

How could you quantify the value of an ancient queen-sized bed, whose worth stemmed from the memory of them having the audacity to buy it when penniless? This extravagant purchase had been their statement of intent. Tables and chairs could wait: this bed was the centre of their world. Over the years they could have easily afforded to replace it with a more deluxe version. Every other item of furniture was upgraded. He changed the windows twice, and replaced the slate kitchen floor before ripping it up again to install underfloor heating. Yet they never changed their bed, knowing that its memories could not be replicated.

Trying to place a value on that bed would be like attempting to value the oil painting which Miriam had admired in a gallery in a remote Tuscany village. Its worth stemmed from the surprise on Miriam's face at discovering it hanging in the downstairs toilet, unaware that Ronan had secretly arranged its shipment to Dublin. The true value of possessions lay in the memories they unlocked. Each of their chillingly itemised possessions had represented memories of a love that grew obscured, like rings of bark trapped inside a tree truck. Divorce was an axe taken to that tree. Only after the axe blows of a court case had rendered the trunk asunder could Ronan see the luminous rings of their first love made visible again. He needed only to close his eyes to see them as teenagers in jeans walking the crumbling cliff path between Greystones and Bray, penniless young lovers mesmerised by first witnessing a sizzling dish of beef in black bean sauce being served in a Chinese restaurant, a young couple keeping each other awake during the initial weeks of living in sin by trading precious childhood memories they never shared with another soul. This bedrock of childhood secrets had congealed into their private code, unbreakable until it was destroyed by dry legal terms in communiqués issued through solicitors.

'I can always tell exactly what you want,' Miriam used to say. 'It's whatever you can't have. Once you possess anything, you want to run away from it.' Ronan knew that he should go to bed and curl up against his new bride, who possessed the wondrous gift of being content. But Miriam's observation had captured him properly. Kim was not enough tonight because her sexual compliance was attainable. It was Miriam he wanted here now, just so he could tell her that, even when they had reached a stage of being unable to bear the sight of each other, they always amounted to more than an inventory of possessions. Of course, being honest, the last thing he wanted was for Miriam to materialise: he could cope with her scorn, but not with her pity.

Not that anyone had reason to pity him. Ronan had always handled himself well until Hughes swindled him. This town house had become a nightmare. To top it all, after manoeuvring Chris through the latest crisis, the fool had disappeared. Where was he? Not hanging from a tree: successfully tying a noose involved a level of mechanical competence that Chris lacked. Ronan suspected that he was stuck on a metaphorical ledge, paralysed by indecision, failing to summon sufficient courage to confess to the police. Hunger or hyperthermia or the need for a clean shirt would eventually lure him home. Ronan would soothe his conscience, or terrify him into silence, because he was good at analysing other people's weaknesses. He understood his own weaknesses too. What was really keeping him awake was an unfathomable dissatisfaction with his life, which verged on self-disgust.

He associated its onset with the time when he was finally acquiring the outward trappings of success, when his ability to navigate shortcuts allowed him to become a bit-player in the property bonanza. But the more that he was allowed to glimpse this world – with enormous fortunes made by investors with the courage to buy derelict sites and sell them for twice the price – the more he became aware of being excluded from the real action. He was unable to decide which league he aspired to belong to. One reason for his friendship with Chris was that Chris's paralysing caution allowed Ronan to feel good about himself. Compared to Chris, Ronan was a shrewd success. Likewise, he seemed a big man to migrants like Jiri and Ezal because he could conjure the only currency that they and his late father understood: a roll of banknotes so thick no elastic band could hold it.

In the opulent echelons where Ronan barely registered, however, cash was vulgar and prehistoric. Transactions happened electronically, assets changing ownership through impenetrable mazes of shelf companies in remote tax havens. Developers assembled portfolios with the brutal greed of conquistadors accumulating gold. Ronan was excluded from this world, apart from a drip-feed of hints dropped by

Hughes, who had used him for the same purpose as Ronan sometimes used Chris: an inconsequential nonentity against whom to measure his success. Hughes was a dead man walking now. But for all his love of the limelight, and gossip columnists' love of him, he was always only chicken shit compared to the real players, who already owned most of London and New York, and were buying up Eastern Europe. These maestros had grasped the true secret of money: that it is not actually real. After it soared beyond a certain figure, money was only an abstraction – the most important abstraction on earth. Nobody needed to possess the colossal figures bandied about. Nobody could even comprehend their magnitude. They just needed the balls to scrawl their signatures on loan forms. The bonus commission was so enormous that no bank executive could afford to fret about people's ability to repay. Their job was to sanction loans and then get them off their books and bully the staff below them to achieve targets, with the same intensity with which they were being bullied from above.

If Ronan's bluff were ever called, and he was asked to repay all his loans, his only option would be to enter his study and shoot himself. He suspected that Ezal could supply the gun. Ezal looked like a man to supply anything for the right price. But how could the banks ask him for what he couldn't repay when they knew that everyone was in similar hock in this frantic race to buy Ireland from each other? People owned so much that nobody really owned anything any more.

If he died tomorrow, what was he truly worth? How could he answer that when he no longer knew how to quantify anything? Maybe his father was right: the only worthwhile measure of wealth was a wad of banknotes held together by a rubber band. When he found the dead workman's body, it was his father's mocking tones he heard in his mind. Ronan's ruthless actions had been one way to block out that ghostly voice. But only now, when the crisis was over, did he realise that the workman's death had shocked him even more profoundly than he had previously imagined. He felt flattened, like he had felt as a boy for days after a particularly savage tackle on the rugby pitch would leave him sapped of energy as if the life-force were knocked out of him. In the immediate adrenalin rush of the crisis his brain had broken down the problem into a set of logistical hurdles, and he was adept at making problems disappear. Only afterwards do you realise that problems don't disappear simply because, like a magician, you make them appear to do so. On Sunday night he had done the smart thing. Squeamish people might call it immoral, but his actions were the practical solution to his family's security being threatened. But every time he was forced to make such a moral judgement call a part of him died – the boy who had once shared his dreams with a girl in jeans on the cliff path between Greystones and Bray, the youth whose judgement Ronan feared the most.

Ronan opened the conservatory doors and stepped onto the moonlit patio. He longed to be magically transported to the safety of his bed beside Kim. Surely a tangible lover was what any rational man would want? But reality made demands, and exposed you to the possibility of sexual humiliation. Ronan was fighting against compulsion, staving off the moment when he re-entered the house en route to bed. He knew that he was unable to pass his office without turning on his computer in the pretence of checking email. This happened every night; all that varied was for how long he held out against the impulse. Afterwards, he barely remembered what videos he viewed: they merged into a nightmare narrative without a beginning or end. It was no longer a way to forget his problems, but a way to lose his identity. Once he clicked on that mouse, it took possession of him. He lost his sense of responsibility, and was freed from the need to think. He became a hollowed-out shell without any free will. Ronan knew that he could not hold out for much longer against the lure of this cyberworld. Compulsion would compel him to enter his office and become a cipher, or maybe his true self – the ravaged Dorian Gray portrait locked in the attic. Pornography was the loneliest way to keep loneliness at bay, the crack cocaine of the respectable classes, a nightmare in which nobody could reach him or make demands. Just now it seemed to be the only place where he could truly feel at home.

Chapter Twenty-Six

Chris

Tuesday 7th, 1.30 a.m.

How long was it since he left the Mass rock? Chris found it impossible to retain a sense of time. He was struggling through woodland again. When had he last spent a night on these hills? Not since being in the Catholic Boy Scouts. He could recall his pride in his uniform, how it bestowed a sense of belonging, and more importantly, of preparation. Camping up here as a scout had seemed to mark another stage in the audition to enter the unfathomable state of adulthood, an induction and rite of passage towards a time when he would be able to handle every situation. But nothing prepared you for adulthood. As a boy he had been propelled by an anticipation of great feats to come. Even during Alice's illness he had believed that time would compensate them for their bad years. But now, walking exhausted through this forest, he accepted that this too had been a childish illusion.

His body felt so cold that he worried about hyperthermia. He also had an irrational sensation of being watched, as if somebody were tracking him, a hunter practised at soundlessly stalking deer or men. What did he know about the men building his town house; taciturn, muscular figures like Ezal, who rarely wasted words? Disbanded Special Forces were rumoured to work alongside carpenters and bricklayers on Irish building sites. What skills did such militiamen learn? Could they fake their own deaths? Surely that workman was dead when they placed him in the car boot, but who else would be stalking him, unless unknown forces were involved in that man's death, using Chris as a pawn in their bigger game?

He felt certain of nothing, unable to think straight, plagued by delusions and paranoia. But how could something be paranoia when it was true? As he emerged from the trees, Chris saw the moonlit sheen of a small lake a hundred yards below him. The foreign workman had not bothered tracking Chris: instead, he had patiently waited for Chris to find his way to him. Accepting the futility of trying to avoid his retribution, Chris walked down to confront the workman whose body he had dumped over that cliff. The man was stripped to the waist, his naked torso illuminated by a small fire, which revealed an open-backed van parked on the lakeside track. Calmly glancing towards Chris, the workman shrugged and reached down to pick up a weapon. He swung the weapon, but swung it away from Chris, out across the lake. Chris realised that it was a fishing rod.

The figure turned his back on him, impassive, incurious and indifferent, and as Chris studied him in the glow of the fire, he knew he had been mistaken. This man was also East European, possessing the same solid build, shaven head and seriousness of purpose as Jiri's workmen, but up close his features were unfamiliar, and certainly not those of the plasterer. Chris always tried to make such foreigners feel welcome when they worked in his garden. Now Chris felt like the intruder, the foreigner out of his depth, especially when the silence was broken by laughter from a young woman lying on a blanket near the fire. Several beer cans lay at her feet, but her amused tone contained no trace of drunkenness. At first Chris imagined that she was laughing at his torn clothes and dishevelled appearance, but she was eyeing her companion, who solemnly adjusted the amount of drag on the line while turning the handle of his closed-faced spincast reel. She only glanced up at Chris when he approached the fire, shivering with cold, suddenly so exhausted that he was unsure if his legs could take his weight.

'Lajos works so many night shifts that he even thinks the fish in this lake clock in at midnight. The only fish still biting are in the sea.'

Her companion acknowledged neither her teasing nor Chris's presence. He seemed absorbed in winding in his line, as if he had trained his mind to deal with one problem at a time. Chris couldn't decide if he were hostile or welcoming. He suspected they would have been less hospitable if Chris had stumbled across them an hour earlier. The young woman's playful tone and the way she languidly stretched on the blanket suggested that they had recently made love. Chris thought that Lajos intended to ignore her remark, but then the man replied without looking back.

'We caught enough trout before the light went. We would be gone from here hours ago if you hadn't distracted me. I am making sure this rod is working before we meet the others on Kilcoole Beach.'

'Do you do anything at night other than fish, Lajos?' the young woman asked in her East European accent.

Setting down his rod, the man turned to observe them both. 'I have other uses.'

She pulled a face. This coquettish mockery seemed part of a post-coital ritual, made more intimate for being played out before a stranger.

'I told you to pack up,' the man added. 'At Kilcoole you can wander between the tilly lamps and gas heaters and annoy other people with your silly talk.'

'I'll talk so loudly I'll frighten away the fish in the sea. Then I might see my bed before dawn.'

Lajos shrugged, dismantling his rod. 'All you've been doing since sunset is lying down.'

The woman looked fifteen years younger than Lajos. Their teasing playfulness stung Chris, reminding him of how, after Alice and he used to make love unexpectedly, they would find excuses to brush against each other, the afterglow infusing every seemingly trivial comment. He felt such a ravenous hunger now that he couldn't stop eyeing the discarded food near the fire: a meatloaf with an inner lining of hard-boiled eggs, and an unfamiliar type of flatbread. The woman followed his gaze.

'When did you last eat?' Concern replaced playfulness in her voice.

'I'm not sure. What day is this?'

She laughed, and then realised Chris was serious.

'You do not know the day?'

'My car broke down, and then I fell down a cliff. I've been walking for so long I have no idea what time it is.'

Lajos said something, and she replied in English, as if insulted. 'Do you think I would let him go hungry?' Chris hunched beside the fire, unable to stop his teeth chattering. She washed a plate in the lake, dried it with her skirt and brought it over to him, filled with food. 'We call this *stefánia szelet*. The bread is *lángos* … like Hungarian pizza. I made plenty to share with the others later. It is half past two. Do you want a beer?'

Chris nodded. When she handed him the can, his fingers were too freezing to open it. The fisherman prised it open and hunched down beside Chris, glancing back towards the woods from which he had emerged. The taste of the alcohol sickened Chris, yet also revived him. He tried not to eat too fast under the gaze of these foreigners.

'The beer is strong,' Chris said. 'I've never heard of this brand.'

The girl laughed, tidying up her possessions. 'That is because you do not buy your beer from behind a grille in Booze-to-Go.'

'You look more like a wine man,' Lajos said. 'Port, brandy ….'

'Do I smell of brandy?'

'You smell of fear.' Chris's eye was drawn to the bloodstained knife on the grass, which the man had used to gut the fish he caught earlier. 'Is someone following you?'

'What makes you say that?'

The woman paused as she loaded up the van. 'You keep glancing back at those trees.'

'I'm nervous.'

'You should be, all alone up here. You look like you need another beer.'

Chris had drained the first. It might be dangerous to get drunk among strangers, but his throat was so parched that he could not refuse when the young woman knelt to offer him the second beer. The alcohol went straight to his head, and he realised that he didn't know what to say to these people. The usual questions, like 'how long have you been in Ireland?', sounded trite and patronising. The young woman smiled at him. Her skirt was short. In the firelight he saw how the buttons on her blouse were rearranged out of sequence, as if she had been too relaxed after lovemaking to do them up properly. Why had he only noticed this now? Could she have deliberately readjusted the buttons when packing the van so as to toy with Chris? He tried to prevent his gaze lingering on her breasts in case it made the fisherman jealous. Might this be some sort of post-coital game, Chris beaten up when his eyes strayed over some boundary? What type of couple remained this late in the mountains? In recent years several girls had disappeared up here. Chris had no idea where he was, he just knew how alluring the young woman looked and how Lajos was observing him in a sardonic manner.

'You say your car broke down?'

Chris nodded in reply to him.

'The only road for miles is this dirt track. We saw no broken car. Your face is scratched. You should see a doctor.'

'I lost my way in the forest. The branches are sharp.'

'As a woman's nails,' the girl said. Chris couldn't decode what lay behind her teasing. 'Are you a ladies' man? What is the phrase ... a crime of passion?'

'It was nothing like that.' Chris stared out across the lake, deliberately avoiding eye contact with either of them.

'No jealous wife?' she added. 'That would be nice for a change. You must have done something. Did you rob a bank?' Chris realised that she was more drunk than he had previously thought. There was an edge in her remarks not directed not at him.

'Men like him don't rob banks,' Lajos told her. 'They work in them ... white-collar crime. In Ireland you only get arrested if you steal a loaf of bread.'

'I stole nothing,' Chris said quietly. 'I'm trying to go home ... my wife will be worried.'

'Have you children?'

'A daughter of nineteen.'

'My daughter is seventeen. She lives with her mother. I send her things.'

'She sends me back things.' The young woman rose, agitated. 'Swear words no female should call another.' She returned with the blanket, which she placed around Chris's shoulders. 'It feels cold now; I am putting on my jacket.' She moved into the darkness, gathering up any remaining items. She had not raised her voice, but Chris registered her deep upset. Lajos glanced after her, then looked at Chris, his tone confiding, father to father.

'Piroska is closer in age to my daughter than to my wife. It makes it awkward for them both, though they have never met, but with Facebook everyone sees everything. Piroska is a free spirit. She posts photos of us, not thinking that sometimes it is wiser to be cautious. Photos make no difference to my wife. We reach a crossroads long before I leave to find work in Ireland. I send her more money than I could make at home. My separation had nothing to do with Piroska: I only meet her two years after I come here. But my daughter and Piroska are like a wound in each other's side. Daughters expect their fathers' lives to be simple. If life were simple, we would not end up meeting here in the dark.' He observed Chris closely. 'Are you in trouble?'

Chris nodded.

'Woman trouble?'

'All kinds of trouble.'

'Is your daughter waiting at home with your wife?'

Chris nodded. It seemed simpler to lie. Being the fathers of daughters had forged a bond that bridged their circumstances. 'I wanted to protect them. All I've managed to do is fuck everything up.'

The woman had finished packing, and sat at the open van door, smoking, framed by a weak light from inside the vehicle. She seemed lost in her own thoughts.

'Fathers always fuck up. We try too hard, spending our lives trying to see around corners. I don't want to know what trouble you are in, but I envy you having a wife and daughter waiting at home to tear you limb from limb. I thought nobody could scream louder than my wife, until I heard four bare walls scream at me.'

Chris glanced toward the van. 'You and Piroska don't live together?'

'No we don't. But it is what she wants.'

'And you?'

'Piroska wants me all to herself. But I have too many ghosts. Can you fix this thing you've screwed up?'

'I don't know.'

'My daughter is almost a grown woman. But I would still give anything to put her childhood back together for her and make it right.' He rose and called across to Piroska. 'This man refuses my gift of rainbow trout. You will have to cook them all yourself.'

She stubbed out her cigarette and climbed into the van. 'Fish Monday, fish Tuesday, fish Wednesday, what a lucky girl I am!' She slammed the door.

'You're in her bad books,' Chris commented.

The man smiled. 'Sometimes it is good to be in her bad books, for the fun I have becoming her friend again. She is a good person. She deserves better than me. I am one lucky man. We are meeting friends at Kilcoole. There will be night fishermen driving back to Dublin. I will arrange a lift for you. Climb in and get warm so I take my blanket back. Too many good memories are wrapped up in that blanket.'

Chapter Twenty-Seven

Ronan

Tuesday 7th, 2.30 a.m.

Ronan didn't know how long he was standing, lost in thought, on that patio, when he heard a movement behind him, almost imperceptible, but loud enough for him to sense that another human being was watching. It was illogical, but he half-expected to be confronted by the workman's corpse, or Chris's ghost with a noose around his neck. He would have preferred any ghost to the sight of Kim in a white dressing gown. It was out of character for her to come down at night.

'What are you doing out here?' she asked quietly.

'Does it look like I'm doing anything?' Ronan was immediately defensive.

'Are you expecting somebody? You look startled.'

'It's just that you never come down. You'll catch cold in that nightdress.'

'I'm not as fragile as you think.'

'All the same, you should be in bed.'

'You should be there with me.'

Ronan turned to survey his amputated garden. The high wall he intended to build would block off the town house's natural light, but hopefully they could find a first-time buyer unable to afford to care, someone desperate for a good address to use as a springboard up the housing ladder. 'I'm too tired tonight.'

'You know this is not what I mean.'

'How do I know what you mean? I feel old in my bones just now, not able to do things I once took for granted.'

'Life is not a competition, Ronan; you don't always need to compete.'

'Maybe life isn't a competition in Manila, maybe they're happy as pigs in muck over there, but trust me, it's a dog-eat-dog world here.'

He hadn't meant this remark to sound so deliberately cruel, but barbs were his default mechanism to keep people at bay when he felt this vulnerable. Miriam would have responded with equally sharp words, but there was no anger in Kim's reply; her voice so low that he knew he had wounded her deeply.

'I do not come from pigs in muck.'

'I know, Kim. I'm sorry. When I'm rattled I say things I don't mean.'

'You know nothing about Manila.'

'You're right.' Apologetically, he turned to face her. 'Don't be offended, please.'

'The longer I live with you, the less I think you know about life.'

'I know too much.' He smiled in a way that normally made her smile back. 'My bones betray there's almost twenty years between us.'

'Then why are you still a schoolboy, competing to prove you own the biggest toy? Why have you not figured out the meaning of rich and poor?'

'I know what poverty means,' Ronan said firmly. 'My father needed to rebuild his business after losing everything when I was young.'

'He didn't lose everything. Nobody here loses everything, there are always safety nets, welfare payments, supplements … I can show you true poor in Manila, shanty-town poor, mud-floor poor, tin-roof poor. I can show you my father spending every hour making money any way he can; selling bottled water from our kitchen, cooking meals for passing workers, scavenging in rubbish dumps to salvage copper from scrap metal that rich people throw away. He will do this until he gets sick or dies because my father is *poor*. Poor means not having the things your family needs to survive. My sisters think I have married a rich man, but I finally understand I didn't.'

'How can you say that?' he asked, hurt. 'Name one single thing that you want for.'

'A husband who is content,' she replied. 'I always thought that being rich meant having the things you need, but a man like you will never have enough things. You can never show me rich, because no matter what you own you'll still desperately want more. You are poorer than my father is because you will never be satisfied, looking over your shoulder at some other property or woman.'

'That's unfair,' Ronan said, more stung by her composed tone than by any tantrum Miriam ever threw. 'I've never looked at another woman since the day we met.'

'You are too busy looking at other men, watching them eye me like meat. I know you care for me, but you cannot stop looking at other men. It's how you enjoy seeing me best, reflected back in their eyes. You enjoy their envy at you possessing an exotic butterfly. It lets you feel good about yourself.'

'I didn't marry you as a bauble to show off.' Ronan was angry now. 'I wanted a companion to share my life and work hard for. How can you say all this after I lifted you out of poverty?'

Kim drew herself up to her full height, her voice raised slightly. 'I lifted myself out of poverty by working hard to gain the chance to study, by making sacrifices for years before we ever met. I lifted myself up by finding the money to come to Ireland and then sending home money to lift my sisters out of poverty too.'

'You were living in a squalid bedsit when we met, being ripped off by a landlord, until I put the fear of God into him.'

'I never asked you to threaten him with your tacky showbiz solicitor friend with the toupée,' Kim said. 'You did that behind my back. I'm old enough to look after myself.'

'Really?' Ronan could not prevent sarcasm from entering his voice, another automatic defence mode. It provoked an icy anger within Kim.

'Don't use that patronising tone. I'm no child. You do not know what I've seen, what I've lived through. You know nothing about me.'

'I know you're my wife.'

'I fooled myself into believing I was, but I feel like your latest accessory. You acquired me like men acquire villas in Portugal, to make other men jealous.'

'That's unfair.'

'Life isn't fair. It's not fair that my family in Manila own too little and you have too much, yet all you yearn for is more. When will you be happy?'

Ronan stepped towards Kim, trying to put his arms around her.

'Come here,' he whispered. 'It's late; you're just upset.'

'Fuck you. I'm not just upset.' She pushed him away. Her words stung. He never heard her swear before.

'Don't curse, please. It's ugly.'

'You always curse.'

'I'm different.'

'Why?'

'Just don't curse, please.'

'Fuck you.' Her voice rose, as if determined that every neighbour should hear. 'Fuck you for turning me into an ornament. Fuck you for making me lonely.'

She looked different in the moonlight, a puzzling stranger he desperately wanted to know.

'I've tried to give you everything I can,' he said.

'I never wanted *things*,' she said, her anger abating, her voice so low that she sounded lost. 'I just wanted not to be lonely any more.'

'I didn't know you were lonely. I thought you had everything you wanted.'

'So did I, playing my part in your fantasy, emailing my sisters pictures of our kitchen and all your gifts. I was as dumbstruck as they were, grateful that you wanted only to please me, to give me everything I wanted. And you would too, Ronan, because you are a good man.'

'I only ever wanted for you to be happy.'

'You wanted to buy me happiness, and I let you try. I sold myself, like the girls I saw outside bars as a child.'

'Don't say that. Don't compare anything we did with ....'

'I didn't know I was selling myself, any more than you realised you were buying me. I was the little girl who suddenly finds herself inside a sweet shop.'

'And I was the lecherous shopkeeper?'

'No.' Kim softly caressed his cheek. Ronan had explored every part of her body, but this touch from her felt different. It contained a raw sympathy. 'You were a little boy with huge eyes staring in the window, desperate to buy me every sweet. Is this the only way you can be happy, by buying things for other people? What about making yourself happy?'

'Do you love me, Kim?' he asked. 'Forget this house, take away my vanity and bullshit. Look at me for what I am – an ageing man – and say if you love me or not.'

'How can I answer when I don't know you? What are you doing, standing here in the dark?'

'Looking at that blasted town house I want to smash down, brick by brick.'

'Then why build such an ugly thing?'

'Because I saw a business deal that I thought could be done. I genuinely believed I had a buyer. I was lied to.'

'Do you even need the money?'

Ronan looked at her. 'When your father is not slaving at some other job, does he really need to scavenge in a rubbish dump, poisoning himself to extract another few kilos of discarded copper?'

'My father is poor.'

'When would he decide he is rich enough to stop? How much copper would he need before feeling confident his family was secure? Would he ever feel truly secure? Is he so different from me? It's in his DNA to keep working. There's nothing more dangerous than the moment you relax: it's when everything falls apart. I thought my future was sewn up until my divorce settlement cut everything in half. I let Miriam's lawyers fleece me. I only rowed with them when I felt they were fleecing her by charging too big a fee. I made provision for our daughters, even though they refuse to speak to me. I did these things because it's what a man does. It gives him purpose. I honoured my responsibilities, like your father feels he is honouring his, behind goggles in some godforsaken rubbish tip. This is who we are as men. It's why I built this town house, to secure your future, so you would be financially independent, like Miriam and my girls are.'

'You still love Miriam, don't you?'

'I couldn't live with Miriam.'

'My father comes home exhausted, but then he can relax. You are always on edge. Maybe it's yourself you can't live with.'

Her words stung, like echoing remarks that Miriam used to make, recommending life counsellors as if he were someone who needed help. 'When did you become a head shrink?' he asked. 'You were a nursing attendant, grateful that anyone even noticed your lonely existence, when you placed an ad on that internet dating site.'

'We promised to never talk about how we met,' Kim said, wounded.

'I was good enough for you when you were lonely. You had no complaints about me being too old back then.'

'Your age isn't what's making me lonely. I cannot build a marriage out of being grateful, Ronan. I'm finished with being grateful.'

'Is it money then?' he snapped, disconcerted to his core. 'Miriam said that was all you were after. What do you want, half the house? Take the whole fucking house. I'll have Jiri build a higher wall and move into the blasted town house myself.'

'This is not about money,' she said. 'Why do you always think everything is about money?'

'In the end, everything is … money and, in your case, an Irish passport.'

'Why must you always say hurtful things when I try to get close enough to understand what's wrong with you?'

'There's nothing wrong with me. Why do women always think there's something in me that needs fixing? I'm just tired tonight. I'll go upstairs and prove there's nothing wrong with me if you'll give the Viagra time to work. Is that what it will take to leave me alone? If I fuck the living daylights out of you, will that prove there's nothing wrong with me?'

'What's wrong with you is that you are like a fist clenched so tight your knuckles are white. At first I thought you were strong. You made me feel safe here. But you're not strong. My father is poor, but he takes responsibility for his actions like a grown man.'

'What does that mean?'

'Why has Chris disappeared?'

'I don't know.'

'You could be honest … show me what type of husband you really are ….'

Ronan sat down wearily on a patio chair.

'A husband who loves his wife too much to implicate her in anything.'

'Husbands and wives don't have secrets.'

Ronan nodded. 'In a perfect world, yes, but the real world is messy and sordid. I try to do my best for people. I think I have every angle covered, but life never works out the way you expect. I'm scared, Kim. Ever since we married I've been scared of losing you. You're the one thing that makes me feel good about myself. If you want to leave, that's okay. I'll ask my own solicitor to represent you. He's a pit bull, but he won't have to be; I won't contest anything. We're mature adults. We can separate without falling out. If that's what you really came down here to tell me tonight, then I won't stop you. If you're unhappy I won't try and make you stay.'

'I came down to try and find out what type of husband I have,' Kim said. 'Bricks and mortar won't make me stay. Money won't make me stay, no more than being shouted at when you're scared will drive me away. Only loneliness will drive me away. If I must be lonely, I'd sooner be lonely on my own. Before we met, I needed to work hard for everything. You seduced me with comfort; you cocooned me inside this soft world. But luxury is not what I need you to give me. Find Chris and bring him back safe, no matter what trouble that causes. If you want to give me something special, give me a husband I can respect as much as I respect my father.'

Chapter Twenty-Eight

Chris

Tuesday 7th, 3 a.m.

Chris tried to watch out for his car on the tiny roads that Lajos drove along, but they travelled at such speed in the dark that he doubted whether he would spot it. Piroska sat between them. She remained quiet for a time, lost in thought, then leaned forward to switch on the radio and flick between stations until she found one playing 1980s' hits. Her foreign accent as she sang along made the familiar songs sound different, as if Chris was hearing them in a new way.

There again, it felt like he was seeing his whole life in a new way. He had never felt more exhausted, yet more alive. He fingered his stubble, realising that he had not shaved for forty-eight hours. He had taken a day out from his life, and now he didn't know if that life fitted him any more. Maybe this unshaven passenger, with a scratched face and torn clothes, was the person he had always secretly been during the years when he needed to concoct a disguise to bear the weight of being responsible for others. A poem came back to him that his English teacher had read aloud to the class during his leaving certificate year. All he could recall were half-lines and phrases:

> *In depths of rain among the tree shapes …*

> *Two trunks in their infinitesimal dance of growth*
> *Have turned completely about one another, their join*
> *A slowly twisted scar …*

He had rarely thought about that poem in the decades since. But whenever Alice would mention how – once they found their dream home – she planned to erect a wooden sign to christen it *Tanglewood*, this nightmarish image from the poem had flitted uninvited across his consciousness. Two trees growing too closely together in a wood so that they leaned into each other; their branches gradually entwining in an act of intimate embrace, but also of strangulation, supporting one another's weight as they competed for space and oxygen until, rendered inseparable, they slowly suffocated each other.

As Lajos's van hurtled towards Kilcoole, Chris felt that he was returning from a journey that had lasted far longer than one day. He was going home to Alice, even if he no longer truly knew who Alice was. He felt as much a foreigner in a foreign land as Piroska who sang along to the radio, or Lajos who teased her softly until they laughed, relaxed with each other again. They left Chris to stare out at his own face staring back in at him through the passenger window.

Lajos briefly joined the motorway and manoeuvred past a complex series of roundabouts, the last of which was overlooked by an apartment block incongruously perched beside it. The main street of the sleeping village of Kilcoole looked the same as Chris remembered it from years before. Then Lajos swung left onto an unlit lane leading towards the sea. Half a mile down it they passed a new housing estate amid empty fields, and eventually Lajos stopped where the lane ended, beside a tiny commuter station in the middle of nowhere, where Chris suspected that trains only stopped twice a day.

Seven cars were parked along the narrow roadway. Lajos got out and led the way across the train tracks, which straddled the shoreline. A wall of boulders had been erected to defend against coastal erosion above the shingle beach, but so many had collapsed during storms that Chris needed to pick his way carefully. By day this view might look beautiful, but it felt desolate in the dark. It was odd to discover this unknown world of night fishermen, though only a handful remained on the narrow stretch of shingle at this hour. Companionship radiated between these solitary figures, lit by white waves against the stones, by occasional lamps and Primus stoves. It took Chris a moment to realise that Lajos and Piroska had slipped away. He was unsure if they had deserted him until Lajos returned through the dark with an older grey-haired man in a woollen hat, wrapped up in several layers of jackets. Lajos handed Chris a chipped mug of coffee.

'This is Simon,' he said. 'Simon is heading back to Dublin.'

'I should have headed home hours ago,' the old man explained, 'but there's a decent run of surf with the easterly breeze. It's hard to leave when you get a bite on every cast, though they're hardy little buggers, turning on a sixpence to drag you back along the shoreline. You'd swear you had Moby Dick hooked, but all I reeled in was flounder and whiting so small it's a good thing I've only myself to feed. What part of Dublin are you aiming for?'

'Anywhere near Blackrock would be great.' Chris savoured the warm coffee.

'I'll be going straight through it, heading for the East Link Bridge.' Simon turned to Lajos. 'There's frozen peeler crab in a bag if you're low on bait.'

'I've bait in the van, and if Piroska drives me crazy I can throw her in.'

Simon laughed. 'Every man on this beach will hurl you in after her. She's the only reason half of us are still out here in the cold.' He surveyed Chris's scratched face without comment. 'Are we for the road?'

'We are.'

Piroska appeared from the darkness to give Simon a kiss on the check.

'Look after yourself,' she scolded. 'Even with three coats you look cold.'

'You needn't worry about me.' The man was unable to hide his pleasure. 'I'm one of the unkillable children of the poor.'

Piroska shook Chris's hand. 'I wish your scratch were marks from a woman: it would make a better story.'

'Thank you both for rescuing me.' Chris handed back the mug, and shook Lajos's hand also.

Simon's car was parked on the small road. Chris walked with him in silence, and sat in the passenger seat while the old man loaded his gear into the boot. Stripping off two of his jackets, Simon threw them onto the back seat before climbing into the vehicle. He looked at Chris.

'Do you know what I'm going to ask you?'

'What?'

'Fuck all, because it's none of my business. After I lost my missus to cancer I felt like a *Mastermind* contestant I had so many questions fired at me by concerned neighbours and my children if I did anything remotely odd. Sure, the only way I survived was by doing odd things. Shout when we reach wherever you want to jump out along the Blackrock bypass.'

'I'll do that.'

It was the last words they spoke on their journey to join the motorway, snaking through the Glen of the Downs and on towards the city. They travelled in the sociable silence of tired men unencumbered by curiosity, the polar opposite of the tense silence in which he had traversed this motorway with Ronan twenty-four hours ago. Going through Blackrock would take the old man out of his way, but Chris knew that he was in no hurry. Simon was not keeping loneliness at bay: he had made a pact to live with it, unashamed and unafraid. When they reached Blackrock, Chris tapped his shoulder at the traffic lights for Carysfort Avenue.

'I'll walk from here.'

The old man watched Chris step from the car. 'Good luck.'

'I'll need it.'

The lights changed. Chris crossed the carriageway and walked along the deserted main street towards the coast. A hoarding was erected around the Victorian building which burnt down on the night before Chris had lost at auction in the spring. He remembered walking these streets that night, pent up with anxiety, worried about what else he might lose if he lost that auction. Had the developer not outbid him, none of this would have occurred; there would be no unfinished town house, no dead workman, no secret binding him and Ronan. It tormented him that he didn't know where Ronan had buried the workman's body. But this was not the question really torturing him as he walked, the question he needed to ask the woman asleep in a house that no longer felt like home. Did Alice still love him, despite his flaws, as himself, the only true version of himself he could be?

Chapter Twenty-Nine

Alice

Tuesday 7th, 3.30 a.m.

Alice had no notion of how long she had been asleep, nor of how long she had previously lain awake, consumed with worry. The secret with insomnia was to lie still, not allowing her mind to race from one worry to the next. She had trained herself to think about characters in library books, to speculate on fictional lives instead of her own. Characters in books, no matter what ludicrous emotional webs entangled them, possessed a sense of knowing where their lives were going. The only certainty in Alice's life was that, without regular sleep, she was terrified of slipping back into illness. Tonight she had lain awake for hours, trying to block out her suffocating worries before eventually drifting asleep. She had no notion of how long ago that was. Alice just knew that she was suddenly wide awake.

A creak had woken her, someone sitting on her mattress. This intruder could only be Chris: if their house were in flames he would sit this quietly, hesitant to wake her, aware of how precious her sleep was and her inconsolability when woken. She sensed how this fear prevented him from stroking her hair. Alice ached for his touch, for the unselfconscious intimacy that existed before a cancer of secrets corrupted every cell.

Back when their love was uncomplicatedly absolute, Alice would have raged at him for waking her. Now she needed to remain calm and use these seconds, while he thought her still asleep, to prepare for whatever was coming. She felt flooded by relief at his return, yet dreaded what he intended to say. Alice knew her husband inside out. She knew that he longed to strip and lie beside her. He had always been such a comforting hugger, content to spoon for hours into her naked back, but now their relationship was so askew that he was incapable of doing so. Slowly raising a hand to remove her black-out sleeping mask, she saw Chris in the thin shafts of moonlight filtering through the wooden blinds. She expected a torturously complicated apology, but Chris was waiting for her to speak.

'Where have you been?' she asked softly, rubbing sleep from her eyes.

'I took a day off from my life.'

'That's not like you.'

His voice was low. 'We used to love taking time off from our everyday lives when we were just getting to know each other. We'd dare each other to phone in sick at work so we could cycle into the Wicklow Mountains. Remember starving ourselves to savour dinner in a restaurant we could barely afford, then lying awake in each other's arms in a remote B&B, exhausted from lovemaking but too wonderstruck at the magic of being together to fall asleep?'

Alice felt perturbed by this conjuring of precious memories. 'What has that got to do with you vanishing for a day?'

'You disappeared on me months ago.'

'Don't say that,' she said defensively.

'I came home one night to find this bedroom door locked. Suddenly I felt like an intruder in my own marriage.'

'Maybe I needed space,' Alice said.

Chris reached across the duvet and tentatively brushed his fingers along her bare arm. It felt like the ghost of a touch from a previous life.

'I've forgotten what it feels like to be loved,' he said. 'We were so close once that we shared the same heartbeat. Even when we bickered, we were like two halves of one soul feuding.'

'When a woman needs space, maybe it's because she's hurt.'

'What does that mean?'

His bewilderment annoyed her. Why did he need every emotion to be defined?

'I've been worried sick, and now you barge in, saying you ran away because I don't show you enough affection. Where have you been?'

'Off trying to regain my self-respect,' Chris replied. 'It's too late to regain yours. You saw me crack too often at auctions.'

'What's broken between us won't be fixed by buying another house,' she said quietly.

He nodded. 'I know that now. We've used our dream house as a panacea. It allowed us to never deal with our problems. We imagined they'd be miraculously solved when we unpacked them in a new set of rooms. I never needed a big house to feel wealthy. I felt rich beyond measure for simply having you. I only became poor the day you stopped believing in me. Today I resolved to win back the self-respect I lost watching you get dressed to meet strangers I don't know.'

'I've the right to a private life.' Alice longed to turn this into an ordinary quarrel: it sounded too much like a post-mortem on their marriage.

'Do you know how lonely it feels to stand at an upstairs window and watch the person I love disappear into another world?'

'I was lonely at a bedroom window for years,' Alice said. 'You can't just barge in at this hour and drag up things I don't want to discuss.'

'Are they too close to the bone?'

'Have you ever taken one risk in your life?'

'I stopped taking risks the day we met,' Chris said. 'Even before your accident you needed someone to wrap you in cotton wool. I was trying to mind you and raise Sophie.'

'I did everything I could for Sophie,' Alice replied. 'I brought her to medical appointments when I could barely walk. When she was sick I'd sit up all night watching over her. It killed me to hear you bang pots downstairs every evening. I grew to hate the rattle of my dinner tray being carried upstairs. This bedroom became a living tomb.'

'I know.' Chris entwined his fingers with hers, but this intimacy felt too much. Alice untwined her fingers, curling her body into a ball beneath the duvet.

'You don't know,' she whispered. 'I remember your every kindness, but also every time you cursed under your breath when the stress grew too much. I remember each slight, because words cut through me like a knife. You loved me, but it didn't stop you finding subtle ways to belittle me.'

'At times I reached the end of my tether,' Chris admitted, 'but I never belittled you, and certainly never in front of Sophie.'

'Not intentionally, but Sophie saw you throw your eyes to heaven when I couldn't cope with something that seemed minor to you. I could sense her eyes raised in reply, the silent code between you.'

'Sophie loves you,' Chris protested. 'What man wouldn't lose his rag occasionally, under all that pressure?'

'Another man might have walked away from all you had to cope with, especially with a wife too ill to respond to any caress. Another man might have found consolation elsewhere. Maybe you did likewise. You're only human, Chris.'

Chris reached beneath the duvet for her hand. Despite her reluctance, he held it firm. 'I was never unfaithful. I swear.'

'How can I know that?'

'Why would you think such a thing?'

Her fingers tentatively pressed against his. Her voice was hesitant.

'Things can play on a woman's mind.'

'What things?'

The duvet still separated them, but this moment felt as intimate as if he were curled naked against her. This was the conversation she longed to have, but had never been able to break free of the reticence instilled by her parents.

'I was such a worrier that I infected you with worry,' she replied softly. 'You'd have gladly borne all my pain … though I never understood why, because I felt worthless, especially after the crash. You couldn't take away my physical injuries, so you took on the burden of my worries and made them your own. One day when I felt stronger I looked up and saw that all the worries I wanted to escape from transferred onto you. I can't bear seeing you scrunched up in a ball of anxiety: it's too much like seeing my former self. My great terror is relapsing.' Alice paused. 'Maybe I need new friends who don't remember me crying with tiredness. A woman is entitled to secrets if they harm no one.'

'If secrets come between us they harm us.'

Alice withdrew her fingers. 'Is that what today was about, punishing me for wanting to keep one part of my life private?'

'Everything I've done for years was to try and make you happy,' Chris said. 'But today was about me. I was going to stop being manipulated by Ronan. I planned to recover a workman's body from the mountains, but when I found the spot there was no police cordon or corpse, like it never happened and we got away scot-free. But nobody escapes scot-free; everyone loses part of their soul. I can't run away from myself, so here I am, back to face the music.'

'What workman?' Alice was scared. 'Has Ronan led you into some sort of trouble?'

'I let myself be led. I have to confess something.'

'Tell me nothing that might hurt me, because I don't want to tell you anything that might hurt you.' She felt overwhelmed, woken from sleep to be confronted like this. 'Maybe we've both done stupid things, but we can save our marriage by not asking each other about them. You look so intense that I'm worried.'

'You fell in love with me because I loved you so intensely.'

Alice hesitated. 'Before you, a boyfriend hurt me badly. I never talk about it, but after him you seemed like burnished gold because I knew you'd never leave me.'

'I'd still walk through fire for you.'

'I realise now that I don't want firewalkers or fireworks. All I want is our old life back.'

'And I want no secrets between us.'

Looking away, she lifted her finger lifting a wooden blind to allow a wider slat of moonlight to fall across the bed. 'Most marriages are Sellotaped together with secrets. Whatever trouble you're in, I bet Ronan caused it.'

'There's a dead man involved.'

She looked at Chris. 'Did you kill him?'

'No.'

'Or cause his death?'

'Not knowingly … but I could be partly responsible … through negligence.'

'Whatever mischief Ronan has been at, you'd never knowingly hurt anyone.'

'I often hurt you by losing my temper when stressed,' Chris said. 'But no matter how intensely we fought, we'd always make love more intensely afterwards. When did we last make love, Alice?'

Alice adjusted the wooden blind and the shaft of light disappeared.

'I get hot flushes. I can't bear having you beside me in bed like a furnace,' she said. 'It kills me to see you make halves of yourself trying to please everyone. You set standards the rest of us can't live up to.'

'Are you saying you don't need me any more?'

'Since Sophie left I've needed the space to make my own mistakes and discover certain things for myself and about myself. Can't you just tell me if you still love me, and if so, let's pretend that everything else never happened?'

'I can't live with lies any more,' Chris said.

Alice reached for his hand. 'Lies are how marriages endure,' she whispered.

Chris withdrew his hand. 'These new friends have warped you.'

'I don't have any true friends,' Alice paused. 'I've been angry, Chris. I thought you'd cheated on me. Last September you went out one evening, acting so ill-at-ease as you made a fuss of saying you were going to the driving range with Ronan that I knew you weren't. Some instinct made me search the wardrobe. What I found caused me such panic that I asked Ronan on the following day if he had been out with you. He gave a typically ambiguous reply, delighted that my obvious anxiety gave him a sense of power.'

'What did he say?'

'Does it matter?'

'It matters to me.'

'He complimented me on still having such a nice body, almost as nice as when I was eighteen. But even if I had aged a bit, he said, my scar compensated for that … it gave my face a certain mystique.'

'The bastard.'

'Then he turned all solicitous and assured me that you had both been practising your golf and had a drink afterwards. But he knew that he had worked his mischief in planting a seed of doubt that maybe you were secretly seeing a younger woman. It was his revenge for me having taken Miriam's side. He knew I'd never dare repeat it back to you. He also knew that the more he kept trying to convince me that the pair of you had been out together, the more convinced I'd be that you weren't. His insinuation was that, if you were meeting someone, it was my own fault for not being as attractive any more.'

'I'd have killed him for speaking to you like that,' Chris said.

'You couldn't; you needed him as an alibi two weeks later when you went off again, mysterious and evasive. That second time I knew you weren't going anywhere with Ronan. You were going to see a woman, weren't you?'

Chris nodded slowly in the half-light.

'And not a woman you wanted to tell me about.'

He shook his head in discomfiture. 'I didn't want you to feel hurt.'

Alice was silent for a moment. 'It wasn't just the physical betrayal,' she said quietly. 'Your lie destroyed the intimacy we shared. Our marriage was like a warm room where I felt safe. Suddenly you'd opened the door to let in an icy wind. Was it worth it, whatever you and this woman did together?'

'We drank tea,' Chris replied, 'She opened a box of Jacob's biscuits some neighbour gave her at Christmas.'

Alice stared at him. 'Do you take me for a fool? You met some woman you can't tell me about and claim that you just drank tea?'

'We talked, more about your father than you. I'd have felt disloyal discussing you. She didn't want to talk about you either: your relationship got off on the wrong foot. I could see you were both too alike, too stubborn to ever reach out to each other again. Mainly we discussed Sophie … she seemed obsessed about Sophie.'

'You talked about our family to a stranger?'

'It was her family too … even if she spent her life cutting herself off. I knew you'd kill me if I said I was going to meet her. The only time she was ever in this house – the day she screamed abuse at you after finding her bewildered brother sitting on his doorstep – you made Sophie and me swear to never have anything to do with her. You'd get annoyed if I even mentioned that you had an aunt.'

'*Aunt Patricia*?! I can't believe she's still alive.' Amid her incredulity, Alice felt anger at Chris for going behind her back, but also at herself for letting her suspicions run wild. Chris had no business meeting her aunt, but so much loneliness and recklessness might never have occurred if he had told her.

'She was a formidable age and a formidable woman,' Chris said. 'The longest sitting tenant in the Mespil flats. Her walls were white once, but were now the colour of cigarette smoke. I doubt if anything had changed in her flat for decades, except for a new television set and the fact that she owned a laptop.'

'You had no right to seek her out,' Alice insisted. 'She never even bothered to attend her brother's funeral.'

'I didn't seek her out,' Chris replied. 'She sought out Sophie.'

'Then she has no right to barge in on our daughter's life.'

'That's what I knew you'd say, and you'd accuse me of always taking someone else's side against yours. But I wasn't taking sides in a family quarrel: I just didn't want to leave Sophie in the position of having to decide whether to risk annoying you by responding to a mysterious aunt who contacted her out of the blue. Last August Sophie showed me a friend request that Patricia posted on her Facebook page.'

'Are you telling me a ninety-year-old woman can use Facebook?'

'If they're as formidable as Patricia, yes. Sophie came to me for advice. I didn't like the idea of this woman trawling through Sophie's online photos, so I paid Patricia a visit. You're her closest living relative. I figured it might be better that I tell you how she was doing rather than have a social worker phone you up one day to inform you that you were once again legally responsible for an elderly person losing their mind.'

'You should have told me you were going to see her,' Alice protested.

Chris nodded. 'I know. But would you have come with me?'

Alice hesitated and then shook her head.

'You see?' Chris said. 'There was a pair of you in it. Patricia had no interest in being reconciled either. The more she kept insisting that she was no Prendeville, the more she sounded exactly your father. I planned to tell you everything after my first visit. I had even hoped that you and she might become friends so that Sophie would get to know one relation on your side, but things got complicated ….'

'Are you still in touch with her?'

Chris shook his head.

'But I remember you going out on other nights, acting shifty and feeding me lies. The last night you came back looking like you'd been jilted.'

'Patricia's physical heath was frail,' Chris said. 'A neighbour needed to bring her an *Irish Times* every morning, but she'd complete the Crosaire and Simplex crosswords by noon. She had a razor-sharp mind, and no desire for cosy family reunions. The only thing she wanted me to bring on my second visit was Sophie's PPS number.'

'Why?'

'Patricia had savings invested in An Post certs and bonds that were coming up for renewal. She needed Sophie's PPS number because she wanted to transfer some certs into Sophie's name. They won't mature for several years yet, but Patricia hoped that when Sophie finishes college this money will allow her to spread her wings and see the world if she wishes.'

'You let her give Sophie money without asking me?'

'It was Patricia's money … she wasn't giving it to you or me.'

'And Sophie knows about this?'

'Patricia swore me to secrecy on my second visit. She was a fiercely private woman. She insisted that neither you nor Sophie should know anything until the certs mature.'

'And you agreed with a stranger to keep your wife in the dark?'

Chris shrugged with sheepish awkwardness. 'She caught me off guard. I wasn't sure how you'd react, and to be honest I got greedy, not for myself but for Sophie. I didn't want to deny Sophie this money. I worry so much about money, how to find enough to move house, and how, after saddling ourselves with a huge mortgage, we'll have anything left to give Sophie a start in life. Sophie's not a child any more, she's a young woman suddenly, and kids barely older than her in Blackrock already have one foot on the property ladder. Patricia's money will give Sophie's opportunities that we can't give her. All I focused on was Sophie getting money for free in a world where nothing is free. It blinded me to everything, even the necessity of lying to you.'

'And did it never occur to you how panicked I'd feel at watching you go out, knowing from your body language that you were lying to me?'

He nodded. 'It felt so terrible to be keeping a secret from you that on my third visit to Patricia, when I was due to collect the certs reissued in Sophie's name, I was determined to demand the right to tell you. I wanted no more cloak-and-dagger stuff. If Patricia wished to give Sophie a gift then she'd need to meet Sophie and meet you, even though I knew that you'd go ballistic at me for suggesting such a family reunion.'

'Instead, you let Patricia bully you into submission. Is that why you came home looking so shaken?'

Chris shook his head. 'She wasn't there to bully me. She'd once told me that if I got no reply to my knock I could let myself in, using the key under her mat. Everything was the same, except that she was gone from her armchair and three envelopes were left on the coffee table. The first one contained €120,000 of saving certs in Sophie's name, alongside a photo of Patricia at Sophie's age.'

'How do you know it was Patricia?'

'She looked the spit of you at that age.'

'What was in the other envelopes?'

Chris shrugged, a wry admission of having been outfoxed. 'The second envelope was crammed with receipts from Dignitas in Zurich. They specialise in assisted suicides. She even left a receipt to show how she had paid in advance to have her body cremated and her ashes disposed of without ceremony in Switzerland. I felt stupid for not having realised how she'd been planning this from the start. She told me she once made a promise to you never to become someone else's burden. She was a resolutely independent woman who always took command of her life. She was still doing so, down to the last detail.'

'And in the last envelope?'

'A curt note to me with three instructions. Firstly, the name of the charity shop I should donate her furniture to. Secondly, an instruction that no memorial service should be held and no death notice printed in a newspaper. Thirdly, she repeated that you and Sophie were to know nothing about her death until the certs matured. I should have ignored her instructions, but you and I were going through a bad patch, and I was scared of making things worse because I didn't know how you'd react.'

Alice could vividly recall Patricia's flat. She had never returned, not wanting to give her aunt a chance to say *I told you you'd waste your life looking after a father who'd never thank you*. Alice could never decide whether, by offering to buy her a plane ticket back to Canada, Patricia had wanted to help her start a new life, or wished to score a victory over her brother, separating him from his daughter when grief had him at his most vulnerable. Nor did she know what motives lay behind Patricia's posthumous generosity to Sophie. Did she want to surprise Sophie with an unexpected inheritance, or ensure that the child had the money to flee if Sophie ever felt as estranged from her parents as Alice and Patricia had been from theirs? But by biding her time to surreptitiously re-enter Alice's life, Patricia had driven a wedge between a husband and wife who once implicitly trusted each other. Had paranoia caused Alice to make the greatest mistake of her life?

'The first evening you went out I found a packet of Viagra with three tablets missing,' she said. 'I knew from the purchase date that you hadn't used them with me. The moment just never seemed right to make love for weeks. Besides, surely you'd have told me.'

Chris held his head in his hands. 'Maybe I was too ashamed to confess to needing to use them. A woman can talk about how her body is changing. Mine is changing too, but I don't feel comfortable discussing it. I took Viagra on three evenings when Sophie was meant to go out and I hoped you and I might get some time together, but the opportunity never came because someone phoned or Sophie changed her mind. Viagra takes an hour to work, and I couldn't tell you in advance because our lovemaking, back when we made love, needed to be spontaneous. I was trying to prepare my body for such a moment, but it never came. I wound up feeling stupid for having swallowed them. My body gets tired. I didn't want you to imagine that it was you I was tired of.'

'Finding something hidden can make a woman scared and flustered,' Alice said, 'especially if she feels that something is going on behind her back. That's why I locked this bedroom that night in September. It wasn't just because I didn't want you beside me: I needed the space to silently cry without having to lock myself in the bathroom. I felt betrayed. I didn't know if I could ever trust you again. I wondered if you'd had other affairs when I was sick, or if you'd grown jealous at Ronan suddenly having a wife half his age. I know you find Kim attractive; I see you try so hard at times not to undress her with your eyes. I had no one to talk to. I could hardly ask Kim for advice. Every time I say hello to Kim I feel I'm letting Miriam down.'

'So what did you do?'

Alice was silent for a moment. 'I can never tell you anything because you're incapable of letting things go. You'll be forever harking back to it.'

'I've only ever wanted to make you happy,' Chris said.

'Nobody can make me happy except myself,' Alice replied. 'That's what I've realised. Not you, and certainly not the person I can't tell you about.'

Chris rose from the bed, his mind reluctantly trying to digest the meaning of her words. He retreated to the armchair, which was piled with her loose clothes.

'That's what you were doing, when I was trying to build this monstrosity in the garden so we'd finally have the money for our dream house?'

'We got so caught up in talk of a dream house that we stopped living in the present. I saw you worry yourself sick over a problem you'll never solve. There was this ball of tension in the place of the man I loved. Maybe I needed something more, someone who made me feel good about myself. Maybe at forty-eight I needed to rediscover what I'd already discovered at nineteen.'

'What's that?' Chris asked in a broken voice.

'That you're like a dull, burnished gold,' Alice said. 'The gold that dazzles is only wielded by schemers who take what they want and leave.'

'You slept with Ronan, didn't you?'

'What?' Incredulity entered Alice's voice.

'Before going to Canada. You never told me.'

'How was I to know that he'd end up moving in next door to us?'

'You claimed you were a virgin when we first made love. I wouldn't have cared if you'd had ten boyfriends, so why lie to me from the start?'

'I wanted to forget that my one night with Ronan ever happened, but I always knew he'd eventually use the knowledge to divide us.'

'Who else have you slept with?'

'I was faithful to you from the day we met.'

'Until when? I know there's something going on.'

In the past this was the sort of tilting point when their arguments descended into a cacophony of hurled allegations, but Alice's voice was bereft of emotion.

'I was angry. I felt insecure, and the menopause magnifies insecurities. But who says I've been unfaithful? Why must everything be black and white?'

'That's no answer.'

'Until recently I never knew how other people live,' Alice said. 'It might surprise you what women discuss after a few drinks. It surprised me. I was so naïve that I considered you to be a man of the world. Now I realise you're one of life's innocents.'

'Is this what you've been doing?'

'Maybe I needed to be around people with an edge of danger,' Alice said, defensively. 'I liked how when I went out some men admired me for who I am now, a good-looking woman for my age. I liked how they expressed an interest in my opinions.'

'Your opinions were the last thing they were interested in.'

'Well then, maybe I liked how some men still looked at me in that way, despite the scar on my cheek.'

'That scar is barely noticeable.'

'It's noticeable to me when I see the judgemental way that people around here continually look at it. Is it so terribly wrong to feel good about myself? Though I always need to keep one eye on my watch, knowing you'll be waiting up like a disapproving father, making me feel guilty the minute I walk in the door.'

'I'd the right to at least know who you were out with,' Chris said quietly.

'I was out with myself,' Alice replied, 'the person I'm not allowed to be when I go out with you. Sophie's absence gave me a glimpse into what the future might be like with just us two alone here.'

'So you found another man.'

'You don't know what I did.'

'Then tell me.'

'We've agreed to keep our secrets.'

'We never agreed,' Chris said. 'You simply decided.'

Alice was quiet for a moment. 'You're the only man who has ever counted in my life. Anything else would simply be sex, and would mean nothing afterwards.'

'How can you say that?'

'Maybe that's the truth for grown-ups, or the lie I consoled myself with when I thought of you sleeping with someone else. I wish to God I'd never found that blasted Viagra. Nobody gets hurt if nobody discovers anything.'

'Is that how your new friends taught you to think? Do you imagine they walk away scot-free in their hearts after each betrayal?'

'I can think for myself.'

'And what were you thinking, getting dressed up to meet this man?'

'It wasn't just one man. I fell into company with a circle of people.'

Alice looked away, agitatedly, her heart pounding. This conversation was intensely painful: it went against every instinct ingrained into her by her parents never to confront problems directly. Maybe her recent actions, so utterly out of character, had been another symptom of avoidance. Maybe all the subterfuge and risk had felt easier than having to open her heart and talk about her innermost feelings.

'Are you saying there was more than one man?' Chris asked.

She looked at him. 'One man made me feel especially good about myself.'

'And he's your secret … the man you slept with?'

'The man I nearly slept with. The man who brought me to the precipice of adultery, who rented a bedroom in the D4 Hotel in Ballsbridge every Sunday night for these past six weeks, who held my hand in the lobby when I said I just wasn't ready to go upstairs yet, and hid his impatience, claiming there was no hurry. He could wait until I felt ready. He would be patient with me when the moment came, and I'd know the sort of pleasure you haven't been able to give me for years. There's too much baggage between us, too many disappointments and harsh words. You treat me like I still need looking after, but I've desires I'm barely starting to understand. Sex with this man would be light as a feather, an interlude of pleasure with no future or past. Was it so wrong to just once want to feel uncomplicated pleasure?'

'You tell me. I barely know who I'm looking at.'

Alice's voice was low. 'I can't tell you because I never found out. On Sunday night I sat in that hotel lobby one last time. I knew his patience was over. Part of me wanted to enter the elevator, the part that never takes risks. Another part of me, the real me, who grips your hand tight at auctions, wanted to be back home with you. I wanted Sophie to be waiting up in her pyjamas, aged seven again. I wanted to return to a time when I felt an absolute sense of purpose, when I knew who I was because my child needed me. As I hesitated yet again, I saw this man's eyes harden. He had big-game-hunter's eyes, salesman's eyes, ready to clinch the deal or find another customer. He was as insincere as he was sexy. I realised what attracted me: he had Ronan's eyes. He wanted me in the same way that Ronan had wanted me at seventeen, as a challenge to his ego. Being wanted like that had made me feel seventeen again. But I'm not. Men will never look at me like they look at Kim and Sophie. Once this man bedded me I would cease to exist for him; he would be too busy seeking his next conquest.'

'What did you do?'

'I told him that if he went upstairs I'd follow and knock on the door. I watched him smile back at me in triumph as he entered the lift. I waited until the lift doors closed, then I ran from the hotel, where I felt that everyone was watching me, knowing exactly why I was there. I broke every red light as I drove to Dun Laoghaire Harbour and parked crookedly on double yellow lines. I didn't care if I was clamped. I barely cared if I lived or died. I walked out along the dark pier and sat on the cold stone, shaking because one part of me still longed to be living out a fantasy in that hotel bedroom. The part of me which always wants to hurt myself, which has been unable to see any good in myself. I realised that I hadn't wanted revenge on you, but on life itself for making me old and forcing me to accept that my dreams will never be realised. I walked on through the dark to the end of the deserted pier. I wanted to throw myself in. Instead, I took out my second phone, the one with those people's numbers, and hurled it as far into the waves as I could. Then I drove home, ready to snap your head off if you asked where I'd been. But you weren't here, and I never felt more alone than sitting up in this empty house waiting for you ....'

She paused, startled at having found the courage to address the contradictions she had locked away in her heart until they festered.

'Don't just sit there, Chris,' she pleaded. 'This is who I am, more naked than you've ever seen me. Say something.'

Chris shook his head. 'I can't think straight.'

Alice stretched out her hand. 'Chris, listen ….'

She could see his hands tightly clutch her discarded clothes on the chair beneath him. He released his grip and headed for the door.

'I'll show you I'm not just a cuckolded coward,' he said. 'I'm going to turn that blasted town house into a pile of ash.'

Chapter Thirty

Ronan

Tuesday 7th, 4 a.m.

It was Kim who woke first; Kim who always slept soundly, yet constantly surprised Ronan with her ability to wake at any unfamiliar sound, not in Miriam's perturbed, sleepy way, but instantly composed and alert. She shook Ronan awake. He was unsure of how long it was since he blacked out after downing one last brandy, poured over crushed ice.

'Someone's in the garden,' Kim said softly. 'There's shouting.'

Ronan became utterly alert. Getting out of bed, he lifted the window blind. Kim's movements were so quiet that he was unaware of her beside him until she spoke.

'You should go down. He's like a tortured soul.'

'Tortured soul my arse … he's like a lunatic. He'll torch the place and set himself alight in the process.'

Maybe she was upset by his language, but Ronan only realised after he had hurriedly pulled on trousers and a jumper to run downstairs that Kim had not spoken again. She remained at the window, watching Alice and Chris shout in the garden. At first Ronan thought that his coarse tone had shocked her into silence, but then he realised that Kim was cutting him adrift, using her impenetrable impassiveness as a barrier.

By the time he unlocked the conservatory doors to run down towards the town house, the building site reeked of paraffin, which

Chris was frantically splashing from a can that Jiri had left out on what remained of the lawn. Ronan was shocked at his neighbour's altered appearance. It wasn't just the scratched face or torn clothes; there was something manic about his eyes, like a man pushed so far that he could find no way back. Alice stood in her bare feet in a nightdress, trying to approach Chris and yet constrained by fear that he would set himself alight. Ronan was relieved at how rattled Chris looked. His father always claimed that it was easier to cajole a deranged workman down from a ledge than to reason with a calm one. This situation just needed someone to take control. But his instincts told him not to stray too close to Chris: the tactic was to calm him like you would a frightened animal.

Alice was so desperately pleading with Chris that she didn't notice Ronan's arrival. This allowed him covertly to observe her body through the thin nightdress. There was something quietly erotic to Ronan about her involuntary shivering.

'Chris, look at me,' Ronan said, keeping his tone sardonic. 'Then look at your half-frozen wife and tell me what the fuck you're doing?'

'I'm burning down this town house.'

'What will that solve? Now stop splashing around paraffin like an altar boy with holy water. You're hysterical. Take a deep breath and listen ….'

'I'm finished listening to you,' Chris said. 'Finished having you make a mockery of me!'

'When did I ever mock you?'

'You never let me in to the big joke that you once slept with my wife.'

Ronan rolled his eyes upwards in amused exasperation. 'The Bay City Rollers were on *Top of the Pops*,' he said. 'U2 were struggling to play in the same key in the Dandelion Market. That's prehistory, and even then it didn't mean anything.'

'Thanks very much.' Alice flushed with indignity. 'You broke my heart at seventeen.'

Ronan turned to reason with her. 'Having your heart broken is part of being seventeen. We were kids in flared jeans. We're adults now, so get your husband to start behaving like one.'

'Chris is ten times the man you ever were,' Alice said defiantly.

Ronan ignored her and addressed Chris. 'Put down the paraffin. This town house is your passport out of here.'

'Maybe I don't want a bloodstained passport.' Chris lowered his voice, his fury dissipating as he meekly approached Ronan. Chris's clothing was so drenched that Ronan still needed to be cautious, but he experienced a relieved elation at having brought this situation under control. Chris bowed his head, exhausted.

'Everything will be okay,' Ronan whispered. 'Jiri just shrugged when I told him his plasterer never showed. He got Andrzej to finish the job. Look behind you, the scaffolding is gone. That safety inspector can do fuck all to us. I told you to trust me.'

Chris slowly raised his head and reached out his right hand unexpectedly, his fingers so tight around Ronan's neck that Ronan struggled to breathe.

'Don't fuck with me.' Chris's whisper was chilling. 'I'm sick of your games.'

'Let go!' Ronan could barely speak, panicked that Chris might not release his grip. Slowly those fingers relaxed their pressure, but Chris didn't let go fully, his face inches from Ronan's, as if afraid that Ronan would disappear if he glanced away.

'Tell me what you did with his body.'

'Keep your voice down.' Ronan glanced towards Alice. 'What happened in Wicklow stays in Wicklow.'

'You drove back there at dawn. Tell me where you dumped his fucking body.'

Ronan eased his neck free from Chris's grip and eyed him warily. 'Don't say you honestly risked going back up there?'

'You knew that I would after I sobered up. You always think one step ahead.'

'Do you know how hard it was to stop Alice phoning the police after you disappeared?' Ronan hissed.

'What are you both whispering about?' Alice called out. 'Chris, I want us to go back inside.'

'Take her advice,' Ronan said angrily. 'Clean yourself up and sober up.'

'I'm deadly sober.'

'I didn't move him,' Ronan insisted. 'If you went back up there, you broke our agreement.'

'When did you keep an agreement in your life? Now stop lying.'

'Why would I lie?'

'Lying comes as naturally as breathing to you,' Chris said.

'I was here all day.' Ronan looked at Chris, genuinely alarmed. 'If his body is gone, somebody else moved it.'

'Does Kim know?'

'Kim doesn't need to know.' He looked at Chris. 'We need to go back up there.'

'I'm going nowhere with you.'

The conservatory door opened, and Kim appeared, a silk dressing gown loosely tied over her nightdress. Ronan saw Chris glance at her exposed calves and look away. Her voice was barely above a whisper as she asked why everyone was shouting. Ronan tried to usher her back inside, but Kim ignored Ronan's restraining hand and walked past her husband towards Chris, who lifted the paraffin can as if it were a bargaining tool that might buy him space to think. He sprinkled more paraffin over the loose timbers.

'You look exhausted, Chris,' she said quietly. 'What are you doing?'

'He's having a nervous breakdown,' Ronan said. 'Now go inside, it's dangerous out here.' He raised his voice. 'Chris, get some sleep and this will seem like a bad dream. Maybe you don't want the money from selling this town house, but your wife is desperate to get away. Stop thinking about yourself and put your wife first.' Ronan turned to Alice. 'Forget anything you've heard tonight, Alice. An unfortunate incident occurred, not of our making. We needed to tidy things up, for everyone's sake.'

Ronan was anxious for Kim to get no closer to Chris, who looked almost overcome by fumes from the paraffin saturating his clothes. Kim was vainly asking them to listen to something she wished to say, but Alice ignored her, begging Chris to drop the can.

'Starting a fire will only bring attention down on our heads,' she said. 'I don't care if we ever move house; I just want our old life together back.'

'Our life together is an empty shell,' Chris replied.

'Don't say that,' Alice begged. 'We still have each other.'

'Do we?' Chris's voice sounded lost.

'Listen to her,' Ronan urged.

Alice turned to him furiously. 'Stay out of our lives.'

Kim took another step towards Chris. 'Chris, please, listen to me.'

'Stay out of this, Kim,' Alice cautioned. 'It has nothing to do with you.'

Kim stared at Alice. 'Your husband is standing in my back garden splattered in paraffin,' she pointed out.

'We're dealing with things that happened before you ever set foot in Ireland.' Alice tried to make her voice conciliatory. 'They simply don't concern you.'

Ronan was surprised by Kim's steely reply. 'Do you think I am some sort of maid to be sent indoors, Alice?'

It wasn't the change in Kim's tone that perturbed Ronan; it was how she kept steadily encroaching into Chris's space. Dropping the can, Chris produced the matchbox that Ronan had given him on Sunday night to light a cigar with. He looked at Alice. 'I keep seeing you in that hotel foyer with a conniving snake-oil-salesman smiling at you from the lift. One part of you longed to go upstairs.'

'But I never did,' Alice insisted. 'It was a stupid, girlish fantasy. I stepped back from the edge before it was too late.' She looked at him beseechingly. 'Tell me it's not too late.'

Kim took a step closer, and Chris struck a match, holding it aloft. Ronan felt that Chris hadn't the courage to drop it, but his hand shook so much it could fall from his grasp.

'Please, Kim, this isn't safe,' Ronan begged. He raised his voice. 'Blow out that blasted match, Chris. Are you listening?'

'No,' Chris tilted the match horizontally so the flame burnt slowly along the stick. 'I'm taking a proper long look at you. It's the first time I've ever seen you scared. You can't manipulate me any more. Take one step closer and I'll drop this.'

'My husband will stay where he's told to,' Kim said firmly. 'It's me who's going to take those matches from you.'

'Stay back, Kim,' Chris pleaded. 'Alice is right, this doesn't concern you.'

'Are you all so stupid that you cannot see how you are intruding on my life?'

'Chris!' Alice sounded terrified. 'It's about to burn your fingers.'

At any second the paraffin soaking his fingers would ignite, but still Chris seemed paralysed until Kim barked an order.

'Put it out!'

He blew out the match, scared now in case the smouldering, blackened stick ignited the paraffin at his feet as it twirled to the ground.

Kim held out her palm. 'Hand me the matches.'

Mute and exhausted, Chris surrendered them.

'You could have burnt my wife alive!' Ronan shouted, but was silenced by how Kim turned to survey him and Alice.

'I know the remarks some wives make, Alice, about Ronan only marrying me because he couldn't cope with a real woman. I am a real woman. Maybe I'm not fancy, educated in a private school, but that doesn't make me a mail-order bride. I owe nothing to anybody.' Kim placed the matches in her silk dressing gown. 'Every evening from my kitchen window I watched the workmen building this town house, labouring into the dark like my father and brothers do in Manila.'

'I watch them too,' Alice told her. 'I try to befriend those men, make them tea and sandwiches when I know they must be hungry, but they just look through me like it's no longer even my garden. They only want to talk to Ronan.'

'That's because my husband pays their wages, and therefore so do I,' Kim replied. 'I own half of everything Ronan owns, which means that I also owe half his debts, even if he tries to hide them, as if I'm a child who needs to be shielded. I wanted to draw up a document that stated if our marriage failed I would walk away with nothing except my pride, but Ronan insisted I must be entitled to half. He did so because he is a good man, no matter what you think. He is insecure and constantly needs to prove himself, but he is not a bad man. I say this as his wife.' Kim tapped her breast. 'That's who I am: myself, not some second-rate replacement for Miriam. Maybe you thought Chris was perfect when you married him, Alice, but I always knew I was marrying a flawed man with goodness at his core. I watch you and Chris mentally torture each other over the realisation that you both have flaws. But I accept my husband in all his contradictions, because I've seen truly bad men. I saw evil none of you will ever see.' Kim looked at Ronan. 'You spend so much time hiding things from me, that just this once I hid something from you.'

'What?'

'I found that workman's corpse.'

'What are you saying?' Chris asked, having sunk to his knees after Kim confiscated the matches. Rubble pressed into his kneecaps, but he did not possess enough energy to shift position.

'It was nearly dark on Sunday when I saw that workman climb the scaffolding,' Kim said. 'He seemed a solitary type. His grey beard reminded me of my Uncle Rosito, who often rested in our kitchen between jobs, too tired to talk. Because he was alone, I decided to bring him out coffee and bread. I was cutting thick slices when I looked out the window again and saw him stand, very straight and still, one hand clutching his chest and one gripping the scaffolding. His back was to me, but I saw him staring straight ahead, like a saint looking at an apparition. I knew something was wrong. He took a step back, but there was nothing to step onto. He let go of the scaffolding and fell without fuss onto the grass beside the pond at the end of our garden.'

'You're wrong,' Chris said. 'He fell onto rubble beneath the faulty scaffolding.'

Then Chris went silent as Kim's gaze made him feel like a gullible child.

'There was nothing wrong with the scaffolding, the fault was his heart. I've worked in hospitals. Even at that distance I could tell it was a heart attack, so intense he was already dead before he fell off the scaffolding.'

'You saw this and did nothing?' Chris asked, bewildered.

'I did all I could, Chris. I ran out to kneel beside him. I felt his pulse and listened to his heart. There were no vital signs, no heartbeat, nothing any doctor could do for him. So I stayed kneeling and said an act of contrition in his ear. I prayed for him in English and in Tagalog, and then I said the few prayers I know in Spanish and in Ilokano. I cried for him and for my Uncle Rosito, whom I had found dead when I was sent to wake him one morning. Then I cried for myself out of self-pity, feeling homesick and scared. Ronan was meeting that slimeball, Hughes, and only Alice was next door.' Kim glanced at Alice. 'Whoever I was going to turn to for help, it would never be you.'

'What did you do, Kim?' Ronan asked, his voice barely a whisper.

'I went inside to call an ambulance. I picked up the phone but I couldn't press the dial button. I was waiting for guidance. Then God told me what I needed to do.'

'God told you?' Alice asked incredulously.

'Yes,' Kim said. 'My God is not your soft, anaemic God. My Christ has no time for scented candles or holistic healing. My Christ is a carpenter with weathered hands. He told me that there was nothing I could do for the workman, but I could do something for myself and for my husband. I could leave the body where I found it, to discover the true nature of the man I married.'

'I could tell you his true nature,' Alice began, but a look from Kim silenced her.

'You couldn't, and nor could I. But I could set a test to make Ronan take responsibility. I had seen the safety inspector close down this site, and knew that when Ronan found the body he would blame the loose scaffolding. But if he found the courage not to duck and dive, an autopsy would clear him of blame and prove that the scaffolding played no part: that man could have as easily died in bed.'

Ronan looked at her, intensely hurt. 'I've always taken responsibility,' he said, 'responsibility for you.'

'Maybe it was time to take it for yourself. Maybe I did wrong … I don't know … I'm not perfect … but I poured myself a large gin – something I never do – then cooked us a late dinner and pulled down my kitchen blind. I washed up after we ate and waited for you to venture out and find the body.' She turned to Alice. 'You were going out somewhere, Alice, and Chris arrived over. He seemed upset, so I made our husbands coffee. I went to bed and listened to them downstairs, drinking and talking big talk. I was longing to go down and confess, but my God instructed me not to interfere in this test to see into the soul of the man I have wed.'

'So all that time you lay awake,' Ronan murmured.

Kim looked at him. 'I stayed up, shivering in my nightdress, staring through the window blinds until I finally saw you go outside for your usual, secret smoke. How old you looked when you stumbled upon his body and slumped down beside it.'

'I had no time to think,' Ronan said helplessly.

'You found time. You were slumped there for so long that I thought you were praying. Instead, as always, you were scheming, devising ways to avoid responsibility.'

'Why didn't I see the body when I came out?' Chris asked, breaking his silence.

'You were too busy peeping up at my lit window like a guilty schoolboy as you urinated against a tree. You were so eager for a flash of bare thigh that you missed the sight of Ronan quietly dragging the body across our lawn to deposit him on your property, transferring the problem onto your shoulders.'

'I was scared.' Ronan raised his voice, momentarily ceasing to care if other neighbours heard. 'Is it such a crime to simply be scared? What is it you expected from me?'

'You couldn't have been more scared than me,' Kim said, 'scared for all of us. I expected you to have the courage to summon an ambulance. I saw you re-enter and still hoped you were going to take out your phone. Instead, you picked up the bloodstained rock that the poor man's head had struck after his heart attack. You placed the rock next to his body beside the scaffolding and hunched down to cry out to Chris for help.'

'Heart attack or not, there was still a closure order on this site,' Ronan protested. 'I did whatever was needed to protect you.'

'You incriminated me,' Chris said.

'You let him incriminate you,' Kim said. 'From my window I watched your agony in the garden. I could second-guess every move my husband would make. I watched Ronan orchestrate the cover-up, distancing himself even further by using your car. I watched you struggle with your conscience, knowing that your conscience would never win.'

'I was stocious drunk.' Chris turned on Ronan. 'You gave me no time to think.'

'For Jesus' sake,' Ronan snapped, 'if I'd been waiting for you to make a decision we'd still be kneeling out here! I needed to take the responsibility of thinking for us both.' He lowered his voice and pointed to the conservatory doors. 'Let's go indoors; this is too dangerous a conversation to have out here. The ceramic floor tiles in my kitchen have a ten-year guarantee against self-immolating Buddhist monks, but all the same you can leave your drenched clothes at the door. We'll find you a blanket.'

'We'll stay exactly where we are,' Alice said firmly. 'I've never liked your house, in any of its incarnations.'

Ronan snorted. 'That's rich from someone living in a poky pigsty.'

'My house may be small, but it's no pigsty. It's decorated in my own way, not simply copied from pages ripped from the latest glossy magazine, like you, always aping someone else's tastes. You moved that dead man's body onto our land.'

'And what does it matter if I did? Regardless of where his body landed, the fact is that he still fell from unsafe scaffolding on your property.' Ronan glared at Kim. 'If you'd told me it was a heart attack we could have been saved all this … I could have moved his body up the garden and pretended he was weeding our flower beds when he got chest pains.'

'My God told me not to interfere.'

'Your God … your God ….' Ronan wheeled around in exasperation. 'Your God is great for issuing instructions, but I've yet to see him help with our mortgage repayments! Indeed, he takes a singular disinterest in servicing any of our loans. Your God doesn't magically pay the bill for the Visa card you can flash in any shop.'

'I don't flash any cards; I use our Visa card sparingly, for essentials,' Kim responded. 'I don't need wealth; I need to live with a man I can respect.'

Alice interrupted their argument, her voice low. 'What have you put us all through, Kim?'

Kim turned to her with quiet defiance. 'Did I place a corpse in your husband's car boot for him to dump it like an old fridge?'

'All the same, you could have saved us from this.'

'From what? From looking into your souls?'

'I was willing to look into my soul or face any court case,' Chris said quietly. 'I just couldn't face Alice telling me I'd screwed up by trusting Ronan.'

'Thanks a lot,' Ronan said.

Chris ignored him. 'I was so drunk that I acted out of cowardice … but what I was truly scared of was facing my wife.'

'Is that really how you see me?' Alice asked, near tears. 'Is this what we've come to?'

'After all our trouble trying to move house ....'

'Forget about the blasted house. I was never really angry with you about moving house. I was angry because I thought you were seeing another woman. The thought that maybe you no longer found me attractive scared me. But I never forced you to put a workman in a car. I wasn't even involved, yet you blame me.'

'You were involved because I was involved,' Chris said. 'Remember the trauma of those months we spent waiting for the inquest into the death of the child in that crash, and then the agony of waiting for the court case and all the publicity? Another court case looming over our heads would fester and drive us even further apart.'

Ronan produced his mobile phone and raised a hand to request silence, trying to regain control of the situation.

'This has gone far enough,' he said. 'From this moment on we all sing from the same hymn sheet.' He glanced at Kim. 'I'll show you that I'm capable of taking full responsibility. I'm telling the police that I was alone when I found the body in my garden, and that I took Chris's car keys without his knowledge. Let's face it: Chris knew nothing about the closure order, so he's not at fault for the scaffolding still being used. And you had no real hand either in dumping the corpse, Chris. I goaded and cajoled you into playing your bit-part. I'm telling the cops that I dumped his body alone, and I'll give them directions how to find it.'

'We acted together,' Chris said. 'And his body is gone. I scoured every lane around Lough Dan until I found the spot where we dumped him.'

Ronan raised his eyes to heaven. 'We never drove near Lough Dan. Wherever you wound up, it wasn't where we dumped the body. We left him at the end of a boreen beyond Annamoe. Face it, Chris: left alone you couldn't find your own arse in a paper bag.'

Kim's words silenced them. 'Hillwalkers found the body this evening. There were pictures on the late news. The state pathologist is at the scene. Her autopsy report is not completed, but police are treating it as a heart attack and don't suspect foul play.'

Ronan took a deep breath. 'So you're saying we're in the clear?'

'With the police, yes.'

'What does your carpenter God tell you to do now, Kim?' Alice asked.

Pulling her dressing gown closed, Kim stared at Alice, woman to woman.

'To go on living my flawed life with this flawed man I love.'

'To carry on like nothing has happened?'

'Oh no,' Kim replied. 'What's happened cannot be undone. But for the first time I feel that Ronan and I are equals. We were equally petrified when we each found that body. My sisters imagine that I live a perfect life, but perfection is too hard an illusion to maintain. Ronan and I are both flawed. Maybe that's good. If we were perfect we wouldn't need each other. We finish this town house and sell it. Then, with no disrespect, hopefully you'll move away so we can all start again. But I know who my husband is now, and he knows me. We'll sink or swim together.'

'Maybe I don't intend moving now,' Alice protested. 'And how do we know this man died from a heart attack? All we have is your word.'

'I am a trained nursing attendant.'

'That doesn't make you a heart surgeon,' Alice retorted, flustered.

'You know what I did, and what Chris and Ronan did when we found the body,' Kim replied. 'So tell me, what does your God tell you to do?'

Alice stared around. 'It's not fair to put this decision on me.'

'You're the only innocent person left,' Kim said. 'You judge everyone, but I never see you make actual decisions. So would you have called the police?'

'It's the first thing I'd have done if I'd seen him fall,' Alice replied.

'Then do it now.' Kim held out her phone.

Alice looked at Chris. 'What will happen if I do?' she asked him, scared. 'Can they jail you for moving his body? Answer me. I know that at times I give out to you, but I never say a bad word about you to anyone else. How could I when you're a good man? It makes you hard to live with, when sometimes I feel that I can't be as good, when you hide yourself so much behind goodness that at times you're impossible to reach as a man I just want to touch and fuck and bicker with like any normal couple. Now I'm desperately sorry about that poor workman, but, God forgive me, these past twenty-four hours have made me realise that I only care about you. I love you, Chris, so don't just kneel there. Get up on your feet and tell me what to do.'

'All I've ever wanted is to make you happy,' Chris replied.

'And who says I'm not happy? I've done crazy things lately and hated myself afterwards, but that's me rattling the bars of my cage. It doesn't mean I want to end up alone. I'm no different from any woman on this street. I'm happily unhappy.'

'But I'm not happy,' Chris replied. 'I want a wife who respects me. Hand me your phone, Kim. I'm calling the police.'

Chris's fingers were closing in on Kim's phone when Alice grabbed it from her palm. It was the latest lightweight touchscreen model. Alice could imagine Ronan bringing it home and insisting, over Kim's protests, that her previous phone go in the bin. Alice flung it across the patio, not caring if it broke.

'Calling the police won't bring that workman back to life,' she told Chris, 'and I don't want to lose what we have left.'

'What have we left?' Chris asked.

'You are the only man who's ever meant anything to me. Let's get those clothes off you and get you into the shower.'

'Alice,' Ronan touched her arm lightly, 'none of this was supposed to happen.'

'Just sell this town house, Ronan,' Alice said, and then turned to Kim. 'I'm sorry I broke your phone, Kim. You think I've something against you because you took Miriam's place, but let me tell you a secret … I never liked Miriam. We were always laughing, but we never talked about anything real. She brimmed with confidence, and on days when my heart was low I was glad to be dragged along in her slipstream, but we were never friends. I envied her for her energy, and at times I envied the clothes she flaunted, but I never envied her for who she was. I wish that you and I hadn't been thrown together as neighbours like this. You're the sort of friend I would love to make if we fell into conversation by fluke in a coffee shop or on the Dart. I've ten times more in common with you than I ever had with Miriam. But it always felt like it would be an act of disloyalty to become pally with you. Don't ask me why I felt bound by a sense of loyalty to a woman I never truly liked, but you're ten times the person Miriam ever was, whether your husband knows it or not.'

Ronan wanted to speak, but he felt oddly invisible and diminished as he watched Alice walk away, grasping Chris's hand while his body shook from exhaustion. 'Let's get you inside, pet,' Alice coaxed, 'into our own home. There's so much I want to talk to you about. These neighbours, they have no business in our lives.'

Left alone, Kim and Ronan confronted each other in silence. Kim turned and walked inside, knowing that Ronan would follow her up the stairs and lie awake in bed holding her tightly, bound together and torn apart.

PART THREE

October, 2007

Chapter Thirty-One

Ezal

Friday 19th, 6.30 p.m.

T he workmen started to gather in the laneway outside the completed town house at half past six, most on their way back from full-time jobs, and some en route to commence several more hours of labour for cash. But this was final payment night, when all debts would be settled by Jiri. There was little need for Ezal or the others to accompany Jiri to this last meeting with Ronan: Jiri had his own methods to discreetly circulate messages and cash. But an unspoken pride made the workmen wish to be present to witness the completion of this house they had built from scratch. They wanted the satisfaction of receiving an envelope crammed with banknotes, and of giving the plastered walls one final slap before they departed to another unregulated site.

Ezal sensed how the workmen found it odd to be gathered together without shovels or wheelbarrows. Their silence had the awkwardness that men possess when standing around at a funeral. The eight men present had been hand-picked by Jiri – three Czechs, two Poles, a Moldovan, a Romanian and Ezal. The functional English of the building site was their only common language, but not a language in which any of them thought. Not that these men shared their inner thoughts. Ezal's knowledge of the others was confined to what they wished him to know, or what he had unobtrusively observed.

The Moldovan plasterer, Andrzej, had a gravely ill daughter to whom he sang lullabies from call centres, never betraying evidence of his grief until the call was over. Andrzej was terrified that if he did not return to Moldova soon he might never see his daughter alive, but needed to balance his torment against the fact that four other children were dependant on the money he sent home from working illegally in Ireland. To fly home, even for one day, ran the risk that, without a valid work permit, he might not be allowed back into Ireland.

Ezal was aware that Luan, the youngest man present, sent every euro he could save back to Albania. His girlfriend, whose photograph Luan carried in his wallet, planned to open a shop with the cash Luan earned from untaxed jobs like this. Unlike Luan, both the Poles intended to settle in Ireland. They were renting poorly built apartments near Shankill, but would add tonight's cash to the deposits they intended to place on houses after the market fell. One of them had a son who was captain of an under-elevens hurling team.

As they waited to get paid, Ezal suspected that each workman fleetingly thought about Pavle. These thoughts were less about the inexplicable puzzle of why such a man would go hillwalking instead of earning a day's wage, and more about whether Jiri would hold on to the plasterer's share of the proceeds. His cut would not be much, as Pavle had only worked there on a few occasions. Ezal had not discussed this matter with Jiri – they rarely held unnecessary discussions – but he knew that Jiri would subdivide this small windfall among the others. Not only was it fair, but it would leave no unfinished business. In some way it made them all complicit in the plasterer's disappearance, because, though they would never wish to have dealings with policemen, most of the men present harboured suspicions that Pavle had not died on a Wicklow hillside.

Ezal knew that Ronan and Chris would never offload this town house, or would need to sell it for only half of what they expected. In recent months he had overheard frantic discussions in makeshift offices on building sites, worried developers shouting into mobile phones as if he were invisible. The disappearance of Paul Hughes and his wife to America with whatever cash he could scavenge, hours before receivers were appointed to his sites, had spooked the market. Building work was drying up. Soon this bubble would end in the way of all bubbles. The Irish liked to consider themselves sophisticated, but their inflated sense of destiny, and their optimism that their debts could be eternally long-fingered, reminded Ezal of peasant villagers, meekly surrendering their savings to pyramid scam conmen promising endless wealth.

Ronan emerged from his conservatory and walked down his truncated garden to join them in the lane. The Irishman looked overdressed, perspiring as if his business suit were too tight. But Ezal knew why he was sweating, why his hand shook as he counted out an extra €1,500 in cash to be shared among the workmen. Ronan wanted them gone, along with every other potentially incriminating witness. Jiri publicly thanked him, and the other men murmured their appreciation. They were equally anxious to get rid of Ronan so they could receive their cut. Jiri appeared neither impressed nor unimpressed by Ronan's largesse. He accepted this bonus like he accepted all news, good or bad. Every workman knew that Jiri would be scrupulously fair in sharing it out. Jiri would survive the forthcoming crash: shrewd entrepreneurs like him always did, immigrants who methodically and unemotionally built empires by thinking ahead. If he stayed around, Ezal absolutely trusted that Jiri would find him work in the straitened times to come, because Jiri valued Ezal's skills and his lack of curiosity.

Jiri was the closest thing to a friend that Ezal allowed himself, but he always had to think one step ahead and trust no one. A city like Dublin was a good place to be invisible when people needed him to lay bricks in the freezing cold, to tear down old houses and erect apartment blocks he could never afford. Being paid was not always easy, but you had to expect that businessmen, who paid you to cut corners with safety standards, would similarly try to cut corners with you. Once you stood up to such men they caved in, as if trying to cheat you was part of an elaborate social ritual in which you were each required to play a token part.

Ireland had proven less good for other migrants he sometimes encountered on isolated sites, pimped-out men who spoke no English and never saw their wages. All interactions with Irish employers were handled by the subcontractor thugs from their own countries who had lured them here with false promises. Ezal had seen their famished faces and wondered how Irish employers could not see this exploitation occurring. The answer was that the Irish had no wish to see; they only had time to marvel at the sums of money they were juggling. They were too busy coping with being rich, and too terrified of being left behind to notice the unsold apartments starting to clog up the outskirts of towns. They were so accustomed to wealth that they could not conceive of it ending. Ezal remembered how the inhabitants of his native village were so accustomed to peace that they were could not conceive of it ending, until the week of Ezal's sixteenth birthday. His family and friends had possessed that same innocence as the Irish did now, believing that when something became the norm it would exist forever.

Ronan was shaking hands with each workman. The men laughed at his jokes to make him feel big and reward him for the bonus money handed over to appease his conscience. Guilt was so clearly written on his face that Ezal wondered if every workman recognised it. Jiri could spot this look of guilt, though he did not fully understand it. Ezal knew this because Jiri spotted almost everything. But not everything. During three years of working together, Jiri had never fully seen into Ezal's soul. Jiri would be surprised to find him gone tomorrow, but surprise was a luxury Jiri could not dwell on. Ezal was confident of finding work somewhere: he travelled light, alert to opportunities. The cash from this town house would be stored with cash earned from other jobs that Jiri had arranged and jobs Jiri knew nothing about. It was easy to save when you have nobody to send money home to.

Ezal's only luxury was to allow himself three beers before going to sleep at night, but he always bought cheap cans from off-licences. He didn't like Irish pubs. In fact, he did not especially like company. But this year he had allowed himself a second luxury by joining a gym. The downstairs area contained treadmills crammed with Irish girls, their tied-up dyed-blonde hair making them resemble photofits of each other as they listened to music on headphones. Ezal preferred the upstairs weightlifting area where he was surrounded by silent men from Moldavia and Belarus, working on bench presses and free weights. Their seriousness of purpose appealed to him, the occasional anguished grunts when pushing through pain barriers. The gym was a place where you could be alone for hours in the seeming midst of company.

It was in the gym that he had started to notice Chris running on a treadmill, his eyes fixed in the distance. The gym contained a leisure centre. He had started to sit opposite Chris in the sauna, watching the Irishman trying to sweat off excess kilos, or emerging from the steam room on the verge of collapse, as if endurance might cleanse him of the weight of sin. Ezal could observe Chris candidly there, realising that Chris did not recognise him when removed from the context of the building site. In the gym, Ezal was just another of the shaven-headed East Europeans who all merged into a blur.

Ezal could not understand such face blindness. He never forgot a face, even though there were faces he wanted to forget, times when he slaved all day so that, when he closed his eyes, exhaustion, not memories, would claim him. Ireland was meant to be a land where he could escape the past and stop seeing the faces of former neighbours staring out from passing buses, faces that could not exist because they belonged to the dead. Ezal was still alive, not through divine intervention but simple fluke. Similarly, it was not destiny but simple fluke that made him spot Pavle's face six months ago. Twenty-two years had aged Pavle, whose workday clothes were different from the black uniform he had worn on the day he came to Ezal's village. In retrospect it was not a proper uniform, just a black outfit embossed with the makeshift insignia of a makeshift militia, finished off with black gloves and a black balaclava that Pavle only made the mistake of removing for a few seconds.

Back then, Pavle would have been too young to be a senior officer. Indeed, initially there seemed to be no command structure when Pavle's militia unit took control of Ezal's village, rounding up former neighbours with whom they had once chatted in town squares or on the terraces of football stadiums, back when everyone was awkwardly bound together by the brutal glue of dictatorship. It had taken longer for the Marshal to die from gangrene than for his cobbled-together Yugoslavia to rend itself asunder. Not even his colossal state funeral, with four kings, thirty-one presidents and twenty-two prime ministers attending to check that he was finally dead, could hold back the factions starting to splinter apart. There were too many rekindled whisperings of nationalism, too many historical scores to be settled, too many boils festering, too many cracks that the Marshal had concealed behind a façade of unity.

Not that Ezal cared much about history back then. If the future had been different he would have drank in the same bars as Pavle when they migrated for work to the nearest town and chased the same girls in cavernous nightclubs, with sweat on the walls and urinals stinking of ammonia. They might have become friends, or perhaps never met. As it was, they never properly met. But Ezal had never forgotten his one glimpse of Pavle in the village he once called home.

Ezal hadn't possessed time for philosophical observations at sixteen. He was too preoccupied in tinkering with his patched-up motorbike and contemplating the heft of his girlfriend Sanja's breasts at night when she sometimes allowed him to unbutton her dress on the edge of the forest. His mind was too caught up with kisses, and memories of his exploring hands and her reciprocating fingers, to be concerned about home-grown militias operating close to his village. He could laugh at the lies parroted on state television and his mother's needless apprehension. He felt invincible from rumours sweeping in of other villages being uprooted or, some claimed, made to disappear. How could the weight of history compete with the weight of Sanja's breasts? His neighbours could talk about arming to defend themselves amid these curious upheavals, but he was an incurious boy, and there is no safer feeling than being in your native place.

He had no idea that history possessed a face until the day he looked up when playing a football match on waste ground, alerted by the sudden arrival of trucks. He saw a makeshift militia, ragtag puppets of an unrecognised breakaway state. At first he only ran towards the woods because other youths started running, but then he increased his speed as fear manifested itself into a cold trickle of sweat down his backbone after he heard shots and screams. Almost every instinct made him veer left towards his house to check that his family was safe, but an overriding instinct for survival made him run straight. This straight line became jagged, gunshots making him dart like a veering rabbit. Adrenaline alone carried him forward; his brain had gone numb. He finally stopped running after he collided with branches in the woods. He lay panting, deeper in the undergrowth than Sanja had ever let him bring her. At that moment Ezal knew with dazzling clarity that he was utterly alone.

If he returned to his village, he would need to step over the bodies of fellow footballers, their startled eyes unblinking at the sun. He could not run any farther away; his limbs refused to move. They trembled in uncontrollable shock. He longed to throw up, yet when glancing at his clothes saw that he had already vomited up everything inside him without any memory of doing so. The stink from his trousers betrayed that he had soiled himself. He could not lie there shaking forever. He needed to go forward, but could only do so by firstly crawling back, trying to make no sound in that silence, where even the dying seemed to moderate their anguished whimpers so as not to attract attention among the scattered dead. Buses had arrived. Women and children were being crammed onto them, and onto the trucks in which the militia had arrived, with no time to gather possessions. Ezal did not know where they were being taken.

Ezal could see that this ragtag local militia was now being instructed by new arrivals, who wore more quasi-official blue uniforms. He sensed that these proper officers came from outside the region, trained soldiers whose superiors could deny all knowledge of such events. He wished he could spot Sanja or his mother among the women in the vehicles, but the women didn't look like themselves any more, as if terror had stolen away the imprint of their features.

It was late when the last bus and truck left. The village looked empty, but Ezal knew that it was not. Shouts of angry men and frightened boys arose from the old cinema, shouts quietened at intervals by a solitary gunshot. Forty women and children also remained, for whom there was no transport. They huddled in the square while officers argued over what to do with them. This was the only time that the makeshift militia showed any hesitation, as if the adrenaline of barbarism had deserted them and they were reverting to being factory workers and farm labourers, perplexed at how they could have inflicted such horror on a neighbouring village. An army officer shouted at them, but only when he fired his pistol into the air did they obey his command to push the women and children towards the doors of the cinema. It was briefly reopened, with a fight breaking out as the men trapped inside tried to flee.

Soon every door was locked again and guarded by militia, until, after an eternity, the original trucks returned, now empty. The militia moved away from the cinema, occasionally unleashing bursts of automatic gunfire into the air with fearful bravado. They boarded the trucks. Only one militiaman remained, bowing his head in the gloom to listen to quiet instructions being issued by an officer. Ezal was too far away amid the bushes to hear what was said, or maybe he was shaking so much with cold and shock to take in the words. It was so dark that the officer briefly shone a flashlight to allow the militiaman to see what he was doing.

During the two decades that followed, Ezal often wondered what made Pavle remove his balaclava. Maybe he felt unable to breathe with the stench of paraffin after he opened the heavy container. Or maybe he felt able to work better without his balaclava. Pavle was a quick and efficient worker. His real name was not Pavle back then, no more than Ezal's birth name was Ezal. Certain events require you to reinvent yourself, events you desperately try to forget. But some faces cannot be forgotten. Pavle's movements were unhurried when the uniformed officer boarded the truck and left him alone to splatter each container of paraffin calmly against the cinema doors and walls. The doors were wooden, the inside walls studded with chipboard. The high ceiling had wooden rafters where stray birds occasionally perched, having found a way in through gaps amid the roof tiles.

How many people were inside that building? His father? His older brothers, if not already shot? Pavle had not yet struck a match. Ezal could have run towards the cinema and grappled with him before the militiamen in the trucks riddled him with bullets, but Ezal did nothing except watch from the undergrowth, because he was sixteen years old in shit-soiled trousers. He could see why the officer delegated this task to Pavle: even then, he possessed the perfect temperament to torch a building. He had the calmest movements Ezal ever saw. There was no tremor in his fingers when he lit the match to ignite the whoosh of paraffin that caused Ezal to become fatherless and stateless. Within seconds, the cinema was an inferno.

That fire exiled Ezal from the place he called home. It made him exchange the dangerous currency of his real name for a succession of nondescript aliases. It propelled him into a futile search for his mother and Sanja through refugee camps that UN soldiers were too weak and preoccupied with protocol to protect. In such camps a young man's life was always in danger. There were raids by enemy militias to abduct boys. There was incitement to join splinter factions intent on seeking revenge, or territory for the various fragmented states that emerged from the death pangs of the Marshal's nation being hung, quartered and redrawn. Embryonic nations arose, mired in states of ectopic pregnancy, or in mass pregnancies from the rape of girls with Sanja's features and the eyes of the walking dead.

Ezal slipped free from these camps where the horizon was constrained by guarded sacks of relief supplies, where water and hope was rationed and the only uncurtailed commodity was hatred. He fled for his safety after being stabbed. Mainly he fled for his sanity because he so often mistakenly thought he had caught sight of his mother and Sanja that he longer trusted his own memory. Only one face remained truly real, a face he could never forget, even though he only glimpsed it when a balaclava was briefly removed. His flight took him through farmland with food to rob, across fixed borders, and borders in permanent flux. He moved in the guise of numerous identities in sealed containers stored for days at port, through a purgatory of stale air and dehydration where he thought he would never be found alive. He passed through hands of criminals and conmen into German cities, where twice he was certain he glimpsed his dead brother's face staring out from a restaurant window. He slept in doorways or hostels where you kept your shoes under your pillow and a knife inside them.

In time he negotiated a truce with himself, a pact to disremember. He retreated into an impenetrable essence where memory was sealed and love untenable, where he neither truly feared nor trusted any living person. He slipped illegally into an Ireland whose burghers were too preoccupied with their position at the epicentre of the world to wonder about people's past. Here he found a common language with others of his ilk, a factual vocabulary of phrases to describe the legal depth of foundations required by safely inspectors, and the actual depth they were told to dig by subcontractors.

In Jiri he found the type of trustworthy man his father had been. With Jiri no workman felt exploited; they were part of an honest, back-breaking crew. Men who knew not to ask too many questions. Men unperturbed by your silence provided you did your share of work. Men who included Ezal in everyday chat until he almost felt that he belonged among them. His past remained quarantined until the afternoon when Jiri recruited a plasterer rumoured to work for little and to say even less. Pavle seemed to have no past. All Jiri knew was a rumour that Irish developers trusted his discretion in torching old buildings for which planning permission had been refused. On the first evening they worked together, Ezal was unsure if this was the same man. Two decades had aged them both. There were no questions Ezal could ask. If Pavle were aware of Ezal discreetly scrutinising him, he did not betray it.

Pavle's undocumented past did not concern Jiri, but it mattered to Ezal. Pavle's face came between him and his sleep. Ezal had been glimpsing dead faces in café windows for two decades, mirages induced by guilt and grief. How could he be sure that his mind was not playing tricks once more? But from the moment he saw Pavle again, Ezal was certain that this was the rendezvous he had been patiently and unconsciously awaiting for two decades.

When a man cannot sleep, he goes walking. When haunted by another man, he stalks him. Seven months ago, on the night when Ezal tracked Pavle to a derelict seafront building in Blackrock, the temptation to follow him inside had been strong. It would be the perfect place, with no witnesses, but Ezal had needed to be certain he was not condemning an innocent man. He waited across the road until Pavle re-emerged. By then Ezal could see flames through a curtained window. But only when Pavle closed the front door with a calm deliberation was Ezal absolutely convinced that he was the same person. Pavle's unhurried nonchalance was a mirror reflection of his exact movements after igniting the conflagration in Ezal's village twenty-two years before.

Even then, Ezal waited for his moment. An execution should not be hurried. He had befriended Pavle whenever Jiri put them working together, treating him with the impeccable respect that should always be bestowed on the dead. The fact of Pavle being unaware that in essence he was already dead did not lessen this burden of courtesy. Ezal counted down the remaining days of Pavle's posthumous existence in a way that echoed Pavle's unhurried manner. Jiri was the closest thing Ezal had to a friend, but he was not really close to Jiri. His physical needs necessitated him taking occasional lovers, but he was never able to feel close to these women because he needed to hold things back from them. With Pavle, such intimate memories did not need to be mentioned: they shared them without Pavle being aware of it. Sitting beside Pavle on some site, sharing an unhurried supper in silence because Pavle rarely spoke, Ezal had not felt so close to anyone since he was sixteen.

He felt like confiding personal details from that time, like how much he had loved his motorbike, or how the frayed stitching on Sanja's dress used to make him afraid that his clumsy fingers would cause a button to fall off. There were questions he wished to ask, but one stray remark would give Pavle the chance to disappear. Occasionally Ezal saw Pavle scrutinise him with a considered look, but Ezal soon realised that Pavle observed anyone who sat too close to him like that. This gave Ezal the key to Pavle's quietude. It was the silence of a condemned man patiently waiting to be found, the watchfulness of someone who knows that retribution would only come in that moment when he finally relaxed and thought he was safe.

Ezal was with Jiri when he decided to take his chief plasterer, Andrzej, off this small town house job and send him instead to a house in Rathmines that some rich architect was renovating as a vanity project. He had not directly suggested Pavle as a replacement, but as soon as Jiri mentioned his name, Ezal indicated that he could easily get a message to this taciturn man to come, late on the afternoon of the bank holiday Sunday, when the plasterer would have the site to himself.

After finishing work at lunchtime on that Sunday, Ezal had gone to the gym, lying in a full-length Jacuzzi where there was room for eight people to stretch out. When he closed his eyes, the jets of water pounding against his skin seemed to take on the colour of blood. The jets were hot as they sprayed his flesh, yet they could not wash away the stench of dried-in shit on his legs from when he was a terrified sixteen-year-old. That smell followed him into the steam room. The vapour was so thick that it was impossible to discern the shapes of the people on the opposite bench, but he knew that if the steam cleared he would see the faces of boys he had been playing football with on that day, or of girls herded onto buses. He remained in the steam room, even when the heat grew impossible. He stayed until the steam was turned off, the gym closing early. He was the last to leave the empty changing room.

He walked through the quiet streets, waiting until dusk, knowing that Pavle was a methodical worker who would keep plastering until every workable trace of daylight was gone.

When there was barely enough light left to see, Ezal climbed the rickety scaffolding attached to the town house. Pavle was mixing plaster with his back to him. Ronan's wife worked at the sink by the window. Ezal waited until Kim moved away so she would not see him; then he stepped forward, quietly calling out that he had a message from Jiri. He watched Pavle slowly turn and knew that, in this moment, Pavle still believed he was safe. Ezal needed this moment of trust: it allowed him to approach until they were face-to-face. He stared into Pavle's eyes without a need to say anything else; words are unnecessary when two men feel suddenly as close as brothers. Pavle did not recognise him – back when they were young, the man had never glimpsed Ezal's face before he ran away – but Pavle recognised the single word that Ezal uttered, the name of a village that no longer existed. In his jacket pocket Ezal was fingering a heavy rock, but the rock was unneeded. The mere mention of this village caused Pavle to step backwards. Pavle's eyes remained calm, almost as if relieved that the ordeal of waiting for retribution was over. All debts must eventually be paid, all loans called in. Pavle nodded in the half-second before Ezal pushed him, the half-second when Ezal wanted to scream his rage. Ezal did not scream because Pavle made no sound. There was no time. Pavle fell sideways in silence and landed in silence beside the ornamental water feature on Ronan's lawn. The only sound was a dull thud as his skull collided with one of the rocks that framed that small pond.

Ezal stepped back, seeing Ronan's wife return to the window just before Pavle fell. She stood there in shock, looking impossibly lost. When she moved from the window, Ezal knew he only had a few seconds before she emerged into the garden. Peering over the scaffolding, he knew he would not need to climb down and finish off his victim. Even in the dusk, he saw Pavle gaze up unblinkingly. From the disjointed angle of his neck he knew that Pavle could see nothing, but perhaps in that last remembered second he had seen flames ignite around him as he hurtled through the darkening air, careering to his death while regaining his true identity.

Ezal's memories were suddenly disturbed by Jiri's voice at his shoulder. The other workers had been paid off and were moving away. Jiri held out Ezal's share of the money. Ezal accepted it with a nod of thanks, wondering for how long Jiri had been observing him with his careful avoidance of curiosity. Ezal touched the plastered wall one final time and looked up at the house, where he saw Chris stand against a bedroom window, hands outstretched in purgatory. Ezal turned and silently walked away with Jiri, carefully folding the pile of banknotes inside his pocket.

PART FOUR

17th May 2009

Chapter Thirty-Two

Sophie

Things were different when I returned from my Erasmus year. For a start, a squat, ugly town house occupied the end of our garden. A wall divided us from it, but did not block out the roof or the *For Sale* sign in the lane. Over the next eighteen months the *For Sale* sign blew down during storms and changed shape as different estate agents tried to sell the town house – for a vast fortune, for a small fortune, and then for a pittance. It was built at the worst time, months before everything collapsed. Every commentator was wise after the property bubble burst, claiming they had warned that it was a house of cards, a vast Ponzi scheme that made the banks and speculators rich until the banks collapsed, the speculators declared themselves bankrupt after transferring all remaining assets to their wives, and in time the state almost collapsed, until the International Monetary Fund saved Ireland from going under.

I was still never sure who owned the town house – Mum just said it was complicated. Legally it was in my parents' names, but Kim next door took control of it. I saw her in the laneway instructing the estate agent to remove their sign two days before four nursing aides moved in. They were different nationalities, but worked in the hospital where Kim had worked before marrying Ronan, and where she now returned to work. Kim didn't just manage the rent, she managed most things next door where Ronan no longer acted like Peter Pan. He seemed older and quieter. Maybe this was because I saw so little of him; Dad and he avoided each other. Ronan didn't get much work any more

– being a quantity surveyor in a recession is as useful as being a eunuch in places where being a eunuch is a bad career choice. Certainly, he worked shorter hours. If I woke during the night I would no longer see him through the skylight of his study, gazing intently at his computer, absorbed in whatever grandiose scheme he was being asked to cost. Now at half past eleven every night Kim entered his study, and from my bedroom window I could see Ronan meekly hand over his laptop. He would sit on alone, staring into space, nursing a single glass of whatever cheap red wine was on offer in Tesco. At midnight, he invariably rose and turned off his light.

Maybe because the town house remained unsold, the tension between the two houses spilled over to my mother and Kim. They were careful never to be in their back gardens at the same time. Mum rarely opened our front door without checking through the window that Kim was not getting into her car in her driveway. No cards were exchanged at Christmas, but once a month, after the nursing aides moved in, Kim slipped an envelope through our letterbox, containing half of whatever rent she received.

Things were not only different between the two houses: relations had also changed between my parents. Mum could still be distant from Dad, adrift in her own thoughts, but then at unlikely moments she would ask him for a hug. It felt embarrassing to witness them locked in silent embraces on the sofa like teenagers, but the shouting matches that occurred before I went to Italy had stopped, and I didn't feel an unbearable pressure to be a peacemaker. It was as if another unspoken buffer now existed. It sometimes unnerved me to see them cling to each other with such love and desperation. Mostly, though, I was happy that they had worked out a compromise which allowed them to muddle on with what seemed like unnecessarily complicated lives. Occasionally, glancing through Dad's computer search history, I saw that he couldn't stop looking at estate agents' websites. These now displayed numerous examples of the sort of house he always longed to buy Mum, on sale for a fraction of the prices he had anguished over when bidding against more foolhardy couples who soared as high as Icarus.

Those triumphant winning bidders are now in negative equity, saddled with mortgages they will never pay off and trophy homes from which they can't escape. Dad could easily buy Mum her dream house now if he hadn't been lured by Ronan into squandering their life savings on that dinky town house. Some evenings I still see him tot up figures, but these are about retirement now, although he is barely in his fifties. But the international troika, which governs our government, has issued its edicts, and if Dad doesn't retire from the Civil Service soon his pension entitlements will be slashed. Irish banks don't give mortgages to people who suddenly become retirees in their fifties. Dad and Mum remain stuck in this small house at its peculiar angle: the house that I loved and never wished to leave when growing up.

The problem is that I have grown up. When I returned from Italy everything had changed, and this no longer felt like my home. That's not strictly true, though: this house is as much my home as any physical dwelling can be. I continued to live here while completing my final year in UCD. Last Tuesday in a hired gown I was applauded in the O'Reilly Hall after receiving my degree. I hugged the friends graduating with me in a changed Ireland. Posing for group photos by the artificial lake, one girl dolefully murmured that we were 'All dressed up with nowhere to go,' and we fell about laughing at her black joke. We had shared years of study, but also years filled with an expectation that we would inherit the earth. Now those of us who stay in Ireland will inherit an island of debt, but I'm not sure how many will be able to stay.

Could I stay? Financially it would be no problem. A week after I finished my final exams, Mum and Dad called me down to the kitchen and handed me an envelope with such solemnity that at first I feared it was the bad results of a medical test on one of them. Instead it contained An Post saving certs about to mature in my name, along with an old photograph of a young woman who vaguely resembled Mum. I knew instinctively that it wasn't my grandmother – married women of her generation never had any income of their own. But Mum needed to mention her Aunt Patricia twice before I even remembered meeting that stranger just once, when poor Granddad was losing his mind and my only recollection was of a shouting match. I vaguely recall a Patricia Prendeville leaving a friend request on my Facebook page three years ago, but in truth I have no idea why this unknown woman would wish to leave me a small fortune.

I'll light a candle for her on my travels, even though Dad assured me firmly that Patricia was a devout atheist. This seems to be the only thing they know about her, beyond the fact that she died somewhere abroad. I offered to share the money with them, to compensate for their life savings lost on that town house, but they insisted that this stranger wanted the money to go to me. She was anxious that I should have choices in life. But I have already made my choices, and this unexpected windfall changes nothing. My honours degree enables me to do a Master's or a PhD in any Irish university, but doing so would only delay my life's true journey.

I feel sorry for Mum and Dad, who would love me to stay. But I have my own life to lead, and my heart tells me that I have already delayed for long enough. In Italy I found my true home. I don't mean Italy itself; I mean that I now possess a place where I feel I properly belong. Home is between the sheets of any bed where I am able to lie alongside the girl I love. I don't just feel this inseparable bond between us during exhilarating moments when our hair is matted with sweat, and we lie, exhausted, from having repeatedly made each other climax. I feel an equal sense that I have reached home when I wake and lie quietly, listening to Jessie breathing beside me. I feel it on those mornings when rain lashes against the window of a borrowed flat and Jessie and I sit up in our pyjamas, giggling as we try not to scatter crumbs everywhere from her home-made brownies.

I went to Urbino to immerse myself in everything Italian, from the exoticness of Caravaggio and Tintoretto to watching families loudly talk over each other on outdoor café terraces. I thought there could be nowhere deeper to lose yourself than in Dante Alighieri's imagination. I was wrong. As a student abroad you get thrown together with people you would normally never meet. I was nine days in Urbino when I spied a note advertising two rooms to rent in a shared apartment. The apartment already contained two untidy Italian sisters, and a Danish student suffering from such an unhealthy compulsion towards neatness that the tins on her shelf in the kitchen were organised into pairs and arrayed by height. I got the first spare room. Three days later, Jessie, a Canadian girl, rented the second one.

The Italian sisters constantly fought in the big bedroom they shared. The Danish student suffered silent apoplexy any time she suspected someone of moving her toothpaste from where she carefully placed it. Jessie and I learnt to barricade ourselves into one of our rooms, trying to suppress our laughter at their antics. How long did it take us to recognise our feeling towards each other? I think we knew from the start, and I liked it that we said nothing and did nothing. The attraction was huge, but it could wait – it only heightened the expectation of our first kiss. It was too special to be cheapened by sisters bickering over some boy who rattled around on a Vespa motor scooter, or the neurosis of a girl who hoovered the communal living room every time anybody walked across it.

It was Jessie who spied the ad for a dilapidated one-bedroom flat on the third floor of a nineteenth-century building. We inspected the tiny flat, the wooden shutters with two slats missing, the toilet bowl that was the town's best example of its Gothic and Romanesque heritage, and the garishly modern cheap kitchen presses colonised by cockroaches. The double bed barely fitted in the small bedroom. The mattress was filthy, but the bedstead was made of brass, which made the evening light dance across the drab walls. This bedstead was the most beautiful artefact I have ever seen. The old woman who owned the flat stood behind us, asking no questions. I said nothing to Jessie. Jessie said nothing to me. We looked at the brass bed and then at each other, before Jessie turned to the landlady and said, '*Lo prendiamo, Signora.*'

The night before we moved out, the younger Italian sister brought home the Vespa boy over whom they were fighting. The older sister sulked on the communal sofa, her sighs louder than the soundtrack of a dubbed blue movie. The Danish girl quarantined her toothbrush in case he touched it. Our menagerie of flatmates had left next morning by the time we finished packing. The door was wide open into the sister's room, a used condom discarded among the jumbled clothes beside the bed. Jessie retrieved it gingerly and draped it over the Danish girl's toothbrush. We were still giggling like wayward children as we struggled to carry the new mattress we had purchased up the narrow staircase to our new flat. We decontaminated the kitchen. We scrubbed the toilet. We commuted death sentences on any cockroach that left of their own volition. We shared the bread and ham we had purchased. Then we made up the bed and closed over the broken shutters. When Jessie turned after fastening them, I kissed her for the first time, standing in whatever moonlight filtered through the broken slats. Kissing her was the most natural thing I had ever done. Its naturalness was matched by every caress that occurred throughout that night and most of the following morning until, reluctantly and ravenously, I ventured out to find breakfast and bring it home.

Dante and Caravaggio were outshone. I was lost in something more exotic, a twenty-one-year-old girl from Cape Breton Island. I told her about Blackrock and how much I loved and fretted about Mum and Dad. Jessie told me how Cape Breton faces west onto the Gulf of Saint Lawrence and east onto the Northumberland Strait. She described the views out over Smelt Brook and the huge saltwater lake in the middle of the island, which French settlers had christened the Arm of Gold. She told me how people in Cape Breton talked in a dialect that contains hints of French, but also echoes of Irish and Scots Gaelic, because many immigrants fled there from the Irish Famine and the Highland Clearances. I told her how people in Blackrock talked in a dialect that primarily revolved around property prices. When she laughed at this I loved her laughter. But there again, there is nothing I don't love about her. I love how her shoulder-length hair is one shade of natural blonde and her pubic hair is another. I love the generosity within her kiss, and her absolute absence of guile. I love how I don't need to mine a second seam of meaning from her remarks, unlike in Ireland, where sentences must be decoded as carefully as encrypted Cold War secrets.

One night in Urbino I looked at her face in the moonlight and I started crying. I couldn't stop, even when Jessie repeatedly asked me what was wrong. I couldn't really explain, though eventually I tried. But at that moment I realised that I was leading my mother's other life, the life she might have led if she had not dutifully returned home from Toronto. My tears made no sense in one way: I could never imagine Mum in bed with another woman. But I realised that the first thing that attracted me to Jessie was the fact that she was Canadian. Jessie seemed to step forth from the picture calendar of Canadian cities that Mum had kept in our kitchen for years after it expired. I realised that I was a free spirit in a way which Mum never could be. Mum would have been too

274

insecure, naïve and fragile to survive as an emigrant. She needed Dad as her rock to rail against.

But lying in bed, with my tears causing Jessie to shed bewildered tears, upset because I was upset, I knew that I was on the verge of the life that Mum had desperately wanted at my age. I was remembering the day when Mum continued to stare into space after the traffic lights changed, when we were bringing Granddad to John of God's Hospital. I had felt occluded that day, watching her retreat into an imaginary world where traffic was not bumper-to-bumper along the Stillorgan dual carriageway. In that other life she was free to cruise along Lake Shore Boulevard and reach her dream house in Tanglewood, Ontario, where a perfect husband and children waited for her, phantoms that Dad and I could never live up to no matter how deeply she loves us.

If it had been me living in Toronto, would I have come home and stayed like Mum did? I don't know. I've never stood in a foreign phone booth, confronted by the dilemma that a parent is dying. 'You lead a charmed life,' Mum once said during a Skype conversation when I was in Urbino, delighted that I sounded so happy. Maybe I do lead a charmed life, gliding up here on this tightrope of happiness, and perhaps one day I am due a huge fall. But thinking of Mum and Dad, and of poor Granddad who lost his mind, or his sister, my unknown benefactress, who smoked her way through a half-century of cigarettes in some flat that sounds as tiny as a nun's cell, I sometimes feel that, as a family, we have incrementally been crawling our way out of a giant chrysalis.

I don't really know much about Granddad and Gran's world of subterfuge and silence. I sometimes wonder what dreams my unknown grandmother possessed as a girl. Maybe the same dreams that her daughter almost achieved in Toronto, the dreams that I am packing into the single suitcase I will take with me tomorrow when I fly to Canada on a one-year work visa. I keep calling this my gap year. It seems easier on Mum and Dad rather than to say that I am irrevocably leaving home. If I cannot find an employer in Cape Breton to sponsor me for a residency work permit, perhaps this trip may only last for one year. But I cannot imagine myself ever sleeping in this small bedroom again, except as a guest returning to revisit my childhood home. I feel no nostalgia for Blackrock as a place. The only thing that binds me to this suburb is my love for Mum and Dad. I know that they love me too. I am the epicentre of their world, even though they conceal their sadness at my departure. This is why, that night in Urbino when I finished crying and hugged Jessie tight until she also stopped crying, Jessie and I made love like a couple needing to atone for a quarrel we have never actually had. I experienced a climax that night more intense than I had ever previously known. I felt cleansed and calmed by it, despite the palpitations of my heart. It felt like I had climaxed for somebody else's sake to heal a hurt that had gone beyond rational healing. It was the craziest sensation, but when I stretched out my hand in the dark, it felt as if Mum were sitting there on the edge of that brass bed in our tiny Urbino flat. She was whispering that love is not love if it suffocates the person you love. She was whispering that she loved me, and if I loved her I should spread my wings, like she never could, and truly take flight.

Needless to say, I never shared this particular memory with Mum and Dad when I returned from Urbino. I did, however, tell them for the first time that I was a lesbian. They accepted it with such distracted amiability that I cursed myself for not having confided in them at fourteen but I sensed that if I had told them before leaving for Italy it would have been a huge deal, not from any moral disapproval but in case it represented another source of stress that might impede Mum's recovery. Something happened in the year I was away to change all that. Even Dad, the most open of men, never discusses that time with me. All I know is that when I am gone this house will no longer be too small for them. I also know that they are now trapped here beside neighbours they dislike, thanks to an unsold monstrosity which straddles two gardens.

Last week when Jessie was visiting her aunt in Toronto she drove out to find this little place called Tanglewood. '*It's perfect,*' she wrote in her email. '*When we reach retirement age we should buy a condo there and fill it with stray cats. Once you pass the eyesore of the Gardiner Expressway the place is full of great little shops – awesome European delicatessens and loads of churches. We'll ward off old age with Kielbasa, rye bread and finding Jesus. I searched for the hardware store your mother remembers near Yonge Street, but it has vanished. I wanted to buy her a wooden plaque and get a plaque made for us. Ours, of course, would have the word "Tumbleweed" on it so that it will look equally at home in all the places I want us to explore. There are a million places I want to bring you to. The first one is my bed – which will take care of your first week in Canada. I've made you a mixtape of awesome Canadian bands to get you into the swing of the place. Just promise not to fall in love with any of the lead singers ….'*

I have been listening to Jessie's music all evening as I pack. Only when the music stopped did I realise how quiet the rest of the house was. I went downstairs, touching each bannister, my old school pictures on the wall and the knick-knacks on the hall sideboard that Mum loves to bring home as holiday souvenirs. I was storing up the feel of everything, knowing that I will never lose my love of these small rooms that helped to shape me. A card was jammed through the letter box with my name in Ronan's writing. I knew it contained Canadian dollars he can ill afford. I also knew that he would be uncomfortable, in the strange miasma which now exists between our two houses, if I called over to thank him. The living-room door was ajar. I spied Mum and Dad sitting there with their backs to me, saying nothing, just holding hands like an old couple patiently waiting for a bus. I felt like an intruder and realised why they had not come upstairs: they would equally feel like intruders if they walked into my room when I was packing. I felt flooded by memories of so many moments of great happiness between them, an awareness of how deeply they loved each other despite their occasional rows. Then I realised that the rows did not occur because they were growing apart but because they had grown too close, so tangled up in each other's needs and desires that at times they needed to row so as to shatter their entwined closeness, briefly allowing them to surface for light and air. Mum became aware of me watching from the doorway.

'Are you all right, Sophie?'

'Jessie says just to bring one bag. I know she's right, but I haven't a clue what to pack and what to leave behind. Can you help?'

Mum knew that this was a white lie, but it gave us an excuse to be together in my room one last time, busily opening drawers, laying out skirts and tops on the bed, remembering when I bought a certain pair of shoes or she bought me a dress she saw in a shop and immediately sensed that it was perfect for me. Mum has such exquisite taste that I sometimes think she was born in the wrong generation. We made slow progress, fussing over every item because neither of us wanted to finish packing. It gave us an excuse to talk, woman to woman.

'Did your mother help you to pack when you went to Canada?' I asked.

Mum laughed. 'If your Gran had packed for me I'd have been mistaken for a nun going through customs. I had no real clothes to bring: I owned one pair of flared jeans and had to find work in a shop at weekends to save for them. Your Gran didn't approve of girls wearing jeans. I don't think she approved of me full stop, though she loved me. She made me feel odd for wanting to be normal. It took me years to realise that I was normal. She could never understand me wanting to go to Canada when I could have joined the Civil Service. I'd have hated the Civil Service, but she was mystified that anyone would seek happiness when they could settle for security instead.'

'And are you happy?' I asked. 'If I could be granted one wish in the world, it would be for you and Dad to be happy.'

'What makes you think we're unhappy?'

'You've always wanted to move from here. Now it looks like you never will.'

'Maybe we were trying to get away from ourselves.'

'From each other?'

Mum folded a blouse we both loved and placed it carefully into my case. 'Not from each other, but from ourselves ... from our own flaws. We imagined we'd become different people if we woke up in a different place. Life doesn't work that way. If you're not careful you can waste your life waiting for it to begin when you should already be living every day of it.'

I sat on the bed and touched her hand. 'Mum, I need to know if you and Dad will be okay. I feel guilty leaving.'

She took my shoulders and held them tightly. 'Go to Jessie,' she said. 'Just don't expect too much of each other. Don't expect Jessie to solve all your problems, or that you'll be able to solve all of hers. Be there for each other without becoming dependent. Dependency isn't healthy. I'm glad you're going. I just ask one favour ... don't look back. Your dad and I will be fine. I'll never be happier than when thinking of you being happy. If you feel free then I'll feel free. Can you understand that?'

I shook my head. 'Not really. Do you love Dad?'

'Yes, but not in the way you love Jessie.'

'What does that mean?'

'Love is like gold: it must be tested before you know if it's real. You have to endure bad times with someone before you can truly say you love them. Chris drives me demented, yet there's nobody I feel safer with. I love him in my own way. He's a precious jewel no one else can see.'

'That sounds too complicated.'

Mum released my shoulders and surveyed the clothes on the bed. 'There's only one thing in life that's uncomplicated: the Aer Lingus baggage allowance. There's a weighing scales on your dad's side of the bed in our bedroom. Fetch it or we'll never get you packed properly. You can't bring too much.'

'I'm taking all the important stuff,' I said. 'Not in this suitcase, but where it matters, in my heart and my head.'

I stopped speaking, suddenly aware of Dad watching from the doorway. I stood up and held out one hand towards him and one towards Mum. I saw them hesitate before they came towards me and towards each other. Then they both slowly wrapped me up in one last embrace in my small bedroom, none of us saying anything because there was nothing more that needed to be said.

Also by Dermot Bolger

Novels
Night Shift
The Woman's Daughter
The Journey Home
Emily's Shoes
Father's Music
Temptation
The Valparaiso Voyage
The Family on Paradise Pier

Collaborative Novels
Finbar's Hotel
Ladies' Night at Finbar's Hotel

Plays
The Lament for Arthur Cleary
Blinded by the Light
In High Germany
The Holy Ground
One Last White Horse
April Bright
The Passion of Jerome
Consenting Adults
Tea Chests & Dreams